Birthquake

B.L. BERRY

© 2017 by B.L. Berry
All rights reserved.

Editing: Jennifer Roberts-Hall
Proofreading: Virginia Carey
Cover Designer: Najla Qamber, Najla Qamber Designs
Interior Designer: The Write Assistants

No part of this book may be reproduced or transmitted in any form or by any means, electronic or mechanical, including photocopying, recording, or by any information storage and retrieval system without written permission of the author, except for the use of brief quotations in a book review.

This is a work of fiction. Names, characters, businesses, places, brands, events and incidents are either the products of the author's imagination or used in a fictitious manner. Any resemblance to actual persons, living or dead, actual events, or locales is entirely coincidental.

ISBN-13: 978-1975960001
ISBN-10: 1975960009

To Karma,
For bestowing upon me a little girl who is just as sassy and smartassy as I was at this age.
May what goes around come back around to her in twenty-five years.

This one's for you, Betsy!
I'd say thank you for letting me be your mom, but you're kinda stuck with me, kiddo. I love you more than all the unicorns in the galaxy!

Prologue

BIG THINGS AND TIGHT SPACES
JEFF

Beads of sweat race down the back of my neck and adrenaline pulsates through my veins. I can feel my heartbeat in my head all the way down to my toes, and I know that if I don't get there fast, I'm going to explode. And not just metaphorically.

Pull your shit together, Jeff! This isn't like you.

My legs quiver and the harder I go, the more I feel like my body is going to give out from underneath me.

"*Fuck,*" I mutter under my breath as I lick my lips and gasp for air. I swallow hard, doing my best to keep it together. This moment will *not* end before it even begins. I quickly wipe at the sheen of sweat building on my forehead. I send silent prayers above.

Dear, God, please. Just hold out a little longer. Come on ...

My breath is short and fast, and it all hurts so good, and my body aches from the incessant pounding this morning. And then all of my muscles tense simultaneously, and it's almost euphoric.

Almost.

Because the radiant woman before me finally comes into focus. And from the looks of it, she's pissed.

"Hold the plane!" I beg in my final sprint toward the Southwest Airlines gate agent, waving my ticket in the air. My brother Chris will string me up by my balls if I'm not there for tee time later this morning. "*Please* ... wait!" I beg.

The woman is starting to close the door to the tarmac but notices me moments before she shuts it. Her glare pierces right through me, and I can't tell if she's annoyed or if that look is just permanent resting bitch face. Either way, it doesn't matter because, at this moment, she hates me. I'm likely the reason the entire day has started off with a delay. I went so far as to call the Southwest Airlines desk at the Kansas City Airport from my taxi, letting them know I would be there before takeoff, but depending on the security line, I would be cutting it close. In true Midwest hospitality, the agent on the other end of the line informed me that, "We can't hold the plane for you, but I'll call the gate agent and see if they can stall closing the doors until the last possible moment."

The woman guarding the door at the gate looks down at her wristwatch and raises her eyebrows, silently scolding me. Without so much as a word, she holds out her hand, palm up.

So much for that Midwest hospitality.

I hand her my ticket to scan and give her my best apologetic smile.

"Running a bit late are we?"

"I know. I injured myself trying to get into my skinny jeans," I say breathlessly, my lungs still on fire from my unexpected morning run.

The woman looks me up and down, unamused. "You're not even wearing skinny jeans, sir."

Okay, so humor isn't immune from her sour mood.

"I know. Ironic, right?" I don't know why I'm making excuses to this woman. I don't owe her anything. She doesn't *know* me.

"Whatever," she sighs. "This is a nearly full flight, so take the first seat you can find." The machine between us beeps, and she hands my ticket back to me as I silently curse the fact I didn't book an airline that actually assigns seats. "Have a nice trip."

Clearly, this is code for get the hell out of my face.

I hustle down the tarmac, and when I turn into the aisle of the plane, all eyes are on me. It reminds me of the recurring dream I had in junior high where I'd show up to school naked, and everyone would double over in fits of laughter. That dream was far different from my fantasy where I'd show up to school naked and the entire varsity cheerleading squad would fawn over just how ginormous I was. I blame my older brother Kyle's retro VHS porn collection for my unrealistic expectations of high school and sex and girls.

Ah, those were the days.

"It's all middle seats now, and there's only a handful left. Also, the overhead bins are full, so you'll need to put your bag underneath the seat in front of you." The flight attendant is a little too perky for this ungodly hour of the morning. She must be running on three pots of extra strong coffee. What I'd give for a hit of caffeine.

I'm close to halfway through the plane when I cross the first open seat and I clumsily climb over a businessman in the aisle and plop into the chair with an exasperated *oomph!* I take the backpack from my lap and wrestle to stuff it underneath the seat in front of me, which means my long legs are going to be cramped for the duration of the flight. I silently curse myself for not putting more into my checked bag.

"Winning the war against physics, I see." A woman's voice jests with a delicate laugh.

I turn toward her and my whole world freezes. And for the first time ever, I have the elusive *Dream Weaver* moment. You know, where everything moves in slow motion, and you see heinous special effects stars and glitter and Gary Wright's terrible song plays in the background? It happened to Wayne when he first saw Cassandra rocking out on stage in Wayne's World. Yeah. *That* is this exact moment for me, including the part where I have to physically pick my jaw up off of the floor as I mentally go *sha-wing*!

She raises her eyebrows at me, seemingly pleased with herself. Her auburn hair cascades down her back and perfectly frames her face, and her perfectly glossed lips just beg to be tasted. Even seated, I can tell she's fit, and it's easy to imagine what she looks like under all those clothes.

And I'm instantly a believer.

I believe you can get me through the night.

I try to recall what she said exactly three seconds ago before I was dumbstruck by her beauty. Yes. Physics. The fact my backpack can barely fit underneath the seat in front of me.

I clear my throat and try to sound suave. "Uh … yeah, I'm kind of the master of fitting big things into tight spaces." *What the fuck kind of comment was that?* Although the prospect of fitting *my* big thing in *her* tight space is not lost on me, that is *not* an appropriate conversation with a stranger, and certainly not something you say to a woman whose beauty has stunned you into stupidity.

Her cheeks flush red as she purses her lips and turns to look out the window. "Ooookay, then …" she mutters under her breath.

Shit.

I shift in my seat, rattle the thought from my brain, and try to avoid my junk from springing into action. And while I subscribe to the theory that it's never too early for a hard on, I do believe that I need to keep my junk in check when I'm on a plane.

Unless, of course, I'm being inducted into The Mile High Club. Which I wouldn't say no to, especially if *she* were to do the honors.

"I'm sorry. I ... I didn't mean that to come out so ... sexually. I just meant that I'm the master of getting things to go exactly where they belong." *You're making no sense. This conversation is so stupid. You need to stop talking and close your eyes and stop looking at the pretty girl and simply sleep this flight away.*

But I don't. Because I'm an idiot.

"You should see what I'm packing down below."

"Excuse me?"

"I meant my bag! Under the plane!" I shut my eyes tight, willing everything I've said to her back into my mouth. Heat rises in my cheeks. "I can pack a bag like it's nobody's business." *I'm just going to shut now. And die up. I mean I'm just going to shut up and then die. Jesus! She's even infiltrated my internal monologue!*

"I see," she responds slowly.

I'm desperate to escape this whole scenario, so I grab a magazine from the seat back pocket and start thumbing through, pretending to read some article that appears to be about weight loss based on the pictures on the page.

The flight attendants go through the safety procedures while no one pays attention, and before I know it, we're barreling down the runway, thrusting hundreds of thousands of pounds into the air, defying all laws of gravity. It's kind of terrifying when you think about it.

Just like this woman.

She terrifies me in all the best ways possible.

"So ..." She turns back toward me, and I'm pleasantly surprised that she's still engaging with me. Maybe I'm not royally screwing this up after all? "Good article?"

"Yeah. It's pretty good." *Okay, I can handle short, casual*

phrases *if I don't look at her. This is improvement. Keep it quick.*
"This is one of my favorite mags."

She tilts her head and flashes me her pearly whites. "Long-time reader?"

"Yeah. For years." I keep my eyes trained to the page, interest feigned. *Good! This is good! We're connecting on common ground.*

"I never would have pegged you as a *Senior Women's Weekly* aficionado."

I shut the magazine and look at the silver-haired grandmother on the cover. *Shit.* I shrug it off and focus on being casual. Cool. Someone she would want to get to know. I turn to look at her. "There's a lot of things you probably wouldn't peg me as."

"Is that so?"

"Yeah." I smile smugly.

"Let me guess." She shifts in her seat, trying to turn toward me and folds her arms over her chest. "You're a professional snuggler, who prefers taco Tuesdays to wine Wednesdays. In your spare time you enjoy playing video games on the couch in your mom's basement. You secretly fancy cats over dogs. And you were late this morning because you accidentally took an ex-lax instead of your daily vitamins and had a rough time getting here." The teasing smile that plays her lips is enough to make my dick twitch.

"Close. While I am good at being the big spoon in a snuggle sandwich, I'm actually a software engineer who enjoys a good ole fashioned Kentucky Bourbon. The last time I played video games on the couch in my mother's basement was when I was fifteen alongside my two brothers. I was late this morning not because I couldn't control my bowels, but rather because I had a love affair with my snooze button." I lean in closer and lower my voice, looking for any excuse to be close enough to breathe her in. "But yes, I do secretly prefer cats over dogs, and if you ever divulge that to anyone, I will hunt you down and force you to listen to the song *Tom's Diner* on repeat until your ears bleed."

The words don't come out as confidently as I'd like, but at least it was a coherent sentence, so I'll take that as a win given my track record with this conversation.

She stares right through me and my mouth suddenly goes dry. I swallow hard before grabbing my bottle of water for a satisfying swig. "So ..." She cocks an eyebrow like she's deep in thought. "You like pussy?"

I choke on my water and nearly cough up a lung as I try to collect myself. I take a few deep breaths. "Excuse me?" *Is she offering hers? What the hell is with this woman?*

"You admitted you like cats. I was just fucking with you." She laughs and gently touches her fingers to my forearm, and it sets my entire body on high alert.

She goes on to tell me random thoughts about her childhood dog, Zeus, her best friend, Tara, and how last night she managed to ruin a batch of instant pudding and instead of trying to clean the pot she simply threw it away.

I hang on her every last word. She could be reading me the dictionary, and I'd still grasp onto her every last syllable like a talisman. She's unlike any girl I've ever met before. And that notion makes me uneasy because every girl I've ever met has been candidly predictable. But in spite of how she makes me feel, I want more.

"So are you from Kansas City? Or are you heading home to Denver?"

Please don't be from Denver. Please don't be from Denver. If she's from Denver, the likelihood of me seeing her again is slim. And that would suck. But if she is from Denver, please don't let her be a Broncos fan.

"Nah. I'm a Kansas City girl through and through. Born and raised in the suburbs. I'm just headed to Denver on business."

She gestures to the leather satchel at her feet as if I should have known this little fact based on her handbag choices. "What about yourself? Are you from Denver? You're not one of those obnoxious Broncos fans, are you? Because if you are, I'm going to have to change seats. I was sitting over there, and then *that* sat next to me." She nods toward the aisle where a grown ass man is sporting a beer belly, a lumberjack beard dyed orange and blue, and the Denver Broncos logo shaved into the side of his head. "His mother must be so proud."

Oh my god. I think I love you.

"Yes. I mean no. No, I'm not a Broncos fan." *Please don't change seats on me!* "But yes, I *am* from Denver ... was ... originally ... I mean ... not originally *originally*. I'm originally from Seattle. But we moved to Denver when I was little. And then I moved to KC. Not when I was little, but after college. Kansas City lives me. I mean, I live in Kansas City. Downtown. On the plaza. Where I work. On the plaza. As a software engineer." *What the ever living fuck is my problem?*

She smiles and snickers politely. "So you live ... and work ... on the plaza," she repeats slowly.

I swallow hard. *Idiot!* "Yeah, I do." I can feel all the blood rushing to my face. I reach up and turn the knob to increase the airflow. *Would it be too much trouble to get some god damned air back here?*

"I don't work too far from there."

So not only is she local, she's in close proximity. *There is a god looking down on me!*

She nails me with an expectant look, and I think I should just keep my mouth shut. "I'm a teacher, by the way. I teach sixth grade Language Arts at Waterview Elementary."

I can practically hear the *'Thanks for asking, douche canoe!'* in her voice. My mind runs wild with all the questions I want to ask, but don't trust myself to form complete sentences.

Do you get summers off?
Can you put me in detention?
Will you marry me?
What is it about this woman that makes it impossible to talk to her like a normal human being?

She looks up at me from underneath her mile long lashes. And there it is.

Her eyes.

Holy shit.

Those eyes are remarkable. A mysterious, rich shade of chocolate brown that is disarming. And kind. Each time I look into her eyes, I turn into a bumbling bumblefuck. *Whatever the hell that means.* I can't talk to her when I'm actually looking *at* her, so I shift my gaze downward, hoping the change in scenery will allow me to regain my composure. I smile as I'm greeted by what are, quite possibly, the world's most perfect pair of breasts perfectly contoured in this perfect little black v-neck top. I can feel the corners of my lips curl up in a dopey-ass grin. But I can't even care because...

"Perfection."

Oh shit. I said that out loud, didn't I?

"Hey!" She snaps her fingers in front of my face. "If you want to talk to my boobs, the least you could do is buy them a drink first."

"Sorry," I mutter under my breath and silently curse myself. Why the hell did I sit here? Why couldn't there have been an empty seat next to a little old lady who'd show me photos of her thirty-seven cats for the duration of the flight? Or even a seat next to Mr. Bronco over there. I turn my head to see him digging for gold. If his finger were up there any further, his brain might gnaw it off. But no, I'm sitting here making an ass of myself next to a beautiful woman.

"You think I'm beautiful?"

My eyes flash to her, and there's no hiding the panic on my face. "Well ... uh ..." *No use backpedaling, dumbass. Don't be the guy who compliments a woman and then denies it. Ridiculous novels are full of assholes. Don't be the asshole in this stranger's life. Don't be the guy she texts her girlfriends about in some horror meeting on an airplane.*

"Yeah, I do. From the little I've gathered about you, I think you're beautiful."

Dammit! Now I sound shallow.

"And nice. I think you're nice, too." I hate that it sounds like an afterthought. I hate that I can't be remotely coherent around her.

"Nice?" she asks cautiously.

"What's wrong with being nice? I'm a nice guy."

"That remains to be determined." She smirks and playfully nudges me in the shoulder, quickly recovering by casually leaning against the window. "But if natural disasters are nice, then yeah ... I guess you could say that I'm nice."

She's a natural disaster, all right. This woman is an earthquake with a heartbeat and a smile capable of shifting the earth beneath your feet, but powerful enough to bring your whole world crumbling down. It absolutely terrifies me. And all I know is I want more of it.

Of her.

I shift in my seat and look more closely at her, trying to read in between the lines. "What's that supposed to mean?" I ask.

"It means that I am arguably one of the klutziest humans to grace this planet. Murphy's Law exists because of me."

Has she not noticed my ridiculousness over the past hour?

"Well, if you're a self-proclaimed disaster, you are easily one of the most beautiful disasters I've ever laid eyes on." I didn't mean to call her beautiful, but I love that she's fighting a smile as her cheeks blush, nearly turning the color of her fiery, glowing hair.

"Thanks," she says underneath her breath.

The hum of the airplane's engines take over, and she looks at me wordlessly. Dare I say awkwardly? I have absolutely no idea where to go from here. And so we fly ...

In complete silence.

The descent into the Denver airport is brutal at best. I've never had a turbulent-free landing here. So when the plane seemingly drops three hundred feet from the sky, she panics and grabs for the armrest. However, she misses the armrest by a long shot and takes a death grip on my upper thigh, mere millimeters from my manhood.

I'd be lying if I said I didn't enjoy it ... just a little bit.

"Oh my God! I am *so* sorry!" She immediately retracts her hands like she's just touched a hot stove.

No! Don't be sorry. It is totally okay with me if you want to put your hand back there. "You know, if you want to grab my junk the least you could do is buy me a drink first," I jest, mimicking her words from a few minutes ago. "Actually, that's a lie. No drink needed. I'm easy like that."

She closes her eyes and shakes her head as she recovers from the moment. "Seriously ... I'm sorry ... I didn't mean ..." her voice trails off softly.

"It's okay. Really."

She offers me a small, apologetic smile. The sunlight angles through the window in just the right way where her hair catches fire light.

And I'm a fucking goner.

Marry me, you hilarious, kind and beautiful creature.

As the wheels touch down, I'm desperate for us to ascend back into the clouds. The hour and twenty minutes in the air with her were not nearly enough for me.

"Do you think when we both get back to Kansas City, I could eat you out sometime?" *Shit! Fuck! God, just kill me now.* "I mean, do you think I could *take* you out to eat sometime?"

She nervously bites her nail as she considers my offer. "Yeah ... I'd like that." Her nerves subside, and she smiles sweetly, then reaches into her purse underneath the seat in front of her. She takes out a crumpled up receipt and scribbles something down on the back side. When she passes me the soft paper, she extends her hand to shake mine. "I'm Henley, by the way." Her skin is soft, and I resist pulling it up to my lips to kiss her hand. There's no way this woman tastes anything less than incredible.

"Henley," I muse softly. I love her name. I love her eyes. I love her boobs. I love how her hand feels tucked inside mine. I love that she hates the Broncos almost as much as I do.

Awkwardly, Henley keeps her hand in mine, and we're holding hands for a few moments too long for this to just be casual. She raises her eyebrows at me curiously and laughs before pulling her hand away from mine. I instantly feel the void and regret allowing her to let it go.

But I'm quickly soothed when I look down at the paper in my hand and see her number scrawled underneath her scrolled name.

"Um..." She hesitates for a moment. "You're ... *charming.*" She bites her lower lip coyly like she is starting to understand the stronghold she has over me. But damn, I don't care.

And then it dawns on me what she's looking for.

"No, not *charming.* Jeff. My name is Jeff."

Chapter One

THE UNICORN

"Things between you and lovah-boy seem to be going well. How long has it been now? Four months?"

Tara is perched on the edge of my bed, speaking into her vodka glass like a microphone. She's less Oprah and more Wendy Williams. Oprah wouldn't conduct gossip interviews with a vodkaphone, would she? She'd be classier and come to the table with a cosmophone or maybe even a belliniphone for good measure.

When Tara pushes the vodkaphone my way, I pluck the glass from her fingers and take a swig before handing it back to her.

"Yeah ... it's been almost five, actually." I smile at my best friend as I pull my skirt up my legs and around my hips. I'm pretty sure I've fallen in love with him, but I don't make mention of that yet. I'd never hear the end of it. Part of me fell in love with him at ten thousand feet amid all of his glorious awkwardness. Thankfully that subsided by our third date — just in time for *my* true awkwardness to arrive. I admit I put on a good front. But once you get to know me, it's impossible for me to hide how utterly ridiculous I am. But apparently, he adores me in spite of that.

"So you think he's the one?"

I turn back toward my closet to scour the hangers for my favorite cobalt blouse. "I think he's the one for right now."

"Seriously, Hen? You haven't dated in centuries. And now you have an awesome guy, with — and I quote 'a package that makes your vajayjay squeal with fright and delight' — who worships the ground you walk on, and you're claiming he's Mr. Right Now? I call bullshit. That man is a goddamned unicorn, and you know it."

"Whatever, Tara." She knows it takes a lot to get me to open up about my relationships. It took me *how* long to pick up the pieces after Leo and I broke up. I'm guarded—and rightfully so.

Ever since I first mentioned Jeff when I returned from my Denver trip, Tara has taken a keen interest in my love life. Probably because the last time I had a love life, she was a free-spirited single gal sowing her wild oats in college. Now that her days are spent knee-deep in peanut butter sandwiches and yelling at her kids to stop playing Star Wars with their penises, she's hell-bent on reliving the glory days through me.

I guess I can't blame her though.

I pull my shirt off the hanger and slip it over my head, smoothing the wrinkles out with my palms. I turn to face Tara and raise my arms to ask *what do you think?*

"Oh God. You're not wearing *that* shirt, are you?" Tara guffaws as she tosses back the last of her vodka cranberry. She doesn't get out very often these days with three toddler boys of her own and a husband who is one giant man-child—so anytime we're together without the accompaniment of impressionable ears, she's quick to hit the mommy sauce.

"What's wrong with this top?" Sure, it's from college, but it fits, there are no stains, and it makes the ladies look great. "It's always been one of my favorites."

"Do I really need to remind you?"

I throw a questioning look over my shoulder at her and head over to my jewelry box to pull out a coral necklace for a pop of color.

"This is *the* top."

"*Theeeeee* top?" I question in over-exaggeration and fist my hands to my hips. "That's pretty vague, T."

"I can't believe you don't remember." She sets her empty glass down on my nightstand and begins raiding my closet, tossing shirt after shirt onto the bed. "This is the shirt you wore the day that crusty knob shiner broke your heart."

Ugh. I don't want to be reminded of him before my date tonight. "He didn't break my—"

"Shlllrrrp!!" Tara sounds, effectively shutting me up. "You refused to take that shirt off for four days because you said it still smelled of his aftershave and cologne from the last time he hugged you. You were pathetic. I deliberately spilled an ice cream sundae all over it while you loused around on the couch in hopes you'd finally change your clothes, but no. You didn't. You took the damn spoon and scooped that shit up right off your tits and shoveled it in your mouth."

She's right. I found little colored sprinkles and dried chocolate sauce on my boobs later that weekend. Not exactly one of my finer moments.

"Dude," I sigh. "Point taken. Those were some dark times. Let's not revisit it, okay?"

"So then change your damn top."

Fine.

Hastily, I pull the shirt back up and over my head and grab the pink ballerina blouse that's in her hands, making quick work of the pearl buttons. "Did I tell you he asked me to meet his family?"

"No! When?"

I bite the inside of my cheek to avoid a shit eating smile. "At the beginning of February. I'm headed back to Denver with him for his brother Chris's wedding."

"Shut up! Not only are you meeting them, but you're meeting them *at* his brother's wedding? This *is* serious. Do you know what this means?"

I roll my eyes. "It means I'm going to meet his family when we're in town for his brother's wedding. Nothing more. Nothing less." I'm not doing a very good job of *not* getting my hopes up because I can read between the lines. I'm more than just a wedding date. I'm his girlfriend. A serious girlfriend. His girlfriend that he's so serious about, he's schlepping me across the Midwest to spend time with his family at an intimate affair. It means that he can see some kind of future with me beyond just this given moment. Because you don't take just *anyone* to your brother's wedding. And that? *That* is huge.

Tara gives me a knowing look. She knows I've never been someone's wedding date. She knows it's huge, too.

"It's no big deal ... *really*," I bite back as I step into my nude-colored flats.

I turn to the mirror, tousle my long auburn locks, and smile. I've always considered myself to be girl next door cute, but with these legs for days, I feel unstoppable.

"You look hot, by the way."

"Thanks." I smile, pleased with myself. If my memory serves me correctly, this is the same outfit I wore on date number four. The glorious date in which I gave him permission to dip his wick in the land down under. And dip he did.

God, that was beyond incredible.

I was quickly schooled in what is, and more importantly what is not, an orgasm through physical penetration. A lesson brought to me by the Female Orgasm Ad Council. Also known as Jeff Carrington, my current love interest.

What I had assumed was the big O with Leo was apparently nothing more than a tiny blip in the ocean. A ripple from a small pebble on a glass lake. A ... wait a minute ... was that little twitch between my legs it? Let's just call it what it was: a sad, little disappointment, and an opportunity for me to perfect my acting skills.

But sex with Jeff was no act. Oh, no! Sex with Jeff was a toe-curling, hair-fisting, back-arching, neighbors calling to make sure nobody is being murdered kind of affair that resulted in ten million angels dancing upon my g-spot. Yes, his cock was heavenly, and the experience was downright spiritual. It was enough to make me sing God's praises, and not just mid-thrust either.

Tara's right. He *is* a goddamned unicorn. And I can't believe he's mine.

More often than not, I spare Tara those intimate details. It's one thing to experience them for yourself and relive those memories on a rainy day with your vibrator. But it's another when your best friend is probing you for more information about how his "meat scepter makes my fish flaps feel." And those are her repulsive and disturbing words, not mine.

"So what else is new with you?"

"Oh, the same old, same old. Cam is keeping busy at work, I'm keeping busy with the boys, and the boys are keeping busy with plotting my demise. It's just another day in paradise."

I laugh because I know it's true. Ever since the triplets started walking, Tara has grown more gray hairs than I can count. Wes, Miles, and Jack are ornery little terrors, and it's a miracle that she hasn't sold one of them off to the circus. Or considered running away herself.

"And how are they?" It's been a few weeks since I last saw them.

"They're fine. Growing like weeds. I'm looking forward to the day where I can drink *with* them and not because of them. They're with Cam for the next little bit until grandma picks them up for a sleepover. You're not the only one with a date tonight, and we are long overdue." She wiggles her eyebrows at me.

I love how much she and Cam are still head over heels for each other after all these years.

"Oh! And thanks again for the series of books you gave the boys for their birthday."

"No problem. I hope they like them."

I had found this amazing ten book set of all the classic tales with a twist that appealed to boys. I figured the last thing Tara and Cameron wanted was a deluxe Lego set. I can only imagine the hell that comes with stepping on one of those fuckers barefoot.

"Yeah, they're awesome and are the cornerstone of our bedtime routine. But I've learned that no matter which fairy tale I read to them, the moral of the story that *I* take away is to always get your tubes tied." Tara checks her watch and slips her shoes back on her feet.

"Okay. Well, I'm gonna go. Grandma is picking the kids up in fifteen minutes, and the heavens need me right now."

I should be used to this kind of random remark from Tara, and after all these years of friendship, I should really know better than to ask. But still, I can't help myself.

"The *heavens* need you? Is that so?" I inspect my makeup in the mirror and pull out the gloss to touch up my lips.

"Yeah." She turns toward me and pauses a beat. "The kids are gone. And every time I climax, an angel gets its wings."

"Seriously, Tara?" I can't help but laugh at her.

She blows me a kiss as she heads for the door. "I just hope I'm not the only one getting a little lust and thrust tonight, love muffin. Just don't make a mistake. Make sure he covers his snake!"

I shake my head at her, trying my best not to smile.

"What? If he goes into heat, make sure to package his meat!"

"TARA!" *God, she's so crass! And apparently, she's also a walking, talking billboard for safe sex, and not just because she has triplets.*

Tara slips through the door and pops her head back through the crack. "All I'm saying is that there's nothing wrong with a little latex protection before his flesh injection! So sock that wang before you bang. Have fun tonight, Henley!"

And then the door shuts before I can get another word in.

Chapter Two

PACKING BAGGAGE

"Would you just try and relax, Henley?" Jeff says, stuffing some underwear into the side pocket of his suitcase. My nail beds are destroyed as I've been picking and chewing at them thoughtlessly for the past hour. I have been nothing but a basket case of epic proportions ever since the magnitude of this wedding invitation truly slapped me upside the head.

It's one thing for him to tell me to relax. It's another to actually achieve desired levels of relaxation without the assistance of a Xanax, a bottle of wine, and my trusty vibrator.

I fold my fingers in my lap and take a few slow and calming breaths, willing my nerves to settle the fuck down. But I still feel like I'm going to lose it.

Jeff looks back to his dresser and pulls out an armful of fancy, colorful dress socks. I like to think I've done a pretty bang up job of hiding my annoyance this evening. But with each drawer shut and shirt ripped down from a closet hanger, I mentally shoot daggers in Jeff's direction.

Come to my brother's wedding! he said.

You can meet my family! he said.

It'll be fun! he said!

What he failed to mention was that the Carrington last name causes people to stop and stare at the mere mention of it. Revelation that his family is kind of a big deal surprised me. Apparently, it carries more weight than an elephant tap dancing to mariachi music once we crossed the Colorado border. An imaginary line we'll be crossing in a few short hours since we're taking the first flight out at o'dark thirty tomorrow.

I've been packed, repacked and then packed again for this weekend since Monday night, but leave it to Romeo to wait until the last minute, effectively causing us to miss our dinner reservations, making me hangry and wound up tighter than a minister's wife's panties at a Vegas strip show.

"Let the record show that I was doing just fine until you told me that this wedding was going to be a two hundred thousand dollar black tie affair at The Little Nell in Aspen. I looked up photos. We have to take a motherfucking private gondola three miles up the side of a mountain to get to the ceremony, Jeff. Our room alone is more than eleven hundred dollars a night! You could buy a private island in the Caribbean for that price tag."

Seems like a smarter investment at least.

The online photos showed me a little piece of snowy heaven on earth. But the only way I could ever afford to visit this place is if I blew my life savings and worked a street corner for a few weeks for good measure.

I know I shouldn't complain. It's not like *I'm* paying for any of this. The property looks immaculate. The kind of place where the three-second rule doesn't apply when you drop food on the floor. But I already know that I'm going to be the odd man out in the game of *one of these things is not like the other* when we arrive. Even still, I hope it will be worth the mental anguish. I need to get away if only for a little bit in the height of frozen mountain tops. And if I have my way, my presence will go virtually undetected, and I can hide by the top shelf open bar most of the night.

"Aww, come on. It's not *that* much." Jeff gives me a knowing look.

"Says the man whose last name automatically qualifies him for the friends and family discount at every five-star ski lodge in North America." A little-known fact that only came up days ago.

I can't even begin to wrap my brain around the thought of dropping two hundred thousand dollars on one party that'll last maybe half the day. Jeff's parents insisted on paying for the wedding, with his mom lamenting the fact she never had a daughter. But that kind of money is just a drop in the bucket for Colorado's leading environmental lawyer, who singlehandedly defended the National Parks in a huge corporate lawsuit, and the woman whose family nine-figure inheritance comes from the Snowfalls chain of luxury ski resorts.

For coming from money, it's amazing how grounded and headstrong Jeff is. *"I'm not rich. My parents are. And from an early age they were clear that if Chris, Kyle, and I wanted that kind of life, we had to be the ones to work for it,"* he had told me during a recent conversation.

I'm *just* a teacher. His parents probably make a year's worth of my salary in one week of work. From the stories he's told me, they certainly don't live—or act—like their bank accounts could purchase a Major League franchise.

"I promise it'll be okay. I love you, so I know for a fact that they are going to love you, too."

I try to take his word for it, but the whole meeting the parents thing is foreign territory, and damn near maddening under *any* circumstance. Let alone *this* particular scenario that requires me to be on my game for everyone.

"That's easy for you to say. They're your parents. They *have* to love you," I sigh in defeat.

"Besides, everyone is going to be so busy with the wedding, they'll probably forget we're even there."

I roll my eyes. Jeff is in the wedding, so his presence—or absence—will be quite obvious. The best I can hope for is to fly under the radar without incident.

I sit down on the end of his bed and watch him finish packing sweater after sweater. Colorado in February seems like a risky idea for a wedding, but hopefully, Mother Nature has an unseasonal hot flash and avoids a deluge of snow. With my luck, we'll get snowed in.

"Okay. Let me see if I've got this right. Kyle's your oldest brother, and he's been dating Kayla for a while."

"That's correct."

"Chris and Erin met while volunteering at an animal shelter in downtown Denver last year, and knew each other for five months before deciding to get hitched."

Jeff listens to me prattle on as he moves into his bathroom to gather his toiletries. "See? You know what's up!" He returns with his arms full of face soap and shaving cream and razors and shampoo and ...

Is that premium organic moisturizer?

No wonder his skin is so soft. Most men can get away with just one bottle of generic travel stuff: an all-in-one type cleanser that not only takes care of the hair on your head but also the hair on your feet and ass, too. But Jeff isn't most men.

"Hardly," I scoff. It's one thing to recall what I've been told. It's another to experience it first hand while trying to avoid their judge-y eyes. "Your family is big."

A tinge of jealousy washes over me at the thought of his big family. I am an only child, born to two only children, so beyond my immediate family, there wasn't ever anyone around. It made for some boring summers and lonely holidays being the sole person under the age of forty at family affairs. I guess that's why any close friends I made, I latched onto like a sibling.

"Beyond my brothers, you'll probably meet a gaggle of cousins, many of whose names I can't keep straight, and a few overbearing aunts and uncles. But watch out for my Uncle Russ. He's pushing sixty but claims he's only as old as the women he dates. He likes 'em young and pretty."

Ew!

He kisses my forehead, and I make a mental note to simply steer clear of his extended family.

"And what about your parents?"

"What about them?" he asks without making eye contact while zipping his bag up.

Jeff rarely mentions his parents, and I can only imagine that's for good reason. Isn't there some legal or moral parental obligation that they embarrass their children regardless of how old they are? Whenever I have kids, I'm going to be the cool mom. At least I hope to be.

"It's just that I know absolutely nothing about them."

He presses his lips together in a hard line and thinks for a long moment before speaking. No doubt meticulously plucking the right words from his brain so not to scare me. "My parents are a bit ... eclectic. Martha has very little interest and awareness in personal space and my dad—his name is Colin—as daft as he can sometimes be, does his best to reign her in. They're good people. Just ... *different*. Try not to get worked up about it. I know my mom is really excited to meet you and make you feel all sorts of awkward."

He's joking, right?

I laugh politely and uncomfortably all at once. He must sense my unrest because he stops what he's doing and sits down next to me on the bed. "But like I said, they're going to love you. You've got nothing to worry about." His eyes turn soft, and he grabs my hand, giving it a gentle squeeze. "I really appreciate you taking off a few days to come with me. I know you don't like to leave your students but—"

"It's really okay," I cut him off. "We're just going over some basics for the standardized tests they're taking in a few weeks. I left thorough notes, and if they finish early, I've got some educational videos they can watch." And by educational I mean some snoozefest about our Founding Fathers since the principal wouldn't approve me showing *Dangerous Minds*. I don't care what anybody says, there are *a lot* of valuable life lessons to be learned from that movie. "It's nothing the substitute can't handle."

His face lights up, and he takes my face in his hands, studying my lips. His grip is firm, and his eyes are longing. Before I know it, he's lowering me back onto the bed, quenching my hunger with a slow, deep kiss that slingshots an insatiable ache straight to my nether regions.

He pulls back to sweep some of my long auburn hair from my face. "God, I love it when you talk teacher to me. It's so hot," he marvels just before he buries his face, kissing me between my breasts, straight through my blouse.

"Seriously, Jeff?" My jaw drops and my eyes roll as I swat his shoulder away. "You are so weird!"

He looks up my body and pounds me with a coy, mischievous smirk. "Oh? And what are you going to do about that? Send me to detention?"

We both pause a beat, me trying to determine if he's serious about some teacher-student role playing action, and him undoubtedly trying to gauge my interest. But before I can even form a response he doubles over in laughter, rolling off of me and onto his back.

"Oh my God, you should see your face right now, Henley."

I throw an arm over my eyes and silently feel relief. Because as much as I love this guy, I'm not sure I have it in me to actually do any role playing. Let alone role playing in my daily profession.

"Come on. Let's go forage for food so we can get to bed. Because if I have my way, I'd like to feast on you for dessert."

He pulls me up off his bed, and I follow him to the kitchen, noting that the most dangerous mind in my life is his.

Chapter Three

CRIMES AGAINST CRAMPING

"Shhh!"

Jeff tugs on my hand as he leads me away from the bustling ballroom. I'm not sure why he wants me to be quiet because there's no way anyone at the reception can possibly hear us right now. I should feel guilty sneaking off before the toasts and the throwing of the bride's bouquet, but I don't think anyone will miss us. They're all a bit preoccupied with dancing and the alcohol that's flowing as freely as our inhibitions.

My laughter echoes down the empty marble hallway, which makes me laugh even harder. In the distance, the wedding band is in the middle of their latest crowd-pleasing set. Jeff's family didn't notice our escape as they were too busy belting the lyrics to Robin Thicke's *Blurred Lines* right alongside that horrible wedding singer. Fortunately for all, enough booze has been consumed that nobody even cares when the wedding singer goes off on a three-minute tangent answering Thicke's million dollar question of "what rhymes with hug me?" I think the real million dollar question here is who sings *Blurred Lines* at a wedding? That's about as appropriate as playing Nine Inch Nails' *Closer* at a Beastiality Anonymous meeting, but I digress.

Other than the music, this wedding has been pretty incredible. I practically threw myself on top of Jeff right in the middle of the dance floor earlier in the evening. His epic, white guy dance moves were certainly not the way into my panties, but when his eyes smiled, and there was a glint of mischief, I nearly mauled him.

But that's not how we got here in the hallway.

I'm not sure when I made the decision to slip away with my boyfriend for a mid-wedding celebration quickie, but when he looked at me with his ocean blue eyes and lazy drunken smile and jokingly said, "There's something about weddings that makes me horny," I knew it was hopeless to fight my libido. My ears perked up at the magic "H" word. It's not the first time he's told me that line, but it's the first time I was drunk enough to react to them like I did roughly ninety seconds ago.

The room was dim, my fingertips were curious, and I leaned over into his ear and whispered, "There's something about *you* that makes me horny," just before brushing my fingertips up the length of his inner thigh to discover that he was telling the truth. I am *never* that forward. But imagine my surprise when I learned those weren't just words ... weddings actually *do* make him horny. Jeff grabbed me in a flash and had me sprinting out the double doors behind him.

Maybe it was the bottle and a half of champagne I'd downed during the happy hour that made me follow him? No, it was *definitely* the bottle and a half of champagne I downed during happy hour. I don't care, though. Because this man, my boyfriend, is all I want right now. Provided we can actually find a few minutes of peace and quiet.

That's a lie.

I'm probably drunk enough to entertain an audience with him.

The first two doors Jeff tries are locked, but on the third try, he throws his weight against a door and opens a room that is pitch black. Before I know it, our lips mesh as Jeff pushes my shoulders against the door.

He moans into my mouth. "You taste like strawberries, woman."

I giggle and reach for his shirt, enthusiastically unbuttoning it from the top down.

"Don't bother, Henley, we only have a few minutes," he reminds me, then nips my collarbone with his teeth before flicking his tongue up my neck, retracting the path with relentless kisses.

His hot breath against my skin causes me to writhe and my head slams against the backside of the door. "Ow!" I cry through my laughter. Noting that the copious amount of champagne has deadened my nerves.

"Are you okay, baby?" he whispers in concern. I can barely see his face lit up by the dim glow of a red exit sign above us.

"Yeah," I breathe out heavily and fumble with the belt wrapped around his waist.

"Hold on, let me find a light really quick."

"Fuck the lights, Jeff." I pull his chin toward me and kiss him with an unrivaled ferocity all while unzipping his tuxedo pants, slipping my hand into his boxers and pumping my hand up and down his cock a few times. It comes back to life instantly in my palm.

Jeff presses his forehead against mine, and a purr escapes from the back of his throat. "Shit, Henley, I want you so bad right now."

Jeff reaches around my body and attempts to take my dress off, which is ridiculous if I'm not even allowed to take off his shirt. "Don't even try. It's too much effort." And it's true. My navy strapless dress has a corset back, and there's no way I can get in — or out — of it without the assistance of an army. I reach down and gather the fabric and hoist it up to my waist. Jeff slides his hands up my calves and thighs to slip my panties off.

"What the fuck?" he slurs in surprise. If I weren't so caught off guard by his comment, I'd probably find his tone adorable.

"What do you mean?"

"What the hell is this, Henley?"

Oh, God. Shit! "Um ..."

"Are you wearing granny panties?"

I grind my teeth in horror. "Shit. No! Those are Spanx. They were undoubtedly made by some guy as a torture device, but they do a damn good job keeping everything in place." *There goes my lady in the streets but a freak in the sheets reputation I'll never get.*

"Mmm ... I'd like to spank you right about now," Jeff growls.

Involuntarily, I snort at his comment. It reminds me of the time we tried dirty talking and failed miserably. We both ended up in fits of laughter.

"Just get them off, will you?"

"Yes, ma'am."

Jeff kneels down and peels the Spanx off my ass, and I step out of them, kicking them to the side. My body instantly feels free from the tight confines of those wretched unmentionables. He makes quick work of the rest of his pants and boxers, dropping them to his ankles. He leans my body back against the door and in one fell swoop, pushes himself inside of me, filling me to the brim.

I melt around his body.

My head is light from all the champagne and from the dizzying spell he casts upon me. It becomes increasingly difficult to hold my body up as my legs turn weak and, instinctively, Jeff takes on more and more of my body weight in his arms as we lean back against the door.

"It feels wrong to be having sex before the bride and groom," I pant mid-thrust.

"It's not wrong. We're celebrating love. They'd commend us for celebrating so passionately," Jeff whispers in my ear before nipping my earlobe with his teeth.

"To love," I cry out and clench his body tighter. Our tongues are at war with one another as our bodies mesh together.

"Oh my God, Henley, I'm so close. I'm so close ... I'm gonna come," he growls in my ear like he's a freaking sports announcer calling a grand slam, game-winning play at the bottom of the ninth inning of the final World Series match up.

Why do guys do that anyway?

I hitch my leg tighter around his waist and sink my fingernails into his perfectly tight ass, bringing him impossibly closer to my body.

"Oh, shit! Henley! My calf ... I ... I'm cramping ... Oh, God ... I'm coming! CRAMP!" Jeff's body tenses right as the overhead lights flash on, blinding us both.

What the fuck?

My gaze snaps to his, and I feel the color draining from my face in one fast, sobering moment. The same moment Jeff's body shudders as he finds his release.

"Holy fuck nuggets" he whispers, clenching his eyes shut.

"Hey! You! You can't be in here!" a man's voice echoes through the space, chopped up into bits and pieces of broken English. "Stop that! Now! That is bad!"

When I look over Jeff's shoulder, a portly old man in a hunter green security uniform crosses the space across the empty ballroom, hastily waving his finger at us.

"Oh, shit!" I whisper, trying to contain my laughter.

Jeff stares at me wide-eyed and full of panic as he processes exactly what is happening here. He stands eerily still like he believes that he's camouflaged with the door behind me and if he moves even a fraction of an inch he'll be exposed. *No pun intended.* Don't get me wrong, his ass cheeks are pale. Just not *that* pale. This is one of those moments where I'd give my left tit to have my childhood wish of being invisible actually come true.

When I look over Jeff's shoulder and see the guard glaring at me, he speaks louder. You know, just in case I didn't hear him the first time he chided my first experience of sex in a public place.

"You bad for doing that here! You dirty! You bad! Go! Go now!" With each syllable, he stabs his finger into the air, and even from the other side of the room, I can see his thick, caterpillar eyebrows furrow angrily.

I give Jeff's arm a subtle squeeze, reminding him that we're not, in fact, invisible, and that we actually need to make a move before this five-foot cock-blocker takes a step toward us.

Jeff kisses my lips quickly as he pulls himself out from my body and hoists his pants back up in a flash, narrowly missing catching his manhood in the zipper. I let the skirt of my dress fall to my ankles and smooth out the fabric. We slip out the door and hightail it back down the hallway to his brother's wedding reception.

"Holy hell. Did that really just happen?" he asks over his shoulder as he reaches back for my hand.

"What? The realization that we just had a run in with Long Duk Dong thirty years after his movie debut in Sixteen Candles, or the fact you cramped up like a little bitch in the throes of passion?"

Jeff stops dead in his tracks and gives me a pointed look. "Hey, there was nothing bitchy about my moves back there. Or little for that matter."

I can't help but laugh softly.

"I love you," he says with a smile that reaches his eyes.

"I love you, too," I pant, still trying to catch my breath from the sexcapades that happened over the past ten minutes. I roll up onto my tip toes to lay another kiss on him and—

"You!"

Jeff and I both turn toward the distinct voice echoing from the far end of the hallway.

"Jesus! This guy is a stage five clinger," I say.

"Let's go. The last thing I want is to get kicked out during my brother's wedding reception for indecent exposure."

We slip inside the doorway, back into the reception hall full of Jeff's intoxicated family and friends, but the security guard is *still* chasing after us, yelling about something I can't make out while waving a tan-colored towel in the air like he's trying to land a goddamned Boeing 747.

Oh shit.

I swallow hard and make a beeline to the bar with Jeff hot on my heels. "A glass of champagne—actually, two. Please." I throw the last word in as an afterthought. I should probably try to be more polite in front of my boyfriend's family.

"Uh, just one," Jeff corrects the bartender before adding, "I'll take a glass of scotch, I was done with the bubbles hours ago."

"I know," I deadpan and then look back over the counter to catch the barkeep's attention. "Champagne, two glasses. Not one."

He nods in compliance and quickly produces two glasses, one for each hand, then grabs the bottle of Johnny Walker Black and a low ball glass for Jeff. I toss back the first champagne flute in one swift motion and squeeze my eyes tight as the bubbles quickly take effect.

"Whoa, babe, slow down! The sex wasn't *that* bad, was it?"

I shake my head no because, if I'm honest, having spontaneous wedding reception sex now tops my nonexistent list of sexual experiences outside of the bedroom.

Jeff laces his fingers through mine and lifts my chin toward his face. "Then what is it? Is everything okay?"

"No ... I mean yes ..." I sigh in defeat. *Or maybe it's embarrassment?*

Tap ... tap ... tap ... "Excuse me!" a man says in broken English from the microphone at the front of the stage.

Fuck.

"No. I'm not okay. That security guy is holding my Spanx hostage." I bury my face in the crook of Jeff's neck.

"Would da young lady in navy dress who left these," he waves my unmentionables far above his head and the crowd begins to snicker, "come see me to take back?"

I groan and want for nothing more than the floor to swallow me whole.

The man's eyes finally find mine in the crowd, and he smiles like he's just discovered the golden ticket into the Wonka's Chocolate Factory. "You!" He points excitedly, gesturing me to come up and see him. "Here you go! These belong to you!"

More than a hundred pairs of eyes look from my underwear and then straight to me, standing in Jeff's arms. They're quickly doing the math as to how I'm standing here and my Spanx are not plastered to my ass. The best I can hope for is that everyone is so completely wasted that they'll have no memory of this moment when they wake up in the morning. I'd also settle for a cameo from Will Smith and Tommy Lee Jones with those nifty mind eraser thingies from *Men in Black*.

Mrs. Carrington's eyes find mine, and her expression changes no less than fifteen times, teetering between horror and amusement in the span of three seconds.

Just kill me. Kill me now!

And without hesitation, Jeff thrusts his glass of scotch in the air and shouts, "To Love!" mirroring my words from our moment of glory in the other ballroom.

For a fraction of a second, the room is frozen as they process the moment. Then everyone else lifts their drink in the air, echoing the sentiment and a valiant cheer.

The band resumes.

The chatter commences.

And I exit stage left in sheer mortification.

The First Trimester

Chapter Four

DEATH BY CHOCOLATE

"You know what I love most about you?"

"What's that?" I stretch out on the other end of the couch and put my feet up in his lap.

"How even after all these months, I'm still learning something new about you every day."

I smile at the sentiment, knowing it's true. And I love how it goes both ways. Just this morning I learned that he prefers peanut butter on his waffles in addition to maple syrup. And not the store bought syrup. It has to be real Canadian Maple Syrup because, as he says, "That shit is legit."

"So what'd you learn about me today?"

He stretches his arm across the back of the couch and looks at me curiously. "Hmm, not sure. The day's not over, though, so I've still got time to figure it out."

I wiggle my toes in the air, a silent invitation for him to rub my feet, and he complies without hesitation. "Why don't you just ask me something?"

"Really?"

"Yes, really. I'm an open book with you."

"Well, this could take a while because I want to know everything about you."

I roll my eyes at his ridiculousness. "I highly doubt you want to know *everything*. Most of my life has been boring and by the book."

"What? It's true. I love you, and since I didn't get to spend the past twenty-seven years with you, the least you can do it tell me the highlights of what I've missed." He rubs the pads of his thumbs in tiny circles along the arches of my feet. It feels glorious.

"Well, I'm not about to wax poetic about my awkward years with the permed bangs and braces, or how I was convinced as a child that if I stayed in the bathtub too long, I would shrink into nothing. So if there's anything specific you're curious about, speak now or forever hold your peace."

Jeff snorts. "You really thought that?"

"Yep, that and many other ridiculous things you're never going to learn if you make fun of me!" I poke my toes into his belly.

"I would never." He feigns defensiveness.

I laugh so hard my stomach starts to hurt. We both know better than that. I'm an easy target, and I'm okay with it. The jokes are just one of the many ways he shows that he loves me.

"*Suuuuuuuure.*"

The look on his face makes my heart melt. Actually, everything about him makes me melt. Jeff opens his mouth to speak but quickly snaps it shut. "I'm gonna go against my better judgment here, but I feel like it's something I should know."

"Oh? What's that?"

He wets his lips and smirks at me knowingly. "I want to know about your first time?"

"My first time?" I cringe.

"Yeah. I mean, I'm not naive. I know there were other guys before me."

I feel my face flush crimson and heat rises to my cheeks. I really don't want to get into details with him, but it would be nice to know more about his past, too. I wonder if he'll let me get away with ambiguity here? I pull my legs back underneath me and instantly miss his touch.

"Mine was pretty lackluster," I sigh, trying to downplay the whole ordeal. "I was nineteen and had been dating this guy for a while. He was in a fraternity, and there are only so many places you get an iota of privacy in a frat house. So we snuck into the sleeping dorm during a party."

"Sleeping dorm? What's that?"

"Oh, it's a big room with bunk beds where everyone slept. At any rate, I lost my virginity in a freaking sleeping dorm. It was painful and lasted all of three minutes—*if that*! And to add insult to injury, one of the party's designated drivers was in there *trying to* sleep before his shift started at the end of the party. Said, "Thanks for the show," when we were done. It was the epitome of romance." I laugh at how foolish I was.

"No way."

"Yeah." I swallow hard. "At the time, I thought it was love. But really, he was just looking for a quick fix." When my gaze meets his, Jeff gives me a sad smile. "Stop that, I don't want your pity. Besides, things have drastically improved since then. And *you* showed me what love actually is." I wink at him so he knows I'm okay with how losing my v-card played out, even though I'm anything but okay with how it all went down. "So what about yourself? It's only fair that you tell me about your first time now, too."

"Um, I must have been fifteen or sixteen. I was at my girlfriend's house, and her parents ran to the grocery store for hamburger buns which gave us about a thirty-minute window —

at that age, I only needed a fraction of that. Even so, her bedroom was right above the garage, and I was finishing right as the garage door was opening. I think her dad knew what we were up to when I couldn't look him in the eye. But looking back, I didn't have a fucking clue what I was doing."

"Does anyone ever really have a clue?"

"Of course I do. I've had over a decade of women ... I mean, of practice," he quickly corrects himself, "so I'd like to think I've improved my game over the course of a decade."

"A decade of women?" I snort. As much as I love this adorable, ridiculous man, you'd think after his decade of women he'd know where to find the clitoris in a drunken stupor. Sober? He's completely fine. But with that much 'practice' as he calls it, you'd think he'd know where it is based on muscle memory to really pack a punch after happy hour. It's not like it's a magic bean that is hidden in a different place on every different chick that has graced his mattress. It's in the same general vicinity regardless of whether or not you're sober. It's really not that hard if you pay attention.

"What? You don't believe me? Between exes and hook ups, there have been at least a half-dozen women every year."

I quickly run the numbers in my head.

"More than sixty women?" I give him a pointed look and fold my arms over my chest. I never felt inadequate with my number until now. "That's just wrong."

Jeff stretches his arms out wide in defeat and shrugs. "Yeah ... give or take, I guess it's around sixty. I don't know what to tell you. None of them mattered because they weren't you." He leans over and kisses the tip of my nose.

"It's a good thing I love you." I narrow my eyes at him playfully.

Jeff settles back in his seat. "Sooo ... tell me."

"Tell you what?"

"You know my number ... *loosely* ... what's yours?"

I really don't want to get into this with him today. It's enough that he already knows how miserable my first time was. And there's absolutely nothing romantic about sharing old bedroom war stories with your boyfriend about past lovers.

"In my defense, I never actually asked you how many women you slept with before me." My stomach turns at the thought of his *decades* of women, but I try not to let it get to me. Because, like he said, none of them mattered because they weren't me.

"I know, it's just that we should be able to tell each other everything. We should *want* to tell each other everything. You weren't a part of my past, but you're my future. Point blank, you're it for me. I want you to know everything in my life that happened before the day we met."

I really shouldn't complain because that sentiment is incredibly sweet. But I could do without some of the gritty, intimate details.

Jeff cocks one exaggerated eyebrow up at me like he's a cartoon or something. "Well?"

My secret hangs in the balance between us. And I don't want there to be any secrets between us. I take a deep breath and steel myself. "Two."

"There were only two guys before me?"

I swallow hard, and my pride goes right down with it. "No ... two ... total. Including you."

His eyes go wide, and my insides do a funny little flip flop. "Two?" he asks, like he didn't hear me correctly the first time I told him. The tone of his voice makes me feel inadequate. Inexperienced. And suddenly unworthy because I wasn't a leg spreading trollop in my college years.

I nod, hold up two fingers, and whisper, "Two."

"Whoa."

I shift uncomfortably in my seat. I don't think the number

would bother me so much if it had been anybody other than Leo who was my first. I was naive and, admittedly, feeling desperate to lose the proverbial v-card. We only slept together a few times before our relationship went to shit—if you could even call it a relationship. Relationship implies that more than one person was involved. And looking back, I was the only one making any effort.

"It's not something I really talk about." I've done a damn good job skirting around the Leo conversation since we started dating, and I'm hoping he'll just let this go because, really, I don't want to get into the nitty gritty details.

Jeff wraps his arm around me, pulling my body closer to his. "That's nothing to be ashamed of, Henley. I just, I don't know. With your moves, I thought it would've been significantly more, that's all."

I snort at the mere insinuation of having moves in the sack, though the compliment feels a little good. However, I am anything *but* seasoned.

"So ...how do I compare with Mr. Three Minute Wonder Pants?" he asks with a wink. "I mean, should I track him down to thank him for setting the bar so low?"

I swat his shoulder with the back of my hand. "Shut up, you! There is no comparison."

And it's true. Being with Jeff quickly showed me how sex is so much more awesome when there's emotion involved. It's like comparing a Tootsie Roll to a glorious gourmet five tier chocolate cake, when you really, really, really love chocolate and want your tombstone to one day read "Here lies Henley. Death by Chocolate with an orgasmic smile on her face."

Jeff laughs lightly and kisses my cheek. "I love you, woman."

"I know. I love me, too."

Chapter Five

PERFORMANCE ANXIETY

I have a lot of "things" that I can say are "my thing."

Being able to sing all of the lyrics to every Coolio and Salt-N-Peppa song ever released? My thing.

Knowing an abundance of useless eighties movie trivia? My thing. In fact, I am the reigning undisputed champion.

Tying a knot in a cherry stem using only my tongue? Totally my thing. And also a great way to score a date while out at the bars. Because if I can do *that* with my tongue, I must have mad skills with other tongue-related activities, right?

Wrong.

But peeing on command? Yeah, that is sooo *not* my thing. Even after a liter of apple juice.

This one time at Christmas, when I was in college, my mom told my then boyfriend Leo how I used to sing *America the Beautiful* when I would go to the bathroom when I was little like the music would somehow coax my body into compliance. For the rest of the visit, Leo would stand outside the bathroom door humming patriotic tunes whenever I was trying to take care of business.

I look at the white stick in my hand and anxiously bounce my foot against the tile floor of Tara's guest bathroom.

Oh, why the hell not?

"O' beautiful, for spacious skies ... for amber waves of grain ... " I start singing softly before I am so rudely interrupted.

"How's it going in there?" Tara asks from the other side of the door as she taps her knuckles against the wood.

"I have stage fright!"

"Um, okay? Is *that* why you're serenading me?"

"No," I sheepishly retort. "My bladder is shy."

"So you were serenading your bladder? Okay, then," Tara says matter-of-factly.

I hear her footsteps trail off down the hall, and I look at a random hole in my undies. I'm a mess. It's a miracle that Jeff even wants to have sex with me.

Then it happens.

I hear Tara belting at the top of her lungs from a few rooms away. "For purple mountain majesties, above the fruited plains!"

By the time she gets to from "sea to shining sea," the moment of relief has come, and I'm peeing faster than a racehorse.

At the sound of the flushing toilet, Tara bursts into the bathroom. We've never been friends with personal barriers. She probably would have held the stick in between my legs if I'd asked her.

"Did you do the deed?"

Oh, I did the deed all right. A few weeks ago when a security guard held my Spanx ransom in front of my boyfriend's family and closest friends.

"Yeah. And now we wait."

I set the stick of fate on the side of the sink and wash my hands. Tara closes the door behind her and leans against it, examining the pregnancy test without actually touching it.

"Well, it looks like we don't have to wait for long."

I dry my hands on my shirt and look at her, then down at the test. My heart is in my throat and my stomach at my feet. A faint little pink plus sign slowly appears and grows increasingly bolder over the next minute.

Stupid little stick.

"Maybe it's a false positive?" I try to convince myself weakly.

"Or maybe you really are pregnant?" Tara wraps her arm around my shoulder. My breath quivers and my body starts to shake even though no tears fall. "Hey now, this is really exciting. Babies are good things."

"Right. Babies are good things when you're emotionally and financially and mentally equipped to handle it. I'm not even married. Jeff is gonna freak out. He's going to leave."

"Don't you even worry about him. Women have been having babies without men for ages, and now, more than ever. I can go with you to all of your appointments if you want. We'll let the doctors think we're the ultimate lesbian tag team."

"Do you have any idea how totally un-p.c. that is of you to say?"

Tara just shrugs and brushes me off. My eyes zero back in on the little white stick and the pink plus sign that has changed everything forever.

"Maybe ...? Maybe he simply won't notice?"

"And maybe, just maybe, you're going to give birth to a polka-dotted unicorn that will sing *America the Beautiful* to you every time you head to the bathroom?"

My glare at her says it all without even muttering a word.

"Oh, sorry. The thought of a unicorn horn ripping through your vag probably isn't one you want. It'd be like a self-inflicted episiotomy."

"Episioto-what?"

"Never mind." Tara's shoulders rise and fall as she sighs. "But you are going to tell him, right?" I hesitate, and she shoots me the silent scolding look that she's perfected over the years with her triplets.

"Right." The word comes out more like a question than an affirmation, but I know she's right. In a few months, I'm not going to be able to convince him that I look ginormous because I ate a really big burger for lunch. I mean, that will probably stop working once I hit the second trimester.

"Everything will be okay, Henley. You ... You will be okay." Tara gives me a small, friendly smile like the kind you'd give a persnickety old lady you nearly ran into with your shopping cart at the grocery store. It feels all too polite, and I don't like it. I know she's being genuine when she gives me the beefy grin of a fourteen-year-old boy who is hiding a secret stash of porno mags underneath his mattress.

"I'll be okay," I repeat, nodding. Because it's true. In the future, I *will* be okay.

Just not right now.

My heart sinks, and I shut my eyes tightly, trapping the threatening tears.

"Oh, sweetie ..." Tara pulls me into her arms.

"I'm so scared," I whisper into her shoulder.

"Shhh..." Tara runs her fingers through my hair. "You weren't scared of that dick, though," she feebly jokes. I don't find it funny, though.

"What have I gotten myself into?" If you can't have a complete meltdown in front of your best friend, then who can you meltdown in front of?

"Hey now, pregnancy is a little fucked up, but the end result is pretty fantastic. Let's get a few things straight—you don't have contractions. You have birthquakes. Everyone, especially strangers, thinks they're entitled to put their grimy hands on your stomach. Pregnancy brain will make you do a ton of stupid shit, like getting in the tub while you're fully clothed, and don't even get me started on trying to shave your snatch patch once you hit the third trimester. It's as if Edward Scissorhands and Stevie Wonder's secret love child are all up in your business." She cracks a sinister smile that makes me more worried than relieved.

"In short, the next nine months and eighteen years are going to be the most horrifically glorious time of your life, Henley. Come on, let's move this party to the couch and I'll tell you *all* about it."

Chapter Six

THE HOLY GRAIL

I step back into the doorway of the kitchen and admire my work. It's not bad considering I refused to take home economics as an elective back in high school. In fact, it looks like Martha Stewart threw up in here.

"I have turned into a motherfucking Stepford wife. Minus the wife part, of course," I sigh to no one in particular.

Wife. The distinct misnomer in the first comes love, then comes marriage fairy tale that is my life.

The mouthwatering aroma of ribs wafts through the apartment. The kitchen table is set, complete with a pressed sage-colored tablecloth and a small bouquet of daisies and baby's breath in the center. And don't even get me started on what I'm wearing. The floral sundress minimizes my swollen boobs and does a decent job hiding the bloat. But on the bright side, at least I'm having a killer hair day.

Big moments call for the perfect stage. And this moment is arguably the biggest one I've had to face in my twenty-seven years.

And what's worse is that I have no idea how I'm even going to broach the subject. It's not as if I can come right out and say, "Oh, hey! Remember that time I lost my Spanx when we decided to play hide the pickle during your brother's wedding reception? Well, your pickle juice was potent, and now we're in one giant ass jam since I'm knocked up. Be a dear and pass the relish, will you?"

No. It has to be handled delicately. Because *this* is the kind of news that most guys lose their shit over. By the end of the night, my life story could very well be one tragic country song.

Things are officially progressing according to my OBGYN. At Tara's insistence, I made an appointment to officially confirm what a little pee on a stick already told me was true. I'm only a few weeks along, and by my calculations, this kiddo was conceived against a door in a vacant hotel ballroom on the night of his brother Chris's wedding while the band played Strokin' by Clarence Carter a few doors down. If only we had heeded Clarence's instruction and stuck to masturbation or a good ole fashioned handy, we wouldn't be in this child out of wedlock mess.

I am *so* going to hell.

I take a deep breath and squeeze the back of my neck. Before I can even think about how this is going to realistically play out, I hear his key slide into my apartment door and he lets himself in.

I pause to gawk at him when he steps through the door.

Jeff looks especially good today. The sleeves of his white button-down shirt are rolled up to his elbows, and his navy slacks hug his ass perfectly. It looks like he's stepping off the page of a J. Crew catalog rather than coming home from nine hours in the office. He smiles my favorite lazy smile at me.

Sometimes I don't think Jeff realizes just how handsome he is. He's not the kind of hot where your vagina incinerates, and your panties burst into flames or anything. He's a cute guy, but I learned long ago not to call him *cute*. In fact, that four-letter word once got me the silent treatment for three days.

"Puppies are cute. Sloths are cute. But men? Men are *never* cute. It makes me feel like you should be having baby talk with my manhood," he'd said.

But that's not what earned me the silent treatment. Against my better judgment, I'd decided a rousing game of peek-a-boo with his penis in the middle of foreplay would be hilarious. And it was.

For me.

Him? Not so much.

I have never seen a guy pout *that* much in my entire life—and that includes Tara's toddlers. And no matter how secure a man may seem, penis jokes are inevitably off the table.

Lesson learned.

I feel Jeff's arms wrap around my waist, and he kisses my shoulder. "Mmm ... This smells amazing, babe. And you look beautiful tonight. New dress?"

"Thanks, and no. It's just one that I haven't worn in years."

"What's the occasion?"

"Oh, nothing. I just thought we could have a nice meal and talk." I keep my tone nonchalant as to not worry him.

Jeff furrows his brows. "Talk? The last time a girl told me she wanted to talk, I ended up a single man and woke up half-naked in a baby pool filled with empty bottles of tequila."

I force a soft laugh and play with the hair on the back of his neck. Depending on his reaction, we both could very well be single by the time this night is through. "No, no, it's nothing like that. I promise."

"Okay, good. How much time until dinner's ready?"

I check the timer on my cell phone. "About another fifteen minutes."

"Then why don't we go ahead and start chatting now?"

"Sure, just let me go to the bathroom first." I give him a small smile before I slip inside the tiny bathroom, gripping the sides of the sink.

"You can do this, Henley. You love him. He loves you. He's going to be an incredible dad. You are probably going to be the world's most mediocre mother. He's going to take this news like a champ, and the two of you are going to ride off into the sunset and live happily ever after like the Waltons or the Cleavers, and all of your problems will be solved in thirty minutes or less just like the sitcoms," I whisper to myself in the mirror in a lame attempt at self-pep talk. What I really need is Samuel L. Jackson standing behind me telling me to grow a pair and deal with it in his epic, booming voice. I mean, if Samuel L. Jackson told me to dress like a chicken, walk into a KFC and cry because everyone there was eating my babies, I would do it. Because he's freakin' Samuel L. Jackson.

I emerge from the bathroom minutes later, and he's already on the couch with his feet kicked up on the coffee table, drinking a bottle of Boulevard Wheat. He scoots over, inviting me next to him, and I instinctively curl up underneath his arm as he passes me a bottle of beer. I trace the mouth of it with my fingertip, still unsure of exactly what to say.

"So ... you want to *talk*." The last word sounds like shards of glass coming off of his tongue.

"Mm-hmm," I lie. I'd rather be making out than talking right now. Hell, I'd rather be ripping off my toenails with a wrench than having this conversation.

"So, let's talk."

I take a deep breath and brace myself for the pending nuclear bomb I'm about to drop. Jeff gives my shoulder a tender squeeze, and I turn my face to his. "I love you, Jeff. More than you can ever begin to comprehend."

"Aww, babe. I love you, too." He leans over and kisses the tip of my nose. "Is everything all right? You're acting strange."

"I just ... I have a lot on my mind right now. But what I really want to know is ..." I swallow hard and hesitate. "Where do you see *us* going?"

He turns his head away from me and grimaces. "Shit, Henley! I thought you said it wasn't like that."

"It's not!"

"Babe. I love you, you're it for me. But I can't have you give me an ultimatum for a ring. The timing's all wrong, and I still need to ask your father, and there are a billion other things to do before we cross that bridge."

Oh, God. It's impossible not to feel like an asshole right now. Though my insides swoon at the thought of him asking my father for my hand in marriage.

Focus, Henley!

"No, that's not it at all, Jeff."

Without even thinking, I bring the bottle of Boulevard up to my lips and take a long pull. *Fuck.* I shouldn't have done that. Somebody needs to get this bottle away from me! And where is Samuel L. Jackson when I need him?

"Then what is it, Henley?"

I lean over and rest the bottle on the coffee table.

"I ..." My nose wrinkles at a bitter, charred stench in the air. "Oh my God! Something's burning!"

The moment I spring up from the couch, the smoke alarm gives an ear-splitting wail that nearly makes me go deaf. Smoke has already started to fill the kitchen, and when I open the oven door, grey clouds billow out, causing me to choke. Jeff rushes to open the window and fans a dishtowel through the air, trying to clear the space.

I pull the pan out to reveal my feeble attempt at making dinner. Of all the things I could have fucked up on this meal, my dumb ass never even took the bread out of the plastic bag. I laugh so hard that tears prickle the corner of my eyes. Apparently "pregnancy brain" is a real thing.

"What?" Jeff mouths as he frantically fans the air between us.

"I'm pregnant!" I shout over the blaring din of the fire alarm.

"What?" he screams back. I can barely hear him.

"I said, I'm pregnant!"

He stops dead in his tracks and turns toward me.

"You're pregnant?!" I can tell he's screaming, but I can only see him mouthing the words. And so, I nod. Mostly because I can't hear my own thoughts over this insane smoke alarm. "Oh my God! Henley! You're pregnant?!"

"I'm pregnant," I mouth back to him and swallow hard. This is the moment where it all comes tumbling down ...

But it's not.

Whatever hint of panic was on his face moments ago is gone as his face lights up like an awe-struck child watching fireworks for the very first time.

In an instant, he has closed the space between us and I'm airborne as he spins me around, twirling the smoke up around us. "We're having a baby?!" Jeff shouts into my ear. When he pulls back, his face is overcome with joy.

"Yes, you're going to be a father."

Of all the possible reactions I imagined him having, sheer elation was certainly not one of them.

"I'M NEVER GOING to get the scent of smoke out of my hair." I toss a piece of crust into the pizza box and wipe the corners of my mouth with a napkin. Once the smoke detector finally turned off and we slowly regained our hearing, I rendered dinner unsalvageable. The toxic smell of the plastic infiltrated its way into the ribs, and everything smelled disgusting.

"But I'll venture to say this is one night you'll never forget." He beams.

A soft laugh passes my lips. "You could say that again."

"So what *were* we going to have for dinner anyway?"

"Baby back ribs. With a side of baby artichokes. And some buns in the oven and a side of nearly burnt apartment," I sigh. Hopefully the effort doesn't go unnoticed, even if I did nearly burn down the apartment.

"I get it ... all 'baby foods.' He reaches out and softly pinches my cheek. If this had happened before I got pregnant, I would have found it irritating. But instead, the gesture is endearing. "That has to be the cutest thing you've ever done, Henley."

And there's that word again. *Cute*. At least *I* can take it in stride.

I snort. "I've been stressing over how to tell you since I wasn't sure how you'd react. I was secretly hoping you would just look at the meal and get what I was trying to tell you telepathically. I didn't expect it all to come out in such dramatic fanfare." Without warning, my eyes well up again, and these ridiculous tears refuse to stop. "I'm just hormonal and emotional. I've been terrified to tell you."

"Henley, my love for you is unconditional. You're pregnant and hormontional. And even though you're batshit crazy and nearly burned down your apartment, I'm willing to work with that. *That's* how much I love you. And that, right there, is the beginning and the end of everything I need to know in my life."

We eat in silence for a few minutes, and when the pizza starts to make my stomach do somersaults, I pick the sausage off the top of my slice mindlessly and look at Jeff, trying to gauge exactly how he's feeling.

"So how are you doing with all of this? I mean *really* doing. And not the knee-jerk reaction of pretending everything's okay to avoid sending your pregnant girlfriend into a hormonal tailspin all while reaching internal meltdown levels of DEFCON one." I don't mean for the words to fly from my mouth faster than my Spanx at his brother's wedding. But they do.

"Whoa, slow down, Henley. I'm not pretending," Jeff assures me as he tucks a loose strand of hair behind my ear. "Sure, it's a lot to take in without any warning. But this is a good thing— a *great* thing actually. I've always known that you're the one. Who cares if we do things out of order? This is *our* life. Screw everyone else and their opinions. I'm happy. You're happy ... I hope. And only you and me and Jeff Junior matter."

"Jeff Junior?" I laugh out loud. It's impossible *not* to be happy with this man by my side. "And what if little Jeff Junior is born with little lady bits?"

"That's impossible," he proclaims with an exhilarated scoff. "I'm only capable of producing penises. I had a talk with my soldiers once, and my sperm would *never* defy me."

That's the last thing we need more of—penises. Penises are nothing but trouble. And I've had more trouble than I can handle. "We'll see about that, stud."

Jeff takes my plate from my lap and sets it on the coffee table next to his. He pulls me tenderly underneath his arm, and I instantly feel at home. He rests his head against mine and whispers solemnly, "So how are *you* doing with all of this? And I mean *really* doing?"

"I'm good," I lie. I hate that he's turned the tables around on me.

"That doesn't sound very convincing," he says delicately. My shoulders slouch at the realization of just how well Jeff knows me. I bite my lip and steel myself to just come out with the truth. "What's on your mind, babe?"

I sigh and stare at a grease mark on the side of the pizza box. "I'm just terrified," I sputter.

"About ...?"

Everything. Isn't it obvious?

"I can't even make the simplest Brown 'n Serve rolls without causing the fire alarm to sound off. Last night when you were on the phone, a Home Depot commercial sent me into a sobbing mess. And just this morning, I washed my hair with shaving cream instead of shampoo. I can hardly take care of myself most days. I am in no way equipped to raise a child."

"Well, for starters, you're not doing this alone. I'm here with you. We're in this together." He presses his lips against my temple and gives me a firm squeeze. His words and his actions are the perfect counterpoints to my neuroses. "And if it makes you feel any better, if it was the commercial where the father and son are building a defunct tree house together, that one makes me cry like a baby, too."

"Shut up." I sniffle and fight the smile playing at the corners of my mouth.

"What else is bothering you?"

I pause, trying to pinpoint exactly what's rubbing me the wrong way.

"Well?" he probes.

"Some stuff that Tara told me about being pregnant and childbirth. I know it's months away, but still. I can't un-hear those things. It's kind of traumatizing."

"Good grief. What'd she tell you?"

"I'm not sure you really want to know."

"Yes, I do. I told you before, I want to know everything there is to know when it comes to you."

Right. But some of the stuff she told me could change a lot of things between us.

And I firmly believe that there are some things couples should never do. Like, oh ... say ... poop in front of each other. Tara had the audacity to tell me that I will more than likely poop on the table during labor and delivery — so vile! What the hell is that about? I don't care that I'm pushing a baby out. Nobody needs to see me pushing anything else out. And let's not even talk about the fact it'll be like the prom scene in the movie *Carrie* down there. I've already made the executive decision that Jeff is not allowed "down there" to see everything in action. God forbid I did crap. I could never look him in the eye again! *He* would never be able to look at *me* again! There's no way I would be able to salvage the dregs of my dignity by the time all is said and done. Poop is simply something you don't bounce back from.

But I can't possibly tell him about the poop. So I settle for some of the other nuggets of wisdom Tara has traumatized me with.

"Thanks to her, I now know that post-baby sex is like throwing a hot dog down a hallway. And that I should consider keeping my placenta in my freezer after birth and have it dried out, pulverized, and encapsulated into pills to take. And after hearing her horror story about her kids' births, I now have visions of my vagina turning into a clown car."

"Honey, she has triplets. *Her* vagina certainly *is* a clown car." He leans back to avoid my fist weakly slugging him in the shoulder. "Besides, your vagina is magical. Or better yet, it's like the Holy Grail. Except furrier and harder to drink wine out of. Though, given the chance, I'm fairly certain I could make it work."

I swat at his chest and laugh, electing to ignore the fact he called me furry. I'm half-tempted to call his penis cute in retaliation, but I bite my tongue.

"Promise me you'll stop listening to Tara."

"Only if you promise me you won't ever attempt to drink wine out of my vag."

He extends his hand out to shake mine. "You've got yourself a deal."

Chapter Seven

WHERE THE STREETS HAVE NO SHAME

I lie back on the table and push my ass to the edge, doing my best to relax. The speculum is excruciatingly cold against my skin, the stirrups are awkward, and there's an uncomfortable draft breezing through my lady garden down below.

"Henley, I need you to drop your knees out to the sides and take a deep breath." Doctor Highman, whose ironic name is not at all lost on me, pulls a latex glove onto her hand and covers it with a lubricating gel.

I take a deep breath and slowly ease my knees out to the side, doing my best to try and keep everything south of the equator relaxed. I turn my head toward Jeff, who has grown pale and has an obvious sheen of sweat glistening on his forehead.

"You okay?" I ask him soberly.

He swallows hard and shifts in his seat. "Yeah. I just don't do well with doctors or any medical type things, really."

I smile reassuringly, finding humor in the fact that *I'm* the one on the table about to get to third base with her obstetrician and he looks like he's about to toss cookies. In the entire time I've known him, he's never once been sick, but the one time he nicked his finger slicing a zucchini, he couldn't even look at the cut. I had to put the Band-Aid on him ... with the reaction he had, you'd think I was giving him a tourniquet.

He's a big ole' baby.

"Okay now, Henley. The internal should only take a moment. When we're done, we'll be able to get to the fun stuff — the sonogram to see how your baby is progressing." Doctor Highman gives me a warm smile, and then I feel the violation of her hand.

I wince at the pressure, and I'm glad that Jeff doesn't have a front row view on the other side of my gown because as much as any man has a fantasy of seeing their girlfriend be touched intimately by another woman, this moment hardly constitutes as erotic foreplay.

"What are you doing to her? You're going to hurt the baby!" he demands protectively. He still looks ill, but I'm glad he's at least acting spritely.

Doctor Highman stops mid-exam and smiles at him, brows knit with amusement. "You've got nothing to worry about, Jeff. This is all routine. I'm not touching anywhere near your baby," she chirps cheerfully as she's elbow deep in my lady bits.

She goes on to simply explain that she's doing the standard pelvic exam and wants to ensure that both my vagina and cervix are healthy.

But his expression doesn't waver.

"Calm down, hon. It's all right." I instantly question if he actually passed his junior high sex-ed classes. Or maybe he just permanently blocked those graphic memories from his mind? Because that seventies birth video we were forced to watch left emotional scars that I still haven't been able to shake.

"Everything seems good," Doctor Highman says as she takes

off the latex gloves and wheels over the sonogram machine to the side of the bed. "Ready for the fun stuff?"

I squeeze Jeff's hand, and his face finally lights up. It sends flutters through my body. He's just as excited as I am to share this moment.

First, we listen to the beautiful whooshing sound of the heartbeat. It is, singlehandedly, the most magnificent sound in the entire world. It nearly causes my heart to burst.

"It's still too early in the pregnancy for a traditional sonogram over the stomach, but we can get some pretty clear pictures using this guy." Doctor Highman grabs the internal sonogram wand and gets down to business quickly. I don't care that my modesty has gone out the window because I'm so excited about what's to come for the pair of us.

Slowly, but surely, a fuzzy image comes into focus on the screen next to the bed. "Huh," Jeff says, confused by the indiscernible black and white picture on the screen in front of him.

Doctor Highman moves the wand around, searching for a better angle, then clicks a few buttons on the computer. "There we go. There's a bit more detail now than you had before, Henley," she says with a smile.

The last sonogram she'd spent fifteen minutes pointing out a shapeless blob, trying to convince me that this thing was, in fact, a baby. Now I can actually begin to see the head and limbs taking shape ... sorta.

Jeff tilts his head and narrows his eyes, looking at the screen. "*That's* it?" he asks, unimpressed. Jeff didn't accompany me to my previous doctor appointment, so the cluelessness he's feeling now is what I felt the last time I was here.

"See this right here?" Doctor Highman points to the screen. "That is your baby's head."

"It's so ... big," Jeff observes.

"And these little things here and here? Those are the arm and leg buds starting to grow. Right now your child is about the size of a jelly bean or raspberry."

My stomach rumbles at the sheer mention of food.

"Wow," he whispers, positioning himself closer to the screen.

"And you're measuring right on schedule. I'm showing eight weeks, three days right now which gives us a due date of October thirty-first."

Visions of a Halloween baby swell my head. I love the idea of birthday celebrations filled with pumpkins and candy and tiny kids in costume. If I wasn't over the moon excited two minutes ago, I am now.

"He's so perfect," Jeff says in awe, almost inaudibly, hands touching the screen.

Dr. Highman eyes Jeff suspiciously. "Well, it's too early to tell if it's a girl or a boy just yet."

"No ... it's a boy." He's confident, and I don't have it in me to argue or ruin this moment for him.

WHEN WE MAKE it back to the car, Jeff is holding onto the sonogram photos like a talisman. He hasn't looked up from the images once, and I realize I'm witnessing him fall in love first hand. Most women would be jealous watching their man fall in love with someone else, but this is truly something special. The sheer adoration across his face, and the soft, proud smile playing at his lips, makes me a believer.

He really is here to stay.

This really *is* it.

This feeling of love is so overwhelming, I almost don't know what to do with it. Well, I know what I *want* to do with it, but that breaks some kind of social protocol for daylight and public places. And with our track record, we'd probably get arrested.

As I'm driving back home, Jeff reaches over and lovingly puts his hand on my leg, softly rubbing my knee. And he must be some goddamned magician because this simple, innocent, loving touch sets my mind ablaze and wild images of me having my way with him here and now flood my mind. *Damn. Tara was right, again.* I didn't believe her when she said I'd either want it all the time like a sex-starved nymphomaniac or be permanently closed for business like Sister Mary Prudence.

I turn onto an empty side street in an undeveloped part of town and park the car. We're surrounded by nothing but abandoned construction machinery and piles of dirt and rock. So I do what any dignified, revved up woman would do. I crank up the volume on the MP3 player, set it to Justin Timberlake's FutureSex LoveSound album and unbuckle my seatbelt.

Jeff finally looks up from the photo and takes in his surroundings. "What are you doing, Henley?"

"Shh ..." I command, as I quickly reach over to undo his seat belt and crawl into his lap.

"Hen—"

My mouth is on his before he can finish my name, and the tiny ember I previously felt with his hand on my knee has ignited into a five alarm fire that I *need* put out immediately.

What the fuck is happening to me?

I'm pawing at the buttons on his shirt with my left hand and bringing his hands to my breasts with the right. And when I finally break the kiss his eyes are full of surprise. *Okay, then. We're doing this!* his look tells me in unspoken words. I reach down and pull the lever on the side of his seat, reclining us back unexpectedly. I fall onto his chest, and a small laugh escapes my lips.

"You're crazy," he says into my mouth just as he swallows me whole with a passionate kiss, turning the car into an inferno of lust.

And I know I am. Crazy, that is.

Because there are only two things in life that can make someone *this* crazy and this damn stupid.

Pregnancy.

And love.

Chapter Eight

CONFESSIONS OF A MODERN DAY VIRGIN MARY

Deep down I always knew that telling Jeff I was pregnant would be far easier than telling my parents. As an only child, there have always been unspoken expectations set upon me. Simply stated, it was to be the best at pretty much everything.

Sell the most Girl Scout cookies in your troop, Henley.

Don't just be on the cheerleading squad, Henley. You have to be captain.

Make the dean's list, Henley.

Don't get drunk and have sex in a public place and get knocked up out of wedlock, Henley.

Okay, maybe that last one wasn't something they actually said, but I'm pretty sure it probably crossed their minds at some point. So when it actually came time to officially announce that I was more scandalous than the canoodling whore of Babylon and that I was, in fact, harboring a bastard child within my loins, I braced myself for the worst.

Jeff's parents took it surprisingly well. Mostly, I think they were relieved that they were simply getting *a* grandchild. They didn't care which son gave it to them.

Jeff wanted to break the news to them in some silly Hallmark-esque fanfare, with a cute puzzle they had to solve or with a matching set of "Grandparents in Training" tea cups or something equally absurd. I was so anxious about the entire situation I accidentally blurted it out in the middle of a FaceTime call.

Jeff's mom, Martha, wanted his opinion of a few potential wall colors for the downstairs bathroom. Why? I don't know, considering he has the home decorating sense of a drunk clown. But Martha had just finished showing us a dozen swaths of grey paint above the toilet when I blurted out, "I'm pregnant!". Jeff beamed, and I had that pained, toothy, uncomfortable grin on my face. The kind of smile you get when you ask a toddler to say "Cheese!" for the camera and everything gets awkward.

We both watched his mother in stunned silence as the world hesitated for one breathless moment.

No, literally.

Everything stopped.

Technology failed, and the screen froze, distorting Martha into a kaleidoscope of pixels across the screen as a "Bad Connection" error message flashed. We could hear her flailing about, shouting for her husband to come join her in the bathroom on the call, but we couldn't actually see her reaction. I could only hope that the tears we heard were tears of joy.

When the screen finally came back into focus, Jeff's parents were gleefully jumping up and down and immediately began discussing the whereabouts of my boyfriend's childhood toy collection.

My folks, on the other hand, didn't take the news as well—*or at all*.

I learned early on that bringing guys home to meet my folks was a bad idea. No man would ever be good enough for me, at least according to my parents, so they tended to alienate anyone with a penis who passed through their threshold next to me. I think they accepted Leo as well as they did because his mere existence was confirmation that I didn't play for the other team.

"I don't understand why you're so worked up about telling them, Henley. This is really exciting news. Any parent should be thrilled to learn their child is expecting. Mine were overjoyed beyond measure."

"Yeah. But you haven't met my parents." *And this is hardly the ideal circumstance to meet them.*

Jeff sighs, dread slowly filling his eyes. "So what's the likelihood of them believing you're a modern day Virgin Mary? It worked once. Maybe it could work again?" Jeff massages my shoulder, trying to chase the building tension away.

"Well, they're Catholic, but that's about the only thing that's working in our favor."

"Aren't Catholics supposed to be all super forgiving and what not?"

"My parents have perfected guilt and judgment to an art form."

I spent the entire first trimester thinking through the scenario:

Mom, Dad, this is my boyfriend, Jeff. And this is his unborn child I'm carrying.

"Would you like to see my gun collection?"

Mom, Dad, I know you haven't met Jeff, yet. But we've decided to combine DNA and breed new life into the world!

"Son, can I show you my Purple Heart?"

Hey, guys! I slipped and fell on Jeff's dick, and his man seeds ended up inside my flower, and now I'm carrying his spawn.

"Let me tell you something ... Whatever you have done to my little girl, I will personally do to you."

For weeks I played the prospective conversation over and

over in my head, all with the same inevitable outcome: death and possible dismemberment of Jeff's member.
　But what happened was worse.
　Much, much worse.
　Against my better judgment, Jeff came with me. I know we're inseparable these days, but I had insisted that I do this alone. Give them a chance to get comfortable with the idea that their little daughter dearest was with child. But my boyfriend extraordinaire insisted that this was a *we* thing. *We* got ourselves into this situation, and *we* will take it on together.
　As he always tells me, "Where you walk, I walk."
　And so together we would walk into the depths of hell and hopefully emerge out the other side together and in one piece.
　It was a Sunday afternoon. We had met my parents for brunch after they attended the ten o'clock service at Good Shepherd Church. My mother had worn a long flowery dress and ivory shawl while my dad picked his usual suit and tie. Nothing less than their best for an ordinary Sunday. But little did they know they were dressing for their funeral because I was sure this news was going to knock them over dead.
　The conversation over brunch went well. My parents used the opportunity to ask Jeff questions and learn about his upbringing, make sure he was well educated (or well enough educated for their only daughter), and dance around his career to confirm his financial stability. In short, they wanted to make sure this gentleman caller was an acceptable suitor. It took all the energy I could muster to bite my tongue instead of cueing a southern drawl and proclaiming, "Well, I do declare he'd make a fine husband for me, one day!"
　By the time we returned to my parents' house, the nerves had taken over. I continually wiped my palms against my thighs and found myself concentrating on my breathing like I did when I

went to yoga classes every Tuesday night before I traded up to participate in Taco Tuesday adventures instead.

I took a large sip of water, and with a shaky hand set the glass down on the table. As Jeff squeezed my leg, my dad cleared his throat and shot him a cutting glare as if to say, "Get your hands off my daughter before I knock your ass back to fifth grade."

"Mom ... Dad ... I have something I want to tell you."

Jeff made some weird sniffling sound that rivaled my dad's throat clearing as he put his arm around my shoulders, drawing me near.

"I mean, *we*, have something to tell you."

My dad leaned over, resting his elbows on his knees as my mom smiled brightly at us, her gaze traveling to my left hand in anticipation of a proposal announcement.

"What is it, dear?" Her voice was light and full of hope.

Most parents would be ecstatic about their grown ass daughter having a baby. But my parents weren't most parents. And I knew that this was going to smash that hopeful voice into a million tiny pieces.

I paused, momentarily paralyzed.

"Well ...?" she begged.

I watched her eyes drift to my naked left ring finger and then looked to Jeff. He proffers a timid but encouraging smile.

"We ... um ...Jeff and I ... are ... um ... " I stumbled over every damn syllable. I knew that no matter how I scripted this in my head it would inevitably be a disaster.

"Mr. and Mrs. Carson, what Henley is trying to say is—"

"I'm pregnant!" I exclaimed.

I knew Jeff was only trying to help the situation, but if I don't own up to this in front of my parents, I would never live it down. I was a grown woman who made grown up decisions and was facing the grown up consequences of telling her parents. Even still, I couldn't help but feel like a teenage girl confessing to wrecking the car on the way home from a party I never should have been at in the first place.

My parents looked at me, then at Jeff and then each other in a terrifying silence. Then as if on cue, they both doubled over in laughter at the same time, slapping their knees, hemming and hawing over how hilarious our little prank was.

I swallowed hard as Jeff and I stared at each other awkwardly.

"That's a good one, Hen!" My dad wiped tears away from his eyes as he continued to howl in hysterics. "Our little girl ... pregnant!" He barely spit the words out as he gasped for air between full blown belly laughs.

My heart fell to my stomach, and I tried to steady my breath.

"I ... um ... this isn't a joke." I looked at my hands in my lap. "I'm eleven weeks, today."

And for an awkward ten seconds, that terrifying silence returned, only to be broken by the wailing sobs of my mother as she ran from the room, my father quick on her heels, presumably to console her.

"Wow," Jeff breathed. "I wasn't quite expecting ... *that*."

There's no better word than *that*.

That was unexpected.

That was the precise moment I tore my mother's heart in two.

That was possibly the best situation I could have hoped for knowing those two.

"They're a bit ... traditional. They'll come around ... I promise."

I hoped.

I place my hand on his knee and run my thumb back and forth, but it does nothing to soothe either of us.

LATER THAT EVENING my father called and asked to speak

with Jeff. I cautiously handed him the phone and lingered close by, just in case.

To my surprise, I wasn't able to hear my dad screaming at Jeff through the line. And thankfully, my dad didn't show up unannounced with a hit man in tow. They both spoke in hushed tones, and I could only hear Jeff's side of the conversation which was made up of direct phrases like "Yes, sir," and "No, it's not like that," and "I promise". I could only imagine the menacing threats he was continuing to make against my boyfriend.

When Jeff hung up the phone, my heart crumbled. "They didn't want to talk to me?" I asked softly.

"No, it's not that they didn't want to talk to you. They had some questions for me."

"How bad?" I deadpanned, my face expressionless but my mind moving fast enough to break a speedometer on a formula one race car.

He squeezes the back of his neck with his hand, presumably weighing the options of truth and fabrication.

"Don't you dare lie to me. Like you said, we're in this together." I stared at him, silently willing him to tell me about the conversation.

Jeff approached me and took my hands in his. "Your mom and dad love you, and all they wanted to do was make sure that I love you, too. And that I'm serious about a future with both you and our baby, which I am." He leaned over and kissed my forehead.

"That's all?" I wasn't convinced.

Jeff sighed. "Let's put it this way. What would happen if the roles were reversed and that was *our* child telling us they were expecting out of wedlock to someone they'd been dating for less than a year?" He looked at me poignantly.

Okay. I got it.

"You can't fault them for wanting to talk to me a little more.

Your dad even invited me fishing in a few weeks. He wants to get to know me better."

"No, he wants to throw you off a boat for taking his daughter's virginity away. It's all under the guise of a getting to know you fishing trip."

"Babe, you weren't a virgin when we met." He released my hand and touched my cheek softly.

"Yeah, but he doesn't know that. I guarantee that he wholeheartedly believes that I've only had sex one time, and once was enough to get knocked up."

He caressed my cheek in his palm, and gently rubbed his thumb against my jawline. "They may be traditional, but they're not stupid, babe. But if your dad has ulterior motives, let's get an extra life insurance policy on me before I hit the lake with him. My parting gift to you, aside from my undying love from beyond the grave, would be a nice little sum of dough."

I snorted, and he pressed his lips against mine in the tenderest of kisses. When he pulled back, he smirked, and there was a boyish twinkle in his eye. "But even in death, you can't get rid of me. I love you so much that I'd come back to haunt your sweet ass just so you'd know you're still top of mind in the afterlife."

I playfully swatted at his shoulder. "If that's not love, then I don't know what is."

The Second Trimester

Chapter Nine

THE SPANK BANK

"Can I get you a beer, man?" Cameron asks Jeff as we walk through the tiny foyer of their home.

"Uh …" Jeff looks at Cameron and then to me, silently asking for permission. It's a sweet gesture, much like most of his gestures, but completely unnecessary.

"It's fine, babe. It's bad enough that *I'm* not allowed to drink. It doesn't mean that both of us need to commit ourselves to nine months of sobriety."

The guys grab a beer from the fridge and walk into the living room. I head into the kitchen, setting down the store-bought french silk pie on the counter. I've never been one to show up empty-handed and usually try to make something sweet from scratch whenever we are invited to dinner. In my defense, I did bake brownies earlier this morning, but the baby got hungry. And one brownie turned into twelve, and I quickly realized just *why* I've gained so much weight in this first trimester.

Whoopsie!

Tara rests a spoon next to the stove and comes over to hug me. "Hey, Momma! You're lookin' good."

I smile at her then wrap my arms around her. It's a good thing I *look* good because I feel like crap. Then again, that's probably just the brownies talking. "Thanks, how was Florida?"

The Carmichael clan got back from their annual trip to the South a few days ago. I'm secretly jealous of all their family bonding time. The only family vacation I was privy to in my childhood was when my great aunt Bernice died, and we road tripped up to Lancaster, Pennsylvania when I was twelve years old. My parents told me I didn't have to go to the actual burial, so I wandered around town and befriended some Amish kids who made wood furniture "for fun." I quickly learned there wasn't anything fun about sanding a headboard to perfection, but Elmer (yes, one of them was actually named *Elmer*) did learn just how much fun it was to swap gum without the use of one's hands. *Oh, those were the days!*

"Oh, it was wonderful, but I am all Mickey-ed out. I even sent the trio over to Cam's folks for the night so we could have some uninterrupted adult time. But if I have to hear *It's a Small World* one more time I am going to willingly put some kind of flesh eating bacteria in my ears."

"That bad, eh?"

Tara's eyebrows jump to her hairline as she nods enthusiastically. I mentally plan to avoid the land of oversized fake plastic characters on Prozac and long lines for as long as humanly possible.

"The flight home, however, was the worst. I asked to switch seats on the plane because I was seated next to a screeching toddler. But apparently, that's not allowed if the child belongs to you."

I laugh, and Tara shoots me her infamous *I'm not fucking joking* glare. "Well, I'm glad you're back." And it's true. I am. Even though Tara and I don't see each other as much as we'd like to, we do a kick ass job at keeping in touch. But for those long stretches where we have life-induced radio silence, we always seem to pick things up exactly where they were left off. We're kind of like a couple of dudes in that respect. Low maintenance friendships bonded by alcohol and a general love at yelling at things such as sports on TV, children, and significant others.

"By the way, this smells delicious. What are we having?"

"Well, we *were* going to grill steak, but a storm is rolling through so that's out. Instead, I'm making this awesome bacon and pasta dish. There's enough garlic in it to ward off any vampire in a one hundred mile radius."

I know. I could smell it from outside. Not that I'm complaining, though. "Edward Cullen will be so sad. What can I do to help?"

Tara points to the stool at the island. "Nothing, I'm almost done. You can just sit your tush down and watch me cook." She quickly returns to the stove to stir the sauce and turn on the oven. "So I take it Jeff took the news well?"

"He did. Though I think I caught him off guard since I nearly burned my apartment down in the process."

"You what!?" She snaps her head back toward me so fast, I fear the girl will give herself whiplash.

I shake my head. "Long story, don't ask. He seems genuinely excited though. I know he'll be a good dad. I just keep waiting for the news to really hit and for him to tailspin into panic mode."

Tara nods her head. "Aaaaand what's this about your apartment?"

"Eh, it's no big deal. Let's just say I wasn't focused, and I accidentally burned dinner. And by burned dinner I mean I may or may not have caused a small kitchen fire in the oven causing the smoke detectors to go off. It was pretty bad, T. I haven't been back to my place all week. The pungent smell of melted plastic nearly makes me choke every time I'm home. I've been staying at Jeff's until my apartment airs out. He even had to run back to get my clothes for me. Every time I step foot in there my gag reflexes kick in." I wait for her to make a joke about my weak gag reflexes, but her expression turns semi-serious, and she surprises me.

"Maybe you should just move in with him? I mean, you *are* going to have a kid together."

I rest my hand on my chin and look at her. It makes sense. And I'm pretty sure Jeff is *the one*. Or at least I think he is. At the very least he's *the one* of the moment. That has to count for something, right?

"I know. I've been thinking about it a lot. It's just ... I like my space. Even though we're practically living together right now, the illusion of independence is nice."

Tara turns toward me and puts one hand on her hip and points her wooden spoon at me with the other. "You *do* realize that you're about to lose *all* of your space for the next eighteen years, right?"

"I know, but—"

"Nope. No buts. The only butts allowed is the one you'll be wiping. You need to get used to it. No boundaries. No privacy. No nothing. Your quiet 'me time' of a bubble bath complete with wine and your favorite book is going to turn into sneaking the last cookie into the bathroom simply because you don't want to share it, all while listening to your monster squad cry from the other side of the door as they stuff their sticky little fingers underneath it because they 'miss you.'"

Oh, God.

"If you want to tackle that solo, more power to you. But it just makes sense for you two to do this *together*."

She's right. And I know we need to talk about it at some point, but I'm just not ready. Not yet at least.

I sigh.

"All I'm saying is this parenting shit is a lot easier to swallow when you tag team. And trust me, when you've got a tiny terror finger painting the crib and the walls and his body with poop, *you* want to be the one to give him the bath. Because the *other* parent is the one cleaning up the nursery in full body armor and a gas mask."

"You make everything sound so glamorous," I deadpan.

"Because it is. And the sooner you can accept the fact that motherhood is the most glamorous job where you'll be covered in snot and sticky fingers, and your purse will forever be the keeper of stale snacks and crumbs, the better off you'll be."

SURPRISINGLY, dinner tasted as good as it smelled, which is a rarity in this household. So score one for Tara because it was actually edible.

Tara has never really been a good cook as she likes to veer off-recipe, adding liberal amounts of spices to dishes because she thinks the name sounds cool. Paprika pot pie where the filling was three parts paprika, one part potatoes, chicken, and carrots. Curry in a coconut cake. But my favorite incident was the great wasabi disaster of 2014. Tara cut full chunks of wasabi root into a pot roast and Cameron and I ate it to simply be polite. We each spent the following three days with our asses glued to the toilet seat. Not the same toilet seat, of course. Needless to say, she's been banned from making pot roast and buying any form of wasabi ever since.

"Hey, babe, come over here," Cameron says, standing at the head of the dinner table.

Tara looks from Cameron to me and then back to her husband again. "I'm right here."

"No, I mean come *here*. I want to do something really quick." Cameron makes his way around the table and reaches for Tara's hand, pulling her up and out of the chair.

"What are you doing?" she asks cautiously.

"We're going outside really quick. There's something I need to do."

Just as the words leave his mouth, thunder crashes and the room fills with white hot light from the latest lightning strike.

"Um, no. There's a monsoon out there. You sit your ass back down. Whatever is outside can wait."

"Quit being a baby. You're not going to melt."

Tara folds her arms in protest and looks at her husband unamused.

"I just want to kiss you!" he exclaims.

"You can kiss me right here. But I highly doubt Henley and Jeff want a front row seat to a tonsil hockey match."

"No, not in *front* of them. I want to kiss you in the rain." He pauses for a beat, and a glint of mischief takes over his expression. "That way you'll be twice as wet."

Tara swats his shoulder with her mouth agape in mock audacity. She can hardly talk over the sound of her own laughter. "You are so vile."

Jeff shifts uncomfortably in his seat. Some days I feel bad for the guy. Tara and I are a package deal, and with Tara comes Cameron who is just as bad as my best girlfriend. Those two are a match made in heaven if heaven were a high school locker room full of fart jokes and ridiculous sexual innuendos. Some people just never grow up. But it works for them, and I love them all the more for it.

"You guys are utterly ridiculous," I chime in. *And utterly in love.*

When we're done with dinner, I help Tara clear the table as Jeff and Cam head back into the living room to watch the rest of the Royals game. I love that they get along well, but they are awfully chatty tonight.

I turn to Tara and speak softly, to ensure there's no way that Jeff can hear me. "How did you know that Cam was *the one?*"

Tara puts the serving bowl down on the counter and looks at me thoughtfully. "Oh, that's easy. At least it was for me."

I find that hard to believe. Nothing about love is ever easy. Love is confusing and messy and hard.

"I knew it was real the day he confessed that he jerked off to pictures of me," Tara confesses.

"Gross! You're joking, right?"

Tara is delusional. And disgusting. And the last thing I needed tonight was the visual of Cameron with a bottle of lotion in one hand and a box of tissues in the other.

"What? Out of all the women in the world and all the porn in existence, he chose to knock his rocks off to *me*. It was his subtle way of saying, 'you're the only one.' Now if *that's* not love, I don't know what is."

"Huh," I breathe in a moment of clarity. I hate that she actually makes sense right now. Even still, the last thing I want is the mental image of Cam spanking it to thoughts of Tara. I silently shudder.

"You know I'm right." She pauses with her hand upon her hip. "Why don't you ask Jeff?"

"Ask him what?"

"Ask him if you're in his spank bank."

I guffaw. "That is *not* something you just come out and ask your boyfriend."

"No, but it's something you can ask your baby daddy. Watch …" She walks toward the family room where the guys are sitting. "Hey, babe," she calls out to Cameron, "when the kids are busy cock blocking you from getting into my pants, what do you do?"

"Ah! I whip out—"

"NO!" I interject, throwing a hand out motioning him to end this conversation immediately. "You stop right there, Cameron Carmichael! I don't want to know about you *whipping* things out!

All friendships need boundaries. And this is where I draw the hard line."

Cameron gasps and clutches his chest like a damsel in distress. "What? Gross, Henley. I wasn't going to tell you about unleashing the snake. *I'm a gentleman.* I would never dare tell a lady about the time I spend choking my chicken. About cranking the love pump. Or spouting old faithful. Or fiddling the flesh flute. Or—"

"Okay, okay, okay! I get it. Just stop!" My hands fly to my head, and I can feel my cheeks flushing red. *God, what is with these two!? I can't even tell you which one is worse!*

"All I was going to say is when the three musketeers make it impossible for a quickie with my lady love, I have a nice little collection of photos and dirty texts on my phone all courtesy of my bride." He flashes a megawatt smile to Tara.

"Seriously? You do?" Jeff looks at Cam in awe. Maybe even pride. Cam nods, and I can practically see the gears turning over in Jeff's head. "Aww, babe, why don't we do that?" Jeff asks me in all seriousness.

I put a fist on my hip and raise my eyebrows. "Because we don't have triplets?" But I can pretty much guarantee that if we *did* have triplets, sex would be the furthest thing from both of our minds.

"Don't mock it 'til you try it, guys," Tara snaps. Jeff opens his mouth to speak, but my best friend cuts it off. "And no, you cannot try *my* photos, Jeffrey. As much as we've become friends over the past several months, I'm never touching you in any capacity."

Jeff presses his left hand against his heart with a pained expression. "You wound me, Tara."

"Seriously though, the older you get and the longer you two are together, you're going to need to find ways to show that you still care. That baby is going to take nearly all of your love. But you need to remember that first and foremost, you love one another. It doesn't matter if you leave a love note in his car or send him a gratuitous boob pic taken in the bathroom at the grocery store. The point is you have to make a conscious effort each and every day to show one another just how much you're in love."

Jeff looks toward Tara thoughtfully and his expression softens. "Tara ..." Jeff says sincerely, grabbing her attention. "I know you just said you never would ... but right now, you've actually touched me."

JUST AS WE open the front door to slip into the rainy night, we overhear the rest of their conversation. "I'm going to head down to the man cave for a bit," Cameron says from the hallway behind us.

"Like hell you are. The only man cave you need is right here between my thighs. Now get your sweet ass over here and help me clean up. *Then*, and only then will you get a pass to the beloved man cave."

Cameron groans jokingly.

Jeff and I look at each other and exchange silent laughter. "If they're not careful, Tara is going to be knocked up right alongside you." He closes the door behind us, and we assess the storm from the coverage of their front porch.

"The last thing this world needs is more little Carmichaels raising hell. Let's get going."

Jeff makes a mad sprint to open the passenger side door for me as I walk quickly behind him. Just as I'm about to climb in, he spins me around and takes my face in his hands. The look in his eyes says it all.

He hesitates for half a heartbeat and then his lips are wild upon mine. Jeff's grip is firm. His tongue is frantic. And there's a carnal fire building inside us both that the storm cannot put out.

The rain beats down over both of us, and we're quickly getting soaked in this summer storm, melting into each other. He kisses me hard and deep, and even though the frigid rain makes us both shiver, neither of us are cold. It's not about us standing in the storm. It's about us *feeling* the rain.

When Jeff finally pulls away, we're both trying to catch our breath. "What was that for?"

The edges of his lips curl up in delight. "Nothing, I was just thinking about something Cam said earlier," he says innocently.

"I hope you're not thinking of my best friend's husband every time you kiss me like that."

"Nah ..." Jeff reaches around my waist to pinch my butt. "I just wanted to see if I could make you twice as wet. Now let's get you home so I can do all sorts of unmentionable things to you."

Chapter Ten

PERSONAL SPACE

"I love this picture of you two." I smile at the framed photo that Cam and Tara took after a few weeks of dating. They look so young and blissfully in love.

It wasn't always like that, though.

"Me, too." She smiles at the image of her getting a piggyback ride from Cam during the annual beer festival held by the local breweries.

Cam and Tara met at a bar in the Power and Light District of Kansas City shortly after we'd all graduated from the University of Kansas. Tara was all about spreading her wild oats and jumped off the deep end. *"I want to give my vagina the wild adventure it deserves!"* she had said. In an intoxicated stupor, she brought Cameron home to our apartment on the Plaza for a night of regretless tomfoolery. Later that night, they had sex for the first time, and in the heat of the moment, she slapped him clear across the face so hard her handprint left a lasting mark.

When I'd heard the screams, I ran into her room with a baseball bat ready to come to my best friend's defense. Cam was tied to Tara's headboard, and she was wearing what I can only assume were his Gumby boxer shorts.

"Why do you keep hitting me, Kandi?!" he shouted, completely oblivious to my presence.

"I'm hitting you because you're calling me another woman's name! Why do you keep calling me Kandi?!" she asked as she slapped his leg in anger.

"Because that's what you told me your name was!"

Tara stopped dead in her tracks and quickly untied him from her bedpost. "Oh my God, I'm so sorry. I completely forgot." Her voice was sobering, yet sheepish and alarmed.

I slowly backed out of her room and closed the door behind me, staying nearby just in case. And by staying nearby, I really mean pressing my ear up against the door eavesdropping on their conversation.

"Huh? What are you talking about?"

There was an awkward pause. And I smiled because I knew there was no easy way for Tara to get herself out of this mess.

"My name isn't Kandi. I give fake names when I'm out at the bars to distance myself from the creepers."

More awkward silence.

"But you're not a creeper. I, uh ... I actually think you're kind of cool."

There's an indisputable sincerity in her voice, and the next part of the conversation happened in hushed tones, and I was unable to make out what they were saying. Just as I was heading back to my bedroom, I heard Cam say, "God, you're so hot. Get over here." And a few moments later, the earlier screams were replaced with moans and the undeniable sound of sweaty flesh slapping together.

I slept with a pillow over my head that night.

From what Tara had told me the next morning, she finished taming the wild beast and then sent him on his way, keeping the Gumby boxers for good measure. She'd genuinely felt bad about what happened, and was even a little upset when she didn't hear from him for three weeks. Until one day, I came home from the grocery store and they were on the couch sharing a pint of ice cream. He kept calling her Kandi, and she let him.

They've been inseparable ever since.

And Kandi is now the name of her sexual alter ego whenever they need a little spice in the bedroom.

"How'd the doctor appointment go?" she asks, breaking me from the memory.

"It went well. Everything looks good."

"Are you going to find out the gender?"

I shake my head. "Everything in life is so planned these days. We thought we'd leave this as the last great surprise. Plus I think there's something really cool about the notion of having the doctor call out 'It's a ...!' in the middle of the moment."

"That is so freakin' awesome, Hen."

"Though Jeff is convinced it's a boy. I'm not sure what he'll do if this kid actually ends up being a little girl."

"He'd love her all the same. Probably even more since she'd be *his* little girl."

I look around at Tara and the incredible life she's built with Cam, and I am so happy for my friend. If I can find a fraction of her happiness with Jeff and our baby, my life will be a resounding success.

"How do you do it?" I say, completely out of the blue.

"Do what?"

"The mom thing. How do you do it? Because I've spent plenty of time thinking about this lately and I have no clue what I'm doing."

I follow her to the couch and move an empty sippy cup, a toy truck, and a pile of well-loved books to the coffee table so I can sit down, too. It's nothing but chaos and love here, and I wish that motherhood could be like this for everyone.

"Nobody does. The day your child is born, a mother is born, too. And we're all born exactly the same way: excited, clueless and terrified. But you figure it out because that's what parents do. As much as you want the baby to come tattooed with an instruction manual on its ass, it doesn't. And no matter how much you beg for the postpartum nurses to come home with you to make sure you're changing diapers properly and that your baby latches on correctly when nursing, they won't. So you simply do what every parent before you has done. You wing it."

I know she's right. But the notion of fake it till you make it when the life of an unsuspecting infant is in your hands seems a little risky. Though I'm not sure if I'm more nervous about the mom thing after the fact, or the disgusting process of actually getting the baby out of my body. She must sense the underlying fear in my eyes.

"I know this won't be the last time I tell you this, but you're gonna be a great mom, Henley. And if ya fuck up with this one, I've got a kid or two to spare." She winks at me.

With that we hear the thunderous footsteps of a three foot four inch, freckled-face boy barrel down the hallway and finally stop in front of Tara, stamping his foot to command her attention.

"May I help you, sir?" Tara folds her arm and stares curiously at Wes. He's the youngest of the three boys by about three minutes, and he does everything he can to make sure he has the most attention from his parents. They're having a staring contest with an unspoken conversation, and I *think* that Tara is actually winning.

"You're in my personal space, woman!" Wes purses his lips and glares at his mother.

My mouth drops and I don't bother containing my laughter. I'm pretty sure keeping a straight face when your offspring has outrageously naughty — yet hysterical — behavior is going to be one of the hardest parts of parenthood. It's surreal hearing this three-year-old speak like a pissed-off grown man.

"Excuse me? What did you just say?" Tara puts her fists on her hips and looks down at this little curly-haired blond cherub in astonishment.

Surely little Wes is going to cower. Right?

"I said you're in my personal space, woman!" He annunciates each word as clearly as possible, which doesn't say much for a three-year-old.

"You listen here, Wesley Kane Carmichael, you *came* from my personal space. Hell, you and your tribe of brothers inhabited my personal space for more than seven months. Don't you *dare* tell me to get out of *your* personal space."

Wes's eyes grow wide, and he stands frozen, listening to his mother. I feel like I should grab a pen and paper and start taking notes.

"I don't care how old you grow, you are in for a lifetime of me in your personal space. The first time you take a girl out on a date? I'm going to be there in the restaurant or movie theatre watching you. College? You will no doubt feel my presence on campus, but you'll never know where I am. And the day you're all up in some special woman's personal space? I want you to have visions of you in *my* personal space. I will, no doubt, be the most effective birth control in the history of contraceptives. So don't you dare lecture *me* about being in *your* personal space. You started this! I'm your mother. I brought you into this world, and I can take you right back out of it!"

She hammers him with a stern look that instills the fear of God in *me*. Wes's lip quivers and he scampers out of the room, looking back over his shoulder with a terrified expression on his face. I bite my lip hard and do everything in my power to not lose my shit right here in the heat of this magical moment of motherhood. But as soon as he's out of sight, Tara and I both start laughing.

"I'm really impressed, Tara!" I wipe my eyes with the back of my hand and gasp for air. She's fighting a toothy grin.

She takes a sip of her iced tea and smiles at me. "Oh?"

"I don't know how you got through that with such a straight face. That was epic."

"I've got years of practice with Cameron."

Chapter Eleven

THE WAKE-UP CALL

"Henley, sweetie. Are you awake?" I feel Jeff's lips right against my ear and my body shivers at the heat of his breath on my skin. "Honey? It's morning."

He's a little *too* chipper for the sun not even being up. I groan and pull the comforter over my shoulder tightly. Delicately, he traces tiny circles between my shoulder blades with his fingertip. I want to be annoyed, but I can't help but melt at his touch.

"Heeeeenley," he sings softly.

"What time is it?" I yawn, begrudgingly.

"It's six thirty-three. Rise and shine."

"What the hell, Jeff? Go back to bed."

This boy is as dumb as a rock if he thinks he's going to earn any brownie points by waking me up at this ungodly hour. Jeff curls up close to me and begins kissing the exposed skin on the back of my neck. I immediately feel his rock hard length pressing into my leg.

Yep.

Stupidity confirmed.

His dick has stolen seven inches worth of blood from

his brain.

"Not this morning, babe. I've gotten up to pee no less than eight times since I saw the clock turn three A.M. I'm cranky, and I haven't shaved my legs in two weeks."

"Huh? What are you talking about, babe?"

I roll my eyes as he feigns ignorance, then in a huff, I reach out to grab his cock to show him *exactly* what I'm talking about, except the palm of my hand wraps around the remote that was wedged between us.

Oh.

"Hen, I'm not in the mood for TV. I just wanted to talk to you."

"Can't it wait? We can talk when I wake up at a normal hour. You know, after I've had the only eight ounces of caffeine I've been granted to consume each morning." *And those eight ounces of caffeine I require daily to make sure I don't stab anyone. God, I miss drinking a full coffeepot on my own. Stupid doctor rules about pregnancy.*

"No."

I sigh and then roll over to face him, raising my eyebrows. This had better be good.

A softness overtakes his expression, and his eyes crinkle around the edges as he smiles. "Did you know that exactly one year ago today, at this exact moment ... well, this moment *two minutes ago when I first tried waking you up*, we first met?"

And suddenly, *I'm* the asshole.

I love how this crazy, thoughtful man loves me even when I'm at my worst. "I ... I didn't realize that was today." I smile fondly at the memory of Jeff taking the seat next to me on the plane to Denver. I was headed there for work, and he was off to visit his family and celebrate his brother's engagement. I had planned on working on a presentation during the short ninety-minute flight from Kansas City, but instead, I listened to him nervously prattle about nothing and everything. It was quite endearing. I slipped him my number as we deplaned and told him to call me when he was back in Kansas City if he ever wanted to meet up for drinks.

"Yep, it was today. I overslept and nearly missed the flight, and the first available seat I saw was next to a gorgeous, fiery, redhead. I never imagined the course of my life would change all because I'd accidentally turned my alarm off. If I had been there on time, I would have been one of the first people on the plane, finding a way to bogart an entire row to myself, and our paths would never have crossed."

I giggle and lean over to kiss the tip of his nose. "Happy day-we-met-iversary, Jeff. It's a shame you couldn't oversleep this morning too, babe. I am seriously sleep deprived."

"I know, but this will only take a minute." He sits up and reaches over to his nightstand and takes out a small slip of paper, then hands it to me. I push myself up and wipe the sleep away from my eyes. I scan the small square, and it's the stub from his boarding pass from last year.

After all this time, he kept it.

"Flip it over."

Scrawled in his chicken scratch in faded blue ink he wrote, *Today I met Henley. The woman I'm going to marry.*

My breath hitches and when I look up, he is down on one knee on the floor holding the most ridiculous rock I've ever laid eyes on.

"Oh my God," I whisper, then swallow hard, suddenly wide awake.

"Henley Louise Carson, it took an hour and a half at ten thousand feet to fall in love with you one year ago this morning. And now my favorite part of every morning is waking up next to you and falling in love with you all over again. Would you give me the privilege of spending every morning, noon, and night with you for the rest of our lives?"

"Oh my God!" Excitement floods my veins like a runaway train, and all I want to do is kiss him in spite of my horrendous morning breath. "Oh my God, yes!"

Jeff takes my hand and slips the princess cut stone encased in white gold onto my ring finger — except it gets stuck at the knuckle.

"I'm sorry, I swell in the morning. Just one of the many joys of pregnancy." I laugh with tears of happiness prickling my eyes.

He smiles, then kisses my knuckle, licking it in the process so he can maneuver the ring on the rest of the way. "It's okay, we can get it resized."

Jeff climbs back up onto the bed, and I throw my arms around him tightly. We quickly lose balance and fall backward into a pile of pillows. The awkward way he lands on top of me triggers an urgent and insatiable need to relieve myself.

"Oh, shit! Move! Now! I gotta pee!" I playfully swat at his chest, pushing him away.

He howls with laughter as he rolls onto his back and I hustle into the bathroom to avoid embarrassing myself right here in front of my fiancé.

Fiancé.

I roll the strange word around in my mind while I admire Jeff's excellent taste in fine jewelry from the confines of the porcelain throne. The ring truly really is stunning and looks enormous on my delicate fingers. But the moment my body feels relief, my mind takes a hairpin turn, and those nagging fucking voices taunt me.

What if he's proposing out of obligation?

Because if he's doing this because he thinks *I* want him to, or because he feels he *has* to, I will be devastated. Getting married just because I'm pregnant is a terrible idea. I've thought a lot about all of the heart to hearts Tara and I have had about Jeff. And I know without any shadow of a doubt, that he's the Chachi to my Joanie and the Ross to my Rachel. This isn't the plot to some modern day rendition of *For Keeps*. Is it?

"Henley? You okay in there?" Jeff calls out from his bed.

I look down at the floor and see a pile of toilet paper shredded into confetti. I hadn't even realized I was ripping it apart.

I know I'm stalling.

And I know I need to set the record straight about this so I don't spend the next lifetime wondering.

"Yeah, I'm fine! Just a minute!"

I lean down and pick up the scraps of toilet paper and flush them down with uncertainty I felt moments ago. When I come back to bed, Jeff is propped up on his arm, watching me intently.

"Are you're sure you're not just proposing because I'm pregnant?" I mean, I've always known that Jeff and I would one day get married. I just figured it wouldn't be for a while.

Jeff looks at me earnestly and pats the empty spot next to him on the bed. I snuggle into his chest, and he threads his fingers between mine. "First of all, *we're* pregnant, not just you. You may be carrying my baby, but we're a team. We're in this together — I am with you every step of the way. Where you walk, *I walk*. And secondly, I've never been more sure of anything in my entire life."

He leans down and presses his lips to mine in a feverish kiss. This kiss is full of hope and unspoken promises. It makes my heart soar. When we pull apart, there's a truth in his eyes that reassures my soul.

This man is it.

He's it for me.

"I wish you knew just how much I love you, Henley. But I can't wait to spend the rest of our lives showing you just how much."

"I do. I not only feel it in my bones but because I love you just the same."

Chapter Twelve

VAGINAS AND VAJUDGMENTS

"Welcome! Welcome, everyone! Please, come in, select a mat on the floor and take a seat," a spritely, wiry-haired woman proclaims from the hallway, clapping her hands twice.

The swarm of round-bellied women and their significant others that I've found myself in breaks up and follows her command. Quickly, Jeff and I settle down on a mossy green yoga mat on the far side of the circle. Most of the men are seated, straddling their partner, but Jeff sits next to me, and I rest my head on his shoulder.

A few weeks ago Doctor Highman recommended we sign up for one of the hospital recommended child birthing classes, and she provided me with a list of classes ranging from traditional baby and me to Lamaze to hypno-births (who knew that was actually a thing?). The class wasn't a requirement by any means, but I figured it would give Jeff and me a solid peace of mind when coming to terms with what's to come.

I had no idea that I should have signed up for this nonsense before conception even occurred because I was waitlisted for nearly every one I called. But I finally found success when I was able to register for a four-class series called Mother Flower. After quickly perusing the description, I deduced it was good enough to get us through this thing called childbirth alive and in one piece.

The woman walks into the classroom. Her floral tunic swallows her whole as it's easily three sizes too big and her John Lennon-style glasses sport lenses thicker than Coke bottles. I was expecting a nurse to be leading the course, and this woman is most certainly not a nurse.

"Hello, everyone!" she regales in what I can only describe is an over-charismatic theatre voice. "I'm Deborah, and welcome to Mother Flower: A Blossoming Birth. Over the next month we're going to explore the zen of childbirth and learn all about the alternative coping mechanisms that you can use in labor and delivery."

Um ... exsqueeze me?

"Alternative coping mechanisms? Like blaring Nirvana and Pearl Jam during labor to drown out my harrowing screams?" I whisper to Jeff.

"No, babe. Alternative ... like drug-free."

I whip my head toward Jeff so fast that my hair slaps him in the face. "What?" My voice jumps three octaves, and Deborah stops her overdramatic monologue to look at me.

"I'm sorry? Did you have a question?" Her palms are pressed together in front of her chest like she's praying and I'm only now realizing just how much of a loon this woman actually is.

"Oh, no. I just ... I just thought a spider was on my ankle." I swat at the cuff of my pants, pretending to brush away an imaginary insect.

I want the drugs.

I like the drugs.

I definitely will *need* the drugs.

Jeff leans back to my ear. "Yeah, I thought you realized this was an alternative birthing class."

My face contorts in horror, and I can feel my blood pressure jump in a panic. "Does this look like the face of someone who intentionally signed up for some hippy dippy alternative birthing class? Drugs are totally natural!" I whisper, but it's loud enough that the entire class can hear me. I swallow hard and divert my attention back to Deborah, but find it challenging to focus on her words.

"Before we really get into the ins and outs of your bodies and childbirth, I thought we'd do a little ice breaker? You know, since we'll be spending a few hours each week together for the next month. Let's each go around the room, introduce ourselves, and tell us about the last movie you saw?" I softly groan at the suggestion, loathing any kind of group activity that involves sharing. "How about we start with ... *you*." Thankfully she gestures to a young mocha skinned woman with a man who could easily be in his fifties.

The woman perks up. "I'm Jade, this is my husband Walter and *this*," she places her hands on her stomach adoringly, "is little Kitty Sunshine."

For some reason unbeknownst to me, the entire class breaks out into a polite golf clap. I lean over and whisper to Jeff, "Is she having a baby or giving birth to a My Little Pony?"

"And let's see ... The last movie we saw was The Quince Tree Sun. It's this incredible biography of a Spanish artist named Antonio Lopez. It closely follows his agonizing plight to paint the perfect tree in his backyard."

Um ... That sounds ... riveting?

"Seriously? I'd rather watch paint dry than be subjected to that torture," Jeff whispers.

Couple after couple introduces themselves and I realize just how uncultured I am. Stuart and Jane? They quite enjoyed Ma

Vie en Rose. They lost me at the word "subtitles." The lesbian couple across from us? They're obsessed with this drama called Maria Full of Grace where a pregnant teenager from Colombia works as a drug mule transporting cocaine in her stomach to the U.S. And the androgynous hipsters also known as Sawyer and Bennie? They don't believe in televisions or movies or anything remotely entertaining, but they do spin their own organic yarn in their spare time and make baby blankets and tiny hats for the NICU floor. So obviously they are far better people than Jeff and me.

I shift uncomfortably on the floor as the couple next to us prattles on about Selma. I tried watching it, I really did, but after about twenty minutes I traded civil rights for a home renovation show that was far more interesting. Hey now, don't judge. I never said I was a *good* person. And yes, I'm well aware I am probably going to hell.

Jeff squeezes my hips when the silence in the room lasts a beat too long, and I realize that everyone is staring at me. "Hi, everyone." I raise my hand awkwardly in a half wave, trying to hide the anguish of this exercise on my face. "I'm Henley. This is my fiancé, Jeff. And the last movie I saw was this award-winning British documentary about the struggles of a modern day woman on the path of self-discovery. In the process, she falls in love with not one, but two men, who fight for her returned affection." Kitty Sunshine's mother looks at me expectantly, and I quickly continue. "The film was so powerful it made me cry. And the cast was truly outstanding."

"This sounds empowering! What's the film called?" Jane asks from across the room.

I bite my lip and swallow hard. "Um, the name escapes me right now, but this was a moving and life changing film. Everyone *has* to see it! I'll look up the name and let everyone know next time." Which is a blatant lie because there's no way in hell I'm ever coming back here. But the class blissfully nods in approval and moves on to the next couple in the circle.

Jeff's breath tickles just below the curve of my jaw. He speaks softly so he doesn't interrupt the next couple giving their introduction. "What on earth are you talking about, Henley? The last movie we saw had Hugh Grant, Renee Zellweger, and that guy from The King's Speech."

"Yeah, the last movie we saw was Bridget Jones's Diary. But I can't let *them* know that!" I gesture to the gaggle of vultures mentally criticizing my every word. These were, no doubt, the kinds of parents who will only allow their children to eat organic foods, exclusively use essential oils instead of over the counter drugs, and have had their children listening to Mozart in utero since the moment they peed on a stick.

I can feel my eyes roll to the back of my head as the final couple begins to wax poetic about some obscure award-winning indie movie that their dog walker's next door neighbor directed.

"Oh my God. I am *so* shallow!" I hiss into Jeff's ear.

"Babe, you're not shallow. Nobody here is judging you."

I snort inadvertently. Does this man *not* know me at all?

"I know nobody is judging *me*. But my twat is judging them!"

"So you're vajudging them?" He snickers to himself, amused.

"I'm going to be vajudging you if you don't start behaving." I elbow him in the ribs playfully.

MUCH TO MY SURPRISE, the class doesn't focus on the anatomical part of childbirth. I suppose that's because we all know which pieces go in which parts that led us into this glorious predicament. What this particular class *does* cover is more along the lines of a new age therapy session.

"I want to make sure that beyond the birthing basics, everyone here is getting something personal out of the class. So if you ever have any questions, please feel free to interrupt and ask away. Now, tell me, what are some of your biggest fears? It could be about pregnancy or the birthing process or anything that is weighing on your mind?"

A tiny woman with mocha skin shoots her hand into the air and doesn't wait to be called upon to answer. "The pain! I am absolutely terrified of the physical pain. I know I want a drug-free birth, but I know this is going to hurt." Her boyfriend, husband, whoever, rubs his hands up and down her arms, trying to calm her down.

"Ah, yes, the pain. Everyone seems to be so focused on how much it will hurt rather than what awaits you on the other end of the birthing process. Let me tell you this, ladies and gentlemen. That pain? That pain is *all* in your head. And the epidural you crave is actually a crutch and can—and will—prolong your labor. Drug-free childbirth is a very euphoric experience and better for both you and the baby."

"How is being in excruciating pain better for *me?*" I whisper to Jeff. He squeezes my hand reassuringly, and I direct my attention back to Deborah.

"It's a natural high. Those endorphins will kick in, and you won't feel a thing. If anything, you'll feel ah-mazing! But I can promise you this—the eighteen years that follow your child's birth day will be far more painful than the duration of labor and delivery."

The class laughs, but good ole Deb has immediately lost all street cred in my book. Sure, women have been having babies for thousands of years with the vast majority pushing that kid out in less than ideal places without drugs—behind a tree in the wilds of Africa, or on the Oregon Trail while her partner died of dysentery as the oxen pulling the wagon drowned in a river. Or hell, even in a McDonald's bathroom. But in the era of modern medicine, there is absolutely no reason why I should subject myself to such torture.

And for her to insinuate that *my* decisions are wrong just because I want a little cocktail of anesthetics to wash down each contraction? That's just ... just ... deplorable! Just because I *can* get a root canal without the use of laughing gas doesn't mean I should.

I shoot my hand up into the air, ignoring the drug-free diatribe. "So for those of us who, in theory, may want to experiment with said drugs, you know, in case the pain that is in my head is actually manifesting in my vagina considering a child is trying to claw its way out, when would you recommend asking for the epidural?" My tone is snarkier than I expected. But if she can be smug about it all, I can too.

"What I would recommend for anyone wanting an epidural is to register for a traditional birthing class where you can learn all about the toxic chemicals they inject into your body, and therefore, the baby's bloodstream." Deborah gives a dramatic moment of pause and nails me with a look that screams *shut the hell up, woman.*

But right or wrong, the last thing I need—or want—is more judgment. My decisions are mine and no one else's. Except for maybe Jeff. He's part of this, too.

"Rather than focus on your need for an epidural and pain that may or may not happen, what are *you* most afraid of, Henley?"

Pooping. I'm still terrified that I'm going to deliver a six-pound deuce right alongside a six-pound baby.

I hate that she's calling me out in front of everyone, but I know that I can't be entirely truthful here. And my mind goes back to the day Tara traumatized me. "Tearing. I'm scared that this baby will literally tear me in two."

"Ah, yes. The episiotomy ..."

I zone out and try to redirect my anger and annoyance as Deborah goes off on a tangent about tearing and stitches and how the body can miraculously heal itself probably with the help of a concoction of unicorn hair, petals from a silver orchid, and essential oils.

Jeff pulls me closer against him. "That's nothing a little duct tape and Gorilla Glue can't fix, Henley."

"That sounds like a scene from a Godzilla horror film."

"Pretty much. But then again, isn't that childbirth?"

AFTER ALL OF our questions and fears have been addressed, Deborah takes the last part of the class to guide us through a series of body positions and breathing exercises. It's part Kama Sutra and part yoga.

Arch your back this way.
And hold your partner like this.
Apply pressure here.
No, not there. Here.
Focus on opening your soul to new life.
And blah ... blah ... blah ...

Good Lord, this woman is ridiculous. And just when I think it can't get any worse, it does.

"Your body is a wild rose. And as you prepare to give birth, your body blossoms and your rose petals open, and your sweet nectar is exposed."

Jeff hides his head behind me and stifles a laugh. I elbow him again, trying to keep a straight face. Somehow everyone else around us is capable of keeping themselves together, and all eyes are on us.

Deborah clears her throat. She dares not look in our direction, but I'm sure that if she did, the glare would be our murder. And to my utter mortification, she demonstrates how she wants all of us to lay back and bend our knees, exposing our 'sweet nectar' to the world. When she stands, she walks around the circle, correcting our bodies and continuing with the lesson.

"Now breathe in through your nose ... and out through your mouth ... do it with me now. In slowly through your nose ... and exhale through your mouth."

She makes a high-pitched wheezing sound with each and every breath. I'm pretty sure I heard this same sound during a fifth-grade field trip to the zoo where I witnessed two hyenas going at it. It's not very becoming of her.

Deborah walks throughout the room, making sure we're breathing properly. She stops in front of us and kneels down beside me, putting her hand on my knee. "Henley, I know you feel silly. But when you breathe through your whole body without inhibition, you're breathing life into your baby and helping bring him or her into this world. Just try it with me." Her gaze pierces right through me, as serious as a flesh eating bacteria.

I will myself to keep a straight face, swallow my pride and follow her lead, wheezing in and out with an animalistic sound I didn't know I had in me.

"Very good." She pats my leg and gets up to assist another couple.

Jeff turns to me. "We're never coming back here, are we?"

God, I love how this man practically lives in my brain.

"Nope."

ONCE WE'VE RECOVERED from Deborah and her insane attempts to turn my loins into a flowering blossom, or whatever she called it, we take up residence in a hole in the wall coffee shop for a late afternoon snack.

Jeff hands me a croissant and a hot cup of tea, then goes back to the counter to grab his coffee and slice of pound cake. I love the strong smell of this place. The glorious aroma makes me wish more than anything that I could indulge in a cup of Joe. And by cup, I mean the whole damn pot. *Stupid pregnancy rules about avoiding caffeine.*

He takes a seat across from me and breaks off a piece of his pound cake, popping it into his mouth.

"We should probably start talking about names," Jeff says, his mouth full of food.

I haven't thought about names because I've always subscribed to the philosophy that you need to actually *see* the baby before you can choose the name they'll be called for the rest of their life. It's a heavy responsibility when you think about it. I mean, what if little Miss Kitty Sunshine has the disposition of Maleficent on meth? Or was born to rock the resting bitch face? That name simply would not suit her.

Even still. I suppose we can at least *start* to talk about it. Nobody is going to make us decide right here and now. But if he's asking to discuss potential names, he obviously has something he's gunning for.

"What'd you have in mind?" I ask before taking a sip of tea.

"Well, I've always like the name Clinton. Clint for short." He pauses, examining my reaction, but I don't give him one. "It's strong. Presidential. Masculine. Any guy named Clint is a real man's man. Like Clint Eastwood!"

I narrow my eyes, rolling the name around in my mind. I don't hate the name Clint by any means, but it just doesn't feel right.

"Clint?" I ask.

Jeff nods with a proud smile plastered to his face like he's solved world hunger. "Mm-hmm. It's impossible to make fun of a kid named Clinton."

"Really? It's impossible?" I guffaw. How is this not more

obvious to him? "You'd be welcoming him to years of torture in high school once sex ed classes happen."

Jeff raises an eyebrow, challenging me in disbelief. And I'm shocked that this isn't more apparent to him.

"It's true!" I say. "Aside from the obvious 'Clit' nickname snafu, you also run the risk of Clintoris. And God forbid someone forgets to dot the 'i' in his name, it'll look like his name is—" I lean over onto my elbows and whisper, "—*you know* ... the c-word. You may as well name him Vulva or Fallopian."

Jeff drops his jaw, processing the thought of his strapping young boy being named after female anatomy, and doesn't say a word.

I lean back in my chair again and add, "Besides, you still don't know if it's a boy or a girl."

He purses his lips. "Touche."

I split my croissant in half and take a bite, absorbing his silence for a few moments.

I swallow hard and suggest the obvious. "What if we just wait and see what this baby looks like? We could fall in love with a name now, and it may not even suit the child."

I don't want to tell him that no matter what happens, I get veto power over the name. Everyone knows that the mother is supposed to win the name game. No man in his right mind would watch his significant other go through the whole painful and dramatic ordeal of childbirth and say "no" when she asks, "Doesn't she look like a Eunice VonKlepto?" as she cradles the baby in her arms the first time. Sure, naming the kid is a joint effort, but he's not the one pushing it out.

"I can agree to that ... on one condition." He smirks knowingly.

"What's that?"

"The names of any ex-boyfriends are off the table."

I snort. He's delusional if he thinks I'd name this child Leo or the name of any of the buffoons I dated long ago. Even still, his request is reasonable, and one I can agree on.

"Same goes for ex-girlfriends then, too." I nod in agreement. "I do have one name I'd like to veto now, if that's okay with you."

He opens his palm, gesturing me to continue.

"No Kitty Sunshine."

He narrows his eyes and gives me his best cat that ate the canary smile.

"No Kitty Sunshine? No problem. Because no son of mine is going to have a name worthy of an eighties Saturday morning cartoon character.

Chapter Thirteen

SILENCE AND STRETCHY PANTS

"Well? What'd your folks say?" Jeff asks with a little too much enthusiasm as I walk back into the room and set my cell phone down on the coffee table.

My entire demeanor is heavy, and the weight of my body and my mind and all the hormonal baggage I carry with me these days sinks into the couch next to him.

"They ... uh ... they didn't say anything, sweetie." And not for lack of trying. When the phone picked up, I was nothing but sweet and upbeat and hopeful as I let her know we're engaged, but all she gave me was silence.

I extend my hand, palm up on his leg, and he threads his fingers through mine exhaling in an audible *humph*. We had wanted to tell my parents about our engagement in person, and by *we* I mean Jeff. I just wanted them to know, period. Considering how swimmingly they took the news of their pending grandchild, I had (wrongly) assumed that my mother might actually show an iota of excitement for our engagement.

"What?" His incredulous tone matches my exact reaction.

"I know. It was weird. I was putting a few things away in the bedroom when she answered, and so I quickly got down to it. I mean, no sense in beating around the bush, right? So I had said something along the lines of, *hey Mom! I've got some really exciting news!,* and I took her silence as a prompt to continue, and so I told her about how you proposed, and reassured her that this wasn't just some spur of the moment decision because we were expecting, and I told her not to expect a shotgun wedding because we don't want to rush into things so we can focus on the baby, and that we'll keep them posted on details and—"

"Whoa! Slow down, babe. Take a breath. You're talking faster than that Micro Machine guy from the commercials when we were kids."

I take a deep breath and give his hand a tender squeeze. "I'm sorry. I'm just a little bummed out, ya know?"

And like someone flipped a damn light switch, the tears fall without any warning whatsoever. It's not every day you get the cold shoulder from your parents, but apparently, they're doing the silent treatment thing right now. It's clear she's unhappy with me and the situation Jeff and I have found ourselves in. But if I can't get what I want, it's best to simply ignore my folks if they're going to be such a killjoy. Besides, Jeff's parents were happy enough for everyone, so I choose to focus on joy.

I lean over and wipe my eyes and runny nose on the sleeve of Jeff's T-shirt.

"I can't believe they didn't say anything. I thought for sure they would be excited."

"I know," I agree with him in between sobs.

"This is almost worse than their reaction when we told them about the baby." He clumsily runs his free hand against the adorable scruff on his jawline and contemplates the situation. "Maybe I should try calling them? I could help smooth things over. When I asked your dad for your hand in marriage, he was really positive about it all."

Ugh. I'd really rather not be hit twice in one day. Being bruised over the silent treatment one time is enough for the week. No need to drag him into my parents' social ineptitude and hurt his ego, too.

They can be such assholes sometimes!

Their silent treatment is a force to be reckoned with. *Trust me.* When I was a teenager, I came home with a B minus on my U.S. History midterm paper. My folks were so upset they didn't talk to me for a week. The nothingness meant disappointment and contempt. It was my dad who cracked first, and I had to swear to raise my grade before the final—which I did. But for the daughter who fails at nothing, that week *hurt!* If we could bottle their unspoken displeasure and unleash it upon unsuspecting individuals, we'd have a real weapon on our hands.

Before I can ask him to give it a day or two before he reaches out, Jeff has his phone in hand and he's dialing my mom's number. He smiles confidently at me. After a few moments, he whispers, "Voice mail" in my direction and raises up a single finger silently asking me to hold on a second.

"Hey, Mrs. Carson, it's Jeff. I just wanted to chat really quickly about the conversation you and Henley just had. I know our situation is a lot to take in, in a very short amount of time. But I just wanted to reassure you that I love your daughter more than a fat kid loves ice cream and cake, and I'm marrying her out of necessity. Not in the way that a baby needs a mom and dad who are married kind of necessity. But rather because Henley is necessary to my existence. Without her, I would be nothing. So when you have a moment, I'd love it if you could give one of us a—"

Jeff stops talking mid-sentence, pulls the phone away from his ear after a moment and then looks at the screen with a puzzled expression on his face.

"What?" I prompt, pulling him from whatever thoughts are

flooding his head.

He hits the red end button on the screen and places his phone next to him on the couch. "That's funny. It cut me off and said the voicemail box was full."

Odd. My parents always keep their voicemail inbox clear.

We sit in silence for a moment, and from the corner of my eye, I see Jeff look from me down to his phone and then back to me.

"Henley ...?" Jeff says my name slowly, almost questioning it.

"Yeah, babe?" I wipe another rogue tear away from my cheek.

"Did you actually hear your mom talking at *any* point during the call?"

I tilt my head and try to recall if she said anything. "No. Nothing beyond whatever she said when she first answered."

"*Henley* ..." He's still saying my name in a delicate tone that makes me feel like a child being encouraged to see the error in their ways. Whatever it is he's trying to say, I wish he'd just come right out and say it already.

"What, Jeff?" I hate that my tone is short. I know it's not his fault my parents are being soulless punks hell-bent on sucking the happiness out of my life, but I'm just ready for this day to be over. At some point all little girls dream of the moment they tell their parents they're getting married. In the movies it's usually followed with squeals of delight and the mom makes a big fuss about how excited she is to go wedding dress shopping and the whole nine yards. But no, not *my* mom. My mom couldn't even show her excitement. Maybe she was so distraught by the news she keeled over and died on the other end of the line?

"Is there *any* chance your mom never actually picked up the phone to begin with, and that you were rambling to her voice mail and getting yourself all worked up over nothing?" His voice is light and non-accusatory like he knows his words could break me.

Whoopsie!

I can feel the heat rising in my cheeks. "God, I am *such* an idiot." I throw my head in my heads, trying not to be embarrassed, but the effort is futile.

Jeff chuckles softly. "Hey now, don't you dare talk smack on my fiancée." He rubs my back softly. "It's okay. Cam warned me that pregnancy brain can rear its silly little head in the most inconvenient of moments."

Ah, pregnancy brain. My go-to excuse for all those things I don't want to do like switching over the laundry or grading papers or paying bills. Which reminds me, I never paid the electric bill, but I digress. All I can do is sigh and fight the urge to crawl into a hole and disappear. My stupidity knows no bounds.

"Come here, you." He pulls me closer to his body and kisses the top of my head. "I can only imagine how tough it is being pregnant..."

I snort instinctively because he really has no freakin' clue.

"What?"

"Let's just say that pregnancy is like a group project for school. There is a lot of excitement and an all hands on deck approach the very first time you get together to work on the project, but now there's one person stuck doing all the work—me. This growing a human thing really is hard." The last part is more of a confession.

"I know it is, babe. But look on the bright side..."

I lift my head up to meet his gaze, wondering what the silver lining here could possibly be.

"You don't have to deal with your period for a few more months, your tits look great, and you get to live in stretchy pants until this baby arrives."

I guffaw. "You're crazy if you think I'm putting the maternity pants away after this kid debuts. They are, hands down, the most comfortable things in existence. They are *never* coming off."

Chapter Fourteen

HAPPY BAT MITZVAH

The coffee table in front of the couch is littered with half empty glasses and paper plates with traces of chocolate cake and vanilla frosting. I stretch my legs out in front of me, resting my feet on a wad of tissue paper from Tara's gift.

"You said you wanted a low key birthday. I hope this was okay." Jeff kisses my temple and sits down next to me, draping his arm across the back of the couch.

"It was perfect. Thank you, baby." I lean my head against him and relax for the first time all day. He invited Tara and Cameron over for dinner and hired a chef to come in and cook so the four of us could simply relax and catch up.

"I still can't believe she bought you leather pants and a sex swing."

I should have raised a red flag when she kept insisting I open my birthday gifts in front of them throughout dinner. I mean, this is the girl who publicly announced she was hosting a panty intervention for me in the middle of Victoria's Secret when she realized I didn't own a single thong. I don't care what anybody says, but dental floss permanently lodged in the crack of your ass simply is not sexy. Maybe helpful if I had some food lodged back there that needed extraction. But *ew — no.* "I know. That's Tara for you, though. She has no shame. And no limits either."

"What'd her card say?" he asks as he runs his fingers through my hair.

I sit up and move some of the paper on the table looking for the card she included with the gift. Jeff inspects the front of it and raises an eyebrow.

"Um ... this is a Bat Mitzvah card," he observes.

"Read the inside," I deadpan.

Jeff slowly opens the card and clears his throat before reading aloud in an overly-perky voice that rivals Tara's. "Henley, you've finally become a woman! So I thought you'd enjoy some womanly things. The leather pants are for when you regain your rockin' ass after you deliver le bebe. And the sex swing is for ... well, the truth is the sex swing was accidentally sent to us twice from Adam and Eve, you know the discreet adult toy store? And it seemed like a waste to return a perfectly good sex swing when I can share the gift of kinky acrobatics with my best friend. So consider this birthday gift as a way to help get the spark back into the sack after the wee one arrives. Just be sure to stretch first—trust me. Love you, Giggle Tits! Tara." He laughs and tosses the card down on the table. "Giggle Tits? Is this a pet name you've had for a while?"

I nudge him with my shoulder. There aren't many people who I let get away with pet names, let alone pet names like Giggle Tits, but she's one of them.

Beyond the sex toys and pants that won't fit for the next year or two, my mother had the foresight to drop off a few gifts before I got home from the office. I am now the proud new owner of a Martha Stewart wedding planning book and waffle iron. Turns out her silent treatment wasn't so silent after all. She ended up calling and congratulating us the very next day, but not without the accompaniment of some passive aggressive jabs about marriage coming *before* the baby in the baby carriage.

Jeff, however, proved that he is the best gift giver between the two of us as he completely spoiled me rotten. I didn't even give him a hint on what I wanted for my birthday, but he hit a home run. For starters, I unwrapped a luxurious ballerina pink maternity nightgown. It is softer than most of the baby blankets I've felt, and I had to fight the urge to wrap myself up in it immediately. Then he gave me a gift card for a full day of pampering — prenatal massage, mani, pedi, and a facial. And *not* the kind of facial that would require his assistance, though he did make that offer under his breath after I unwrapped the gift certificate.

But the most thoughtful gift of all was a jewelry box he made with his own two hands using photos of the two of us and a bottle of Modge Podge. Inside was a delicate silver bracelet with charms of a heart, an airplane, and a rattle.

"For the day we met, for the day I realized I was in love with you, and for our future," he told me with a nervous smile playing on his lips. "And I plan on adding to it throughout the years."

"Tell me that story."

"Which one?"

I touch the elegant silver heart. "When you knew you were in love with me. I don't think I've heard this one before."

He reaches out and threads his fingers through mine. "It's not really exciting. I knew when I first met you that I was going to marry you someday, but I've told you that already." He squeezes my fingers gingerly. "But when I realized just how deep I was in love with you, it was like I had been struck by lightning and ... and I just *knew*."

"And *when* was that?"

He smiles at me knowingly. "Do you remember the night we went bowling with some of my coworkers down at the Power and Light district?"

"Yeah..." And how could I forget? We had only been dating a little over two months at that point, but in a moment of intoxication, Jeff released the twelve-pound bowling ball behind him and nearly took out Doug from accounting.

"Well, when we got home, you escaped into my room to get ready for bed. After brushing my teeth, I went to grab a glass of water and when I came back in you were snoring like a jackhammer."

"I WAS NOT!" I snatch a pillow and try to smack him with it, but he deftly leans out of the way and laughs at me.

"You were! And it was cute! It was at that precise moment that I knew I could never give my heart to anybody else. I knew I wanted to listen to you saw logs every night from then until eternity."

There is nothing love-worthy or endearing or cute about snoring. "You're so weird."

"And you wouldn't have me any other way."

I adjust the way I'm sitting on the couch to try and give the baby a little more space as it's currently doing summersaults. I'm only in the middle of my second trimester, and there is a noticeable belly pop happening. The good news is I'm past the *is she pregnant or is she just eating too many cheeseburgers* phase of my pregnancy, and I no longer have to try and suck in my gut.

My stomach flutters and I'm convinced it's not a feeling I'll ever get used to. "I think I ate too much cake. This kid is in sugar shock." There is, no doubt, a foot trying to wedge itself in the space between two of my left ribs and an elbow using my bladder as a trampoline. "Here ... feel." I reach for his hand and bring his palm to my side. It's only a matter of moments before the baby kicks again. Jeff's face lights up with an awe and wonder that I've never seen before.

"Wow," he whispers, his face beaming. It's the first time he's actually felt it kick. He keeps his hand there until the baby finally settles.

"You know, it's pretty amazing. *You* used to give me butterflies. You still do, in fact. But now I actually feel the fluttering of little feet inside of me, and *that's* something else."

Jeff gently grabs my chin and turns my face to his. "I love you, Henley."

He looks at me like he's about to swallow me whole. And before I have a chance to tell him that I love him too, his lips are on mine, and his hands are in my hair. It's the kind of kiss that leaves you restless, breathless, and senseless.

When we finally pull away from each other, I know that this man, that this moment, is exactly where I am supposed to be … *home*.

"Oh! Before I forget, I have one more present for you."

"You've already done so much, Jeff. You didn't need to get me anything to begin with. I wanted a low key birthday so we could put money aside for the baby." *And you already spent too much money on this ice skating rink on my left ring finger.*

"I know, but I wanted to do this. This one was important … for us." He lays on the floor, flat on his stomach and extends his hand all the way underneath the couch.

"Oh! You got me a dust bunny? You shouldn't have," I say with a laugh.

"Hold on … I almost … have it!" His words are strained, and his face turns cherry red as it contorts.

I watch him struggle for a few moments before finally suggesting we simply move the couch. It seems like the obvious solution for whatever he has hidden. I stand up so he can rearrange the furniture and once he's found the envelope he was searching for, he gestures me down on the middle cushion and then sits on the wooden coffee table in front of me, resting his elbows on his knees.

"Open it!" He's practically jumping out of his skin in excitement. His knee is bouncing, and he can hardly contain his smile.

I rip open the envelope, pull out the slip of paper and scan the words across the page. "We're going to San Diego?"

"Yeah!"

"We're going *tomorrow*? I've got things I need to do!" I try to hide the panic in my voice. I've got a lot on my plate right now and can't afford to take a vacation with all of the lesson plans I'm working on.

I look back at Jeff, and he's absolutely glowing with pride at this little stunt he's pulled. "Don't you even stress about all that. You're all mine for the next few days. I thought it was important for us to take a babymoon before our son comes."

I give him a pointed look at the word "son." Admittedly, I'm a little nervous that if this is a girl, he'll be somewhat disappointed. "A babymoon?"

"Yeah! I was reading in one of your pregnancy books—"

"Wait? You're reading my pregnancy books?" *Oh God. Does he know I may poop in labor?*

Shit.

Literally.

"Of course I'm reading your pregnancy books. I've told you a thousand times, woman, we're in this together. Where you walk, I walk, remember? Anyway, one of the books said a babymoon is a great way to connect as a couple before the baby arrives. And I know we haven't even had a honeymoon yet — hell, we've never even really been on vacation together. And no, I don't count a family affair like my brother's wedding as vacation, no matter how extravagant the weekend was. So I just thought this would be a good idea. And I know you love Southern California. And I found a really great deal. And—"

I grab his face and kiss him hard and fast. The kiss takes him by surprise, and he moans into my mouth. After a few moments, I can feel him smiling against my lips. It's impossible not to smile back. This is hands down one of the sweetest, most thoughtful gifts anyone has ever given me.

"Oh!" I abruptly pull away at the feel of this kid clawing at my insides. I look down at my stomach and then laugh softly at the interruption. We both watch what I can only assume is an elbow or knee pushing out from my abdomen. It *definitely* looks freaky.

"It seems as if this kid is embarrassed by its parents kissing."

"Well, he better get used to the PDA because I have no intentions to ever stop my public displays of affection when it comes to my beautiful ... sexy ... kindhearted ... wife to be."

He softly kisses my lips in between each word. I love how he has the power to make me feel beautiful. I wish all women could be this lucky. When I pull away after his last kiss, there's nothing but sheer adoration for me illuminating his eyes.

"Thank you, Jeff. I couldn't have asked for a more perfect birthday." I lean over and give him the biggest bear hug that my belly allows.

Whoever said it was impossible to throw your arms around the world never hugged their one true love.

Chapter Fifteen

LET YOUR WEIRDO LIGHT SHINE BRIGHTLY

The next morning we quickly pack our bags and catch a cab to the airport by early afternoon. Since there were no tickets available on the non-stop flight from Kansas City to San Diego, we have a short trip to Denver with a layover for about ninety minutes. It's not so bad, though. In fact, it's kind of nostalgic considering this is the same route where Jeff and I first met.

Jeff holds my hand through takeoff and landing, and about halfway through the flight, he falls asleep on my shoulder in a quick power nap. It's truly amazing how so much can change in such a short amount of time. A ninety-minute flight. A nine-month pregnancy. I practically knew nine minutes into our first date that I wanted to keep him around for a long time.

I guess deep down I've always known on some level that Jeff was *it* for me. Sitting next to him on the plane last year, his charming awkwardness was completely disarming. From the moment he smiled, my insides melted. His laughter was the ultimate aphrodisiac, and with every nervous look he shot my way during that flight, a little piece of him burrowed himself in my heart. He genuinely seemed like the kind of guy who had no idea just how awesome he truly was, and I knew I needed to know him better.

Sometimes when you know, you just know.

As always, the descent into Denver is terrible at best. The plane jerks and seemingly stutters with the change of air as visions of the plane falling out of the sky plague me.

We're both so relieved to be back on the ground once we deplane in Denver, I'm half tempted to get down on my knees and kiss the ground. But I don't. I mean I *could*, but the likelihood of me being able to get back up easily is slim, and I don't want to be that pregnant woman who has an army of Good Samaritans trying to hoist her back to vertical.

"Want to grab a bite to eat?" Jeff asks.

My stomach gurgles in response. These days, it gurgles in response to just about everything, because no matter the question the answer is always food.

How are you feeling today? *Let's eat!*

Is the baby kicking? *I'll take fries with that!*

Are you having a boy or a girl? *A cheeseburger well done, please and thank you.*

Jeff laughs. "I'll take that as a yes." He takes my backpack from his hands and pulls it up over his shoulder. "Are burgers okay?"

I smile. "A burger is always okay. In fact, I've never met a burger I didn't like."

I follow Jeff to this hole in the wall airport restaurant, and he stands in line to place our order while I walk into the seating area in search of a table. Based on how crowded this joint is, these burgers must be pretty damn good.

"Ma'am?" a gravelly male voice calls out, and I feel a weak hand on my forearm as I'm walking by a large window overlooking the tarmac.

Ugh. I hate it when people call me ma'am. My mother is ma'am. I am a twenty-something badass. A pregnant badass, but a badass nonetheless.

I turn toward the voice, and I find an older gentleman with a warm smile and kind eyes. He's wearing the kind of starched plaid button-up shirt you'd expect a man of his age to be wearing. His skin is paper thin, and his hair is a platinum crown of faded glory from years gone by.

"We're just about to leave if you'd like to take our table." He looks from me to a spritely woman across the table from him. At the mere sight of her and her dyed magenta and cyan hair, he lights up. She's wearing a cat T-shirt that reads *How you like meow?* And her glasses are as thick as thieves. She can't be younger than eighty, but her wrinkled skin is masked by her youthful lust for life.

I open my mouth to speak, but it appears I have forgotten how to talk. The old man cackles and reaches across the table to the woman. "She keeps me young. Once upon a time, I was a rock and roller, too. Now I prefer to just rock in my chair. Estelle, here, she still rocks."

"I can see that." I don't even bother fighting my smile. I love the way he's looking at her, and the brightness they bring out in each other.

"We're on our way to Vegas to see AC/DC for her birthday. Backstage passes, you know." He leans over and winks as he says the last part like he's letting me in on a little-known secret.

"How long have you been together?" I'm not being polite. I'm genuinely curious how a seemingly ordinary grandpa ended up with modern day Rockstar Barbie complete with a Debbie Harry rebel attitude.

He lights up proudly. "We're going on sixty-two years this fall."

Whoa. I can't even begin to imagine just how much they've

seen together in their lifetime. "That's impressive," I say, wondering what their secret is.

"Now I recognize we're no spring chickens, and the *normal* thing to do would be to hole ourselves up in some questionable old folks community. That's what our kids wanted us to do anyway. But when I met Estelle back in autumn of 1955, standing in line for Mr. Toad's Wild Ride when Disneyland first opened, I never imagined the wild ride we were about to embark on. Later that night we crossed paths by Sleeping Beauty's Castle, and without ever saying a word, she came up to me and kissed me. It was the fifties. Things like that didn't just happen, and they certainly didn't happen to normal guys like me! But I quickly understood that nothing about us would ever be normal, so no sense in fighting that. And I love that about us. Normalcy breeds boredom and a lackluster lifestyle. To get the most out of life and love, you have to constantly evolve together and make sure that the time you share isn't just time, it's quality. Some days that means me losing the last of my hearing at a death metal concert because it makes my love happy. And other days it means she sucks it up and gets lost in an art museum with me."

There's something to be said about wisdom coming from the end of life.

Estelle stretches her arm across the table and rests it gently on the man's hand. She silently gestures down to her watch.

"Oh my! We better skedaddle. Vegas waits for no one!" he says as he makes quick work of their trash before pulling out the chair for Estelle to help her up. Then he does the same for me, helping me and my growing belly down into the seat.

"Thanks ... for the table," I say to the pair of them.

Estelle smiles warmly at me and begins to move her fingers, signing words I don't understand.

Oh.

And it's the moment I realize I've never actually heard her

speak. The dexterity in her fingers is mesmerizing and beautiful. But I still feel at a loss. "I ... I'm sorry, I don't understand," I say softly as she presses her lips in a solid line.

"It's okay, dear. She just said you remind her of herself when she was younger. And she's right. There's a unique spark about you similar to the one I was first drawn to when I met Estelle." He wraps his arm around her waist and pulls her closer. "Youth is wasted on the young. Don't spend your time on normalcy and boring things. Just be your vibrant, sparkly self."

And with that, the pair turn and head toward their gate for Sin City where Estelle will no doubt throw her bra on stage and roam around the rest of the night sporting free range boobies.

When Jeff and I are that old, I hope we're half as cool and carefree as these two. I love our life, and while we may not be as unconventional as an old biddy whose wardrobe comes from Forever XXI, I wouldn't change our ass backwards ways for anything. Okay, strike that from the record. I would totally change a *few* things ...

Like maybe I would have actually waited until we got back to the hotel room before having sex at his brother's wedding, thus avoiding a hundred plus people seeing my Spanx in all their glory. And stretch marks. I could really do without the evidence of my skin's elasticity. And his love of nineties line dances. I don't care what Jeff says, there is nothing fun about doing the Macarena or Cha Cha Slide no matter how crowded the dance floor is.

Dark clouds spill over the mountains and down through the foothills toward the airport. And I pray it's not some metaphorical sign of what's to come.

"Hey, what are you thinking about?" Jeff sets the tray down in front of me, and I practically fall into a cheeseburger-coma from the orgasmic-inducing aroma of pure Angus beef topped with melted aged cheddar cheese. If this love is wrong, I don't want to be right. It's seduction at first sniff.

This is, without a doubt, the most romantic thing he's done for me since ... well, since last night where he unveiled this little surprise. I look from my food to Jeff, and I want to reach up, grab his face and go diving for his tonsils. But one thing will lead to another, and I'm not sure how sanitary these tables are. And it probably couldn't sustain our combined weight. Pre-pregnant Henley? It could totally withstand us. But the combined efforts of feeding this baby late night pizzas and Oreos and that fifteen-pound bag of gummy bears from Costco, gravity would inevitably win out, crumbling the table beneath us.

Jeff raises his eyebrows, trying to read my mind.

"Oh, just that I love how unconventional we are."

He hums softly with a smile. "Me too." He leans down to give me a peck on the lips. It's not quite what I had in mind, but it'll have to do considering the audience. "I love how you let your weird light shine so brightly."

I snort. "I'm not weird. But if I am, the only reason you found me was because you were attracted to my weirdo light in the first place. Which makes *you* a weirdo, too."

But Jeff is right. This *is* the best airport cheeseburger I've ever had.

AFTER WE FINISH, it doesn't take us long to find our gate, and I settle into a chair after another pee break. I turn to see if our plane has arrived, and the sky opens up and unleashes its fury on the ground below. You can barely see ten feet out the window, and the audible pings of hail hitting the roof echo throughout the terminal. We're not going anywhere at the moment, so we do the only thing we can do ...

We watch in awe and wait.

"LADIES AND GENTLEMEN, may I please have your attention. Due to inclement weather, the Denver International Airport is grounding all flights until further notice. The cell is rather large, so we will keep you posted as soon as more information is available."

And just like that, pandemonium ensues. Passengers are sprinting toward desk agents at virtually all of the gates while others frantically make phone calls. It all feels a bit overdramatic to me. And still, I almost wish I had a tub of popcorn to watch it all throw down.

"I'll never understand why people freak out over things that are entirely out of their control."

"Oh?" Jeff cocks an eyebrow at me. "Is that so?"

"Yeah. It's not like they're going to be stuck here forever. Mother Nature doesn't have a personal vendetta against everyone here. I'm sure the airlines are doing what they can to get us out of here as quickly as possible. I mean, the last thing they want to do is inconvenience *everyone*."

"I'm still stuck on *you* of all people talking about people freaking out about things they can't control. I'd need multiple hands to count the number of times you've panicked over some facet of being pregnant." He's not saying it in a demeaning way. More of a *Hey, Henley! Embrace the things you can't control* kind of way.

The next few hours are spent playing card games in a random gate area with Jeff and keeping tabs on the weather on his phone. The cell was much bigger than anyone predicted. What started off as a catty little thunderstorm quickly turned into a bitchy meltdown from Mother Nature herself. If this were January and a blizzard with whiteout conditions, we'd all be prepared. I mean, it's Denver! The state slogan for the 'Big D' should be "In the winter, you don't know when it'll come, how long it'll last, or how many inches you'll get but enjoy it! Because when we get wet in the summer, we just shrivel up and render ourselves useless." But I suppose thrusting ourselves into the air in a giant metal tube as lightning challenges thunder in a battle royale isn't the most intelligent move.

Eventually the novelty of riding out the storm wanes. I watch Jeff have a heated moment with the gate agent from afar and then storm off. "Well, it looks like we have two options," he says when he finally reemerges.

I raise an eyebrow at him curiously.

"We can either stay here at the airport and *hope* to catch a flight out whenever things clear up. But the plane we were taking has been rerouted to Salt Lake City, and there's no contingency plan for our connection at this point in time."

Ugh. The thought of spending another minute here and risk sleeping on the floor while pregnant displeases me greatly. "What's the other option? A hotel?"

"Not exactly." He grimaces. "Pretty much everything is sold out unless you want to stay at a one-star motel known for bedbugs." We both cringe. "Between the Bronco's home game and two conventions that are in town, we'd have to venture upwards of forty-five minutes outside the city to find a place to stay. And in these conditions, we're under a flash flood warning."

"Okay? So what does that mean?"

He chews on his thumb for a moment before sighing. He *really* doesn't want to tell me whatever it is he's thinking. "It means that if we're not camping on the floor of the Denver airport, we're renting a car and driving to my parents' house. They're only about twenty minutes away. Though, at this rate, we may need to build an ark." He looks out the window and sighs.

I can't believe he's serious about venturing out into this mess.

Jeff watches me cautiously, waiting for my reaction, but I

don't allow my expression to falter. Spending part of our babymoon with my future in-laws isn't exactly how I imagined today going. Babymoons should be full of uncomfortable sex positions and annoying sobriety and simply enjoying one last vacation together (or in our case, our *first* ever vacation together) before this baby comes. Not conversations with your future in-laws, the very people you've been avoiding because you were *sorta kinda* caught plowing through the bean field at their family affair. But like I said earlier, the weather is not in our control and this way at least we have a comfortable bed to sleep in.

I sigh in defeat. "Well, let's hope that car comes with a few oars and floatation devices aside from my swollen boobs." I stand up, grab my bag, and head in the direction of the rental cars with a wary Jeff on my heels.

Chapter Sixteen

FULL MOON OVER 1999

"My little Jeffey!"

His mom walks toward him with open arms and puckered lips. The powder blue dress she wears is straight out of the 1950s, and the faint smell of chocolate chip cookies made from scratch lingers in the air. Trust me, my pregnancy nose hasn't failed me yet. Her husband is right on her heels in a matching shirt and sweater vest.

Mrs. Carrington leans in to kiss her son and tussle his hair like he's five years old. "So good to see you, Mom. Thanks for letting us crash here on such short notice."

"Oh, sweetie, it's no trouble at all. I'm just excited to see you both." She turns to me with a smile, and instead of a warm, motherly hug, I'm greeted to her hands upon my belly and her face alarmingly close to my loins. "And hello to you, too, my sweet, darling grandchild. This is your Nana, and we are going to be the best of friends. And when those mean old parents of yours tell you 'no,' you just call me right up and I'll treat you right. Now, come on and kick for Nana. Kick, little one!"

I sigh at her lack of personal space. And tact for that matter.

And as if Mr. Carrington read my mind, he chimes in. "Oh, Martha, give the poor woman some room. Come here, you." He gives me a quick hug and then holds my arms out to the sides of my body. "You're filling out nicely, Henley."

That's an awkward compliment if I've ever heard one. Wait … That *was* a compliment, right? He's not actually calling me fat, is he?

I smile weakly. "Thanks, Mr. Carrington. It's been a rough couple of months, but slowly I've been starting to feel better."

"I sent you that box of remedies a little while ago. Did you use any of those?" Mrs. Carrington chimes in.

Another weak smile, this one of appreciation. I'm not too sure I'd qualify the package she sent as morning sickness remedies, though. It included things like ginger root — like the literal root straight out of the ground. Some mystery pills in an unmarked vile, a few loose tangerines, and something called motherhood brownies, whose ingredients were questionable. Jeff tasted one and quickly spit it back out it was *that* vile. It pained me to see a batch of chocolate desserts sacrificed in the name of hippie sorcery. While the gesture was thoughtful, the contents of said box of remedies quickly went into the trash. Except for the tangerines. Those appeared to be perfectly normal though I never actually ate them.

"Um, yeah, I tried them all, but none of them worked."

"Well, did you rub the ginger root all over your belly? And those little capsules were a suppository meant to bring gas relief."

So *that's* what I was supposed to do.

Jeff catches the stunned look in my eye and wraps his arm around my waist tenderly. "Why don't you sit down and relax? I'll go run our bags upstairs." Jeff kisses my cheek and quickly disappears out of sight.

It's the first time I've even been alone in his parents' presence, and I'm at a loss for small talk. The whole *meet the parents* thing is something I've never had much practice with. And the last time I met them, everyone was preoccupied with last minute wedding details to notice I'd spent the weekend happily buzzed in an effort to keep my anxiety at bay.

I take a seat on the floral couch that is, no doubt, the same couch Jeff sat on as a child. There's a clashing purple and green floral pillow that is misshaped with an uneven ruffle around the trim. It's hideous and makes me question everything about her taste. His dad sits down on the other side of the couch and rubs his palms over his knees. Maybe he's just as uncomfortable as I am?

"Can I get you anything to drink, Henley? Some water? Tea? A cocktail?" Mrs. Carrington offers as she sets a plate of fresh baked cookies down on the coffee table.

A drink? Really? I stretch my arms around my belly to call attention to the fact I'm pregnant and try to be as polite as possible. "No, thank you, Mrs. Carrington. I'm trying to lay off the sauce for the next few months."

She doesn't laugh. Instead, she just cocks her hip out in awkward silence with narrowed eyes. "So, have you thought about when you two will have the wedding?"

Not this again. "Um, not yet. We've got our hands full right now, and we're not in any rush." I wrap my arms around my stomach and smile sweetly. I've done my fair share of evading wedding questions ever since Jeff proposed. It's not that I'm not looking forward to getting married, because I am. But I fear that planning a wedding while planning for a baby and trying to stay sane is seriously going to fuck with the fragile state of my hormones.

"Well, I've got a few ideas to run through you when you decide it's time."

"Oh?" I'm almost afraid to probe, but this woman *is* going to be my future mother-in-law and this child's grandmother, so I'm morally obligated to at least hear her out. "Well, I guess we've got some time if you want to talk about them tonight?" What do I have to lose?

Mrs. Carrington blinds me with her smile and runs over to the desk drawer, pulling out a notebook and presenting it to me with great pride. "Now these," she says poignantly, "these ideas are something special. And I wish I could take credit for some of them, but I simply can't."

I furrow my brow and open the notebook, the front cover soft and worn under my fingertips. I expect to be bombarded with clippings of Martha Stewart inspired wedding bouquets and information on venues in the Denver metropolitan area. But when my eyes hit the page, they're met with something more ... colorful. And spandex-clad.

Oh. My. God.

"This is from Jeff?" I ask in disbelief. I immediately recognize his chicken scratch etched upon the pages. It hasn't changed at all since his childhood.

"Uh-huh!" She looks down at what I can only describe as a superhero vision board. Littering the pages are drawings of Wonder Woman in bridal attire, her red, gold, and blue emblem prominently around her waist, and single star crown adorned with a flowing veil. Superman had his signature "S" peeking out from underneath his tuxedo, his red cape flapping in the wind behind him. There were Batman inspired boutonnieres and invitations in comic-like fonts announcing that his kryptonite had been found and he was sentencing himself to a lifetime of love with Wonder Woman. And, because it begs to be repeated ...

Oh. My. God.

"This one is my personal favorite. I know it's a bit unconventional, but I just love his creativity and vision!" She flips through a few pages, landing on a sketch of what appears to be a four-tiered Spiderman wedding cake, complete with a spiderweb detail in the frosting.

She can't be serious, right? "This is ... I don't know what this is, but it's something else!"

Jeff planned his own wedding growing up? I do my best not to laugh because I have a distinct feeling I'd be laughing *at* him and not *with* him. And frankly, I don't know enough about his mother to determine if she'd be on board with mockery.

Mrs. Carrington's eyes go warm, and she rests her palm on my forearm lovingly. "You aren't the only one who has been dreaming of this day your whole life, sweetie."

I try not to laugh at the thought, but I can't contain myself.

"What?" she asks, almost offended.

"Nothing. It's just that Jeff never mentioned having specific thoughts or suggestions about our wedding, that's all."

Mrs. Carrington adjusts her posture and smiles amiably, but it doesn't feel genuine. "Well, if you like, you can hold onto this. Then when you *finally* start planning for the big day, you can use some of Jeff's ideas as inspiration."

She can't be serious.

"You can't be serious."

I immediately want to stuff the words back into my mouth. Luckily she doesn't hear me. Or, if she does, she has the forethought to pretend she doesn't hear me. I take the notebook and slip it into my backpack, out of sight, but I can still hear it taunting me, like the heartbeat under the rafters in Poe's Tell-Tale Heart. Don't get me wrong. I love that he's put thought into what he wants in a wedding, but I'm not about to go down a path commonly reserved for Comic-Con fanboys.

I shift uncomfortably and pray that Jeff makes a speedy return. I need to relax. These people are going to be my in-laws. And if I keep this up, they're going to have me excommunicated from the family before I'm even technically in it.

"Um, Mom?" Jeff shouts from the top of the stairs. The flat tone of his voice instantly makes me even more uneasy.

"Yes, dear?" She rushes to the bottom of the stairs, doting on her son's every move.

"What happened to the guest room?"

"Oh! Your father and I turned it into a sewing and craft room for me. Isn't it lovely?" Her face is beaming with pride and excitement over all of the crocheted pot holders and sweatshirts decorated with puff paint and sequins that surely occupy her free time.

Jeff slowly starts to make his way down the stairs with a perplexed expression on his face. "But you don't sew?"

"I'm just dabbling in it and starting to learn. Look, I made those throw pillows on the couch. Beautiful, aren't they?"

I shift my weight to pull the pillow out from my back and run my fingers over the sad attempt at a ruffle. Looks like someone could use a tutorial, or better yet, a new hobby.

"Yeah, it's um, great, but where are we supposed to sleep if the guest room is out of commission?"

"Your old bedroom, of course."

Jeff closes his eyes and sighs. I'm pretty sure I'm the only one who notices him shaking his head imperceptibly.

And suddenly it's clear. Sleeping at the airport would have been a much better idea.

LESS THAN AN HOUR LATER, after feigned pleasantries and exactly three and a half cookies, I'm standing in the doorway of Jeff's childhood bedroom.

"Oh ... my ... God. You've got to be kidding me." I peer inside in wonder and slight mortification. It's suddenly clear why he insisted on not stopping by his parents' house when we were in town for the wedding.

This place is Jeff and his brother Chris frozen in time, and I catch an up close glimpse of my fiancé circa 1999. The room is a shrine, encapsulating Jeff and Chris's life from junior high until they both graduated high school and moved out. There's a shelf lined with trophies from baseball and soccer and ribbons from debate. Posters of supermodels spread out against muscle cars, some of them autographed — a true treasure for any teen boy's spank bank, no doubt — hang from the walls.

But the unspoken masterpiece in the room is the giant oak bunk bed against the wall. Complete with matching Star Wars comforter sets.

I walk to set my backpack and purse on the floor and find a stash of Marvel action figures, unopened and stacked meticulously in a pyramid. I walk over to take a closer look.

"Oh! Who do we have here?" I pick up the Wonder Woman and Superman boxes from the top of the pile. "Am I invited to their wedding? *I now pronounce you husband and wife!*" I press the boxes together, making obscene intimate kissing sounds.

Jeff narrows his eyes and looks over his shoulder at me.

"Oh, Superman! I'm so happy to finally be your wife! Thank you for choosing me over that slutty Super Girl," I tease in a high-pitched voice.

Jeff takes a moment to process what I just said and picks his jaw up from the floor. When realization hits, he fists his hair, distraught. "Damn it, Mom!"

I swallow the giggles rising from my belly.

"Did she ... ummmm ... show you the whole thing?" He swallows so hard I can see his Adam's apple bobbing up and down in his throat and his voice cracks, jumping an octave like a prepubescent boy.

"No," I lie, not wanting to embarrass him any more than his mother already has, but I can practically hear the superhero characters calling to me off the pages of the notebook that is safely hidden in my backpack across the room. I'm not ready to surrender this piece of his childhood. At least not yet.

I stand there wordlessly, taking it all in. "This room is something else."

"Yeah, I know." Jeff shoots a sympathetic look at me. "I don't know why my mom didn't turn *this* into the sewing room. Most of this crap should just be thrown away."

"Aww, don't say that. These are your memories." I walk toward the desk and grab what appears to be a prom photo of Jeff with his arms around a braces-clad smiling girl in a poofy golden dress.

He quickly plucks the picture frame from my hands. "And some of these memories I'd much rather forget."

I run my fingers across his desk and walk over to read one of the many ribbons hanging off the book case. "Participation in the 1995 Field Games. *Impressive.*"

"That was Chris's!" he's quick to clarify.

I flip it over to read Jeff's name and smile. "There's nothing to be ashamed about. This is you. A slightly more awkward, nerdier, and pleasantly delightful version of you that I've never seen before." This room is literally a time warp into his childhood. And I love every moment of it.

Jeff rocks back on his heels, probably waiting for me to run out the door and down the stairs, far away from this place. "Well, for what it's worth, I think I just fell in love with you a little bit more."

I stand in front of him, and he wraps his arms around my waist and mine immediately go to his neck. "I've never brought a girl up here before. I always kept them down in the basement."

I laugh. "That sounds so wrong. Hopefully, you aren't harboring any women down there, now. But I get what you mean. I never had guys in my bedroom either." My fingers drift, teasing the hair on the nape of his neck. "But I like that I get to see this side of you."

"I like it, too."

Jeff looks at me with such reverence that I feel it deep inside my bones. There's a vulnerability in him that is so completely irresistible. And so, I give in.

I lean forward and take his bottom lip between my teeth and gently pull. Softly, Jeff groans in my mouth which sets my nerves on fire. Just as I delicately lick his lips, he's quick to move his hands to my face, holding tightly, and kisses me with such ferocity that it literally steals my breath away.

This boy is a damn thief.

"Ahem."

We pull away abruptly like two teenagers illicitly caught in the act and turn toward the door. I cover my mouth and cough, trying to hide my swollen lips. Jeff nonchalantly adjusts his pants, and I continue forcing myself to cough just so I can stifle a laugh.

The look on his dad's face makes me feel like kissing his son under his roof is a felony. "I just wanted to see if you kids needed anything before your mother and I hit the hay." Jeff's dad pulls his bathrobe shut a little tighter and watches us intently.

"Thanks, Dad, but I think we're all set."

"Yes, thank you so much for welcoming me into your home, Mr. Carrington."

His eyes shift between the two of us and then back to the bunk bed. Amusement is written all over his face. "Well, I'll leave you two at it."

"Good night," we say in awkward unison. The door closes behind him, and we both fall into a fit of laughter.

"That's my dad. Successfully blocking cock since the day I hit puberty."

"I just can't believe that *that* little kiss got you so hot and bothered."

"That's because everything about the woman I was kissing gets me hot and bothered. She has no idea how stunningly radiant she is, and how much of a turn on it is knowing that *she's* carrying *my* child."

It's impossible *not* to smile at his words. I pull our pajamas out from the suitcase, signaling that it's time we put this party to bed. It's been a long day of traveling, and we need to be up early to hopefully make our way to sunny California.

"I still can't believe you have a bunk bed," I say in amazement.

Jeff shrugs. "Chris and I shared a bedroom for years. My mother refused to get rid of the bunk bed because she felt they were practical." He rolls his eyes at the statement.

"Well, I think it's sweet."

"I know you like it on top, but all things considered I think you should sleep on the bottom tonight." He shoots a coy wink at me.

We quickly get ready for bed, the pair of us carefully maneuvering around the other in the postage stamp-sized bathroom. Then he turns off the light, and we each settle into our respective mattresses. Jeff on top, and me on the bottom.

"I love you, Hen."

"Love you most, Jeff."

IT'S damn near impossible to get comfortable. And don't even get me started on the sounds of the house as it comes alive in the dead of night. All I can hear is the constant clanking of pipes somewhere inside the walls and the ice maker growling from the kitchen below us. That and the sound of my body shivering, which is ridiculous because these days I'm running at the temperature of an overworked furnace.

"Henley?" he whispers into the darkness after what feels like an hour but is probably only ten minutes.

"Yeah?" I try to control the chattering of my teeth. Apparently, his parents don't believe in running the thermostat in this part of the house.

"Are you awake?"

Obviously, I'm awake. "Yeah, I'm just down here contemplating if I should sneak into your mother's craft room and knit myself a sweater."

"You're cold, too?"

"It's so cold I'm pretty sure a fire could freeze in here."

Jeff jumps down off the top bunk and runs out of the room. I can see, from the light streaming in from the hallway, that he has a pile of blankets in his arms. He kisses the top of my head and then covers me with three additional quilts.

"There. That ought to do it."

I love how he takes such good care of me. But even more, I want him to.

He climbs back on top, and then darkness and silence resume. "I miss you," he says softly.

"I'm right here. You're one lost dog away from sounding like a stereotypical country song."

"That's not what I mean."

I know exactly what he means. We're both laying in bed feel the void of the other person next to us. And if I'm being honest, I miss him too. I sleep so much better when he's curled up next to me. With great effort, I roll over, hoisting my belly to try and make myself more comfortable.

"I know. I miss you, too."

"Want me to come down there and cuddle with you?"

Do I want him to? Well ... yeah. But I'm not certain where he'd go, and while the floor is tempting, it's simply not an option for this pregnant momma.

"I don't think we can both fit down here. These bunk beds are twin size. There's barely enough room for me and this baby."

He sighs in defeat. Though I secretly wish he would come down here. "Okay. Let me rephrase that. Henley, I'm coming down there to snuggle with you. I miss having you next to me. I don't care if we can't fit comfortably. It won't be nearly as uncomfortable as it is up here without you."

The man is a damn mind reader.

There's a thud on the floor in the dark next to me, and I feel his weight cause the mattress to sink down. I scoot my back to the wall as far as I can to make room for him. The poor guy is clinging for dear life with half of his ass hanging off the side of the bed. He wraps his arms around me tight and nestles his face against the crook of my neck. The heat of his breath skimming my skin feels nice. I inhale slowly, savoring the lingering scent of spice from his body wash.

"I am so sorry this hasn't turned out quite as I had planned. I will make it up to you tomorrow when we get to San Diego, I promise."

"It's okay. As long as we're together that's all that really matters."

And that's the truth.

He's silent for a while, and his breathing slows to an even cadence. Just when I think he's fallen asleep, he speaks again.

"Henley?"

"Yeah, babe?" I sigh. At this rate, we're never going to fall asleep.

"We can tell each other anything, right?"

My heart stutters. I'm not sure what the rest of his comment will bring. I'm not sure I want to know either. I swallow hard and brace myself for the pending explosion of his truth bomb. "Of course. You know you can say anything to me. We are an open book with each other."

He gently brushes his hands up and down the length of my arm. It sends shivers of delight down my spine. "Well..." He pauses thoughtfully and speaks the following words softly, almost timidly. "I've always kinda wanted to ... you know ... fool around in my childhood bedroom?" He says it like a question and not a confession. Like he's asking for permission.

My eyes go wide, and I try not to laugh in disbelief. "I think that's a perfectly normal fantasy to have." Though I know that fantasy isn't the right word for the occasion because I can't think of any fantasy that involves bunk beds.

"And I remember what you told me about that guy back in college ... and the sleeping dorms ... and how awful that whole experience was."

I'm thankful it's dark so he can't see the heat rising in my cheeks. *Ugh.* Why did I even tell him that? And furthermore, why is he even bringing it up now? Because if he's insinuating sex, Leo is the last person I want invading my headspace.

"*I* wasn't thinking about that, but I am now," I say with a sigh. But I can tell he's trying. And that's more than what Leo ever did — tenfold. "That's not exactly the best way to seduce me, Mr. I Participated in the 1995 Field Games and have an amazing ribbon to show for it."

"Hey, I took second in the three-legged race, thank you very much." I can hear the smile in his voice. "All I'm saying is that I don't think bunk beds are all that bad, and you got a bad bunk experience. And maybe, just maybe, with the *right* person, you could have a positive bunkin' up moment in a bunk bed memory. Because you're worth a lifetime of positive experiences."

I can't lie. I don't *hate* the suggestion. I just hate that Leo got to it first. "Is that so?"

"Yep."

"You are something else, Jeff."

"I'm that ... among *many* other things." Jeff moves his arm underneath the covers and splays his palm against the outside of my thigh, making small circles with his fingertips as they creep toward the edge of my nightgown. My body is so sensitive I instinctually release a pleasurable, inviting sigh.

His lips find mine, and I can feel him smile against me as he indulges in one of those I-need-to-take-you-right-now kind of kisses. And I oblige, running my hand through his hair to deepen the kiss.

As much as my head says this is a bad idea, we both know I'm going to throw caution to the wind and give Jeff exactly what he wants. We're flirting with disaster with his parents only a few rooms away, but screw flirting. It's time to fuck disaster and give it the goddamned orgasm it deserves.

His kiss becomes more frantic as he kicks the layers of quilts off of us and starts to kiss his way down my neck and to my shoulders.

"Jeff," I breathe. His hands slip under the thin fabric as he delicately kisses my shoulder, slowly at first, then with increasing speed as he makes his way to my collarbone before nipping his teeth against my jawline.

"Yes?" he muses softly, before pulling my nightgown up and over my head.

"Keep doing that. Whatever you do, keep doing *that*."

Jeff continues to nip at my skin playfully while his hand strokes in between my thighs, hitting everywhere except the one spot I crave the most. I do what I can to try and roll toward him, but it's no use. There's too much belly and not enough bed.

"No, no ... just relax," he whispers as he pushes his weight up into his hands and leans down to kiss me deeply. "Let me take care of you tonight."

My knees go weak at the thought, and I surrender any kind of resistance.

Jeff pauses and sits up as much as possible without hitting his head on the underside of the top bunk, surveying the best way to tackle our situation.

"This isn't going to work. At least not like this." I hide the sexual frustration in my voice as best as I can, because the thought of doing it in his childhood bedroom is kind of hot on some bizarre unchartered territory level.

"Just trust me," he says as determination takes over. He nails me with that panty-dropping, adrenaline inducing, clit-searing mischievous smile.

And I do trust him. Implicitly.

"Lock the door," I whisper.

Jeff stands and crosses the floor in record time, kicking his pajama pants and boxers to the floor when he returns. His swollen head springs to life right before my eyes in the soft glow of the streetlight streaming through the blinds. I reach out to stroke him, but he shakes his head slowly.

"Nuh-uh. I said *I'm* taking care of *you*." He groans at me hungrily before hooking his fingers inside the elastic of my panties. Jeff pulls them off ever so slowly, never once taking his carnal eyes off of mine. That look alone sends a shock wave straight to my core. And for the first time ever, I believe those trashy novels where a woman could, in fact, be brought to orgasm without ever being physically touched.

But touching is more than half the fun. And damn, I *never* want to be one of those poor, unfortunate women. Though the thought of an orgasm without the work can't be all bad.

Jeff kneels on the floor next to the bed and pulls my ass close to him in one fell swoop.

His tongue is pressed between my thighs, flicking and sucking as he hitches my left leg over his shoulder. My pulse races, and my head quickly becomes dizzyingly light, and I fight the words crowding in my mouth. I want to shout that if he stops, I'm going to spontaneously combust.

Keep it quiet, Henley.

It's damn near impossible, and before I remember where I am, I'm whimpering, begging for more.

But before I can even articulate the words, Jeff stands and repositions me on my knees on the bed. I'm bent over on all fours to avoid hitting my head on the top bunk, but just when I'm about to protest, he leans down to kiss my shoulder and wraps his arms around my body, caressing my breasts, my stomach and then trails his fingers down to my clit. Jeff's hands are urgent and skillful. He's eager, but it's clear he wants to take his time and appreciate the newfound curves of my changing body.

Holy fucking hell. That feels so damn good. Every inch of my body is on fire, and I rub my backside against him, trying to contain the moans growing in the back of my throat.

With one hand firmly teasing the nipple of my left breast, Jeff runs the fingers of his right hand up and down my slick seam before thrusting them inside me. Instinctively I cry out at the sensation, and I can hear his breath hitch at my readiness.

"Shit, Henley."

And all I can respond with is a breathy, "Please."

Jeff positions himself against my body and without hesitation, plunges deep inside. We both take a moment to collect ourselves as we melt into each other, and then on cue, savage instinct takes over. There's an energy about him that's usually reserved for horny teenage boys.

I have to keep my eyes closed because each time I open them and look at my surroundings, I'm being stared at and judged by tiny figurines atop trophies and well-loved stuffed animals, and it's kind of ruining my buzz. At least with my eyes closed, I can simply pretend that we're back in our bed at home.

We're finding our rhythm and flow in the most precarious of positions, and I reach out and grab part of the headboard to brace myself because I'm getting alarmingly close all too quickly. Tara was right, pregnant sex is completely different — and arguably better — than regular sex. *Everything* is significantly more sensitive, and I feel like I'm this glowing sex goddess and anything with a penis has come to worship my blossoming body. Jeff is hitting all the right spots in all the right ways, and it's fucking glorious.

I mutter a string of obscenities under my breath because I have no idea how I'm expected to silence what is surely building to be an outrageous orgasm of seismic proportions. He quickens his pace and makes swift work on my clit making my body quiver in ecstasy.

"Oh, God," I pray as I'm traipsing dangerously close to the point of no return. I'm short of breath and seeing stars, and I'm covered in lust and sweat, and it's all too much and not nearly enough all at the same time.

"Fuck, Jeff!" I cry out and clench on even harder to the bed.

Then without warning, something shifts and the bottom bunk snaps in half, sending us crashing to the floor.

"Ow! Fuck!" My hand is smashed in between the broken bunk bed and the wall.

"Oh my God! Are you okay?" Jeff panics, pushing himself back to his feet and quickly lifting part of the bed up and off of me.

Suddenly the door flies open, and I'm blinded by the overhead light.

"What was that? Are you guys all right?"

I gasp.

Martha gasps.

And then Jeff gasps, completing the trifecta of *what the fuck just happened*.

"Mother! Get! Out!"

Jeff's full moon is in clear view as he attempts to shield my body amid the splintered wood at our feet, and Martha's face turns as white as her pearl earrings as she processes the scene.

Why do we keep getting interrupted in this position?

"Oh my gosh! I'm so sorry!" she squeaks as she covers her eyes and quickly backs out of the door, closing it behind her. We hear a muffled conversation as we search for our clothes. "No! Don't go in there, they're fine. The uh, the bed is broken. It's no big deal. Jeff's got it under control."

"Fuck," he says, raking his fingers through his hair. "Are you okay?"

I do a quick assessment and realize that I'm not physically in any pain. And then I laugh, a hearty belly laugh. Because that's really all there is to do in the horrifying moment where you're fucking in your finance's childhood bedroom on a bunk bed that is ten sizes too small for two grown adults, break said bunk bed, and then flash a full moon to his mother.

"Thank God," he says as he holds me close. "And the baby?"

I feel a little kick inside, and smile. "It's moving right now. And I'm not in pain, so I think we're okay. But I'll call and get an appointment scheduled tomorrow, just to make sure."

He exhales in relief, probably not even realizing that he was holding his breath.

"Good."

Jeff reaches down to the floor and passes me my nightgown and panties before slipping into his own boxer shorts and pajama pants.

I'm thankful that we escaped this moment without injury and only slight mortification. In retrospect, this could have played out a lot worse.

I turn toward the bathroom to get myself cleaned up. "Oh, and babe?" I say from the doorway.

"Yeah?" He looks up at me as he's pulling the mattresses from the debris to create a makeshift bed on the floor ... something we probably should have done in the first place.

Hindsight's a bitch like that.

"Thanks for locking the door." I throw a wink over my shoulder and close the bathroom door.

Chapter Seventeen

ELEPHANTS

To say the past few months have been rough is an understatement.

"Oh, the morning sickness will subside when you reach the second semester!" they said.

"You'll have more energy and feel great!" they said.

I want to find whoever "they" are and hex them to a lifetime of morning sickness where they can only dry heave glitter. Because let's be honest, glitter is awesome.

And a bitch to clean up.

The toilet and I have become close friends. Jeff has been pretty great about it all. He holds my hair back just like Tara used to do after a long night of binge drinking back in college. All in all, he's a champ considering his track record with anything remotely squeamish and medical. But if he offers me ginger ale and saltines one more time, I may lose my shit. I make sure to remind him that this is all his fault on a regular basis. Because when you really think about it, it is.

I'm no Virgin Mary incarnate!

Being pregnant is just ... *weird*. Like weird in that way that

French kissing is simply tasting someone else's mouth. Or how a balloon is simply a plastic bag of hot air. There's really no other way to describe it. Half the time I can't tell if I'm having gas or premature contractions. The instant I walk out of the bathroom, I have to pee again. That pregnant glow my mom keeps complimenting me on? It's just sweat. Which means I'm "glowing" all the damn time. And my sex drive is a sling shot. I'm either revved and ready to go with a single hungry glance, or repulsed and closed up tighter than Fort Knox. Even so, I recently find myself wanting to punch Jeff in the face every time I look at him in spite of my inexplicable raging horniness.

Feeling the baby kick for the very first time wasn't this amazing, miraculous moment. It was really fucking freaky. It's like this kid already hates me since it's beating me up from the inside out. And just last week I had a nightmare that my labor and delivery mirrored the scene in *Spaceballs* where the tap dancing alien burst through John Hurt's stomach to a rousing rendition of Howard and Emerson's *Hello! Ma Baby*. I woke up traumatized with my pillowcase drenched in sweat. I mean *drenched* in pregnant glow.

Aside from this constantly growing list of amazing moments on the road to motherhood, things have been relatively normal. It's summer break, and I haven't even thought about updating lesson plans for the upcoming year. Nor do I plan on thinking about them until a week or so before school resumes next month.

Nobody warns you about the horrors of being pregnant in the summer. It is akin to being a fiery furnace lounging on the surface of the sun. Whenever I set the thermostat to a temperature *I'm* finally comfortable with, Jeff is wearing wool sweaters and thick socks. And don't get me started on the sweat. There's back sweat, boob sweat, ass sweat, belly sweat, baby sweat, south of the border sweat, and the meat sweat which come regardless of if I've eaten meat or not. Naturally, a cool shower has become my second home.

Which is where I find myself now on this ninety-two-degree day. Actually, night because it's pushing seven o'clock and I'm quite enjoying the feeling of cold water running over my body.

I've finally rinsed the shaving cream out of my long auburn hair because pregnancy brain strikes again and I'm incapable of putting a coherent thought together when I'm this cranky, swollen, and sticky. It's not the first time I've tried to wash my hair with something other than shampoo — and I doubt it'll be my last.

"Babe!" I call out from the bathroom as I turn the water off, prepared to venture back out into the heat. I hear Jeff come stampeding down the tiny hall and watch as his disembodied head pops through the crack in the door.

"Yeah, hon? Need me to help you shave your legs again?" He gives me a hopeful smile.

I feel my face turn red and try to push that memory out of my mind. I still have scars from all the skin he accidentally chipped off my legs. It was the thought that counts. Even in his faults, he's sickeningly perfect for me.

"No, not this time. I was wondering if you could pass me that towel." I point to the backside of the door where a fluffy blue towel is hanging on a hook. The bathroom is long and narrow, making everything virtually out of reach. Whoever designed this apartment was left with a random strip of space and decided it'd be a good bathroom. And if you were the size of a twig, it would serve its purpose well.

"Oh ... sure." Jeff sounds disappointed but hands the towel to me. I cautiously step out of the shower and prop one leg up on the ledge of the tub to dry it off. And that's when I see it. Or rather *don't* see it.

Oh my God.

Traitor tears prick the edges of my eyes, and I suddenly feel short of breath.

Jeff sees the panic and is instantly at my side, worry crinkling the corners of his mouth and eyes. "Henley?" He says my name delicately, like he's afraid to tip the scales and watch his fiancée come crumbling down.

"Oh my God! It's gone … it's gone!!" I gasp as the floodgates open, and I start to sob freely.

"What's gone? Your engagement ring?" Jeff storms through the bathroom, flipping over everything on the counter and searching for my ring.

"No! Not my ring!" I suck in air and snot in a high-pitched wheeze. "My ankle! My ankles have disappeared!!"

Jeff stops in his tracks and whips his head at me in an alarmingly fast snap. When he sees my engagement ring still on my finger, he howls in high-pitched laughter to the point he can't even breathe.

"It's not funny." I scowl and wipe the tears from my eyes. He covers his face and tries to contain his laughter. "I have some really adorable sandals that strap up the ankles that I'll never be able to wear because I have no ankle! I have a swollen, horrible, ugly cankle. I'll be lucky if I can get my big ole feet through the straps of a basic flip flop!"

He has to sense that if he keeps laughing at me, I may inflict bodily harm upon him because somehow he's able to collect himself. He gives me the kind of look that's mixed with love and heartache and every emotion of *I wish I could take this on for you, you crazy batshit woman*. And the next thing I know, he's kneeling on the floor wedged between the bathtub and the toilet, gently massaging the leg and nonexistent ankle I have propped up.

"Shhh …" he whispers as he works his strong hands into my swollen skin as he continues to dry my body off. "Calm down,

Henley. It's sweltering outside. You're adorable, and you're perfect, and you're overreacting, and most importantly, you're pregnant. This is all par for the course. I promise you, when you're holding our son in your arms, it will be totally worth it, and all of this pain in the ass nonsense will be a distant memory."

I focus on his words and controlling the cadence of my breath until the tears cease and he's managed to dry my body. I'm not sure how much time has passed, but he doesn't dare leave me alone. He knows I need him more than words can ever say.

"I don't know what I'd do without you."

He looks up into my eyes with unspoken love. "I'd venture to say you'd be very wet right now ... and sad, because you'd be missing out on all my awesomeness." He smiles and without missing a beat continues, "and probably not pregnant."

He's right across the board.

I stand up and tug his arms, attempting to pull him up to his feet. "Come on, you. Let's get outta here," I say, and he follows me out of the bathroom.

"CAN we address the big purple elephant in the room?" Jeff says as he watches me get dressed.

"What? The fact that your fiancée is a prime candidate for an ankle transplant?"

He smirks, and I'm trying to read his mind as he deliberately looks everywhere in the bedroom but my nearly naked body.

"That was a joke," I clarify. "Not a very funny one considering you had to talk me off the ledge back there, but a joke nonetheless." I grin, trying to make light of my ridiculousness, but his face doesn't falter.

He's silent for a moment, and my heart skips a beat, suddenly worried about this elephant he speaks of. "Why do we still have two places?" he asks with genuine curiosity laced in his voice.

I know I should have seen this coming, but between life and pretending that virgin pina coladas are just as good as the real thing and doing my best to not completely panic over the fact I'm pushing something the weight of a bowling ball through a tiny key hole in a few short months, it honestly slipped my mind. I've spent nearly every night at Jeff's the past few months, though for whatever reason I've never officially moved in.

"I mean, we're having a baby. We're getting married *at some point*. From a resource and financial standpoint, it's stupid to not be living together, even if your super Catholic parents disagree."

Jeff makes a good point. I can say, with certainty, that even though we've *clearly* been doing the devil's dance between the sheets and having a baby together, my mom would no doubt be against us living together before officially tying the knot. At this point, she'd probably disapprove of a shotgun wedding. I'm a little surprised Mom hasn't pushed me to move back home so *they* could help with the baby, but then again, she's probably still convinced I've got some stanky vajanky. I may as well load up the car and pack the snacks, because that guilt trip from my mother will take us all over the damn country.

I know, I know. I shouldn't care what she thinks, or what anyone else thinks for that matter. But still, she's my mom, and some tiny part of me will always strive for her approval.

I think that's what kids do.

But he's right. It's stupid that we still have two places, and arguably, financially irresponsible. I'm not going anywhere. And as long as I don't continue to have meltdowns over silly things like non-existent ankles, I don't think he's going anywhere either.

"Okay," I say after slipping an oversized nightshirt over my growing body.

"Okay?"

"Okay." I nod. "Let's do it."

He smiles.

"But I do have one little request."

Jeff's eyes narrow and he purses his lips at me in consideration. "What's that?" he asks cautiously.

"We find a *new* place together. My apartment is out of the question considering months later it still reeks of plastic on fire. And as much as I love your humble bachelor abode, it's not exactly conducive to a baby."

His forehead wrinkles and I think I may have offended him. "What do you mean? There's plenty of space here!"

Seriously? If I stretch my arms out in his kitchen, I can touch both walls simultaneously. I know he loves this place, but it's just not right for a family of three. So I take the pragmatic approach.

"You're on the third floor. And there's no elevator. It's bad enough making that trek while pregnant. But *you* try that a few times a day with a stroller and a twelve-pound baby."

He stands in front of me and tries to wrap his arms around my body. It's becoming tougher by the day. A smile plays at the edges of his mouth, and he licks his lips slowly like they do in the movies.

"If that's all it takes to get the future Mrs. Carrington to live with me, then I will pack up both of our apartments right now and move you into the castle of your dreams."

Jeff tilts his face and closes in, kissing me softly at first. But rapidly it grows into a deep, hungry kiss that I feel all the way in my toes. Every ounce of absurdity and pregnancy frustration melts away, just like my panties that I wiggle down past my hips and thighs.

Before I know it, we're making out like two horny teenagers playing seven minutes in heaven. Except this heaven is our reality. And the only way this reality could possibly get any better was if this baby would quit kicking and interrupting the moment.

Little cock blocker.

THE HIGHLIGHT of the second trimester was definitely Jeff and I moving in together, finally settling on a rental home we found in the Waldo neighborhood of Kansas City. Our modest three-bedroom is a brownstone walk-up full of charm, and maybe a little asbestos, but the landlord is taking care of that. I love the wood-burning fireplace, though, given my track record, Jeff says I'm not allowed near it with anything remotely flammable.

The nursery is coming along beautifully. We agreed not to find out the sex of the baby since it's one of the last great surprises you can get in life, so we've stocked up on yellow and green clothes that look like they belong on a Cabbage Patch doll, and found an adorable woodland creature theme for his or her bedroom.

We don't have any furniture yet, but at least this kid won't be naked. Hopefully, we nail down the necessities at the baby shower next month. Until then, I've commandeered a chair from the kitchen table so I have somewhere to sit while Jeff works to prep the nursery.

"So, babe, I've been meaning to ask, how does it feel to have a penis growing inside of you?" Jeff asks as he hangs a tiny onesie with an x marked over a baby bottle that says 'I drink straight from the tap' on a baby blue hanger, and places it in the closet.

I scoff in disgusted horror. "You do realize that you have a fifty percent chance of being wrong, don't you?"

He winks at me playfully.

"And that is the most repulsive and disturbing thing you've said in a long time. I have a penis inside of me? *Seriously*? That's as bad as Tara trying to convince me that the few times she and her husband tried to have sex while she was pregnant constituted an orgy since she was expecting triplets."

"Okay, now *that's* just wrong. And incestual. I love your friend, but I don't need that particular visual seared in my mind the next time we're all hanging out together."

I chuckle, and Jeff comes inside the nursery to take a seat on the ottoman in front of me. His face turns serious, and I instantly know where this conversation is headed before he even says a word. We *just* had this conversation last week.

"Please don't."

"Don't what?" He feigns innocence.

"Don't ask me again right now. I beg you."

He places his hands on my legs, gently brushing his thumbs against my knees and sighs audibly. "Hen, our families are asking. We should really give them *some* kind of details of where our heads are at with this wedding."

I shift uncomfortably in the wooden chair. Every time Jeff suggests making plans for our wedding, I have to remind him to come back down to earth. There is no way I am planning a wedding until after this baby has been evicted from my body.

"I know, it's just that I think we should wait to get married. Nobody wants to see a bride waddle down the aisle only to have her go into labor at the altar. If we have a shotgun wedding before this kid debuts, then everyone is going to think I'm a floozy."

"Henley, you're already pregnant. If that makes you a floozy, then you're *my* floozy. Besides, they're not going to think that. This is the twenty-first century. And I've never been one to be conventional. *We* are anything but conventional, remember?"

His beautiful baby blues plead with me to give him something. Anything to get his mother to stop nagging. "Okay. Let's try this. Big or small? If we can give my folks some kind of inkling of what to expect, that ought to buy us another week or two."

I wrap my arms around my belly and slowly rub tiny circles, trying to figure out how to best answer the question. "I know my parents want to throw a big wedding for me, but really I just want a small celebration. If I had my way, we'd elope. It'd be just the two of us."

He raises a knowing eyebrow at me and then looks to my baby bump.

"Okay ... the *three* of us." I smile, gently patting my stomach. It's kind of surreal that *this* is my life now.

"So you wouldn't want your family there *at all*?"

"It's not that I don't want them there. It'd be nice to have them there, for sure. It's just that everything I need is right here in front of me. And my mom tends to overdo things. Heck, she even threw a party when I first got my period. *Congratulations on bleeding without dying every month for the next forty years! Have a cookie cake!*" I laugh then lean over to press my lips against his. Jeff wraps his hand around the back of my neck, deepening the kiss and tangling his fingers in my hair. When he pulls back, there's a look in his eye that can only be described as complete and total adoration.

"I love you, woman."

"I know. What's not to love? I *am* pretty awesome."

"That you are."

The Third Trimester

Chapter Eighteen

ASSHOLES AND APOLOGIES

From the kitchen, I can hear Jeff fumbling with his keys. It's not the first time he's tried to get in using the wrong key, but this sounds like he's murdering our front door.

Death by keying. May the wood rest in peace.

Just as I'm making my way to the front of the house to open it for him, it flings open, and Jeff swings through the entryway, grasping onto the doorknob.

"Oh, I'm sorry Mr. Door," he sings as he props himself up against it and gives it a hearty slap.

What the...?

His eyes are half open, and his tie is unknotted and draped from his neck. His hair is beyond disheveled, and it looks like Beelzebub himself chewed him up and spit him back out. When he finally realizes I'm a few feet away, his expression turns somber.

"Jeff ...?"

This *is* Jeff, right?

He finally releases the door and closes it behind him. "I thought you were going over to Tara's tonight." His words are laced with arsenic, and he narrows his eyes at me. And in some ways, it looks like he's been run over by a steamroller. I don't like the underlying accusation in his voice, but I brush it off and lay blame on the alcohol he cozied up with.

"That was the plan. But Miles ended up with some kind of stomach virus, and we both thought it would be best for me to stay home rather than rent a hazmat suit to hang out with her."

He takes a long exhale and looks at me, pained. I swear I see tears prick the corners of his eyes. Dare I say he looks ... guilty?

"Are you okay, Jeff?"

He presses the length of his body back against the door and exhales slowly. "Yes. No. I mean, I'm fine. I uh ... I just went out after work. Had some drinks with the guys. You know. The usual."

I want to say that no, I don't know. This moment is anything but usual for him. He rarely gets drinks with the guys from work, but calling him out on that now probably isn't the best idea. And so I choose to focus on some of his other words.

"*Some* drinks? How many is *some*?"

I hate the tone in my voice right now, but I can't help it. I'm not the kind of woman who gets upset when her boyfriend goes drinking. But this is absolutely off the rails for him. I don't remember the last time I saw Jeff drunk. At least not while being completely wasted alongside him. I have to admit, it kind of sucks being the sober one at the moment. And not because I miss alcohol — don't get me wrong, I do, but ever since I got pregnant, he's made a diligent effort to avoid any alcohol. Just another testament of how *we're in this together*. But perhaps that effort has turned him into a cheap date as he is now a lightweight.

Jeff's eyelids droop as he starts to slide his back down the door and his ass hits the ground.

"Oh my God! How shit-faced are you right now?"

"I'm not fit-shaced!" he slurs.

I stifle a laugh. "Suuuure you're not. Come on — let's get you into bed." I walk toward him with my arms outstretched ready to pull him back up to his feet. I just hope that by the morning whatever he's feeling can be cured with a little hair of the dog and a greasy hangover burrito from the shady Mexican joint down the road.

Once semi-standing, he trips over his feet before wrapping an arm around my shoulder and teetering himself upright.

"That's it! Do you need to go to the bathroom before you lay down?"

He closes his eyes and shakes his head wordlessly. We're halfway down the hall when he stops dead in his tracks, pausing me with him.

"YOU!" he bellows, stabbing his finger in the air at me. Then his expression melts into a sad smile. "I ... I lo ..." He's on the cusp of tumbling over, and I grab him, keeping him upright. "I love you, Henley ..."

His tone is almost sad as he trails off on my name.

"I love you, too, babe." And I'm unsure if I should be concerned or scared at this moment.

Jeff brings his face down to my stomach. "And I love *you* too, little dude."

When we get to the bedroom, he plows face first into the pile of pillows, not even bothering to undress or get under the covers. I kneel on the edge and wrestle his dress shoes off of his feet before crawling up to the headboard to sit with him. I know I can't leave him alone right now.

"Rough day at the office?"

"Uh huh," he grunts.

"Wanna talk about it?" I run my fingertips through his hair, gently massaging his scalp. He's always been a happy drunk. The kind of drunk that makes everyone laugh and forget all about the troubles in the world. This is definitely a side of Jeff I've never seen.

"Nope." He's short. Curt. And it makes my heart hurt as we can always talk about anything.

I sigh.

He sighs.

And it feels like the whole damn world sighs right along with us.

This is the moment that I've been waiting for. The moment when all of the stress and reality of becoming a dad hits him all at once, and he does a swan dive into the pool of regret. Jeff is finally having that inevitable moment of panic that Tara warned me about.

Cam had left for a fishing trip with the boys and somehow ended up on a three-day bender where upon day three he climbed up onto a highway billboard and fell asleep wearing nothing but a Mexican wrestling mask and a grass hula skirt. The thought of having not one but three sons was enough to send him sprinting leaping off the proverbial edge.

I love him dearly, but this is kind of an asshole move. A little warning would have been nice.

"Okay, well at least let me get you some water."

I roll my big belly off the bed and grab a glass of water from the kitchen, then head to the bathroom for some Tylenol and a vitamin. Jeff will no doubt be in a world of hurt when he wakes up in the morning, so I want to do anything I can to help minimize the damage. Tomorrow's a big day. We're supposed to head to the store to finish building our baby registry since the shower is coming up soon.

By the time I return back to the bedroom less than thirty-seconds later, he's snoring louder than an elephant stampede. I watch the slow rise and fall of his back for a moment before setting the glass of water down on the night stand.

"I love you, you crazy man of mine." I lean down and kiss his temple, then turn to leave to finish cleaning the kitchen. Just as I'm pulling the door shut, Jeff mumbles, "I'm sorry."

And confusion steamrolls over my heart, breaking it into tiny little pieces.

TO SAY I didn't sleep well last night is an understatement. Mostly because that assumes I was actually capable of sleeping. Which I wasn't. And because this wretched baby shower is only a few weeks away, I still have to get my registry ironed out, with or without the help of Captain Hangover.

Thank God for Tara. When I texted her earlier asking if she'd come with me, she simply wrote back, "A day without wiping three asses? I'll pick you up in an hour."

Before I leave I place an orange Gatorade on the kitchen counter next to a note.

Off to finish the registry with T. I hope today's headache is enough punishment for last night's decisions. Feel better.
XOXO - H

A LITTLE PASSIVE AGGRESSIVE? Maybe. But when you're sleeping for two you need as much rest as you can get. And whatever he's dealing with is seriously hindering my sanity.

"This. You definitely want this," Tara says, pulling my focus from my hasty thoughts.

I grab the box and examine it closely, questioning the cartoon design on the packaging. "Nose Frida?"

"Yeah. You place that little plug thing into the nostril, then you put the tube in your mouth. It helps you suck the boogers right outta the kid's nose."

"That's disgusting!" I turn my nose up at the thought of literally sucking a booger out of my child's nostril.

Tara snatches the registry gun from my hands and scans the bar code on the back.

"No, it's genius. And when this little monster of yours can't sleep because he or she is unable to breathe, you'll suck that snot right out and finally see the genius in it, too."

If you say so.

Tara takes charge as she happily scans all the baby essentials and more toys and books than could possibly fit in the nursery. I let her because my mind is replaying last night's words on loop, coming up with the most horrible scenarios imaginable.

"*I'm sorry.*" I can't shake that stupid, pathetic, apologetic voice of his. *Gah!* What the hell are you sorry for, Jeff?

By the time we reach the rockers and nursery furniture, my mind is made up. Jeff is having an affair with some beautiful, leggy, very much *not* pregnant, blonde European woman. And he's leaving me for her and her multi-million dollar inheritance to go live on a boat in the Mediterranean. She's everything I'm not and never will be.

"Are you okay? You look like you're going to throw up." Tara puts her hand gently on my back and rubs it in small circles. "I know shopping for the baby can be a stressful reality check, but you're doing great, Henley. Really."

"No ... that's not it." I walk over to a dark wooden glider with plush ivory cushions and sit down, leaning forward with my head in my hands. I choke back the threatening tears.

"Oh, sweetie!" Tara rushes next to me. "I got crazy emotional when I worked on the registry for the triplets. And the price of this immaculate glider would make me cry, too." She's right. This glider is immaculate. And *way* out of our price range.

I have to say something. Tara won't judge me. I take a deep breath and look her in the eyes. Her face turns stony with concern and she takes my hands in hers.

"Last night Jeff came home completely annihilated. He could barely stand up straight."

"Oh? Was he out partying with the guys?"

"I don't think so. He was ... I dunno. Just not himself."

Tara looks at me and furrows her perfectly plucked brows.

"He was really short and seemed a little secretive. And as he was passing out he said, 'I'm sorry.'"

"Did he do something stupid? Do I need to go over there and kick his ass for you?"

"No. Well ... I don't think so? He wouldn't do anything dumb. But something was definitely wrong."

"Well, that's ominously vague. What the hell does that even mean? *I'm sorry?*" She spits the words like they're razors on her tongue. "I'm sorry I forgot to take out the trash? I'm sorry I ate the last cupcake when I promised it for my very pregnant girlfriend? I'm sorry I got wasted and screwed my ex?"

I wince at her last comment. But the possibilities truly are endless. "I wish I had some idea on where this *I'm sorry* falls on the Scale of Shit," I confess.

The Scale of Shit was something Tara and I came up with our junior year of college. We'd score exceptionally tough exams, multi-day hangovers and even tragically bad dates against the scale of shit. Forget about Professor Krueger's psych midterm? Congratulations! You've achieved SHITCON level three. Spent the evening listening to your blind date pine over his ex-girlfriend? Easily SHITCON level four any day of the week. But the moment said blind date sheds tears as he details how his ex is transitioning into a man? That shit is SHITCON level two, and worthy of tracking down the ex-in-transition and giving him a high-five for being fearless.

But SHITCON level one is reserved for the gravest of life's infractions. And fortunately for us, it has only been reached one time when Tara got high and went streaking through campus only to be caught and taken in by the campus police. She'd pitched a fit about her bare ass sticking to the seat and chewed out the officer. She nearly didn't graduate.

"I'm pretty sure this has the potential to hit a SHITCON level of one if he's really fucked up here. In fact, it may require us to reconfigure our entire SHITCON scale." Tara's trying to be funny, but failing miserably. This is my life we're talking about here, and not just mine but this baby's, too. A fuck up of epic proportions is exactly what I fear.

I bite my tongue to avoid turning into *that* hormonal pregnant woman incapable of being in public without crying. Some things are simply unforgivable. But we are so deeply intertwined that I know the only way I'd cut Jeff off is if he handed me the scissors.

Tara props a hand on her side and juts her hip out ever so slightly. "Why don't you just talk to him about it?"

Because I don't think I want to know the truth just yet? "I don't know. I just can't!"

"So let me get this straight. You can have his baby, and you can put his dick in your mouth, but you can't call him out on his crap to ask just what the hell is going on?"

Well, when she puts it like that I can't exactly argue.

"I know I need to talk to him about it. I just ... It's delicate. I don't know how to even broach the subject without causing him to go immediately on the defense."

"Well, the way I see it is, you both love each other to the point it's almost sickening. You'll figure it out. Just please don't wait too long because I know you, and you and I both know this is going to keep you awake at night and eat you up inside."

I hate that she's right, but love her for knowing me as well as I know myself.

She takes the registry gun and scans the chair I'm sitting in with a sly smile. I open my mouth to protest.

"Stop. We both know this rocker kicks some serious ass. And bottom line, you're worth it. Just like you're worth the truth of what's going on in your relationship."

"THANKS again for coming with me today," I say on the drive back home.

"It's no big deal. Really."

"I know, but you have *triplets*. And I know I've been bogarting a lot of your time lately."

"Shut it! You're my best friend. And we finally have proof that you put out. Besides, *The Three Musketeers* are busy raising hell at their Nana's house right now. Cam says it's payback for all the times his folks grounded him growing up. His mom always threatened that she hoped one day he'd have a son as ornery and rambunctious as him. She got her wish — three fold. And she has to pay her dues for bringing that mayhem into our lives."

I smile weakly. "Well, it took us long enough, but I think we've got it all covered." At least I hope we do. In spite of all the wisdom imparted by my best friend, useless advice from my family, and all of the *What You Need* lists in the pregnancy books I own, I still feel ill-prepared.

"It was a productive four hours."

I still can't believe it took that long. When I wasn't busy having a pity party in the middle of the store, Tara was busy detailing the best diaper rash creams and looking up reviews on car seats, rectal thermometers, and breast pumps. She went so far as to demonstrate the difference between an electric pump and a hand pump (over the clothes, of course) and garnered the attention of the few dads-to-be in the store.

"Hopefully we've put enough stuff on here for your baby shower. Your mom had me invite a stupid amount of people."

Of course she did. Because only my mother would find a way to make this day about her. "I'm sure it'll be fine. Besides, people tend to buy you stuff they *think* they want anyway. The registry is merely a suggestion."

Tara laughs. "Spoken like a true passive aggressive woman. If I recall, *you* bought me a bottle of wine and a wine glass with a spill-proof lid that said, 'Mommy's Sippy Cup' for my shower."

"Hey now! I bought a truckload of diapers, too. Besides, you love that cup."

Tara looks away from the road to me and smiles. "That's true. The glass does kick some serious ass. Jack once knocked it off the coffee table, and it saved the beige carpet underneath from a bottle of cabernet I had been saving for a special occasion. That special occasion just so happened to be a random Tuesday afternoon."

We drive in silence for a few minutes longer.

"Thanks again for planning a baby shower for me, T. It really means a lot."

"Anything for you, my friend. Anything for you."

Chapter Nineteen

UNDERWHELMED BY OVERWHELMED

To say that it's been a long week and a half would be an understatement. Each passing second feels like a minute. A minute feels like an hour. An hour feels like a day. And well a day feels like an eternity.

Which means we've gone through ten eternities since that night. The night I hate thinking about.

I know I should just rip off the Band-Aid and ask him what the hell his deal was. Find out what was so horrible in his life that he had to swan dive off the deep end and straight into a bottle of whiskey.

But I can't. Because the moment I do is the moment the flood gates open. And once the dam of a pregnant woman breaks, there's no closing it. Your hormones overthrow all semblance of logical thinking, and it's nearly impossible to keep your sanity in check.

We've gotten pretty good at pretending.

And I kind of hate myself for allowing it to go on as long as it has.

I'm in the kitchen smothering a waffle with peanut butter

when I hear the floor creak beneath someone's feet behind me. My adrenaline spikes and I spin on my heel, holding the gooey butter knife out in front of my body like a weapon.

Oh, sweet Jesus. It's just Jeff.

I exhale quickly and close my eyes.

"Hey, you," he says almost sheepishly. And when I open my eyes to look at him, his lips press together in a sad smile.

"I didn't hear you come in. You scared me." My voice is shorter than I'd like, but lately, nearly every reaction I have feels out of my control, so I just go with it.

Jeff pulls his arm out from behind his back to reveal a simple, yet beautiful bouquet of daisies. I look at him, to the flowers, and then back again.

"What's this for?" I ask, not making a move to take the bouquet.

His eyes dart from me nervously, and it's obvious he doesn't want to talk about it right now. Jeff's voice is barely a whisper. "Because I love you."

I take a deep breath before taking the flowers from him. I should thank him, or at least say I love you too, but neither passes my lips. The words that do come, however, surprise me.

"Is this an apology?" I ask as I fill a vase with water, hoping the prompt will shed some light on the unmentionable wedge between us.

"An apology?"

Surely he's not this stupid?

I shut off the water and take the daisies from him, putting them in the vase. I pop my hand on my hip. "For the other night?" I say, but it comes out more like a question, and damn the uncertainty in my voice. I watch him swallow hard, and he struggles to maintain eye contact. I hate confrontation, but I run the risk of combustion if I don't at least ask.

"What happened?" The words are barely a whisper.

He shakes his head, but I'm not sure why. "I'm just ... overwhelmed, I guess."

"Overwhelmed," I repeat, making sure I heard him correctly.

Jeff nods.

And it's the most *underwhelming* response he possibly could have delivered.

I laugh maniacally at the word. Overwhelmed. Who isn't overwhelmed? I'd like to meet one soon-to-be-first-time-parent who doesn't feel like they're overwhelmed. I want to tell him that he's full of shit and if he wants out of this relationship then he should speak now so I can pack my things and leave. It's one thing to have a crap boyfriend who keeps things from you. But it's a whole other ballgame the moment you bring that boyfriend into fatherhood status. These games where he's *overwhelmed* and incapable of being an adult will soon impact more than just the two of us.

I want to spit obscenities and yell and smack him upside the head until he realizes what he's doing.

I may be knocked up and certifiably emotionally unstable right now, but even still, I know that words said in haste can easily become the best speech I'll pontificate and live to regret.

And so I do the smartest thing I've done all day.

I choke back the words that would do more harm than good.

"Why?" I challenge, still needing to find a way to connect with him. I need to know what is so bad that he can't talk to me. "We have a great life. A great home. We both have great jobs. What *I* think is a really great relationship. And up until recently, I was under the impression that we both felt this child was a great addition. Rather than internalize everything, you should be able to just talk to me. I'm going to be your wife. The mother of your child. We're a team. Where you walk, I walk ... remember? It's terrifying to think that when things feel overwhelming to you,

you back off like you're looking for someone to tag you out of the ring."

He winces at my words and rakes his palm down his face. "Can we not do this now babe?"

I scoff and throw my arms up in defeat, trying to bite back the tears.

Whatever.

I guess I expected too much from him.

I'm not hungry anymore. I turn back to the counter and throw away the peanut butter waffle that I never even touched. As I'm walking out of the kitchen, Jeff grabs my wrist and gently pulls me to him.

Jeff's eyes carry a pained expression as he slowly rubs his hands up and down my arms. He leans over, and I feel the heat of his breath linger before he presses his lips to my forehead. I can hear him breathing me in. I close my eyes and wish all this drama would just disappear so we can go back to being Henley and Jeff, the carefree and happy couple.

After a painfully slow moment that was probably only ten-seconds, Jeff pulls back and finally speaks. "I meant what I said. I love you. I truthfully am just overwhelmed. There is so much going on in my head and I can't even begin to process everything right now, but when I'm finally able to make sense of it all, I promise we will talk about it."

It's the most he's said to me in a week and a half.

And it's the one promise that I hope he can keep.

I *need* to give him the benefit of the doubt and shut down the demons chriping inside my head because if I can't, at the very least, try to do that, then every last one of these pregnancy hormones is going to eat me alive.

Chapter Twenty

ANTI-ADVICE

"I have never seen so much blue and pink wrapping paper in one place in my entire life," I say looking at the pile of perfectly primped gift boxes and bags on the table across the room.

"What did you expect? It's a baby shower." My mother gives me a warm side hug.

I'm happy that she's here but still confused as to who most of these people are. Besides Tara, I only invited a small handle of co-workers and two sorority sisters who live nearby. On the other hand, it appears that my mother invited everyone she's ever met, regardless of whether or not they know me. I know she means well, but I feel like this has turned into a celebration for her and her grandchild.

"I know ... I just feel weird for some reason," I admit uncomfortably. "Who are those ladies in the corner over there?"

"That's Demelza, Lyla and Anne Marie, of course."

Oh! Of course that's who it is. I knew my mother was aloof, but this is ridiculous. "And *they* would be?" I prompt her for some kind of recognition.

"My book club ladies. You know them."

"No. No, I don't." I shake my head. Truthfully, I had no idea my mother was even in a book club. But Mom simply gives a subtle *huh* under her breath.

"What about the ladies over by the mimosa station?"

She turns to look at the gaggle of wiry grey-haired women gossiping with their backs toward everyone else. "Oh, those are my friends from church." She leans over to whisper in my ear. "Jeanne, there on the left, likes to take advantage of the wine chalice during communion. Everyone knows she likes the sauce, but nobody ever says anything to her about it, so instead, we just pray for her soul. I dropped ten Hail Marys for her this morning when I realized Tara was serving mimosas."

I watch as Jeanne tops off her champagne flute with a single drop of orange juice, and snicker to myself. I begin to question just how many women my mother has asked to pray for my soul. Because with my permanent record of premarital tomfoolery, I've earned myself a full-ride scholarship to hell. Fortunately, I'm saving the seat next to me in the back of the classroom for Tara. It should be a hoot.

"All of these lovely women have gathered here to celebrate the pending birth of *my* grandchild." She places her hand upon my baby bump like she's staking claim to the contents inside. It's a baby, not a lounge chair on the sundeck of a cruise ship. It's all a bit ridiculous if you ask me.

I smile politely. "Excuse me for just a moment, Mom." I sneak into the kitchen to pour myself a tall glass of ice water and start downing it like I'm a camel on the verge of trekking the Sahara. I pour myself a second, and then a third, and toss it back like the Beer Bong Champ of the Midwest that I am.

Seriously. I won a beer bong contest back in college with a red funnel and tube contraption I called Lil' Bill. My ability to open my throat and let it all slide down knows no bounds.

I set my glass on the counter and exchange pleasantries with my Aunt Tillie, who drove up from Wichita for the occasion, and greet a few of my old college friends. While they're all married, none of them have children yet, so it's hard not to feel like they're silently judging me on some level.

When the baby decides to use my bladder as a Jazzercise trampoline, I excuse myself to use the restroom faster than Richard Simmons running into a sequin factory. Even if I hadn't just chugged a gallon of water, I would no doubt still have to pee like a racehorse. I appreciate the moment of silence, and part of me wishes I could just hide out in here for the rest of the afternoon. Attention is something I don't do very well. It doesn't matter if I'm in front of a hundred people or five. When all eyes are on me, I instinctively get nervous.

"Oh, there you are, dear!" Martha walks up to me just as I emerge from the bathroom.

"Mrs. Carrington, I am so excited you made it." I smile widely and stretch my arms out to hug her. Instead of meeting my embrace, her face is down at my stomach, blowing kisses and making ridiculous baby talk to my ever-growing bump.

"Stop that. Just call me Mom — and I wouldn't miss this for the world. You've gotten so much bigger since I saw you in Colorado. I can't believe how much you've popped! Are you being good for your momma? Are you?" She's still talking to my belly, never once having the courtesy to make eye contact with me. Don't get me wrong, I love that she's over the moon about the arrival of this bundle of joy, but a simple hello would certainly be nice.

I've never had large boobs, but I imagine that this is the frustration of men having their eyes glued to a woman's rack when they're trying to have a conversation. *Hey! Look at me! The fetus you're trying to have a conversation with spent the day searching for its thumb. I'm up here! And I can actually converse with you!*

I sigh. "Yes, the baby is being good. The doctor tells me it's the size of a squash now."

"Oh, that's lovely. Do you hear that? You're a squash right now!" And again her face is mere inches from my vagina. Perhaps I should offer her the opportunity to climb right up in there to keep it company?

The baby starts to dance at the sound of her voice, and for the first time, I wish it were actually gas. If she knows this kid will move on her command, she's going to walk around with her face permanently attached to my crotch for the next few months.

"Mrs. Carrington ... I mean ... *Mom* ..." She looks me in the eye for the first time since her arrival and smiles sweetly as if the word 'mom' alone was the greatest gift I could give her after this child. "There's someone I'd like you to meet."

I look into the room and wave to catch my mother's attention. She smiles and quickly comes over. "Mom, this is Jeff's Mom, Martha Carrington." Mom holds her hand out and surveys Mrs. Carrington curiously. "And Martha, this is my mom, Lisa."

She grabs my mom's hand and pulls her into an overwhelming bear hug. It's hard not to laugh at the panic overtaking her face.

"Oh, it's so wonderful to finally meet you! Henley has told me all about you and your husband."

Um, no I haven't.

"Oh? I haven't heard a thing about you other than the fact you're from Colorado." The words sound like glass on her tongue. My mom pulls back and smooths her palms down over her dress.

"Well, that's no worry. Us grandmas will have plenty of time to bond once my sweet little papoose arrives."

Why the hell is everyone laying claim to this kid? He ... She ... *It* belongs to me! Well, me *and* Jeff. Unless it's being naughty. Then it's definitely Jeff's kid and not mine.

"And I'm so glad Henley wasn't injured a few weeks ago."

My mom's brows perk up, and her eyes dart toward me, silently delivering the great maternal inquisition in one single glare.

Fuck.

"Yes ... we were all ... relieved," she says slowly as her eyes narrow, not giving away the fact that this is brand new information to her.

"Fortunately the bed didn't cause any damage to the floor. That really would have been a nightmare to repair. And we were able to get a carpenter to come out and fix the bed." Jeff's mom pats my arm lovingly before continuing to chat with my mom about all the things I don't want her to know. When Mrs. Carrington finally heads over to the mimosa bar, my mother turns to me with a wicked scowl.

"What is this bed nonsense she speaks of?"

"Nothing, Mom." I sigh, but she stabs me with the *you have three seconds to start talking or else* glare that I feared as a teenager. "We just learned that his childhood bunk beds can't sustain the weight of two grown adults, especially when one of them is pregnant."

My mom's eyes go wide, and she gasps in repugnance. "Henley Louise! Well, I never." Her hand is on her chest.

"Mom, it's fine. *We're* fine. Nobody got hurt, and we've lived to tell the tale."

"No! That's not it at all. I cannot believe you shared a bunk bed with that man."

Oh my God! Seriously? A bunk bed isn't even a *real* bed. It's a bed for kids. A bed for broke college students. She's being absolutely ridiculous right now. *Per usual.*

"Mom the guest room is a craft room. A bunk bed was the only option. It's not like you can fit two people on one of those tiny twin mattresses, especially when one of them is with child," I lie.

I watch as she chews on my words for a few moments. "Well, fine, if you say so. I suppose Martha seems nice enough." Her tone is unconvincing. She already feels threatened by Jeff's mom and the entire situation. They've known each other for exactly one hundred and twenty seconds, and she's going to make things difficult for the next however many years.

My mom purses her lips and folds her arms across her chest. "Though she should have taken better care of you. I still can't believe you're going to give me a grandchild before a son-in-law."

Really? Of all the moments to say something about this pregnancy and pending marriage, this is the one she chooses?

"Are you implying you want us to have a shotgun wedding?"

She gasps in horror. "I am implying no such thing. I was simply stating the obvious."

I sigh and put my glass down on the counter. Just as I'm about to chide her, Tara walks in. *Thank the maker! Tara has come to rescue me!*

"Hey Henley, Mrs. Carson. Are you two having a good time?"

I smile at Tara appreciatively. "You've really outdone yourself, T. This is more than I ever imagined." I reach out and squeeze her hand.

"Yes, it's beautiful, Tara," my mom agrees before giving my best friend a hug and leaving the room. Hopefully to stage an intervention before Jeanne polishes off the mimosa bar.

Tara looks back to me cautiously. "Is everything okay? You seemed annoyed when I came in."

I bite the inside of my cheek. "Just the same old passive aggressive bullshit of having a baby out of wedlock."

"She'll come around, I promise. Once she lays eyes on that perfect little baby of yours, she'll forget all about her daughter being a loose little harlot." She nudges my shoulder. *Inappropriate? Yes. But God, I love this chick.* "Look on the bright side, you can always fashion a homemade Mother's Day card for her out of the psychiatric bills you're bound to incur, courtesy of her, of course."

"Did you see that on Pinterest, too?"

"As a matter of fact, I did." She pops a piece of cheese in her mouth from the spread of food on the counter. "How's everything going with Jeff? Have you talked to him yet?" she asks as she chews.

I cringe because while things haven't exactly gotten light years better, they haven't at least gotten worse. He's still a little distracted, but not as rough around the edges as a few nights ago. He hasn't shown up drunk since that night, so I take that as a checkmark in the winning column. And the pair of us? Well, we're going through the motions, but the motions are at least a little less tense and not as forced.

"Eh, kinda," I admit casually.

"Kinda?" Her voice oozes with skepticism.

I shrug. Tara is a no nonsense, take the bull by the horns kind of chick. If she were in my shoes, she would have known exactly what happened before he ever came through the door. Me, on the other hand, I'm a go with the flow, fly by the seat of my pants-er.

"Yeah, kinda. I tried talking to him the other night. He brought me flowers in what I thought was an attempt to apologize, but I didn't get very far with him. He says he's overwhelmed with life. Which—*I know*—doesn't exactly answer why he was that messed up and drunkenly apologized to me before passing out. Things *seem* like they're a little bit better with each passing day, so I'm hopeful we'll get back to normal in due time. But until then, I'm just trying to give him the space he needs to figure out whatever it is that's eating him from the inside out."

"Henley," Tara scolds. "You need to get him to open up. You can't let this consume your relationship. I already know it's consuming most of your thoughts."

I whip a sharp look at her. "Please stop. I already have two mothers here today. Don't you dare turn into a third."

She cocks her hip out to the side and chews her lip, studying my face. "Okay. I'll drop it ... *for now*. But only because you said please, and because angry pregnant women terrify me. Besides, it's time for presents."

Tara tugs my hand and drags me into the family room where most of the guests are sitting, except for Jeanne who is busy wrestling the cork off another bottle of champagne. My mom saddles up in between me and Tara. I love my mom, but her bizarre behavior today is exhausting, and I can't quite figure out what she's trying to overcompensate for. Regardless, it's really getting old.

"Tara, did you ever consider making this a joint shower?"

"Joint shower? We don't have any other friends expecting, Mrs. Carson."

"No, not a joint *baby* shower, silly. We could have celebrated both the baby and the wedding."

The comment strikes me as odd considering she's the kind of woman who has a party for every occasion. Dad recovers from a hernia? Invite our entire church over for a potluck dinner. School canceled due to snow? Impromptu pajama party for all the kids on the street. It's a random Tuesday? Break out the good wine and invite the neighbors over. She doesn't need a reason to have a soiree. And when she finally does have a reason, she wants to consolidate efforts?

What the hell is that about?

Before I'm even able to respond back to my mother, Tara is grabbing me by the elbow and pulling me toward the chair in the center of the room. I instantly feel the eyes of two dozen women gazing upon me. It makes me want to pee.

"I just want to thank you all again for coming today to celebrate Henley and her impending bundle of doom—I mean joy.

Her impending bundle of joy." Tara throws a wink my direction, and everyone snickers politely, including Jeanne who is finally stumbling to a chair, not even bothering with the orange juice portion of the mimosas anymore. "Now, Henley, being a first-time mom we thought it would be fun to give you some of our favorite parenting pointers. So I asked everyone to write down a parenting tip when they arrived. As you open each gift, we'll read the tip aloud."

"Sounds good." I smile and wonder just what kind of advice is in store for me.

Tara claps her hands twice and nods for me to take my seat. "Okay, let's get this started." She hands me a notecard attached to a beautiful box wrapped up in silver. It's the only box not decked out in shades of baby blue and ballerina pink. I instantly recognize the handwriting on the outside of the envelope.

It's my mother's.

I survey the card, take a deep breath and read the *tip* aloud. "Never let your newly added title of mother prevent you from careful grooming and dressing. Being a new mom is no excuse to look less than your best for your husband."

My eyes scan over the words again, and I let the words sink in. *Husband.* Something I don't have, and won't have before this child comes.

The silence is uncomfortable, and Tara and I both look to my mom. She's clueless and living with a nineteen fifties submissive mentality.

"What? I know that they're not married. But even so, Jeff will have needs. Expectations. But most importantly, just because she has a baby doesn't mean she can just let herself go," my mom exclaims defensively.

Okay, then. I remind myself to breathe. I have no idea even how to respond to this.

Tara claps her hands together and breaks the awkward

silence with a little too much enthusiasm. "Let's see what's inside the box, shall we?"

I tear through the silver paper to find a Cuisinart box. "A ... food processor?" I force a smile and look to my mom. "Thank you so much." She knows that this is a baby shower and *not* a wedding shower, right?

"Well, I just thought that every woman needs a good, reliable food processor."

Are you kidding me? This woman is more excited about the wedding that hasn't even been planned than the birth of her own grandchild. And every mom-to-be needs practical baby things like diapers and nipple cream and tiny clothes covered in puppy dogs and rubber duckies. A food processor doesn't even crack the top one hundred list of things a new mom and dad need to take care of a newborn.

"Henley, dear, this is so you can make all of your own baby food."

"People actually do that?" I say, turning the box over in my hands and looking at the packaging. There are more parts and pieces in here than I know what to do with. "That seems like a lot of work."

All eyes are glued to mine, no doubt judging me for my last comment.

"All the best moms do!" she says matter of factly.

I shift uncomfortably, hating the attention of the Judgey McJudgersons around me.

"What I think your mom means to say is that all the moms want to make sure their children are fed, regardless of the methods. As long as you're not giving it Mountain Dew in a bottle, I think you're doing pretty well," Tara says trying to cut the palpable tension in the room.

I set the gift off to the side and look to Tara, who hands me a card, sans gift. It's a generic Halloween card with a momma pumpkin and baby pumpkin on the cover, presumably because this kiddo is due on Halloween. A slip of paper falls down into my lap. When I open it, there's an image of the ridiculously expensive and beautifully meticulous glider from my mid-store meltdown. And scribbled underneath the photo, there's a delivery date.

"Oh, Tara! I can't believe you did this."

"With how hard being a mom is, you deserve a frickin' throne. And I'm still looking for a matching Mommy's Sippy Cup for you, too."

I beam at her.

Tara's advice? *Enjoy every moment, even the stressful and bad ones. One day you'll look back and wish you could slow down time.*

Tara turns to me with an endearing expression on her face. "I know I frequently joke about wanting the triplets to be grown up and out of the house, but I miss the days when they were tiny and wanted to spend all their time cuddling with me. Don't get me wrong, having hellions is fun. But there's something special about having someone so tiny and precious depending on you for everything."

Mrs. Carrington was more than generous with her gift. Not only did she give us the super tricked out car seat with the highest ratings imaginable, but she also gave us a gift certificate for a newborn photo session with a local photographer. She even managed to clean up some of Jeff's newborn outfits from when he was a baby. At the bottom of her card, she included a note saying that even though they live in Colorado, they want to be able to come down frequently to babysit. The sentiment warms my heart, and I wish my mother were as open and thoughtful as this woman.

Her parenting advice? *Wine.*

Even though I'm not a mom yet, I can't disagree with her at

all, though anyone who came here on my mother's accord is beside themselves as whispers of *'How could a mother drink!'* circulate the room. Including Jeanne, *that sauced-up hypocrite.*

I open gift after gift, unveiling everything from safety gadgets for cabinet doors to pee pee teepees (whatever those are) to a breast pump, to a toddler urinal (seriously?), to something called Baby Bangs — a tiny wig made of real hair, complete with blunt cut curtain bangs to ensure your bald bundle of joy is the envy of the nursery.

All in all, a little less than half of this stuff came from my registry. I keep reminding myself that it's the thought that counts and nothing was more thoughtful than the ridiculous advice that came with each and every gift.

If it's acceptable for airlines to have parents put on their oxygen masks before helping their kids put on theirs, it's totally fine to let your kid cry while you shave your legs and make a sandwich.

Never allow your children to play outside by themselves because if you have nosey neighbors, you may get a house call from Child Protective Services.

There's a reason that the word repaid is the reverse of diaper. Payback's a bitch. But don't worry, it'll all come back around with this kid in a few decades.

When your baby starts teething and accidentally bites you, bite him back so he learns his lesson.

Take the time to mourn your "old life." Because things will never be the same again.

AFTER THE LAST pieces of pink tissue paper and blue ribbon fall to the floor, I'm speechless. Not just at the generosity of all these women, but at the fact that I now feel completely and totally unfit to be a mom based on all of the anti-advice other mindless bits of wisdom imparted upon me. Everything is so horrifically overwhelming. And like I've been struck by a lightning bolt, I realize that it's only a few short months before all of these items will be put to good use.

My eyes well up, and before I know it, unexpected tears spill over, and I'm one hot mess of runny mascara and snot. I try to say, "Thank you so much, I'm sorry for crying," but the only words that come out are, "Spank chew doe muck, yam car pee for buyin," as my shoulders quake uncontrollably. I haven't cried this hard since I saw that insurance commercial where the girl had her couch stolen from her bachelorette pad. Don't judge me— it was a really sweet couch.

My mother rushes to my side and offers me a handkerchief from her purse. I dab the edges of my eyes, trying to maintain some sense of femininity. But it's no use. Big, fat, ugly tears stream down my face in droves, and when I finally look up, I can see judgments being passed around like free condoms at a women's clinic, so I voice exactly what they're all probably thinking.

"I know that I am *so* not ready for any of this! I know that I'm going to be a horrible mother! I don't know how to make my own baby food, and I've never changed a diaper, and I don't even know what a pee pee teepee is, and I'm terrified I'm going to be doing this all wrong! I'm *scared!*"

Tara sits on the arm of the chair and puts her hand on my back. "I think it is virtually impossible for you to be a bad mother, Henley. And listen to me closely. It's okay to be scared. Every woman is scared before she has a baby. But the best things in life are waiting for you on the other side of terror," she says slowly and deliberately to me before turning back around to all of the shower guests. "But fuck all of this advice!"

The room turns quiet, save for a few gasps at Tara's f-bomb, no doubt from my mom's church contingency. Jeanne The

Hypocrite goes bug-eyed as she chugs the last of the champagne straight from the bottle. Thankfully, the eyes turn from me and straight to Tara.

"No offense, ladies, but some of your mothering methods are downright questionable at best. Who are we to judge each other? Who are *you* to judge Henley? And shit, why the hell are we incapable of simply celebrating motherhood — *all* kinds of mothers — regardless of our methods? This is *not* okay!" Tara turns her back to the shower guests and focuses her eyes on me. "And, Henley, I'm sorry that my little shower has seeded all of this doubt in you, but you are going to be the best damn mom in the history of moms. And even when you're living and breathing those inevitable mom fail moments, you'll still be the best because you'll be mothering from the heart."

Everyone watches in stupefied silence.

Then, as if on cue, Jeff's mom starts the kind of slow clap reserved for that epic scene in all the great movies, and my heart begins to swell, ever so slightly. Except only a few co-workers and sorority sisters join in.

And Jeanne.

Jeanne The Hypocrite raises her empty glass in solidarity.

"I CAN'T BELIEVE you had a meltdown at your own baby shower," Jeff says over dinner that night as I recall the tale of the baby shower that no one will soon forget.

"It wasn't so much of a meltdown as it was nuclear hysterics," I clarify shamefully. It will be a long time before I'm capable of bringing myself around most of those women. Even as Tara ushered everyone out, the judgments never ended.

I spear the last green bean on my plate with my fork and pop it into my mouth, fearful that if I keep talking about this afternoon, the waterworks will start again.

Jeff eyes me cautiously like he knows I could break again at any moment.

"Well, I'm glad Tara went off on a tangent. And if I've told you once, I'll tell you a million more times, you're going to be a remarkable mother, Henley."

I swallow and take a slow, deep breath.

"I'm just scared. We're going to be raising a human. A little human who can't fend for itself. There is a lot of room to screw this up. I spent the day listening to other moms talk about how much they loved being pregnant and the closeness they felt to their unborn child. This child has taken up residence right on top of my bladder, and I feel like I don't even know him."

Jeff puts his fork down against the side of the plate and reaches across the table, taking my hand in his. "Our baby hasn't even been born yet, but already you're closer to him than I am." There's a tinge of jealousy in his voice that I never even considered.

"That's because my stomach has turned into an Easy Bake Oven. But there are plenty of things you can do to bond with this baby before its debut."

"Oh? Like what?"

I bite my lip for a moment and think back to what the baby books have all said. "Well, for starters, the baby can already distinguish voices, so you could read a book ... or even sing to it. Your mom is making a point to baby talk straight to my vagina. Who knows, maybe she's onto something?"

"She did not!" His mouth drops in mortification as he imagines his mom's face all up in my unmentionables. I can't help but laugh.

"Oh yes, she did. And the kid even fluttered in my stomach at the sound of her voice. I dunno, while highly inappropriate, it was certainly sweet and done with the best intentions," I admit.

"Maybe it's worth a shot?" I can't believe I'm giving him free reign to *talk* to my stomach.

He nods in agreement, then stands to clear the table. "Tonight! Tonight, I *will* do that."

When Jeff leans down to grab my plate, I tilt my chin up and press my lips to his.

"I wonder how little Jeff Junior would feel about me singing to him?" he asks when our lips finally break apart.

I try to avoid laughing because the only time Jeff sounds good singing is when he's alone in his car and the radio is cranked all the way up. Before I say anything, he's practicing under his breath. Except he's not singing. He's rapping his favorite Jay-Z tune. "I got ninety-nine problems, but your mom ain't one..."

I smile, thankful he's singing *his* favorite Jay-Z song and not mine ...

Big Pimpin'.

Chapter Twenty-One

THE MILKMAN

"What does this thing do?"

"Um, that's my breast pump, honey." *Awkward!*

Jeff looks at the machine and all the boxes of funnels and tubing that are piled on top of our bed. The edges of his lips curl up, and the corners of his eyes crinkle in thought. I can tell he's about to say something he may regret.

"Nope, don't even think about saying it. I know that wicked little mind of yours is conjuring up some joke about why would I need a breast pump when I have you to take care of that for me and blah, blah, blah …" I trail off and walk into the bathroom just off our bedroom.

"That's not what I was going to say, Henley. Give me more credit than that," he calls out from the other room.

Suuure.

I pee for the hundredth—no thousandth—time today, then begin splashing water on my face to start removing my makeup. Before I brush my teeth, Jeff is calling me from the other side of the wall.

"Let's give it a whirl."

I pop my head through the bathroom door and glare at him. *He's joking, right?* "I don't think that's such a good idea. I'm pretty sure nothing will come out at this point. Plus I read in one of those pregnancy books that too much nipple stimulation can cause contractions. And frankly, I'm not *that* eager to jump start that process. We don't even have the nursery finished yet."

"I didn't mean for *you* to try it."

Oh, no. No, no, no, no, no!

When I walk back into the room, Jeff already has the breast pump bag laid out on the bed and is opening the boxes of funnels and bottles. He's trying to figure out which parts connect to what pieces without even bothering to look at the directions.

"Jeff, don't you dare. This is *not* a penis pump. This isn't a toy. This is an expensive piece of machinery. You do realize I need this so I can help store milk for our child, right?"

"First of all, my son will drink right off the tap just like his daddy." He gives me a lazy, smug grin. And I realize that this moment, right here, is the first time in a while where we've actually felt like *us*.

We're the normal Henley and Jeff.

And *damn* does that feel good.

I sigh. As much as I love this man, he drives me crazy. "No. No, first of all. Yes, I am going to nurse our *baby* — which could very well end up a *she*. But I can't exactly bring him or her into the classroom with me every day. I'm going to have to pump milk. But let me be clear, even though you may sometimes act like a big ole baby, I am nursing our *newborn*, not *you*."

Jeff throws his arms in the air. "I didn't mean it like that, babe." He turns quiet.

"Oh? What did you mean it like, then?"

He stands and meets me in the middle of the room, wrapping his arms around my waist. He looks down at me, almost with embarrassment. "I ... I just want to see what it feels like, that's all," he says softly with a subtle shrug of his shoulders. He nuzzles his nose down into my shoulder, and the scruff from his five o'clock shadow tickles the bare skin of my neck before he kisses me tenderly.

"You want to see what it feels like?" I repeat slowly, unsure I heard him correctly.

He nods. I'm still not sure if he's joking, so I suppress the laughter bubbling inside of me. "Well, yeah," he says matter of factly. "We're in this together. If I could experience what a contraction feels like right along with you, I would. I love you, and I love this baby. But honestly? I'm just genuinely curious what it feels like to be a woman."

I'm not sure if I should be mortified or sincerely touched by this moment. Or maybe he's just trying too hard? But either way, I'll go with it.

"Okay. If you want to try the breast pump, I'll let you. But only under two conditions." I put my fist on my side and jut my hip out.

"Hmmm ... and what are they?" He eyes me suspiciously, and I give him an innocent, coquettish smile.

"One," I hold my pointer finger in the air between us. "You let me take a photo to commemorate the moment."

"No! No way. That is *not* gonna happen."

"Pics or it *doesn't* happen," I singsong back to him.

He folds his arms in protest, and I take this moment to inform him of the other condition with a second finger in the air. "And two, you aren't allowed to stop until I say when."

He presses his lips into a hard line and looks at me, seriously weighing how badly he wants to test the waters. I can practically see the cogs in his brain turning round and round as he looks at the machine intently. And just when I'm convinced he's about to bail, he surprises me.

"All right," he clips with a slight nod. "I'll do it. I'm man enough to try your breast pump and even let you take a photo. Actually, I'll one up you."

"Oh?" I fold my arms, challenging him. I'm not sure how this night could get any better.

But it does.

"Yeah. I'll let you video me, and then share it with Chris and Kyle."

I laugh so hard I nearly pee myself. And it feels good. *This* feels normal. Like us. The way we're meant to be. "Really? You'll let me show your family? What's the catch?" I smirk. Surely it can't be *this* easy.

"No catch." He stretches his arms wide. "Like I said, I'm man enough."

Wow. He must really want to take this thing for a test drive. "Okay then." I sit down on the bed and pull the breast pump instructions from the discarded box, quickly scanning over the "how to" illustrations and piecing everything together.

I plug the machine into the wall and turn the power dial, watching as my brand new breast pump comes to life, wheezing and humming in an even cadence. Now that I can hear it, I can't lie ... I'm a bit curious how this works, too. I turn the machine off and then look back to Jeff.

"Okay, my hunky piece of man candy. Nipples out!"

Jeff strips his shirt off a little too eagerly if you ask me, and I giggle in anticipation. He sits down next to me on the bed. "So I just put this here over my breasticle?" He takes one of the funnels and presses it against his left pec. "And the other one here?" He takes the other on his right.

I nod and grab my iPhone. "You ready?" I ask.

"Let's do this."

I hit record on my phone and slowly turn the dial to the lowest setting. Again, the breast pump hums to life, and I watch

Jeff intently. "Okay. That's weird. Maybe even a little nice," he admits, "but mostly weird."

"What's it like?"

"I dunno ... just a gentle little tug, I guess. No big deal. If nursing is anything like this, I think you're golden." He watches his pecs subtly get suctioned in and out of the funnel.

"Getting any milk in there, big boy?"

Jeff rolls his eyes at me. "Hah. Hah. Aren't you the comedienne?"

"I'm not the one experimenting with a breast pump." I smile conspiratorially at him. "Want me to turn it up a pinch?"

He looks right at the camera with an unsuspecting grin that makes me melt. "Sure."

Slowly I turn the dial to medium, and the machine instantly wheezes faster, harder.

"Whoa!" Jeff looks down at his chest and smiles at his pecs as they pulsate in unison. Then the uncontrollable laughter begins and he can barely talk. "Oh my gosh, it's ... it's vibrating ... against my skin. It tickles so much! Wait! No ... it's starting to hurt a little!"

The sound coming from his mouth is akin to a little girl being tickled, and I completely lose it.Tears prick my eyes, and I struggle to keep my iPhone camera steady. And suddenly I have to pee. Jeff falls back into a cloud of pillows and goes to pull the funnels away.

"Don't you dare! You haven't even hit the highest setting." I move closer to the bed to get a better shot of Jeff flailing around in hysterics. "Or are you not *man* enough?" I know I'm just goading him now, but how can I not?

"Oh? I'll *show* you how man enough I am. Do it. Turn it up. All the way to eleven."

I shake my head at his ridiculousness, then reach out and turn it about three-quarters of the way to high for a moment.

"Holy shit, woman!" Jeff winces in both discomfort and laughter, and just when he starts to get used to the sensation, I crank it to the maximum setting.

"Shit! Fuck! Lunch truck!" he cries out in agony. Or pleasure. I'm not sure which because the look on his face is a cross of elation and amazement and horror and *what the hell is this torture device.* "Henley! Ow! Make it stop!"

"What? I can't hear you over the sound of your manliness."

"Holy shit! Henley! I can't! This hurts!" But he's still roaring with laughter. "Turn it off!"

"You want me to turn the camera off? If I do, your brothers won't see how manly you are."

"No! The pump! Turn the damn breast pump off! Please!" he pleads as tears start to prick the corners of his eyes.

With a smug smile on my face, I oblige, though I did enjoy this temporary moment of ridiculous suffering. I think all dads-to-be should be open-minded and try to find ways to experience the joys of motherhood like Jeff has.

When Jeff finally rips the funnels from his chest, he has bright red circles over both of his pecs from the extreme suction. It looks like a pair of bloodshot eyes looking at me with tiny erect man nips as the pupils sticking out at me.

Jeff lies flat on his back, staring at the ceiling with his chest heaving as he tries to catch his breath. As I give him a moment to collect himself, I quickly email the file to my account as backup for safe keeping.

"You okay?" I ask, trying not to laugh.

He turns his head toward me, his eyes wild and confused. "If this kid is anything like your breast pump, you're going to have a little vampire trying to eat you alive every feeding." He pants some more. "If I wasn't over the moon about you having my baby, I might even feel bad for knocking you up."

ping out of the shower. Besides, it's one of the few things that actually fit my changing body these days.

Tara folds her arms and glares at me. "And do you have a bra on underneath your *most comfortable terry cloth wrap dress?*" she says with dramatic air quotes. She gives me that scolding motherly look that she's perfected over the past few years and she knows she has me trapped. "Absolutely not. And I know this because a few moments ago you were oblivious to your own wardrobe malfunction and you flashed me some nip."

I bite the inside of my cheek. "Fine. I'll put clothes on. But don't expect me to put makeup on and look cute. I'm a hopeless case right now. Besides, I haven't done laundry in weeks, and nothing fits."

"Nonsense. I'll find you something." She tugs at my hand, trying to pull me off the couch, but I'm sunk so far into the cushions it would take a crane to lift me. When I don't budge, she turns on her heels and whistles as she strolls down the hallway.

It takes a great effort and a few animalistic grunts, but I'm finally able to push myself up and onto my feet. By the time I get to the bedroom, she's got half of my clothes tossed onto the bed. I lean against the wall and watch her *try* to work her magic with my limited wardrobe in amusement. Her eyes light up as she pulls out one of my favorite shirts from the bottom drawer.

"I can't wear that. That would only fit a twelve-year-old the size of my pinky finger." It's true. While a totally adorable shirt, I haven't worn it for at least five years. I was fifteen pounds lighter, and that was *before* my pre-pregnancy weight. I'd be lucky to get an arm through it now.

"Henley, if Winnie the Pooh can wear that slinky little crop top over his big ole belly and not fuck around with pants, so can you!"

"Last I checked, Winnie the Pooh was a cartoon character. And as much as I'd like to be, I am not."

"Eh. Semantics." She flips her blonde locks over her shoulder and continues scavenging through my clothes.

"And besides, nobody but Jeff and my gynecologist want to see what's going on down below. Though I think Pooh Bear was onto something with the pantless trend."

Tara smiles and tosses me a maxi dress that was hiding in a moving box in the back of my closet. I completely forgot I had this dress. I love how flowy and forgiving the style is.

But the best part? It's not pants.

WE'VE BEEN WALKING around a mall a few towns away for a few hours now looking for shoes that Tara doesn't even need. But I have to admit, it's nice to get out of the house.

"So you feel like you're ready?" Tara asks, stuffing her face with a cinnamon sugar pretzel that we picked up from the Auntie Anne's counter in the food court.

"Almost. We have enough clothes to get us through the first few months, and I *think* enough diapers, but the only furniture we have for the nursery is the glider you bought us. We still need to buy the crib and get it assembled."

I try not to panic that the nursery isn't finished yet. I know that newborns are so small they could sleep in a dresser drawer if needed. Not that I would do that. That would be weird. But, if necessity required us to fashion a tiny bed in a small drawer, I could find a way to make it work, much to my mother's horror.

"For starters, you will *never* have enough diapers. Take what you already have and quadruple it. Then that amount should get you through a week, maybe two. I can't tell you how many trips Cam took to the drugstore in the middle of the night to pick up diapers because we *thought* we had enough. And don't worry about the crib thing. You've got time, and you'll get it figured out."

I smile at him and reach for his hand. "Come on, it wasn't *that* bad, was it?"

"You have *no* idea."

Later that night when we lay down for bed, Jeff grabs a book from the stack of baby shower presents. He places his hand upon my belly, clears his throat, and in a grand bravado gives a dramatic reading of *Goodnight Moon*.

Before he even says goodnight to the kittens and mittens, I've practically forgotten about our recent troubles and fallen in love with him that much more.

Chapter Twenty-Two

POOH BEAR LOGIC

"Get dressed, hoe. We're going shopping." Tara chucks a throw pillow at my face as she leaps off of the couch.

I roll my eyes so far back I can practically see my brain. The skin on my legs has permanently fused to the couch, and frankly, I don't wanna.

"When you said you wanted to hang out today, you made no mention of actually going out in public, so I'm not going anywhere."

"We've been sitting here watching reruns of The Golden Girls, and I want to scoop my eyeballs out with a spork. So, yes, you are going shopping. With me. Right now. Because I need some new shoes. So get up and get some clothes on."

I look down at my wardrobe. "I'm *in* clothes."

"You're in a bathrobe. That hardly constitutes as clothing."

I pull the sides of my robe closed a little tighter and sit up straight. "This is *not* a bathrobe. I'm wearing my most comfortable terry cloth wrap dress." Which isn't far from the truth. I've spent many nights wrapped up in nothing but this robe after step-

I hope she's right. As long as I don't go into labor early, we've got all the time in the world.

"Yeah, I guess so. What else do I need to do?"

Normally these are the kinds of questions you ask your mom, but the one time I asked her for some guidance on things to do before the baby comes, she simply responded, "Get married." *Thanks, Mom. Thanks, a lot.*

"Hmm, have you done the pre-registration crap at the hospital?"

"Yeah, and it was the longest two hours of my life."

"That sounds about right. What about pretty panties? You've got a pair of beautiful undies to wear to the hospital?"

Is she on crack? No woman needs to have pretty, expensive undies going into battle. It's not like you actually wear underwear during labor and delivery. And from what I've gathered, I'll be given a diaper of my very own to wear after.

"Um, yeah, that's one thing I don't think I'll need." I pull a piece of pretzel from her hands and lick the sugar off my fingertips. I discard her suggestion to the top of the proverbial pile of random shit my best friend says.

"Um, *no,* you *do* need it. Do you really think Beyonce strutted into the hospital to deliver those twins sporting stretched out cotton granny panties? No. She, no doubt, was wearing a glorious bejeweled thong since she understood that she's about to have a gaggle of voyeurs all up in her Notorious V.A.G." Tara waggles her finger in my direction. "You could learn a thing or two from Queen Bey. Just sayin' ..."

When Tara comes to terms with the fact that we are *not* making a pit stop in Victoria's Secret, and she finally finds a pair of shoes, she musters the courage to ask the one question she has undoubtedly been wanting to ask all freakin' day. The one I'd been hoping to avoid.

"Have you and Jeff made any more progress in the drunken drama department?"

"I really think it was nothing but a little dad-to-be-bender. Things the past two weeks have been back to normal between us. I'm chalking it up to one off night. He gets a freebie. I'm not his mother, but if he wants to go out and get trashed in a blazing glory of panic, who am I to tell him 'no?'"

Tara looks at me cautiously. "Really?"

"Really," I promise, trying to reassure her that her best friend isn't falling apart at the seams over some silly guy antics. "In fact, ever since the shower, he's been a whole new level of awesome. He's been reading and singing to the baby, doing a lot of the prep work. Actually, *he's* been the one doing all of the nesting. It's sweet. And, oh my God, Tara, you will never believe what Jeff asked to try after the baby shower the other night!"

"Anal?" she deadpans in complete seriousness.

Her comment catches me off guard, and I shake my head to rattle the word from my brain. "Ew! Gross! Not anal. You're so weird." My best friend's ability to completely derail a conversation is a gift. *Seriously. Where did I find this girl?*

"What? Don't mock it 'till you try it." She shrugs. "But before you decide you want to try it, let me know. I'll give you some pointers."

I cut her a side glance and silently promise myself that there are places where no man should ever go.

"So what's up? What'd Jeff do?"

I press my lips together and try not to fall into a fit of laughter at the mere thought of Jeff's pecs dancing under the funnels of my breast pump.

"He ... um, he had some fun with some of the baby shower gifts."

The wrinkles on her forehead are pronounced as she looks at

me in confusion. "Fun like he wanted to be swaddled, call you mommy, and begged to be spanked?"

"Seriously, T?"

She simply beams at me in response. Some days I don't even know why I bother trying to have a normal conversation with this girl.

"Here, watch this." I pull up the video on my phone and hand it to her.

Her eyes go wide in disbelief.

"Shut your face! You're joking, right?" she comments after a few seconds of watching.

"Keep watching, it gets better!"

And before we know it, mall patrons are giving us funny looks because Tara is doubled over in booming laughter.

Chapter Twenty-Three

LITTLE WHITE LIES

Tara: *OMG, Hen. Are you guys okay?*

I stare at the words glowing at me from my phone, processing the implications. I can practically hear Tara's concern leaping off the screen of my phone.
    And still, I'm clueless.

Me: Um, Yeah.

Why wouldn't we be okay?
My fingers make swift work on my tiny phone keyboard.

Me: What are you talking about?

    Sure, we were a little … off, but things have gotten better, his drunken night a distant memory. But that's the ebb and flow of relationships. You have good streaks and less than ideal streaks. And when someone screws up, as long as you're not off the charts on the SHITCON scale, you forgive and move on. Hopefully, the good moments outweigh the bad, and you learn to fall in love with each other all over again each day. I watch my phone with bated breath.

Tara: Henley, you don't have to hide it from me. Things will be okay.

Me: ?

Tara: Cam just told me about Jeff.

Umm ... what?

Me: What are you talking about? What about Jeff?

I call Tara for details, and she picks up before it even has a chance to ring.
"Henley, talk to me, sweetie. Are you okay? Why didn't you tell me Jeff lost his job?"
"What are you talking about, Tara? He didn't lose his job. Jeff's at work right now," I interrupt, but she keeps on talking over me.
"I can't imagine what you two are going through. I was upset that you felt you couldn't talk to me about it all. I know you guys are going to be okay, but I cannot even imagine what you're going through right now with Jeff losing his job so close to your due date."
"Tara ... I don't ..."
But she won't let me get a word in edgewise.
"I know school is about to start again, but it's not like a teacher's salary is anything to shake a stick at."
I blanch, trying not to take offense to her comment, even though it's disturbingly true. "Tara—"

"Have you thought about talking to his parents? I know you said they were loaded. Maybe they could help you out right now?"

"TARA!" I shout into the phone, desperate for her attention. She shuts up. After all, there's a first time for everything.

"Jeff's at work right now," I repeat my words from moments ago. I mean, he *is* at work, *right?* Certainly I'd be the first to know if he lost his job. We're going to have a baby together. We're getting married. This isn't the kind of news you keep from your significant other.

Tara's uncomfortably quiet for a beat and then she whispers, "Oh, sweetie ..."

"Wait. You're serious." It's not a question, and all of my insides feel weak.

"Henley. I'm *so sorry*. I really thought you knew ..."

And then it happens.

That moment of free fall into darkness. Where you're not in control of anything, and everything is just barely out of your grasp. And you keep tumbling, tumbling down into the vast nothing, unsure if anything or anyone will be there to break your fall, but you send a silent prayer up, begging for the landing to be pain-free and for it all to end quickly.

"Say something," Tara implores.

"I ... I don't know what to say."

He's been going to work every day the last few weeks and coming home right on schedule. Nothing in his routine has changed. I pause and look at a framed photo of us on a bookshelf across the room. A couple so happy and so in love. The kind of couple that doesn't keep secrets from one another. The kind that doesn't lie about something so important. A few silent moments pass before I'm able to speak again. "How did you find out? When did this happen?"

"Well, Jeff wasn't the only one lying from what I've gathered."

Now she's really not making any sense. But I remain quiet, waiting for an explanation.

"The night Jeff got wasted was the same day he was let go. What started off as a drink of commiseration with some of his teammates, turned into a panic attack in which half the bar was consumed. Supposedly, Jeff was terrified to call you for fear of launching you into a hormonal tailspin, so he called Cam for a ride. Cam picked him up and tried to drive him around until he sobered up a bit, but it was no use. Then, the pair of them sat at a bench at Swope Park for a few hours. Cam thought he was having the whole pre-dad jitters thing and attempted to have a heart to heart, but Jeff broke down, told him that he was let go from his job and that he felt like nothing less of a failure. Then Jeff asked for his help connecting to some industry headhunters and swore Cam to secrecy."

A million words and emotions pulsate through my body and mind. But a soft *"Oh"* is all that I'm able to respond with.

"Don't worry. I'm plenty mad at Cam over all this. But I'm mostly worried about you."

We sit in silence for what feels like hours. It feels like silence and I are becoming fast friends.

"Are you okay?" Tara asks quietly.

No. "I'm okay," I lie, certain she can feel just how betrayed I am.

"Let me rephrase that, are *you guys* going to be okay?"

Tara understands my threshold for lying is nonexistent. Ever since Leo tried to convince me that the tall woman with the blonde hair and big boobs was his cousin when she was, in fact, a chick he had been sleeping with behind my back, I've been a little sensitive to half-truths, partial truths, and lies of omission.

"Henley?"

I take a deep breath through my nose and exhale slowly through my mouth. I have no clue if there's even a *we* to speak of right now. If there's no *we*, how can *I* possibly be remotely okay? There's only one logical answer.

"I'm going to kill him. And then bring him back from the dead so I can murder him again."

Whoa.

The tone of my voice frightens me a little, and I'm starting to realize just how much more pissed off I am than I first thought. This isn't just a little white lie. This is a big fat fucking omission of epic proportions. And big fat fucking lies are worthy of big fat fucking consequences. A consequence like death and dismemberment.

"Don't you think you're overreacting? The man lost his job and is probably sitting at the lowest of lows. He's probably trying to figure out a plan of attack before he tells you. Don't let your crazy pregnant woman hormones do the talking—or homicide—for you."

That was weeks ago. The window for compassion and understanding was slammed shut the moment he decided to not be forthright with what happened. This is the kind of thing we should be tackling *together*. So much for being a team. Where you walk, I walk, *my ass*! Apparently, I'm only allowed to walk whenever and wherever he allows me to walk. And I am *not* that little submissive woman my mom thinks I should be.

I call bullshit!

How dare he blindside me like this? How could he? And Tara, of anyone, should not be calling me out and defending him right now. Whose team is she on?

I grind my teeth, inhale slowly and count to three. "Don't you think that if Cameron lost his job a few weeks ago, and kept it hidden from you with the facade of going to and from work each and every day, you'd lose your shit *just a little bit?*"

Tara's silent, but I can still hear her breathing on the other end of the phone. She's putting herself in my shoes, trying to process it all.

"So *no,* I don't think I'm overreacting, and this is *not* the hormones talking. I'm the size of a beluga whale, I'm back in the classroom again *next week,* anytime I'm standing for more than five minutes I lose my breath, and now I learn that my fiancé — the man who has vowed to take care of this child and me until the ends of the earth — has been *lying* to me about going to work each and every day? If he's not at work, what—*or who*—the hell is he doing?" My voice is shrill and fast and foreign even to my own ears. I gasp for more air, trying to calm myself.

"Okay. Point taken. You're hurt."

"Damn right, I'm hurt! I'm hurt by the one man who's supposed to *not* hurt me! I just ... I can't even!" I throw my right arm in the air at nothing in particular. I can't believe this is happening right now.

"Don't you mean how much can't, can a white girl can't, if a white girl literally couldn't even?"

Grrr! "It's not the time for jokes, T," I clip harshly.

"I know. I'm sorry. I'm just trying to make you laugh. Do you want me to come over? We could eat our feelings and figure this out together?"

"No. I just want to be alone right now. And not just because I'm only a few weeks away from never being physically alone again." I throw my head against the back of the couch and look at the ceiling. I'd give anything to feel numb right now. But I'm hot, sweaty, and feel like an asshole for not growing some balls and actually pressing him to talk to me. All of this could have been avoided. It *should* have been avoided. But our collective inability to actually confront the situation head on has left us in a hot, confused mess.

"Henley, you're two of the most stubborn people I know. And

you're stubbornly in love with each other. You'll get through this."

I'm not sure about that last part. But I certainly hope she's right. "I'll talk to you later," I whisper before turning off my phone, desperate to make my problems disappear.

Chapter Twenty-Four

SPARKLY TASSELS

The carpet in between my fingers is soft and plush.

Slowly, I brush my palms back and forth against the ivory fibers on the floor.

Back and forth. Back and forth. Back and forth.

The touch and cadence are calming.

Being here, in this room, is calming.

Even though this room is void of a crib and the rest of the necessities we need to buy before this kid comes, it's still the most calming place in the whole house.

It won't be calm for long. In the not so distant future, it will be filled with piles of toys and stacks of books and a baby crying to be fed or have its diaper changed.

But right now, it's strangely hopeful and depressing.

And calming.

I look around the empty nursery, and my heart silently breaks into infinite tiny pieces. This child deserves to come barreling into this world and into a family that has their shit together. A mom and dad with an iron clad bond who can—and will— get through anything life throws at them, because they're able to tackle it head on together.

I have no idea how long I sit on the floor.

Minutes, maybe? Hours?

When I finally look up to the doorway. Jeff is there, arms folded, leaning casually against the frame. There's a thin veil of sadness and concern upon his face. He's trying to mask it with a polite smile that doesn't suit him. I'm used to Jeff beaming so brightly that he lights up the whole damn universe. Or, at the very least, *my* universe. As much as I don't want to believe Tara, I can't help but wonder if what she said was really true.

But it just doesn't make any sense.

"What are you doing in here on the floor?" His voice is so soothing it's almost alarming. I wouldn't think anything of it had it not been for Tara.

I take a breath and steady myself. "How was work today, Jeff?" I ask, ignoring his initial question.

He swallows hard, and I can see his Adam's apple hesitate in his throat as shifts his eyes to the window. "Good," he quips. "Same old, same old."

I look at him, eyes pleading, for him to say something, *anything*, to make me believe him. And God, do I *want* to believe him.

"Marty still being an ass?" He and his boss had always struggled with seeing eye to eye. If anything, the mere mention of Marty is enough to send him off on a twenty-minute tangent.

"You could say that." Jeff squeezes the back of his neck and enters the room, taking a seat next to me on the floor. "Did you have a good day?" he asks, shifting the attention to me.

"Mmmm," I hum noncommittally. I know he's trying to avoid the subject. "I talked with Tara earlier."

"Oh? How's she doing?"

I hate how we're making simple pleasantries. It doesn't feel right. It feels like we're strangers. "She's fine. She, um ... She told me something interesting." I look at him out of the corner of my eye, but I'd rather not watch his reaction.

"Like what? Is he the weight of a Chipotle burrito now?"

I sigh, no sense beating around the bush. "No. She told me that you lost your job a few weeks ago." I slowly turn to look him in the eye, and he quickly diverts his gaze. "Which I told her was ridiculous because you were still getting up at six thirty every morning and heading to the office by eight. And that you were back home every night by five thirty. And that there was no way you had lost your job."

Jeff closes his eyes and pinches the bridge of his nose and says nothing. No admittance. No denial.

So I continue.

"But I learned that you unloaded to Cameron about losing your job the same night you came home wasted. You had asked him for the name of the headhunter when he drove your drunk ass home."

"Fucking Cam," he mutters under his breath.

When he finally looks back at me, I nail him with a venomous look. I can tolerate many things in my life, but lies are not one of them. "I've spent the last few weeks internally playing every worst case scenario in my head. I thought you slept with someone else, Jeff!"

"What? No!" He looks at me with pleading eyes. "I never ..." He shakes his head, trying to find the right words to say. The words to make all of this better.

"I know that now," I whisper. "I don't care that you lost your job. I mean ... I *do* care, but it's not the end of the world. I care about the fact you never once even tried to tell me. You lied to me. And that's not okay. Jobs come and go. And if you're not careful, my trust will too."

He closes his eyes and leans his head against the wall.

"Say something ..." I whisper, doing everything I can to keep calm and not letting the overreactive pregnant beast come out to play.

"The company was bought out by a medical software group on the west coast. With the merger, they have nearly triple the number of software engineers they need. More than half the department was let go. Just the directors were kept on board along with two or three other engineers."

I hate the resignation in his voice. It cracks at my already wounded heart. It's hard not to be angry. I get that things happen, things that are completely out of your control come out of the blue and knock you on your ass. But own up to those things, especially when it directly impacts another person.

"Babe, *you* should've been the one to tell me. Not Tara. We're going to have a baby together. We're getting married. We're *family*. If you can't tell me something that big, it scares me that you're not talking to me about the little things that are going on. The healthiest relationships are built on transparency and trust."

"I know!" he snaps back with a voice that's unfamiliar. "I just ... I couldn't. Not right now." He pinches the bridge of his nose tightly before he finally opens his eyes to look at me.

I offer him a small, rueful smile. But I know it does little to console him. "Why?"

"A lot of reasons, I guess. I didn't want to give you another reason to stress out. I didn't want to give you or your family a reason to panic. We're a few short months away from him being born. I mean, what kind of deadbeat dad would I be not having a job to be able to support my new family? I just couldn't live with you being disappointed in me."

It's hard to be angry with him and his honesty. "Sweetie, I could *never* be disappointed in you. The only thing I'm disappointed in is the fact you didn't give me more credit. You've always stressed that we're in this together. That we're a team. Where you walk, I walk, remember?"

His face softens as I repeat his words back to him. "Where you walk, I walk." He laces his fingers between mine and gives my knuckles a soft kiss. "Just so you know, every day when you thought I was at work, I've been busy meeting with recruiters and networking. Some have even led to interviews."

I hum softly to myself, finding reassurance in his hustle.

"But I am sorry, Henley. I'm so, so sorry. I absolutely should have told you right when it happened."

"I know you are. And I understand why you didn't."

It's true. And I'm not one to harbor anger and allow it to fester under the surface. I couldn't stay angry with Jeff for very long, even if I tried. Unless, of course, he truly did reach SHITCON level one. Then all bets are off. Sure, I'm annoyed that he withheld this info from me for so long, but if I have to admit, I'm a little relieved that it wasn't something far worse.

"I promise it won't happen again."

We sit hand-in-hand, wordlessly looking at the empty nursery before us.

"So now what?" Jeff asks.

I push myself to my feet and look down at him with a smile. "Well, the way I see it is we have two choices."

Jeff looks up at me with a curious glint in his eye.

"We can keep on keeping on. I know you're doing everything you can right now to get your feet back on the ground. Me being angry isn't going to rectify the situation any faster."

"And what's the other option?" he asks.

"We can go buy you some blue, sparkly tassels and get you working the street corner. *That* one is my personal favorite," I tease.

He genuinely smiles for what feels like the first time in weeks, and it warms me all over. "Ah! An entrepreneurial approach. I like your spirit." He stands and walks over to my side, wrapping his arm around my shoulder protectively. "Although I'd much prefer to see *you* in those tassels."

"Mm-hmm, I'm sure you would."

I kiss his cheek and casually let my hand graze across the front of his pants, letting it linger just a beat too long against his dick before I walk out of the room.

"Woman," he groans.

I stifle a laugh, loving that even in the toughest of times, I can still elicit this kind of reaction out of him.

Chapter Twenty-Five

NIPPLEGATE

"Henley? Honey?"

"Hey, Mom, what's—"

"Henley Louise? Can you hear me?" she interrupts.

Shit. I pull the phone away from my ear to make sure I didn't accidentally mute the line.

"Yes, Mom. I can hear you." I sigh into the speaker.

"Henley. Was that Jeff I saw on the computer?"

Okay. She's off her technological rocker again. It's not unusual for her to call and ask how to turn on her computer any given day. I suppose it's all part of her charm. But most days it gets old pretty fast.

"Um ... no? I don't think so? Did you try to FaceTime him or something?"

"No, honey. The video. The one on the computer. Mrs. Kensington — you remember Mrs. Kensington, right?"

How could I forget Mrs. Kensington? She's lived across the street from us since I was eleven and she organized the neighborhood ladies euchre league so she could get all the latest gossip. She kept secrets about as well as I keep my legs shut at wedding receptions. So once something was confessed during a rousing Thursday night euchre game, it was only a matter of hours before the whole damn town knew.

"Yeah. I remember Mrs. Kensington. But what does she have to do with Jeff or your computer?"

"Well, dear, if you'd stop interrupting, I could tell you."

I sigh heavily into the phone again. No use in hiding my annoyance. My mom pauses, making sure that I don't have anything else that could possibly interrupt her story.

"Okay ... well, Mrs. Kensington came over this morning with a basket of muffins and some tea." She pauses again, but this time for reasons unknown. If she thinks I'm going to comment on the gesture, she's got another thing coming to her. "So I invited her in, and we got to chatting, and it turns out that she saw a movie on her computer with Jeff. But I told her that Jeff hadn't been in any movies and that she must have him confused with someone else. But you know Mrs. Kensington. She *always* has to be right. And so she brought me to my computer and went to some tube website where the logo is a red tv ... I think it's called Red Tube or something? I can't remember ... and she—"

And that's the precise moment where I don't hear anything else she says. Two seemingly innocent words "red" and "tube" are echoing in the depths of my mind as I have a visual of my mother having a heart attack and falling over in her chair at the sight of her baby girl saving a horse and riding her boyfriend reverse cowgirl style. Once upon a time I jokingly suggested to Jeff that we should record ourselves having sex to see just what our moves looked like. I was drunk. He was drunk. There may have been a good old fashioned blow job while he was playing Mario Kart to set the mood. And then things happened. The kind of things no mother should ever witness their child doing. We were convinced it would be amazingly sexy to watch back at a later time, so we recorded it. Instead, the outcome was more of a comedy of horrors ... or whores. Take your pick because both are entirely applicable in this particular situation.

But the short of it is that video has now ended up on Red Tube, the most infamous amateur porn website, and my mother's nosy neighbor took the liberty of playing it for her.

"Mom! Mom! Stop talking!"

"What, dear?" This time *she's* the one sighing in annoyance.

I squeeze my eyes tight and pinch the bridge of my nose. How do I even broach this subject? This isn't something they teach you how to handle in sex ed class.

Okay ... just rip the bandage off fast.

"Did you say Red Tube?"

She pauses momentarily. "Yes, I *think* that's what it was."

Shit.

I take a deep breath and steel myself for my next question. I'm not sure I want to know, and I would much rather crawl into a hole and die right now. "Mom, why did Mrs. Kensington take you to a porn site?"

My mother gasps audibly and for a moment I think she's fainted or dropped the phone.

"Mom?"

"Henley Louise Carson! I never! What on earth are you talking about? *I'm* not watching pornography! Are *you* watching porn? Oh, Jesus, Mary, and Joseph! I need to pray for your soul."

She starts whispering a Hail Mary underneath her breath, and I quickly realize that I have everything wrong. If our little video experiment ended up on Red Tube, my mother would have shown up on my doorstep and whisked me away to a convent.

"Mom? Mom! Stop that!" And by some miracle she does. I wish she weren't so aloof. I wish she could actually articulate herself and be direct so I know what's *actually* going on here. "Exactly what video are you talking about?"

"If you'd actually *listen* to your mother, you'd know. The

video of Jeff, sweetie. The one on the computer. The one where he's using your breast pump. What on earth was he thinking? That boy is so silly. He can't produce milk. He should have learned all about that in sixth grade. Though I have to admit, it was hilarious watching him try. And oh my heavens, when he started to moo like a cow, I nearly wet my knickers."

Oh.
My.
God.

Ohmygod. Ohmygod. OHMYGOD!

I'm not sure if I should be relieved that it wasn't our sex tape she saw or mortified that my soon-to-be-husband is on the internet proving he's incapable of lactating.

"You saw *that* video? How did you see that video? That video only exists on my phone." The phone that I'm clenching tighter in my hands.

And then I remember ...

I made him keep good on his promise, and we emailed it to his brothers last week.

Those punks must have uploaded it to YouTube.

"I told you. Mrs. Kensington played it for me. Her son thought she'd find it funny, so he sent her an email about it. He's thoughtful like that. *You* never send me emails about things you think are funny."

"That's because nobody sends funny email forwards anymore. It's not 1998, Mom." I shut my eyes so tightly, little bursts of color form behind my eyelids. I'm not sure if I should scream or cry or laugh, but I am one heartbeat away from driving over to my mom's house and ripping her hair out. She is oblivious to the implications of what has been posted online.

"All I'm saying is that it wouldn't kill you to think of your poor mom once in a while. Especially if you've got a funny video to share. Jeff is hilarious. Why weren't you the one to send this to me?"

Because it was never intended for your eyes. It wasn't intended for anyone's eyes. I cannot believe Chris and Kyle posted this online. We all got a good laugh when we sent it their way, but this is low ... even for them.

My mind is running a million miles an hour, and I bolt to the laptop, booting it up as quickly as I can. In the search field I type *man milks himself with breast pump,* and sure enough, Jeff is the first video that pops up. He's clear as day, smiling in all of his shirtless glory with two funnels pressed against his chest. My eyes quickly go to the total number of views.

One million, six hundred forty-three thousand, five hundred ninety-two.

And this was only posted yesterday.

Yesterday!

"Holy fuck nuggets ... My fiancé has gone viral," I whisper underneath my breath. We shared that stupid video with his stupid brothers, and one of them stupidly put it online.

My mom says something about me not speaking profanity, but I don't catch it because I am so focused on the screen in front of me.

After what feels like hours but is probably a few overdramatic seconds, I'm finally capable of forming words. "Um, Mom? I'm gonna have to call you back." I hang up, not even bothering to say good-bye. I will no doubt get an etiquette lesson for that.

Back on the computer, I quickly start scrolling through the countless comments as Jeff's infectious laughter comes through the speakers.

Undeniable proof that nipples on men are pointless!
Dude! You're supposed to put it on your penis!
Looks like someone lost a bet.

Oh man! My husband did this when we had our first child. But he never would have let me watch, let alone record it. Brave man, but I bet he regrets it now.

The comments go on and on and on. And then something peculiar catches my eye, and I pick my phone back up, dial the number, and wait.

"Tara!" I scold.

"Hey, Hen! What's up?" Her voice is casual ... content ... clueless.

"Oh my God, T. Jeff's breast pump video. It's online."

"I know! He's an internet sensation!" Her voice is almost proud.

"How the hell did it get online? Why am I seeing this posted by 98DegreesSupahFan?" Tara has had the same absurd online handle since junior high, refusing to opt for something more mature as she's aged. Anytime you call her out on it, you're met with a resounding proclamation of "98 Degrees for Life!" with a triumphant fist pump in the air.

"Um, because I put it there, *obviously.*"

I take a calming breath and adjust in my seat. "You weren't supposed to show anyone. You weren't supposed to take it. I wasn't supposed to even show you!" My voice is shrill and panicked and fast, and I'm desperate to rewind time and make this all go away.

"I know, but that shit is pure gold. I sent it to myself from your phone so I could show Cameron. How many views is it up to now?"

"Over one point six million." As embarrassing as this whole thing is, that part is pretty impressive.

"No shit? This morning it was just under a million." She's almost bewildered at the power of social media.

"Listen, T. I need you to take it down." If Jeff hasn't seen it yet, it's only a matter of time before he does. Or worse, someone recognizes him and blindsides him with his unknown internet fame.

"Well, I can take it off of YouTube, but it's not going to do you much good."

"What do you mean? You put it up there, you can just take it down."

"I can, but it's already out in the wild. People have saved it. Reposted it. Shared it. A few hours ago I saw it trending over on BuzzFeed. And it made the main page of Reddit. *Reddit!* Can you believe that?"

Holy shit. It's only a matter of time before everyone in the whole world sees this video. He's going to be so pissed at me.

"So this can't be undone? There's *nothing* that we can do?"

"Nope. The internet never forgets. You can't undo Nipplegate. But don't go getting all uptight over it. He's the one who did it to himself, really. Remember? He egged you on to video it because he was '*soooooo secure in his masculinity.*' And now everyone will know just how manly he is." Her statement is almost proud. "Besides, it's like I always say, people in glass houses should never throw orgies."

What? Jesus Christ on a bike, she never makes any sense. I pull the phone away from my ear and let out a blood curling scream, fighting the growing urge to chuck my phone. I can't believe this is happening.

"I'm so mad at you, Tara." I'm in utter disbelief.

"Sweetie, of all the people in the world that this could happen to, Jeff is most likely to take everything in stride. He'll probably find the whole thing hilarious." She's trying to downplay it all.

God, I hope she's right. "I hope so. I need to go and figure out how to break this to Jeff."

"Okay, Hen. But really, it'll be okay. Let me know how it goes?"

When she sees the evening headline of man decapitates pregnant fiancée over milking video she'll know exactly how it went.

"Sure. Whatever," I say, unconvinced that I will actually be talking to her later. But Tara is right about one thing. The internet never forgets.

And unfortunately for her, neither do I.

Me: When do you think you'll be home?

I stare at my phone, willing it to light up with life. I'm not sure exactly how to break it to Jeff that his man boobs are plastered all over the internet to see, but I know I need to tell him before he finds out on his own. With my luck, he'll probably blame me—payback for him not telling me about the job situation. I know I can be cruel at times, but come on, I'm not *that* mean.

Jeff: I'm finishing up with the recruiter right now. Why? Is everything okay? Is the baby coming?

And before I can even respond, my phone lights up with a photo of Jeff and me taken last winter.

"Oh my God, Henley, is it time? I can leave right now and come home. Or wait, should I meet you at the hospital? How far apart are the contractions? Shit! We never packed the hospital bag! You head to the hospital, and I'll come home and grab everything we need." He speaks faster than an auctioneer on speed.

I laugh at this silly, ridiculous man. "No, no, I'm not in labor. Not yet at least. I just wanted to find out what time you'll be home."

He exhales dramatically, and it makes me smile. "Oh, why? What's up?"

"I ... uh..." I fumble over my words. I hadn't quite thought this far ahead when I was playing it through in my mind. Okay. So I panicked and texted him too quickly. I hadn't thought this through *at all*. "I was, um ... I was thinking we should have a talk. Tonight. Whenever you get home."

"Oh, God." His voice goes grave, and I can literally hear him swallowing on the line. "The last time you wanted to have a talk, you told me you were pregnant." I hear the distinct rustling of papers shuffling, and he says something to the recruiter he's working with, but I can't quite make out the words.

"Babe, it's okay. It's nothing, really," I lie, more so for me than for him. "You don't need to come home right now. We can talk about it later tonight."

"I'm halfway to the car already. I'll be there in ten minutes."

Exactly three minutes and forty-five seconds later, he's running through the door, gasping for air. He drops his bag, places his hands on his knees, and takes a few deep breaths while bent over.

"Hey, babe," *gasp*, "what's up?" *Gasp*. "What'd you wanna talk about?"

"Jesus, Jeff, did you sprint home?"

"Well ..." He sucks in a gulp of air and straightens back up to look at me. "When my baby needs me, she needs me, and I come running."

I take a seat on the couch and gently pat the cushion next to me. Jeff slowly moves to take his seat and turns to me, eyes laced with concern. "There's something you should see," I tell him as I open up the laptop in front of us. "And I want you to know that while it wasn't me directly who did this, I accept full responsibility ... and I'm sorry."

I take a deep breath and type the URL for YouTube into the

browser. Just as I'm about to enter "man milks himself with breast pump" into the search bar, Jeff grabs my wrist.

"Holy shit!"

I swallow and look to him and then back to the screen. Sure enough, in the first position under the "Trending" headline, there's a thumbnail of a bare-chested Jeff holding two funnels to his body and mouth wide open in what looks to be an agonizing "O" face.

"That's me!" he shouts proudly. The edges of his lips crinkle in a subtle smile and his eyes narrow as he tries to process exactly what he's witnessing on the screen. Jeff fingers the touch pad and clicks the video open. "Oh my god. Almost two million views since yesterday?" His hand flies to his mouth, covering it as he scrolls through pages and pages of comments.

"And um ... that's not all."

He turns back to me. "It's not?"

I shake my head. "It's made its way through Reddit. Buzz-Feed. Facebook. All of the usual social suspects."

He stifles laughter, and his cheeks puff out like the cat that ate the goddamned canary. There's a moment of recognition on his face. "So *that's* why the girl at the bakery looked at me funny and then moo'ed."

All I can do is shake my head in disbelief at how well he's taking this entire scenario.

"I'm going to kill my brothers." His tone is playful, but his face is strangely cold. I'm pretty sure he's only half kidding right now.

"About that ..." My voice squeaks. "It wasn't them."

"Well, if it wasn't them, and you didn't do it, then how'd it end up on YouTube's greatest hits?"

I look at my hands that are knotted clumsily in my lap and flash my eyes up to him sweetly. I gently push my swollen boobs together with my upper arms and lean over slightly, giving him a good view of the ladies busting out of my shirt. A little skin never hurt an apology.

"I'm sorry!" I whine, batting my lashes and trying to appear all cute and innocent when we both know I am anything but. "I showed Tara the other day when we were out shopping, and the next thing I know my mom is calling to ask how you ended up inside of her computer. Tara texted the video to herself and took it upon herself to unleash it to the masses. Had I known she was going to do that, I never would have shown her. This isn't some revenge video, I swear."

I feel the tears starting to build inside, and my lip quivers as I try to keep my shit together. This whole spontaneous pregnant melt down thing is *really* starting to piss me off.

Jeff's eyes go from mine, straight down to my chest where they linger for just a beat too long and then back up to my face. Silent tears begin to fall, and I know there's not enough gratuitous boobage in the world to make up for launching this video into the wilds of the internet.

"It's okay," he says softly, and he cups his palm to my cheek.

I sniffle and blink away a few tears. "Wha ... What'd you say?"

Jeff shifts in his seat so he's facing me head on. "Henley, it's okay. Seriously. I'm not mad."

What? Is this some kind of joke? "You're not angry?"

"No." He reassures me and leans over to kiss me sweetly, but I can't kiss him back. Because frankly, part of me wishes he *were* mad. He deserves to be mad at me. I don't want him harboring these emotions only to grow to resent me later.

"You should be," I mumble when he breaks my half-assed kiss.

"Why? You didn't do this deliberately. It was all out of your hands, right?"

I nod then swallow hard, speaking to the obvious issue in the room. "But don't you think this could bite you in the ass with your job search? It's not like that video is the most professional thing you've ever done."

I can see the cogs moving in his head for a fleeting moment, but he shakes it off. "You know what? It's really no big deal. If any prospective company sees that and wants to hold it against me, then that's not the right company for me."

I'm not convinced that's the right mentality, but who am I to argue? Tara was right. He really is taking this in stride. I'm kind of impressed.

Jeff's phone chirps and I instantly recognize the ringtone for his older brother, Kyle. He rolls his eyes as the incoming message, then flashes it toward me.

Kyle: Nice work, jackass.

Attached to Kyle's message is a screen shot of Jeff with the breast pump funnels against his body and the caption "GOT MILK?" in bold white letters across the bottom.

I choke back a laugh and place my hand on his knee. "You sure you're okay with all of this?" I ask softly as I close my eyes.

He turns his phone off and tosses it onto the coffee table, then leans back into the couch and stretches his arm around me, pulling me close under his arm. "Yeah, I always thought it'd be cool to become one of those meme things."

I curl up into his body as much as my pregnant body will let me and close my eyes, thankful for his level-headedness.

Chapter Twenty-Six

IS THIS REAL LIFE?

"Good God, I am so freaking uncomfortable right now!" I exclaim as I walk out of the bathroom for the umpteenth time today. I am convinced that the larger my belly grows, my bladder shrinks in direct proportion.

"Would you rather have to sit on an egg for nine months?" Jeff asks as I sit back down on the couch next to him.

Some days I don't think that'd be so bad. Though an elephant would easily be the worst. They're pregnant for close to two years and birth a baby weighing upwards of two hundred and fifty pounds. I may be in my third trimester, but it feels like I've been knocked up for the better part of a century.

"You know, sitting on an egg sure as hell beats the stretch mark alternative."

"Nonsense. Your stretch marks are beautiful. And they make you even more beautiful to me. They're evidence that you're carrying life in there, and that's a fucking miracle, so I wouldn't trade them for the world."

My heart swells, and he nuzzles his nose against mine. It's so sweet it gives me a toothache. Jeff's phone vibrates against the coffee table in obnoxious fanfare, and we jump apart, startled by the sound. He takes a look and shrugs at the number.

"I have no idea who that is. It's probably a telemarketer or something." He hits the reject button and cozies back into the couch with me.

Almost instantly, it lights up again.

Same number.

"Someone's persistent." He rejects the call once again.

"Is that your secret wife calling to tell you she's pregnant and she knows about the affair, but it doesn't matter because she's going to leave your ass and take your inheritance, your car, and your razor because every woman knows a men's razor is superior?"

"What? No! Why would you even say a ridiculous thing like that?"

I shrug. "I blame my overactive imagination ever since you knocked me up."

"That so?"

"Nah. I actually read about that in a book last year. It fucked me up pretty good. Made me doubt everything about relationships in general."

"Maybe you should stop reading?" He nudges my shoulder playfully, knowing that wouldn't happen.

"Yeah well, reading leads to knowledge. Knowledge leads to power. Minute after minute. Hour after hour."

He pulls back abruptly and looks at me bewildered. "Did you just quote Coolio? Gangster's Paradise?"

All I can do is smile. For years it was my go to karaoke jam.

"I love you more now than I did fifteen seconds ago." Jeff softly tugs my chin upward toward him and ever so gently presses his lips against mine. His touch feels so damn good. My mind drifts off to all of the deliciously inappropriate things I *want* to be doing right now, and just as I make the conscious decision to walk my fingertips up his inner thigh, the damn phone rings *again*.

We both groan in frustration and glare at his phone. His stupid, interrupting phone. And then I look more closely at the number. "323? Isn't that a west coast phone area code?"

"I'm not sure. Maybe?"

A moment of recognition strikes. My freshman year college roommate had this area code. "No, it is. That's Los Angeles."

"But I don't know anyone in L.A."

I wrack my brain trying to think of any potential link between California and us. "Didn't you say the firm that bought out your company was from L.A.?"

"Hmmm, do you think it's them calling? What if they want me to come back? What if they want to extend an offer?"

"I don't know..." I go wide eyed. I know he's been struggling to find work again. "But there's only one way to fix out. Answer it." I crack my knuckles anxiously. This could be the answer we've been looking for. I know the job search hasn't been easy for him, but if it's his former company, I know he'd go back in a heartbeat.

Jeff answers the phone with a solemn look plastered on his face. He's gone into business mode. "Hello? ... Yes, this is Jeff." He shoots me a peculiar look and excuses himself to the next room over. I lean toward the hallway to try and hear part of the one-sided conversation. "Yes, that's me. ... Um, I suppose it was a few weeks ago. ... Wow, really? ... Yeah, sure. I'd have to talk with Henley, but I don't see why not ... Yes, that's her name ... in October ... Yes, I do have one."

And then he must have walked toward the back of the house because all I can make out are a series of "Mhmms" and "Yeses." A few minutes later, he re-emerges with a coy smile playing at his lips but says nothing.

"Well? You got a job offer?" I cringe at the fact that my voice is a little too hopeful.

"No, not exactly." He knits his brows together. "That was actually *The Late Night Buzz*. You know, the TV show hosted by that up and coming comedian, Bryan Albertson? He's the guy who plays pranks on unsuspecting shoppers on Rodeo Drive. And that little video you took made its way to one of the producers and ..." His voice trails off, and he laughs, seemingly in disbelief. "They want to do an interview with us on the show."

Oh fuck. "For real?"

He smiles, more amused by the entire situation than I am. I'd much prefer to pack up, change our names, and move to a foreign country. Or maybe dye my hair (after the baby arrives, of course) and find a way to get in on the witness protection program. I've always felt I looked more like a Maggie than a Henley. But this video has already taken a few trips around the sun, and there's no escaping it now.

"For real. They want to talk with us over Skype."

Us?

My stomach twists in anticipation. "When?"

"Tomorrow. The show is live, but our segment would be pre-recorded. She said it'll take less than a half hour. They'll record the conversation and edit before it goes on the air. Oh, and she also asked if we could send the original video file from your phone to them by the morning."

Jeff hands me a slip of paper with an email address on it and sits back down next to me on the couch as I process everything. I'm not sure if this is a blessing or a curse. I'm not one for attention, especially when it's coming from strangers, let alone on the national scale. We will, no doubt, be the epicenter of countless jokes and internet memes.

"You know they're going to show the clip, right? Thousands— no *millions*—of people will see you trying to milk yourself on national television! Do you really think this is a smart idea considering you're looking for a job right now?"

He turns toward me and takes my hands in his. "Babe, millions of people have already seen it. Any damage has likely already been done. And who knows, maybe this will give me the stage to go on and clear the air? Give the video some context?"

"And what context is that exactly?" I cock my brow, challenging him.

"I'm not sure. But I've got about twenty-four hours to figure that out."

Jeff leans over and gives me a quick peck on the lips before heading out of the room. I'm glad that he's able to take this whole debacle in stride, but I wish I could be just as nonchalant about it. Because if I appear on-air alongside him, I will forever be known as the woman whose husband tried to milk himself.

"YOU LOOK TIRED TODAY, babe. Did my little linebacker keep you up all night?" He smiles at me adoringly as he places his palm against my stomach.

Normally when someone says you look tired, it's code for why the hell do you look like such shit? But I suppose pregnancy and all of the glamorous side effects that come with it actually *do* make you legitimately tired all of the damn time. The comment should annoy me, but with the sweet way he asks, all is forgiven.

Jeff stretches over my growing belly and gives me a deep, toe-curling kiss before I can respond. His tongue slips past my lips, and I softly moan into his mouth. His touch is so damn inviting and he tastes so damn good. I'm about two point five seconds away from stripping down and making a man out of him.

Ever since I hit the third trimester, it feels like I have two settings: one — hornier than a three-peckered prairie dog all doped up on Viagra; and two — so repulsed I'd rather dig my own eyeballs out with a spork than touch him. There is no middle ground. But fortunately for him and his libido, I've recently been wavering more on the former.

I force myself to break the kiss before I get into trouble. There's only so much time before this Skype call, and if I look as tired as he says, I need to spend a few extra minutes (okay, hours) getting ready.

"Well, I *am* a little exhausted today. I got up in the middle of the night to pee and get a glass of water. And then I accidentally ate the leftover pizza that was in the fridge. And then I made some brownies because I was stressed about the fact that the one piece of baby furniture we own is the rocker from Tara. This kid will be here before we know it and we don't even have a crib yet."

"So *that's* what happened to the pizza."

I nudge his arm and retreat to the bathroom to get ready. Two hours and one empty hot water heater later, I emerge from our bathroom looking and feeling like a brand new woman. It's amazing what a curling iron, a little concealer, and some mascara can do.

Much to our surprise, the whole process actually did take less than twenty minutes.

First, we tested the internet connection with a tiny blonde producer, the same gal Jeff spoke with yesterday. Then she ran us through a list of potential questions we'd be asked during the segment: What possessed you to do something so *udderly* ridiculous (and yes, she really did say udderly)? Were you under the influence when you discovered the breast pump? What other baby products have you taken for a test drive? If Henley asked, would you willingly hook yourself up to a machine that made you experience the pain of contractions? And, of course, what did I make of my fiance's new found internet fame?

I was secretly thankful that there was only one planned question for me. I was nervous enough as it was, I didn't need more questions circling my head. But even if we managed to goof up when we were recording, she assured us they would handle it all in editing.

She made Jeff change out of his striped shirt into a solid cobalt pullover because, and I quote, "Stripes will make everyone's TV screens vibrate. Blue is calming and attractive. People will be more likely to relate with you if you're in blue." Apparently, my blush pink blouse would be just fine. I'm still not sure what she meant by the television vibrating, but whatever.

Before it was officially time for the interview, Jeff massaged my neck and shoulders. It all did little to ease the nerves brewing in my stomach. At least I thought they were nerves. At this rate, it could have been gas from the Mexican I had at lunch. You don't realize just how awkward it is to sit in front of your laptop, fake smiling like a jackass, waiting for a Skype interview to begin. For all I know, they're recording me right now for some weird blooper reel.

I shouldn't be nervous, but I am.

Bryan Albertson's face fills the screen, and he's just as handsome on my computer as he is on my TV with his perfectly coiffed hair and million dollar smile. Someone should really hire him for a toothpaste commercial.

"Hey guys, thanks for jumping on with me on such short notice. We'll get going here in just a moment," he says, making small talk.

I just sit there staring like a jackass, permagrin etched to my face. Bryan Albertson is in my living room. *Kind of.* Would it be wildly inappropriate if I whip out my cell phone and take a selfie with his face on the screen?

Bryan looks off camera, smiling and nodding to someone we can't see, so I do what any self-respecting woman with a Hollywood crush would do. I turn so my back is to the computer screen, extend my arm and quickly take a series of selfies with

Bryan in the background, complete with bright eyes and a pouty smile.

"Uh, did you get what you were looking for?" a voice from the computer asks.

"Oh! Sorry, I just ..." I trail off without any legitimate excuse.

"It's okay. You got my good side," Bryan jokes.

A few moments later, Jeff returns to the table and sits down next to me, kissing me quickly on the temple. "You ready?" he whispers into my hair.

"About as ready as I'll ever be," I say with an unconvincing sigh. I'm still not convinced going on late night TV is the right move, but Jeff was excited and adamant about it.

When we turn our attention back to the computer screen, Bryan Albertson is waiting for us expectantly. He raises his eyebrows at us, and Jeff gives him an awkward wave of his hand.

"This should be pretty laid back. I'll give a quick intro, and we'll dive right into the questions. After we end our segment, we're going to cut to a commercial, but we'll use your video as the segue. As my producer mentioned, don't worry if you screw anything up or drop a few f-bombs as we'll take care of that in editing before it airs tonight. Sound good?"

Jeff and I both nod, starstruck by the entire situation. *Is this real life?*

"Loosen up, you kids! This is supposed to be fun." We watch as Bryan stretches his neck to the left and then the right before rolling his shoulders. "Here's how it's gonna go. I'll do a quick intro, ask a few questions, yaddy, yaddy, yadda, and we'll peace out. Sound good?"

"Yep! Sounds good," Jeff affirms with a nod, but I'm caught up on the fact that this grown man just said, "Yaddy, yaddy, yadda."

A few minutes later, we hear the voice of a producer off of the screen, and everything begins. "So we've got the latest internet sensation, Jeff Carrington and his fiancée, Henley, here with us on *The Late Night Buzz*. Unless you've been living under a rock, you've probably seen the video that everyone has dubbed 'The Milkman Cometh.' For those of you who *haven't* seen it, Jeff here experiments with some of Henley's new mom hardware to the point where it sounds like he's having an orgasm. Be sure to stick around as we'll be playing it for you at the end of the segment."

Jeff grimaces, and I snicker politely. I don't know who started calling him The Milkman, but it's damn near genius.

"Hi, Jeff, hi, Henley, thanks so much for joining us this evening."

I have to admit, this guy is good. It's amazing how he just comes to life when he knows the cameras are filming.

"Thanks so much for having us, Bryan," Jeff chirps as we wave in unison.

"It takes a special kind of man to attach his bare nipples to what looks—and sounds—like an archaic S&M torture device. No offense, Henley. So tell us, Jeff, where did you get such a bizarre idea?"

Jeff shifts in his chair, and I know it's the question he's been anticipating. And one that he likely still has no answer for. "You know? It was one of those things where I can't even explain where the idea came from. Henley had a baby shower earlier that day and was pulling apart the pieces of the ..." Jeff stalls, unsure of what to say, so instead he takes his hands and mimics like he's cupping a pair of imaginary breasts on his own chest. "pump to get it clean."

"Jeff, it's okay. You can say breasts on national TV," Bryan reassures him. I can't help but laugh. My fiance's face turns red, and he nods. "But based on that gesture, I'd venture to say you're one of those guys who would stay in bed and play with yourself all day if you woke up one morning as a woman."

"And you wouldn't?" Jeff banters back and Bryan laughs. My

cheeks are starting to hurt from smiling, and I have a feeling that my face is contorting into some awkward, forced half smile that would scare away little kids.

"Fair point. I probably would. But I gotta ask why? What would possess you to hook yourself up to your fiancee's breast pump? Were you trying to see if you could produce milk?"

I can see the heat rising in Jeff's face as his cheeks flush crimson. We both knew this question was coming and I'm not sure he knows how he's going to answer it.

Jeff pauses thoughtfully and looks from the screen to me and then back again. He squeezes my hand out of view.

"No, I wasn't trying to milk myself or anything weird like that. First and foremost, Henley was having a rough day, and I wanted nothing more than to make her smile and try to get her to laugh." He nails me with a look of sincerity, and my heart swells inside my chest. I lean over to give him a quick peck on the cheek before he continues.

"But she had just had her baby shower, and our home was taken over by all these baby items. And, with good reason, none of them are really intended for me as a dad. Everything is for Henley and our son."

"Oh! It's a boy! Congratulations," Bryan chimes. I simply shake my head, and Jeff beams proudly.

"Thanks, Bryan. I guess part of me was always a little bit jealous. As a dad-to-be, you feel like you're standing on the sidelines the entire pregnancy. You're a part of it, but beyond the initial participation in getting pregnant in the first place, you aren't a major player. I'm merely playing a supporting role, and I want to be there for Henley in every way imaginable. I guess part of me thinks for me to be able to accomplish this whole heartedly, I need to say that I've experienced at least some of what she's experiencing. And if that means hooking myself up to a breast pump, then so be it!"

I melt.

A school girl crush grin covers my face, and I feel him reach for my hand and give it a squeeze. He's being totally genuine right now. And I love him even more than I did moments ago.

"I get what you mean. I'm a dad, too. And maybe it's my morbid curiosity, but I always wanted to know what a contraction felt like. Is this legit pain? Or are you just milking this pregnancy thing for all its worth?" Bryan jokes.

I snort.

"Now, I gotta hand it to you, man, that was a bold move allowing Henley to record the whole thing. Whose idea was that?"

Jeff looks to me, and just as he's about to place the blame, I intercept the question. "Actually, Bryan, Jeff wanted to prove his manliness to his brothers. So he told me to record it and then promised I could send it to his family. He totally brought it upon himself."

"So *that's* how the video leaked?"

I laugh. "No, my best friend Tara is purely responsible for Jeff's newfound fame. I made the mistake of showing her the video, and the next thing we know, it's on the front page of Buzz-Feed, Reddit and trending on Facebook."

"She means *former* best friend," Jeff interjects, and I playfully shove his shoulder. It's a good thing Jeff knows my sisters before misters and chicks before dicks policy.

Bryan snickers and shakes his head imperceptibly. "Well, me and the entire crew here at *The Late Night Buzz* were so enamored with your antics, we shared your video with our friends over at Baby Bungalow, the nation's leading baby superstore. They loved your humor so much that they wanted to give you ten thousand dollars to go toward all of your baby needs."

Bryan steps back further into the frame and flashes an oversized check at his computer screen. Sure enough, our names are on the "to" line, and a one followed by four zeros is written meticulously in the dollar amount.

"Holy turdburglers!" cries Jeff. "Do you know how much porn you could buy with that much money?"

Bryan Albertson laughs. "Actually yes, I do, but I'm not sure they sell adult videos at Baby Bungalow since you're shopping there *because* of what happens in those movies."

I'm stunned speechless as relief washes over me. Ten thousand dollars is a fuck ton of money. We'll be able to finally buy our nursery furniture and a truckload of diapers and more tiny clothes than we could ever possibly need. Thanks to this, we can actually breathe until Jeff lands a new job.

My hands fly to my mouth, and the hormones take over. I don't just lose it. I completely meltdown into a stereotypical inconsolable pregnant woman.

Jeff rubs my shoulders. "We can't even begin to thank you enough," Jeff speaks.

"Well, it's truly our pleasure, and congratulations to you both. Now, before we say goodbye, could you do one last thing for me, Jeff?"

Home boy better comply with the man who is giving us ten grand. I squeeze his hand tightly, telepathically telling him to do whatever Bryan asks of him. I don't care if it involves shaving his eyebrows, he's doing it.

"Sure! What's that?"

"Send us out to commercial with your signature milkman moo."

And without missing a beat, I become the woman whose fiancé moos on national television.

Chapter Twenty-Seven

TWATSICLES

"I hope you don't mind, but I took the liberty of making you a postpartum emergency kit." She walks past me and sets the brown paper bag down on the counter.

I smile at my best friend, suddenly feeling inadequate. When she gave birth to triplets all I brought her was a casserole and a jumbo box of diapers. I'm still a handful of weeks away from my due date, and this broad has come bearing gifts every time she's visited. Tara is spoiling me rotten. Or maybe I'm just a shitty friend? I'll just chalk it up to being childless and clueless. Tara's a pro at this momming stuff, so I'll listen to everything she tells me. Well, *almost* everything she tells me.

"That's really sweet of you, T! You didn't need to do that." I don't bother fighting my smile.

"Stop that. Of course I did. Lord knows your mother is probably worthless with the *real* stuff. And as your very bestest friend in the whole universe, it is my moral obligation to make sure you are more than prepared for all the shit that's about to throw down *down there.*" She waggles her eyebrows and shoots a look down toward my nether regions.

"Okay, I thought I was prepared after the baby shower. What else could I possibly need, oh wise one? Lay it on me." I hoist my ass and my belly up onto a bar stool at the island and hold onto the edge of the counter to keep from tipping over. The last thing anyone needs is for Humpty Dumpty to have a great fall right now.

"For starters this." She tosses me a bottle of dry shampoo. "You'll be lucky if you're able to shower. And for the days that you don't, dry shampoo will help. But when you *do* get ninety-four seconds of peace and quiet to jump in super fast, don't make the water too hot. You'll start spraying yourself."

Spraying myself? What the ...?

She must catch the look of confusion on my face. "Your boobs. You'll start spraying all over the place like one of those wacky kid's water toys that look like an octopus and shoots water thirty different directions. And that shit is liquid gold. Don't make the water too hot because you don't want to waste it down the drain."

I nod my head firmly, slightly mortified that this is a thing women have to deal with, but admittedly excited that I might be able to put out a small fire using only my boobs. "No hot water. Got it."

"And no matter what Jeff says, him tasting your breast milk isn't kinky. It's disgusting. If you're going to be doing any fifty shades shit, make it the fun kind of kink. Trust me—Cam learned the hard way."

I cringe, willing her sage advice to my long-term memory and trying to erase the thought of Cam indulging in a cocktail courtesy of my best friend's boobs.

"Okay, next we have seasons one through ten of Friends on DVD. All that baby is going to do is sleep the first six weeks. You'll be bored out of your gourd because you're not supposed to wake a sleeping baby and all those other clichés about motherhood. But you will quickly learn that non-baby responsibilities are overrated, and you can milk visiting family into doing all that crap like laundry and dishes for you, at least the first couple of weeks. And selfishly, I need you to have a refresher course in all things Friends because once your ass can drink again, we're going to dominate the Friends trivia night down at our old watering hole. So these are on loan. I want them back. Don't even think about keeping them, woman."

I smile. She knows me too well. But I really want her to rewind and explain a little bit more on how I can convince family members into becoming my short-term personal maid.

"And when you don't feel like watching television, you can always read."

She pulls out a stack of books. I recognize a few from our defunct book club where we never actually read the books, but instead drank wine and gossiped. As I scan the titles, I see a couple of light romances by some indie authors, but the vast majority are erotica. And if there's anything I *don't* read, it's erotica. It's not that I'm stuck up or anything. I just can't get through the absurd alpha dirty talk and impossible sex positions without turning cherry red and choking on fits of laughter. Seriously. How many times have *you* ever had an explosive orgasm at the exact same time as your billionaire boyfriend?

That's what I thought.

"I know these aren't all your cup of tea, but don't judge. You're going to be starved and sexless for weeks—maybe even months! And I can promise that while you will have zero interest in riding the train to pound town in the beginning, reading about it will suffice and at least give you sexy thoughts during this inevitable drought."

"Fine," I lie. "I'll give the books a chance. But I can't promise I'll actually enjoy them." *Yeah. Sooooo not reading them.*

"I bet if you asked Jeff to do a dramatic reading of this one, not only would you get all hot and bothered, you might actually enjoy it." She places a sleek, black paperback in my hands. On the cover is a white flower where the petals are turning to liquid at the tips. It's gorgeous. "Careful, bitch. That one's signed."

I nod, perusing the back cover before placing it down on the coffee table. I think she's right. I just might enjoy this one.

"And finally, I brought everything you need for twatsicles."

I choke on her words. "Excuse me?" I ask once the coughing finally subsides.

"Twatsicles. Surely I told you about the world's greatest postpartum secret, didn't I?"

"Um, you've told me about a lot of things over the past few months, but twatsicles wasn't one of them. Trust me, with a name like that I would have remembered."

She reaches into another shopping bag and pulls out an economy size package of ultra super thick supreme absorbency "these suckers could stop a flash flood" maxi pads and a bottle of store brand witch hazel. Tara rummages through my kitchen drawer and pulls out a measuring cup. She tears open the package of maxi pads that could probably double as a diaper for this baby in a pinch and opens one up on the counter. Next, she carefully measures out a half cup of witch hazel and pours it over the maxi pad.

I blink at her wordlessly. "Usually in the commercials, the liquid in these experiments is blue. Just saying."

"Yeah, I never understood that." She shrugs nonchalantly. "Either way, this isn't an experiment. All you do is pop this puppy in the freezer, and when things start throbbing—because *things will* start throbbing and *not* in a good way—you just slip this in your panties and have yourself a twatsicle. It'll soothe everything and surprisingly bring you a lot of relief."

This girl never ceases to amaze me.

"Sounds cold." I'm not sure what I was expecting a twatsicle to be, but this surely wasn't it.

"It is. Don't mock it till you try it. Your vagina can thank me later."

I take a mental note to hide this magical maxi pad in the back of the freezer to avoid scarring Jeff for life when he goes to grab ice.

"So, you're what — two, three weeks from your due date? Is everything all set?"

"Yes, by some miracle, everything is in order. We were finally able to buy our furniture thanks to The Late Night Buzz. All the tiny clothes have been washed and put away, and the house is as clean as it's going to get. We're pre-registered at the hospital, so the only thing missing is this kiddo." Even though Tara is indirectly the reason we were bestowed with the nursery makeover, I still haven't forgiven her for that stunt she pulled.

"And everything *down there*? It's primed and ready to go?" She points her finger in the general vicinity of my nether regions and raises an eyebrow.

"Um, yeah?" I'm almost afraid to ask.

"Good. Because between the blood and fluids already going on, no doctor also wants to be elbow deep in fur."

Gross. I shake my head at the mental image and shift in my seat. "I'm sure my OB won't give a damn either way." I shrug, trying to brush off the subject.

"Oh, come on. It's common courtesy. You should get a Brazilian blowout before it's too late. Lord knows you can't see anything south of the equator even if you wanted to trim and keep things tidy."

I divert my eyes to the other side of the room trying to remember the last time I even attempted to take care of *things*. Jeff hasn't complained, and frankly, ignorance is bliss. Besides, I've never been one to tolerate the pain of waxing. The one time I had it done back in college, I jumped so I high I grabbed the ceiling tiles as an earsplitting Michael Jackson "Ow!" escaped my lips.

"Based on the disgust drawn all over your face, this is news to you. I'm going to call and make an appointment for tomorrow. We'll grab lunch, run some errands, and get you some new hardwood floors."

"That's okay. You don't have to do that, Tara. Really." I know my effort is futile. Once she sets her mind on something, we're all just along for the ride.

"Nonsense. And don't even think about the pain. It'll pale in comparison to childbirth. Think of it as your pre-birth warm up."

Oh, God. I completely forgot about the white hot searing pain that comes with hair follicles being yanked from one of the most sensitive spots on the body. It took me months to block the memory of the one and only time I got waxed. There is no way in hell she's taking me to get waxed again tomorrow. Besides, I'd probably end up peeing all over the table.

"*Anyway,*" I emphasize, trying to change the subject. Everyone is so keen on talking about my vagina these days, I've nearly become immune to it, but I'm still trying to lose the visual she just created for me. "I've been so preoccupied with getting everything together for the baby, I don't think I told you Jeff got a job offer. *Two* job offers, actually."

"Really? That's so awesome. I knew he'd land back on his feet quickly."

"Well, his newfound fame from that little viral video stunt you pulled came in handy."

I watch as her jaw drops and the corners of her lips curl up in a subtle, wicked smile. "Shut up. No way."

"Yeah," I say, still in disbelief. "Apparently the gal who came across his resume in Human Resources recognized the name from TV and thought he was hilarious. She put him at the top of the candidate pool once she saw his work credentials, and the team loved Jeff during the interview process."

"What's not to love about Jeff?"

I can think of a few things. Like his inability to put dirty underwear in the basket instead of on the floor next to the hamper, or how he leaves soda cans upside down in the sink rather than toss them out, but I bite my tongue because Lord knows I'm not perfect either. But still, I love him because of his flaws, *and* in spite of them.

"Absolutely nothing. He's perfect. He's my lobster." I beam, referencing one of my favorite lines from Friends.

"The One with the Prom Video," Tara exclaims triumphantly. "Season two, episode fourteen."

I cock an eyebrow, unsure if I should be impressed or intimidated.

"Oh, come on. You didn't know that?"

I shake my head.

She puts her fist on her side and cocks her hip with attitude. "On second thought, if we want to have any chance of winning trivia night, I should probably draft you up the season by season CliffNotes for Friends."

Chapter Twenty-Eight

CLEAN UP IN AISLE TWO

"When you invited me out for lunch, this was not what I had in mind."

I carefully climb down from the front seat of Tara's SUV and place my hands on my hips, trying to stretch out my back. I look up at the towering warehouse above me, and my eyes narrow in on the oversized Costco sign.

"Oh, quit complaining. We're killing two birds with one stone. *Your* cute pregnant ass couldn't make up its mind about what it wanted to eat, and *I* needed to get some shopping done for the monster squad. Costco has food samples in nearly every aisle. It's a win for both of us. Then, when we're done, we'll head over to the Beehive Salon to wax that Bieber of yours."

I smile at her monster squad comment and ignore the rest. She knows just how much I hate calling the female lady bits a beaver, so she's grown akin to calling it a Bieber. Fitting since both are hairy little pussies.

Tara's triplet boys are in their ferocious fours and tear everything apart. Literally everything. Last week I walked in and found the inside fluff of her couch cushions scattered across the floor like a giant cloud because of a game of 'Hot and Cold' gone wrong. The small dinosaur figurine was hidden underneath the couch and not inside the back pillow like Jack had assumed. Tara has had many babysitters quit on her after one night because they can't keep up with the F5 tornado that is Jack, Miles, and Wes. Mini monsters, they most certainly are, and it makes me excited about having a monster squad of my own with Jeff.

Just not three.

And not all at once.

Tara and I eat our way through Costco, stopping at nearly every single sample station for a taste. It's surprisingly more fun than it sounds and they have a killer selection. The fried macaroni and cheese balls in the frozen food section have been my favorite, hands down—though I would *never* admit that to her.

My nose curls up when I sample some spinach artichoke dip that was secretly laced with habanero peppers. No doubt this kiddo will make me pay for that later.

"Quit making that face, Henley. This isn't *that* bad."

"What do you have against sit-down dining? When you sold me on a girl's day out, parading around the aisles searching for bulk toilet paper and a bag of one hundred forty-four count nuggets isn't at all what I had in mind."

"Oh, come on, where else can you taste chicken fingers, cheese spread, fruit snacks, and a Swedish meatball all in the same meal?"

I love how she keeps reiterating this whole extravaganza like it's fine dining. "Um, I dunno, any middle school cafeteria in the Kansas City metropolitan area?"

"Touche."

This is what I get for having a *free lunch on her*. I really should know better by now. This is hardly lunch, and there is certainly nothing free about this experience. Judging by the contents of my cart, I probably have two hundred dollars worth of impulse food purchases here, most of which is in the form of fifteen different kinds of cookies. I really shouldn't be shopping on a mostly empty stomach.

We make our way through a few more aisles in silence, pausing to toss in random basics like a gallon of mayonnaise and a jar of taco seasoning the size of my head. Whatever she plans on making with the contents of her cart, I definitely want to steer clear from.

"So how are things going with you and Cameron? I can only imagine how little time you two actually get to spend together with the boys running around all over the place."

"Oh, you know. It's the same old, same old. We've mastered the art of the five-minute quickie in the laundry room while the kids fight over their toys. It's super romantic." Tara grins. I know she's happy and wouldn't change a thing, but I can't even imagine the chaos that is her life now.

"But I don't want to talk about me today. Tell me what's going on with you and Jeff. I'm really happy you found each other, and that things are working out better than you imagined. He's a really good guy, Hen. I mean ... shit. Imagine what your life would be like if you married that muscle-clad, limp dick, Tommy? Or Charlie? Or what's his name? That tall drink of water with the thick-rimmed glasses? Ever wonder what happened to those guys?" She grabs a sample taste of a buffalo chicken egg roll as we walk.

"Not really. But I'm pretty certain Tommy turned out gay, and I'm sure that's somehow my fault. Charlie was too busy getting high to get a real job and has probably entered some hippie compound where he's busy fashioning organic bongs out of cow shit. And that tall, four-eyed drink of water? His name was Leo. And he was a Grade A cheese dick."

Tara whips her head toward me so fast I'm pretty sure it's going to snap off her neck. "Oh my gosh, Henley. Could you imagine having a dick literally made of cheese? Holy shit! That would be amazing. I might actually enjoy giving blow jobs for once. Hey — if Jeff had a dick made of cheese, you probably wouldn't be harboring a bat up there in your bat cave." She grabs a bag of string cheese and tosses it into the cart making a phallic and inappropriate gesture. Her expression suddenly turns serious, and she tilts her head like she's about to say something thought-provoking.

"You know, whoever came up with the phrase 'it is far better to give than it is to receive' clearly wasn't talking about blow jobs."

Good point. Though I've never really minded them much. "Where do you come up with this shit?"

Tara shrugs and goes back to her previous thought. "I forgot his name was Leo. He headed out west for med school after breaking your heart, right?"

"First of all, he didn't break my heart. He was just my greatest disappointment in spite of his supreme douchebaggery." I give her a pointed look, trying to push his memory from my mind. After he took my virginity, he grew accustomed to calling me Fire Crotch, like it was a shock that my carpet matched my drapes, and I became so self-conscious that I didn't sleep with another man until Jeff. Dating Leo was not one of my finer moments.

"But yeah, I think he ended up at UCLA. Orthopedic surgeon or podiatrist or something."

"Huh," Tara grunts as she hoists a bag of Swedish meatballs roughly the size of Montana into the cart. "You know, that idiot simply couldn't see how incredible you were. Anyone that blind to your awesomeness probably gets off with braille porn pictures."

"Is that even a thing?" I double over in laughter at the sheer stupidity of her last comment. I could totally see Leo finding amusement (and orgasms) in something like that.

"I don't know, but it should be."

I freeze mid-step, gripping the handlebar of my shopping cart until my knuckles turn white. "Oh my God."

"What?" Tara whips around then piles on an oversized bag of mixed greens on top of her ever-growing pile of bulk food.

"I ... I think I just peed myself."

Tara fights a smile and cocks an eyebrow at me. "Don't stress about it. All pregnant women pee their pants when they laugh. You get a child. You get some incontinence. Hardly a fair trade if you ask me."

"Stop it. I'm being serious." I wave her off, needing just a moment of space as I try to discreetly assess the damage. "Okay, I think I'm okay."

After a few more steps, what I thought was a little trickle of pee turns into a massive gush that is usually reserved for Hollywood rom-com flicks and overdramatic junior high sex-ed videos to scare you into abstinence.

"Henley, that's not pee. I think your water just broke."

I stand stunned and speechless in the middle of the produce aisle. "Oh ... my ... God ..." My voice is scarily calm, but my insides are running rampant. "What do I do?"

"Um, what do you think we do? You're about to have a baby! We go to the hospital." Tara abandons her cart and grabs my elbow, trying to pull me away from the scene of the crime, but I don't budge.

"We can't just leave ... this ..." I say, gesturing to the bodily fluids I'm leaving as a parting gift at my friendly, neighborhood Costco store.

"Um, sure we can."

"No, that's gross. That's my ... my ... my *stuff*." My eyes dart around the area frantically looking for something, anything, to clean up this mess.

Tara looks at me incredulously. "You're overreacting, Henley. You're about to have a baby, and you're freaking out over a puddle in a bulk grocery store?"

"But that's *my* puddle. Some poor high school kid barely making minimum wage is going to get stuck slopping up my amniotic fluid with a moldy, worn out mop. I can't just leave it here."

"Yes, you can. And you will."

I look around again, hoping for a manager; for someone to flag down and profusely apologize. When I hear the splatter of fluid against the tile, my attention diverts back to the scene of the crime only to find Tara pouring an entire container of chicken broth on the floor, mixing it together like an amniotic soup.

"There. It's not as bad. It looks like the carton just exploded. Which is way better than, oh say, your vagina exploding."

"My God, does this ever stop?"

Tara grabs me by the elbow and tries to pull me toward the door. But as she does, her feet slip out from underneath her in all her cartoon-esque glory, and she lands ass first right into the mess.

She doesn't even falter.

"Clean up, aisle two!" my best friend booms, and my face flashes crimson. I want to crawl into a hole and die.

"Okay, on *that* note, we can leave this mess behind."

Chapter Twenty-Nine

DINNER AND A SHOW

It would be in everyone's best interest if every woman in labor were given a warning label to stick to her forehead upon arriving at the hospital for her significant other, or hell ... even strangers, to read.

Warning: Highly prone to spontaneous fits of delirium, irrational logic, and violent, unpredictable mood swings. This individual has been sober, swollen and hungry for the past nine months, so proceed with caution and handle with care. Anything said during the course of labor and delivery should not be taken seriously. Side effects may last up to eighteen years. Please consult your physician should castration occur. And never forget, this is all your fault.

"Jesus Christ on a cracker! Can you get me into a room already?" I growl at the cute, blonde woman working reception as another contraction cripples my body. I thought the two-hour pre-registration seminar we did a few weeks ago was supposed to eliminate me waiting in reception.

"Simmer down and let the poor woman do her job, Henley."

Blondie behind the desk shoots daggers my direction.

Oh, shit. It's happening again.

I grind my teeth and shut my eyes so tightly that little stars begin to appear behind my eyelids. A primitive growl escapes my mouth, and I don't even recognize myself at this moment. My hands reach out for something ... anything ... to grab onto, and in the process, my left-hand assaults Tara's boob, and my right-hand spills over a cup of pens effectively messing up Hospital Reception Barbie's organization.

"BIRTHQUAKE!" Tara proclaims at the top of her lungs, and I have to remind myself to breathe. I attempt to hone in on my breathing.

In with serenity.

Out with baby bullshit.

Because really contractions are complete and total bullshit. But focus is one thing I've always lacked, and before I know it, I'm unleashing a scream that is akin to the sound of the devil himself trying to claw out of my body. Probably because he is. Only the spawn of Satan could bring this much physical pain. I haven't even met this child, and while I absolutely love him or her to bits, this kid is kind of being a little asshole. He doesn't know it yet, but he's been grounded since the second trimester.

When the moment finally passes, beads of sweat are streaking down my temples, and I'm gasping for air. Everyone in the waiting room is suspended, frozen in time, watching me with their mouth agape.

I slap my hand down on the counter and my palm stings. I didn't mean to do it, but I appreciate the theatrics of the thunderous sound. The edges of my mouth curl up maniacally and, in the sweetest voice I can muster, I say, "Now will you get me a room, or should I head out and find myself a freakin' manger to birth this impending bundle of joy?"

The woman pushes herself up from the desk and in one swift, glorious hair flip, whisks her tiny frame to the printer behind her, gathers my paperwork, and calls for a nurse. I'm not sure who's more anxious for me to become someone else's problem—me or her.

My money's on me.

Within moments, a nurse magically appears in the doorway with a wheelchair, ready to usher me away into motherhood. Or at least the last long, painful stretch of life before becoming a mom.

"WHEN WILL JEFF BE HERE?" My tone is whiny, my body aches, and I am so over all this. If he doesn't make it here soon, he's going to miss the birth.

"He should've been here by now." Tara pulls her cell phone out of her back pocket and turns away to dial his number.

On some levels, I feel bad for Tara. She may be my best friend, but she doesn't deserve the Jekyll and Hyde whiplash I've involuntarily been dishing out. I already told her to go home to her family, but apparently, the dramas of my being in labor are the lesser of two evils when compared to triplet boys. If motherhood is anything like childbirth, I can't blame her.

When she returns, she gives me a half smile. "Not too much longer. He stopped somewhere on his way here. Probably for flowers or something."

That kind of gesture sounds like something he'd do—come running into the hospital room with his arms overflowing with flowers and balloon bouquets and pink and blue stuffed bears. But this is hardly the time to run errands, even if they come from the best intentions.

"So for now, you can call me Jeff, pretend that I'm the reason you're stuck in this mess, and boss my dick around. Now, what can I get you?"

Even if I can't muster a laugh, I appreciate her attempt at

humor and keeping my mind off of the obvious. "Food. I'd give anything for a cheeseburger right now."

"Oh, sweetie, you're not allowed to eat anything." Tara tenderly brushes a loose strand from my eyes.

One of the nurses strolls in with a cup of water and sets it on the side table. "Your, uh, partner is right. You can have some ice chips if you'd like."

Tara's face lights up at the mere mention of 'partner', and she leans over and kisses my cheek. "See, honey? She says I'm right. Now when are you going to learn this little fact of life?"

Just as I'm about to inform her that Tara is actually not my lesbian life partner, another birthquake comes rolling through. It's hard to not focus on anything but the searing, white hot pain slingshotting out from my vagina from my head all the way down to my pinky toes.

The hormones swing drastically, and instead of the post-contraction relief I was feeling earlier, I'm now overcome with emotion. The sheer thought of all the frozen food we abandoned in the cart back at Costco sends me into a weepy tailspin.

What. The. Fuck. Pull yourself together, Henley!

My shoulders tremble and snot streaks down my face. I no doubt look like a goddamned raccoon whore since I'm an idiot who doesn't wear waterproof mascara. I'm a train wreck, and there's only one person who can remedy this situation.

"He needs to get here soon."

"I've got tissues for your issues, girlfriend." Tara grabs a box of Kleenex and balances it on top of my stomach. She looks over her shoulder at the empty doorway, practically willing him to walk through the threshold at that exact moment.

But he doesn't.

"I promise he'll be here soon," she adds softly as an afterthought.

I have visions of Jeff pacing some random hallway trying to

convince himself that this is what he truly wants. He's always been so cool and collected about everything that it has to be a facade. He's going to change his mind, and I'm going to be left abandoned. Exactly like the industrial size bag of frozen meatballs.

"But what if he—"

"Nope. Don't even go there, Henley," Tara says, effectively trying to shut down my train of thought.

"But I don't wanna be a soggy meatball!"

Tara looks at me like I have four heads and laughs. "What the hell are you talking about?"

Before I can explain, the nurse checking the computer screen that monitors the baby's heartbeat walks down to the end of the bed and squeezes my foot with her hand. "Why don't we see how far you've progressed?"

"O-Okay ..." I sniffle pathetically.

She gives me her best, toothy 'everything is gonna be all right' grin, and without so much as buying me a drink, works her hand all the way up into my business.

"Well, it looks like you're at four centimeters which is great progress," she says with a little too much spark in her voice.

But all I hear is you're *only* at four centimeters.

It took me a few hours to get to this point, and I'm not even halfway there. And even then, when I first arrived I was already at a three. Apparently, I'm a snail because that's the only way I can qualify four centimeters as great progress.

"So why don't you try to relax? First-time moms tend to have a longer labor."

The nurse is out the door before I can ask her when I can get an epidural because, frankly, these contractions are overrated. Mine have been nothing but inconsistent and a great big pain in my ass. Well, a great big pain in my hoo-ha is more like it.

After another forty minutes of trying to settle down with

haphazard birthquakes sprinkled throughout, the voice I've been dying to hear echoes into my room.

"I am so sorry, man! I thought that was my fiancée's room!" When he finally appears, he is beet red in the face. "I uh ... I walked into the wrong room," he sheepishly clarifies before rushing to my side and giving me a kiss on the cheek.

"It's the man of the hour!" Tara says, welcoming him to our little party.

Jeff smiles at me and then at Tara before running his fingertips through my hair like he always does. "How are you doing? What's going on?"

"Oh, you know, I'm just sitting here knitting a *fucking* sweater," I spit at him.

Where the hell has he been? And where are all those flowers and balloons he was supposedly grabbing during whatever pit stop he made on his way to the hospital?

"Good luck," Tara says softly to Jeff with a not so subtle eye roll.

"Thanks for being here, T. I can take it from here." She stands from the chair, and he gives her a bear hug, truly appreciating our friendship.

"It's been fun. Are you sure you don't want me to stick around? I don't mind," Tara says, but what I really think she's saying is that she wants a front row seat for whatever epic freakout I'm inevitably going to dish out to Jeff.

"Nah, I got it."

Tara leans over and gives me one last kiss on the cheek while attempting to wrap her arms around my ginormous belly.

"Love you, Hen."

"Love you too, Tara."

"And just so you know, she really doesn't want to be a soggy meatball." They exchange a confused look and Tara shrugs. "Keep me updated. This auntie wants to come back and steal all the fresh baby snuggles as soon as the kiddo is born."

The instant Tara is out of the room, another contraction rips through my body. Jeff stands there helplessly, trying to coach me through some breathing exercises he probably picked up from some late night sitcoms because the cadence resembles something more like dying sloth than actual Lamaze. The boy gets points for trying though.

Then quickly loses them all a few minutes later.

The rustling of a paper bag catches me off guard as I close my eyes in between contractions. When I open them, I see Jeff peeling back the wrapping of a sandwich. A putrid smell assaults my nostrils, and I start to gag.

"What the hell is that?" I ask, covering my face and turning away from him. My stomach has completely dropped, and this baby is trying to deliver a round-ending punch from the inside out. Like its mother, this child doesn't care for deli meat either.

"It's a pastrami sandwich from Mario's," he mumbles with his mouth full of food.

Are you kidding me? The boy stopped at a deli and bought himself a pastrami sandwich to eat during the birth of his child? Mario's is nowhere near the hospital!

"Did you really go clear across town to get yourself a sandwich while I sat here in labor?"

"What? The doctors warned that this could take a while, and I haven't eaten anything since breakfast."

He's failing to see the problem. I've been here working hard at this birthing a human thing, and he is having a goddamned picnic, all while I've been forbidden to eat. "This is not dinner and a show, Jeff! Get that out of here before I puke."

He scurries out the door. Not even thirty-seconds later, he returns to the room with his mouth full and pouty eyes. He shoved the whole damn sandwich into his mouth.

I shake my head and send a silent prayer for this kid to take after me.

FIRE BURNS my body to ash as another unbearable contraction shreds my insides. I try to control the carnal sounds escaping my lips with breathing, but this time, it comes out more like a high-pitched whine that every dog in a five-mile radius can hear. Jeff looks at me with sympathy, the nurse with amusement as she fights a smile.

I'm somewhere between six and seven the next time a nurse violates me to find out just how much longer it'll be before I finally deliver. "If you're going to have an epidural, now is the time we want to make that decision," she says, pleased with herself.

Jeff and I both answer at the exact same time but imagine my surprise when the answers are completely different.

"Yes!" I cheer a little too enthusiastically.

"No."

Why the hell does he want me to be miserable right now? I grab a fistful of Jeff's shirt and pull him toward me. His breath still reeks of pastrami, and I summon all the strength I have not to kill him.

"If you value your life, you will get me the fucking drugs."

"Really?"

I have no idea why he sounds so surprised by this decision. I never swore that I wouldn't have an epidural. I only promised that I'd try to go without one for a little while all because of that stupid natural childbirth class I accidentally signed us up for. And, according to my calculations, it's been more than *a little while* at this juncture.

"You've come so far, and you're doing great, Henley. Are you sure you don't want to try to go au naturel? At least for a little bit longer?"

"Yes, I am *sure* I don't want to try and go *au naturel!* I don't get a special prize for being a masochist. And until you try pushing something the size of a watermelon through something the size of a nickel, you don't get a say!"

Jeff raises his hands up in surrender, and I'm impressed that the anesthesiologist is in my room with a needle the size of the Chrysler Building within a few short minutes. Everyone has to clear the room, so I shut my eyes and try to stay as still as humanly possible.

Within moments, I am blissfully laying back in the hospital bed with a goofy grin on my face as the anesthesiologist looks down on me.

"Holy shit," I breathe in a drug-induced euphoria. If you could feel stars and smell rainbows and taste unicorn tears, I am certain that *this* is what it would feel like—*magic*.

"Yeah?" says my new best friend, the anesthesiologist.

"Yeah," I sigh. I'm pretty sure I just fell in love with this man who so willingly and selflessly has taken away my pain. "Those are some good drugs."

The good doctor smiles, and I see just how handsome he truly is. This man no doubt receives multiple marriage proposals each day from expectant women.

"Can you feel this?" I watch him run a line up my leg with the cap of his pen.

I shake my head no. "I feel nothing. Absolutely nothing. And therefore, I feel ah-mazing." This shit really *is* magical.

"Good, it looks like everything has taken properly. If you feel like you need a little bit more, just push this button here. It'll allow you to control your pain management and release more as you need it. But it will only release a certain amount every ten minutes, so don't get too trigger happy. What I suggest you do is try to close your eyes and get some rest. You're going to need your strength here in a little bit. You won't know when the contractions hit unless you're looking at the monitor."

I nod off and find myself at peace for the first time all day. I don't hear Jeff come back into the room, but I know he's there from the way he squeezes my hand and the rancid, lingering smell of pastrami.

EVENTUALLY, a new nurse stirs me from sleep.

"Do you mind if I see how far you are?" She has skin the color of cinnamon and has one of the warmest smiles I've ever seen. She seems friendlier than the other nurses I've encountered today.

I spread my legs again, inviting her to do her job, and wince at the pressure. "Are you ready to have your baby because you're at ten! I'll go get the doctor. Take a few moments to yourselves and get ready, because it's time."

She turns to walk out the door, but her eyes settle on Jeff in a moment of recognition. Her eyes narrow ever so slightly. "Aren't you ...?"

"Yes, I'm the fucking milkman. Now go get the doctor because we're ready to get this show on the road."

The realization of what is about to happen hits, and I panic. "Oh my God, I'm not ready for this, Jeff. I can't do it. Make it stop! I'm not ready to be a mom. I won't be good at it. There's no way anyone here at the hospital is going to allow me to take home a baby."

Jeff wipes a rogue tear from my cheek, then grabs both of my hands in his and leans in so he's only inches away from my face. "First of all, there's no way that this amazing woman before me is capable of being a bad mother. You're incredible and selfless and kind and giving. You are all of the things that it takes to be an awesome mom." His words melt my insides, and his eyes are zeroed in on mine. He's being completely serious. "And besides, they are absolutely going to send this kid home with us. Babies are built to withstand first-time parents. You've got this. *We've got this.*"

His words bring me serenity and confidence. "Do you always know the right thing to say?"

He beams down at me and kisses my lips gently. "Yep, and all the wrong things, too."

Everything moves in slow motion around us in preparation. I'm caught off guard when another familiar voice calls to me from the doorway, breaking me away from the last pre-baby moment I'm sharing with Jeff. It's a voice that I never thought I'd hear again ... or rather, wanted to hear again.

"Oh my God, Fire Crotch! Is that you?"

My head snaps to see Leo in mint green scrubs, looking at my file as he walks in. You have *got* to be kidding me. The universe has a sick sense of humor. If I wasn't already a nervous wreck, I certainly was now.

"Leo, wha ... What are you doing here?"

"It's Dr. Wallace, actually. I'm an obstetrician," he says, clarifying the obvious.

"I thought you were a podiatrist or something out in California."

He gives me a smirk and a pointed eyebrow raise as if to say, *Nope!*

"You two know each other?" the nurse asks. She continues checking information on the computer without missing a beat.

Leo approaches the side of my bed and gives me a hug. "We do. Henley's my girl."

"Was," I snap at him then look to Jeff. "I uh ... I dated Leo many moons ago. And really, it wasn't even dating. Leo was a small speed bump on the way to finding you." *This isn't awkward or anything.* I give him a reassuring smile.

"Wait. How do you know my fiancée?"

"Oh? You're engaged to Henley?" Leo looks down at my bare hand and smirks. My hands have been so swollen that I haven't worn the engagement ring in weeks.

"Yeah." Jeff stands a little taller and squeezes my hand.

"Right. Sure." The clip in Leo's voice confirms disbelief. "Hang on a second!" Leo's face lights up. "You're that guy ... The one who tried to milk himself on national TV!"

"It wasn't TV. It was the internet," I seethe through my teeth.

"Same thing," Leo clarifies.

No. Not quite.

Jeff looks from me to Leo and back to me again as he's trying to put the pieces of the puzzle in place.

"Leo was ... a *boyfriend* ... of mine ... in *college*," I reiterate.

"Wait a minute! Is this the sleeping dorm dude? Mr. Three Minute Wonder Pants?"

Leo whips his head to look at Jeff. "What'd you say?"

Of all the embarrassing and awkward moments I've ever endured, this one surely tops the list.

"I said, Mr. Three Min—"

"Both of you STOP IT!" I snap, wishing for the peace and quiet after the anesthesiologist left.

Leo seems on board with effectively shutting down that conversation. "Fine. We can talk about this later because right now, it's time to have a baby."

"Wait ... *you're* going to deliver *my* baby?" Jeff says, slow to add the pieces together. He's uneasy with my ex being elbows deep in my lady bits—and he should be!

"*Our* baby," I correct him.

Jeff's expression turns nervous as if he isn't sure if he wants to pee on my leg to stake his claim or cower down to whatever the doctor says. He wrestles his thoughts before speaking again. "You know what, Dr. Wallace? I don't think it's really appropriate for you to be the one here delivering our baby. Isn't there anyone else available?"

Leo folds his arms defensively and gives me a glare that is somehow still laced with kindness and humor. It's almost reminiscent of the man I once dated.

Almost.

The pair bicker back and forth for a few minutes as I grow increasingly more uncomfortable. I push the epidural button a few times, trying to numb me from this reality, but there's no escaping it. It's clear ...

If I'm going to have this baby, I'm stuck with Leo.

"Look, if you like, Henley can simply cross her legs and wait for her primary obstetrician to be out of surgery, but that could take a while. Or, you can buck up, be a man, and let me deliver this baby safely. Your call, champ."

Jeff knows he's been outmatched. "Fine," he grits begrudgingly through his teeth.

And then it happens.

In a snap, the entire room transforms. The number of nurses has doubled, part of the bed drops out, and the stirrups are hoisted up into sight. And just as I swallow hard to brace myself, a blinding light is turned on. It's bad enough that my goodies are about to be on display for my ex-boyfriend to see, but now we have a spotlight shining down upon it. You know, just in case he didn't get a close enough look all those years ago and wants to commit every fold, nook, and cranny to memory.

I take a deep breath and silently hope that the last time I blindly shaved *down there* didn't leave any ridiculous patches because Lord knows I felt like Helen Keller in the shower trying to shave by feel. Tara was right, I should have just gotten waxed.

Leo has thoroughly washed his hands and now sports a stoic,

professional expression. I'm relieved to see he means business now. I can't help but feel nervous as I watch him position himself between my legs, and just before he falls out of sight to help deliver this baby, he has the audacity to wink at me.

The fucker.

"There she is," Leo singsongs from my nether regions. *Nothing ever changes.* I fight the urge to drive the heel of my foot right through his nose. I'm half tempted to cross my legs and wait for another doctor to become available just as he suggested. I mean, it can't be *that* long of a wait, can it?

"Hey! Keep it professional, Doc," Jeff snaps.

"Eh, there's nothing I haven't seen before. Here, come and grab a leg, old sport."

I can only hope the 'nothing I haven't seen before' comment was a testament to his medical background and not a cheap dig at our former sex life. Just as I feel Jeff's hand on my shin, I panic. If he's holding my leg, he's going to see everything.

Everything.

And some things should remain sacred.

My mind wanders to the inevitable poop talk I had with Tara, and I'm eager to keep Jeff up toward my head and shoulders. "No! Stay up here with me ... please!" I cry out desperately.

His eyes dart to mine with concern. "Henley, I'm right here."

"No, I want you to hold my hand."

"Babe, I thought you were okay with me watching the birth of our child."

"I know, it's just that ... I've changed my mind." I bite my lip nervously, willing him to simply read my thoughts and hightail his tush back up here with me.

"Ah, I know what this is about ..." Leo interrupts, looking at me over my stomach.

"You do?" Jeff's head whips back to the base of the hospital bed.

"Yep. Fire Crotch here is afraid she's going to defecate on the table. Classic paranoia. I see it in labor and delivery all the time."

I cringe at his word. So clinical. So gross. And so right on the money.

"That happens?" Jeff tries to hide his mortification.

"Yes, sir." Leo looks back toward me with a serious expression on his face. "Did you have Mexican last night?"

"No."

"Did you eat Chinese food? I remember how that would often upset your stomach."

"No!" I shout, getting angrier by the moment. Surely there is some doctor code where you can't stare down the vagina of a former lover to deliver her baby. It seems like this would be simple, medical law. You know, if that were actually a thing.

"Then stop being so ridiculous," Leo commands. "Jeff, you stay right here and be my right stirrup."

Jeff obeys, and I open my mouth to plead with him one last time, but he speaks before I can even form the word. "Calm down, Henley. You're going to be fine. This is the birth of *our* child. So stop focusing on poop because we're both going to be up to our elbows in it the next few years. Shit happens. I'll deal with it, but you need to find a way to get over it."

And with the next contraction about to overtake my body, I do.

AFTER CLOSE TO thirty minutes of pushing, I feel like we've gotten nowhere. But according to everyone standing south of my equator, I'm making "excellent progress."

They lie.

Because if my progress was so excellent, I'd have a kid in my arms and I'd be blissfully resting without my muff on display like it was the winning prize purse in the Showcase Showdown.

I've been watching Jeff intently, and he's given nothing away. So if I have, indeed, pooped, I am none the wiser. But let's just say that hopefully hasn't been a problem because there are some places that couples simply should not go.

"Okay. This next contraction, I want you to give me a really big push, Henley."

He's joking, right?

"Haven't all of these pushes been really big?"

Leo says nothing, but gives me a pointed look and then up at the monitor to gauge the next contraction. "Push!"

And I oblige.

I close my eyes and push with all of my might. It doesn't hurt as much as I was expecting, but holy crap, this is a lot of uncomfortable pressure. A nurse counts down backward from ten. I wish she'd count faster so I can stop pushing.

"Go, baby, go, baby, go, baby, go," Jeff cheers me on exactly like he has with every push. It's quite endearing. Though I'm not sure if he's calling *me* baby, or trying to convince the baby to crawl out of my body.

"I can see your baby's head. You're crowning," Leo explains. "It has a full head of hair. Do you want to reach down and feel?"

I shake my head.

"Come on, Henley. It's really quite amazing," he coaxes.

"Oh ... my ... God ..." I feel Jeff's fingertips digging harder and harder into the skin of my calves with each word. He's no longer looking me in the eyes, and the next thing I know, he's on the floor, and my leg flops down onto the table as dead weight. It's a damn good thing I'm numb from the waist down because that probably would have hurt a lot. What else could possibly happen to make this day more eventful?

"Man down!" Leo shouts a little too enthusiastically. I half expect him to make fun of my fiancé for hitting the floor, but he's focused on the task at hand, so a nurse rushes into the room to tend to a passed out Jeff.

"Really, Henley? You couldn't find a *real* man to be with?"

And *now* he's just being cruel.

Jeff quickly comes to with his arms flailing around. Then he's in my face, kissing my cheeks and apologizing profusely for missing the birth.

"We're still in labor and delivery, sweetie." I laugh, thankful he was only out for a moment.

A nurse brings him a chair and encourages him to take it easy. He pulls it right up next to my bed and grabs my hand tightly. I'm glad he's okay, but secretly I'm relieved he's relinquished his front row seat. *Maybe that was Karma's way of paying him back for that pastrami sandwich from earlier?*

"So glad you could join us," Leo quips.

"Are you okay, sweetie?" I offer him a soft smile as I relax before the next wave of pushing.

"Henley, stop pussyfooting around. Another contraction is coming, and I need you to push like you mean it."

When the moment comes, I do. And not because he told me to, but because I need this whole ordeal over and a baby in my arms. Just as the nurse begins her countdown again, Leo clears his throat dramatically.

"Oh, beautiful, for spacious skies, for amber waves of grain."

I grit my teeth, clench my eyes shut, and push with every fiber of my being. The longer he sings, the more anger takes over and every muscle in my body tenses. And if I ever hated Leo before, I loathe him now. There is a special circle of hell waiting for this man. I take a mental note to Google voodoo doll curses when I get home. I want to make sure I give this ass a receding hairline and take sick pleasure as I stab the doll's canvas crotch with tiny pins. Anything to make his dick shrivel up and fall off.

"Keep going. The baby is almost out," the nurse holding my left leg says.

"Good, good. This is good, Henley."

"Puh-push it real good," Jeff sings in my ear.

Tears streak the corners of my eyes, and I know that this is both my best work and my hardest work. A sudden wave of pressure relief is met with the glorious cry of a red-faced child.

"It's a girl!" Leo proclaims as he holds our daughter up in the air for us to see.

"What? Where's his penis?" Jeff is genuinely shocked. I'll never understand how or why he convinced himself that he was having a boy. It's always been a fifty-fifty chance.

"It's a little girl — congratulations! Would you like to come and cut the umbilical cord, Dad?"

I wipe the tears from my cheeks and watch as Jeff cuts the cord with a shaky hand. He reaches out to her, and this little human we created wraps her hand around his pinky finger.

"Hi, there. I'm your daddy." It's clear he's smitten.

She doesn't wail inconsolably like newborn babies do in the movies. Her initial cries turn quickly into soft, sweet murmurs, letting us know she's here and that she's okay. That she's perfect.

They whisk her away to clean her up, weigh her, and run the APGAR tests. I watch as a nurse swaddles her in a soft pink blanket. And that's the moment *before*. That single split second before everything in my entire life changes.

The nurse places her into my arms, and instinct takes over. I shower her in kisses and soft whispers of love and savor the feeling of her skin upon mine. Whoever says they don't believe in love at first sight has never held their own newborn child in their arms. Because in an instant, I am enamored, and life revolves around her.

Jeff kisses my temple. "I am so proud of you," he whispers before turning his attention to his daughter. "And you, you are absolutely beautiful. I'm sorry that I'm going to have to lock you up until you're forty."

We're all smiles in our own little bubble until Leo gives a not so subtle interrupting cough. "Okay, the fun's over, Mom and Dad."

"We're not done?"

"Nope! Now it's time to deliver the placenta."

Oh, shit.

The Fourth Trimester

Yeah, it's a thing. And it lasts eighteen years.
(Good luck with that!)

Chapter Thirty

SEMANTICS

Not long after the nurses have cleaned everything up, they transfer us to a private recovery room. That's when the reality of our new normal set in.

Jeff and I haven't so much as put her down for a second. I want her to know how loved and wanted she is. I know these days are numbered, and each one is a gift I want to commit to memory.

My upper body naturally starts to sway as I cradle her in my arms. "What do you think we should name *her*?" I emphasize the last word as my subtle way of saying, *you were wrong!*

"Just so you know, I'm still holding out hope that this baby will grow a penis."

"You are utterly ridiculous, Jeff." I shake my head at him and deeply inhale the delicious new baby smell, savoring every moment of it. "What about Spencer? I've always loved the name Spencer for a little girl."

"Hmm ... Spencer." The name rolls off his tongue gracefully, but I can tell he doesn't love it as much as I do. "That's a fine name and all, but what about something a little more girly? Like Sophie?"

I scrunch my nose up in disgust. While I love the name Sophie, I taught a girl named Sophie last year who was such a little asshole. Those lashes and rosy cheeks may deceive some novice teachers, but I saw right through her charm and conniving ways.

"No. Sophie isn't even up for discussion."

"Ooookay, then. Lillian, perhaps? That was your grandmother's name, right?"

The suggestion steals my breath and makes me smile. "Lillian is perfect. Lillian Elisabeth. For your grandmother, too."

He leans down and kisses Lillian delicately on the forehead so he doesn't stir her, then presses his lips to mine. Ever so gingerly, I pass Lillian to her father and melt as he softly begins to sing to her. Jeff wasn't lying when he said he didn't know any lullabies, but I take great amusement in the fact he's changing the words to the Snoop Dogg's Gin and Juice, rapping "got my mind on my mommy and my mommy on my mind." It's impossible not to fall even further in love with Jeff, watching him dote over his daughter.

"Thank you ..." I say softly, fighting the building tears in my eyes.

"For what?" His forehead creases and his eyes turn curious as he looks at me for a quick moment before diverting his attention back to Lillian.

"For everything. You've been so incredibly supportive throughout all of this."

Everything is such a vague word, but it's the only one I've got. He could have run when he learned I was pregnant. But he didn't. He *gave* me everything. And therefore he *is* my everything.

"Well, you're my girl—my *girls*. I'd do anything for you two." He beams with genuineness.

"About that ..."

Jeff cocks his eyebrow.

"You know how I've always said that I wanted to get married *after* I had the baby, right?"

"Yeah ..." The word lingers in the space between us with uncertainty.

"Well, I just thought that maybe it's time we start thinking about it?" I shift on the bed, my legs still feeling a bit dead from the aftereffects of the epidural.

"Why are you talking about the wedding now? Enjoy this moment. Let's get settled into this parenting thing and find our rhythm. We don't have to plan this wedding until you're completely ready."

"What? You don't want to marry me now?" I try to pout, but a smug smile plays at my lips as I see him consider taking the bait.

"I'll marry you the instant you'll let me. It doesn't matter if that's next month or next year. I love you, and it's the kind of love that isn't going anywhere."

I hit the nurse's call button and wait.

"Hi, this is Nurse Julie. Is everything okay?"

"Hi, Julie. Yes, everything is fine. I was just wondering if you could see if there was a priest in the building who could stop by our room."

Jeff's eyes go wide, and he looks at me with shock, mouth agape. The pieces are starting to fit together in his mind, and I'm not sure if he's panicked or excited about the stunt I'm about to pull.

"Oh sure, honey, I can absolutely see if there is someone available to stop by and bless your baby."

"Thanks," I chime into the speaker.

I sit up a little taller and pat the open space next to me on the bed. "Blessing Lillian is fine and all, but I want to show you just how much I love you. This, right here, is all that matters. It wasn't only a baby born today. It was a family. And with that, I want it to be our marriage, too."

Jeff continues to stare at me, completely lost for words. "What?"

"I can't believe you just did that."

"Why not? I've said all along that I wanted a small, intimate wedding."

He runs his hand through his hair and watches me intently, trying to get a better gauge on the bomb I've just dropped. "This isn't sleep deprivation and exhaustion overtaking your decision-making abilities, right?"

I laugh, shaking my head.

"And this isn't some weird new mom hormone imbalance where you're going to punch me in the junk and shout 'psyche!' is it?"

"I'm pretty sure nobody has said 'psyche!' since the late nineties. And please, rest assured that I am alert and completely ready for this." I reach for his hand and squeeze it tightly. "I have never been more ready for anything in my entire life."

And the words mean more than simply being married. I'm ready for this new life, our new family. As long as I've got Jeff, I have everything I need.

"God, I love you, woman." He leans in and surprises me with the kind of kiss that puts all other kisses to shame, even with a baby balanced in his arms.

A few minutes later there's a soft knock at the door. "That was quick," Jeff comments.

I sit up a little taller in the bed, realizing that not only am I about to get married, but I'm about to do it in a soiled hospital gown. *Meh* ... I've always felt designer wedding dresses were overrated, and weddings were more a party for the parents and their friends than the couple. I can hardly contain my smile.

It's a shame it doesn't last for long.

"*Oh, hell no!*"

Leo cautiously stands just inside the door and puts his hands up in the air like he's trying to surrender. In his right hand is a small pink teddy bear. Leo looks different in his street clothes rather than doctor scrubs. If I squint my eyes just right, he looks like the guy I once thought I loved.

"What are you doing here?" Jeff delicately passes Lillian back into my arms, taking extra care to support her neck.

"I just wanted to stop by and see Henley before I head home."

Jeff stands to meet Leo and extends his arm out for a handshake. "Don't you think you've spent enough time all up in Henley's business?" The look in Leo's eyes tells me Jeff is squeezing his hand just a little too hard.

Good.

When Jeff finally releases his hand, Leo shifts his attention toward me. "Congratulations, Henley. You, too," he says to my soon-to-be husband. "I've always known you'd make an incredible mother, and from the looks of it, I was right."

It's the nicest thing he's ever said to me.

We spend a few minutes catching up, and it's strangely nice to see that Leo isn't *all* asshole. Deep down, underneath the mocking patriotic songs and obnoxious pet names, there is, in fact, a shred of humanity.

"Ahem." A man dressed in black with a white collar clears his throat from the far side of the room. "I'm sorry, I didn't mean to interrupt. Is now a good time or should I come back later?" He looks exhausted with dark pools under his eyes, and something tells me that 'later' would be tomorrow.

"Oh! No, now is a perfect time, Father. Please, come in."

He walks in further and stands at the end of the bed with a smile on his face. "I'm Father O'Donnell. Your child is beautiful."

He looks fondly at Lillian. "May I?" he asks, reaching out his arms.

I pass my daughter to him, and he beams down at her. It's amazing how such a tiny little person can have such a profound impact on a person. "Have you decided on a name yet?"

"Yes, Lillian Elisabeth."

"That's a beautiful name," Father O'Donnell praises.

He asks us to bow our heads as he leads us in a prayer and blesses both the baby and our new family. When he finishes, he makes a small cross gesture on her forehead and passes her gingerly back to Jeff.

"Thank you, Father. That was beautiful."

"My pleasure, and all the best to your family." He turns on his heel and starts toward the door.

"Actually, Father, if we could trouble you for just one more thing before you leave..."

"Yes?" He turns back around to face us.

How on earth do I even broach this? I know you *think* you were here just to bless our little bundle, and I'm pretty sure we've broken at least four—maybe five of the Ten Commandments recently, but would you mind marrying us? I'm fairly certain if I were to step foot in a church, lightning would strike and engulf the building in flames.

Catholic guilt suddenly grips me, and I bite my tongue.

"Father, I am madly in love with this woman. Have been since the moment I met her last year. Every morning I wake up and thank my stars for how lucky I am to have her in my life."

My heart doesn't melt at his words. It soars.

Father O'Donnell folds his hands in his lap, listening intently. And out of the corner of my eye, I see Leo shifting uncomfortably.

"Nothing about our relationship has ever been conventional, but I know that she's the one for me. We've been engaged for a few months now, and the only thing that could possibly make this day more remarkable than it already has been is to spend it with my wife. Sure, we don't have all of the legal hodgepodge filed, and we don't have rings here with us, and heck, our family doesn't even realize we had the baby today. But it would mean the world if you would marry us. Right here, right now."

I hold my breath and await the condescending look...

But it never comes.

"I am not one to judge you or your definition of conventional. I have always believed that love knows no bounds, and it's clear by the way you look at her that this is meant to be. Besides, when you know, *you know*."

He looks to Leo, questioning his presence here. "Would you mind serving as their witness?"

"Uh ... sure," he says unconvincingly.

Thank you, I mouth to him in appreciation.

"Since we don't have all of the formalities in place, maybe we can just hit the highlights, Father?" Jeff smiles.

A light flickers in Father O'Donnell's eyes. He's clearly amused by this whole scenario. "I suppose we can do that. Under the promise that you'll take care of the license and come back to see me officially with your families?"

"Absolutely," I say.

"Of course," Jeff agrees. He comes to sit down next to me on the hospital bed with Lillian in his arms. She's just as much a part of this celebration as we are.

Father O'Donnell begins with a short prayer before cutting to the chase. "I'm sorry, what were your names again?"

I giggle, realizing we never actually told him *our* names, just Lillian's. "I'm Henley. And this is Jeff."

"Ah yes. Okay." He clears his throat. "Before you declare your vows to one another, I need to hear you confirm that it is your intention to be married here today. Henley, do you come here freely and without reservation to give yourself to Jeff in marriage? If so, please answer 'I do.'"

I've never been so sure about anything in my life. "I do," I repeat confidently.

"And Jeff, do you come here freely and without reservation to give yourself to Henley in marriage?"

"I do." Jeff wraps one arm around my waist, trying to pull me closer to him and Lillian.

"Now, do either of you have vows prepared or...?"

"I can wing it," I say to Jeff. Because if I'm being honest, all those nights where I couldn't fall asleep because I had a baby bouncing on my bladder, I was running through one million and one scenarios of what my vows would be.

"Me, too," Jeff says.

"Okay then." Father O'Donnell gestures to me to look at Jeff.

I take a deep breath and look him in the eyes. I love the sincerity on his face and wish I had a picture to capture this moment. "Jeff, you are my light. You've shown me more love than I've ever known before. I promise to have the patience that our love demands, to speak when words are needed and appreciate the silence when they are not. I look forward to laughing with you and crying with you. Caring for you, and sharing with you. I love that I get to build with you and live with you. And I promise to be faithful to you all the days of our lives."

Jeff can't contain the happiness that takes over his entire demeanor. His smile illuminates the world and I can sense his heart is about to burst from his chest in genuine joy.

"Henley, the day I sat down next to you on that plane, my life finally took off. You gave me the kind of feeling that was instant, powerful, and utterly indescribable. Just like you. You're indescribable. I promise to stand by your side, even when our legs are tired and broken. I promise to never sing *America, the Beautiful* to you." He laughs knowingly which makes me blush. "And I promise that I will never be perfect. Because while neither of us is perfect, we are perfect for each other, and together, we share a perfect kind of love. And really, that's all that matters. I swear to you that I will live each day loving you more than I did the day before. Thank you for allowing me into your life."

We sit there in silence for a moment, savoring each other's words.

"This is typically the part where you'd exchange rings."

"Eh, semantics," Jeff interjects.

"Okay then, by the power vested in me by God and man, I pronounce you husband and wife. Those whom God has joined together, let no one separate."

Jeff looks at me desperately, his lips aching to taste mine, and in an instant, our mouths meet in perfect harmony.

Father O'Donnell laughs. "You may now kiss your bride."

"CONGRATULATIONS AGAIN, HENLEY." Leo leans down and kisses me on the cheek before placing the pink teddy bear into the bassinet. He then turns to Jeff and exchanges another firm handshake. "She was the one who got away. Take good care of her, will ya?"

"I will. And I'm glad she got away."

"I am, too," he responds earnestly. "I never saw her this happy when she was with me."

"That's probably because you called her Fire Crotch and sang patriotic anthems at inappropriate times."

Leo simply shrugs. "What can I say? I never claimed to be a good guy. But don't underestimate the power of *America the Beautiful* when it comes to Henley."

"Duly noted."

Jeff follows Leo to the door and closes it behind him. That went significantly better than I ever imagined it going.

"So now what, wifey?"

"I guess we call our parents? I can't imagine that'll go over well. *I got you a special surprise, Mom! How about a granddaughter* and *a son-in-law!*"

"Hmm, you're right. How about we keep this our little secret? We can tell them all about it later."

I know how butt-hurt my folks will be, but the suggestion sounds perfect.

"Okay. You've got yourself a deal. This stays between us, hubby."

"I like the sound of that."

"Me, too."

We both look around the room and soak in the peacefulness of Lilian sleeping in her bassinet.

"So ... Now what do we do?" I imagine every new parent has had this thought at some point once they've gone through the traditional hospital to do list.

Jeff turns toward me with a mischievous light in his eyes. "This is our honeymoon period, right?"

"I guess technically it is."

"You know what they say about honeymoons?" He wiggles his eyebrows at me.

I laugh uncontrollably. I swear this guy always has sex on the brain. "They say you have to wait six weeks—*at least!*"

"I'm counting down the days. Because Lillian needs a baby brother."

"You're just looking for another reason to joke about a penis being inside of me."

Jeff winks. "I love you, woman."

"I love you, too."

Chapter Thirty-One

PUTTING THE FUN IN FUN BAGS

We couldn't have asked for a more perfect baby.

Lillian slept well through the night, only waking up a handful of times. Jeff was a champ, springing into action each time she whimpered to help with any diaper changing and fatherly duties. I'm crossing all of my cross-ables that this momentum continues when we get back home in a few days.

Knowing Jeff, it no doubt will.

Nursing Lillian *appears* to be going well. I have no idea if I'm doing it right. I actually have no idea if I'm doing *any* of this right. In fact, I'm convinced now more than ever that adults are just making their way through life faking it as best as they can because all of us are freaking clueless.

Lillian is in my arms nursing for what feels like the fifteenth time today, and I'm still resting in the hospital bed, thinking about everything that transpired. Lillian's arrival. Freakin' Leo. Getting married, even if it wasn't technically legal. We'll get those details sorted out soon enough.

All in all, it was an incredible day. One I won't soon forget.

Jeff leans against the doorframe leading into our en suite

bathroom. His hair is still damp, but he's sporting a fresh set of clothes — something I'm longing for. This giant maxi pad I'm sporting could probably absorb the contents of the Mississippi River. I can't feel anything south of the equator thanks to the ice packs they keep telling me to shove down there to help ease the swelling. But I'm terrified to put my own clothes on for fear of ruining them, and so the hospital gown and their glorious undergarments it is.

"Motherhood looks amazing on you, Henley," he says with pride.

"Thanks. We'll see if you still feel the same way when I'm covered in poop and spit up at two-thirty some random morning."

"I'm sure I will." He leans down to kiss me but stops just short of my lips. "Whoa!"

"What?" Surely my breath isn't *that* bad.

"Um, sweetie, I don't know how to put this politely, but you grew porn star boobs overnight." His eyes bug out, and I can see him practically roll his tongue back up into his mouth where it belongs. "Believe me, I'm not complaining! I'm just a little shocked, is all. Maybe even a teeny bit jealous that *she* gets to take advantage of them."

I laugh heartily. "It's not like she's putting the fun in fun bags, Jeff. Besides, these aren't the most comfortable things right now. I have no idea how Pamela Anderson and Dolly Parton function on a daily basis." The girls are so big they will no doubt be getting in my way.

When Lillian's done nursing, Jeff takes over burping duties, and I close my eyes to rest for a little bit as Ellen Degeneres prattles on about good deeds and dancing on the TV screen on the wall. I fall asleep to him softly singing Beyonce's *Single Ladies*, but changing the lyrics to be *Single Babies*.

I wake up when the nurses are changing shifts. I feel like a brand new woman, even though it's the same episode of *The*

Ellen Show when my eyes open. It's amazing what a tiny power nap can do for your body and mind. No wonder everyone says to sleep when the baby is sleeping.

"You have a visitor in the waiting room, Mom and Dad," the afternoon nurse informs me while taking my vitals and going through my pain levels.

"Oh? Send them in, I guess."

Jeff and I exchange a confused look. He shrugs. Clearly, he's as lost as I am right now. But really, *we* don't have visitors. Lillian does. But I wouldn't have it any other way. She's only a day old and so incredibly loved.

"Okay. I'll let reception know."

She disappears, and moments later we hear a booming, singsong "*Helloooooo!*" from the doorway. Mr. and Mrs. Carrington thunder into the room with balloons and flowers and suitcases in tow. Are they moving into our hospital room?

"Mom! Dad! What are you guys doing here?" Jeff stands to greet his parents with a hug as they walk through the door.

"Are you kidding? We hopped in the car the instant we realized Henley was in labor and drove through the night."

The comment strikes me as odd because we didn't tell *anyone* we were at the hospital. Not even my own parents. Which reminds me, we should probably get on that before the Catholic guilt rears its ugly head.

Jeff furrows his brow and looks at me inquisitively. I subtly shrug to let him know this wasn't *my* doing.

I sit up a little taller in the hospital bed and gingerly pass Lily to Jeff.

"Mom, Dad, this is Lillian." Jeff smiles proudly as he passes our daughter off wearing a smile so proud it practically screams "Look at what I made in class today!"

Mrs. Carrington carefully supports her neck and instantly starts swaying Lillian to and fro in her arms. "Hi, sweetie," Mrs.

Carrington whispers. "I'm your Nana, and this is your Pop Pop, and the two of us are going to spoil you silly. So if these two knuckleheads ever tell you 'no,' you just call on us. We'll make it right." The pair of them beam down at their newborn granddaughter.

"She's opening her eyes," Mr. Carrington coos in awe. "She's so beautiful and perfect."

Jeff returns to my bedside and squeezes my hand. He leans down to kiss my cheek and then whispers out of his parents' earshot, "I really have no idea how they knew."

I nod subtly. "I do."

Jeff raises his eyebrows and then the realization hits.

"Tara," we both deadpan in unison.

Jeff grabs his phone and checks Facebook. Sure enough, my best friend had checked in at the hospital, tagging Jeff and me along with her. Below her comment of "OMG! FETUS CARSON-CARRINGTON IS ARRIVING!" is a photo of me, mid-birthquake, scowling at the twiggy Barbie doll behind the registration desk. To say I look possessed is an understatement.

"Dammit, T!" Everyone turns to look at me. "Sorry," I mutter, unsure if I'm supposed to be apologizing for swearing in front of a newborn or because I was ruining a moment for everyone else.

I'll deal with her later.

It's heartwarming watching Jeff's parents bond with their new granddaughter. We exchange little pleasantries about how I'm feeling and what the nursery looks like, but mostly the time spent here is silent with the exception of the obligatory ooh's and aah's that come with an infant that still has that fresh baby smell. It's all very soothing.

"So when is the baptism?" I hear Martha ask just as I'm closing my eyes. That birthing shit was exhausting, and really, I just want to close my eyes and hibernate for a day or two or ten.

But for now, I fake sleep, mostly because I'm interested in what Jeff is going to say.

Having Lily baptized is not something we've ever talked about since neither Jeff nor I have ever been truly religious people. Sure, I grew up Catholic, but that was mostly because I was never given the choice and the protest wasn't worth the consequences. I always had the idea that the extent of Jeff's religious education was his mother telling him, "You better pray that orange soda comes out of the carpet." So it's a little surprising that this is coming from *his* folks.

"Umm ... uh. It isn't something we've really talked about yet, Mom." His voice is low, presumably not to wake his fake sleeping wife.

"Well, you *are* going to have her baptized, right?"

He sighs. "We'll talk about it when we get home. I have no idea what I'm doing next week, let alone if we're going to damn our daughter to roam the earth before being free of original sin."

I have to admit, I'm a little impressed he even knew the correct terminology.

"Okay, okay. Where are Henley's parents?"

"Um, we still have to call them." His voice is sheepish.

"What do you mean *you still have to call them?*" his mother booms, and my eyes open wide so I can back Jeff up on this conversation. "Do they not know their grandchild was born yesterday?"

Martha looks from me to Jeff and then back to me again. Our silence is our confession.

"Seriously?" she admonishes, and turns her attention to her husband. "Honey, get me my phone. I'm calling Lisa."

Shit.

Chapter Thirty-Two

THE GIANT TEDDY BEAR SUIT

"What in the hell is that?" Jeff asks as we pull into our driveway. I take my eyes off of our daughter for the first time during the entire drive home and look up at our porch.

Happily perched on the top step and blocking our front door is a giant eight-foot plush teddy bear that I recall seeing at Costco with Tara a few days ago. It is taller than any human I know, even in the seated position. A bright ribbon is tied around the bear's neck in a perfect oversized bow, and it's holding a banner that says "Welcome Home Baby Who is Not a Boy!" with "Sorry, Jeff!" scribbled in parenthesis underneath.

"No way," I squawk at the unwelcome guest and try to contain my laughter. Visions of Lily sitting next to this fluffy beast flood my mind and the thought is downright adorable.

"Who on earth would actually buy one of those things?" he asks, looking at me in the rearview mirror.

I raise my eyebrows at him. Really? He's really questioning who's responsible for this little stunt? Does he *not* know who my best friend is?

"Okay, let me rephrase that. Why on earth would Tara buy

one of those? And more importantly, how did she get it here without the assistance of a moving truck or forklift? That thing is fucking ginormous!"

"Shhh ..." I remind him that we're in the presence of impressionable ears.

Jeff pulls into our driveway and kills the ignition before turning toward me in the back seat. "Well, either way, your folks should be here shortly. I'll have your dad help me haul it inside. But consider yourself warned, if I can't get it through the doorway, I'm going to pull the stuffing out and wear it as a teddy bear suit and scare the crap out of unsuspecting people—including you."

I snort at the thought. Deranged? Maybe a little. Hilarious? Most definitely. But I wouldn't have it any other way.

"Deal, but only if I can record it."

Maybe with our luck, we'll have another viral video on our hands.

LESS THAN AN HOUR LATER, my parents arrive with bags upon bags of clothes covered in little pink polka dots and sparkly tutus with the exception of a single green and orange cartoon dinosaur onesie that my dad picked out—you know, just in case everyone was wrong and Lily really is harboring a penis inside her diaper. But I don't care. It's so cute that I still plan on dressing her in it — screw gender norms!

By some divine intervention, my mom wasn't pissed that I didn't call her the instant I went into labor. As it turns out, she didn't call *her* parents either until the day after I was born.

Like mother, like daughter.

I watch my mom make sweet faces and baby sounds at Lillian for no less than an hour. She even jumped right in and changed a dirty diaper, letting me relax on the couch for a bit. I guess there's something about holding a newborn baby that turns you into a softie.

"So now that the baby is here, does this mean I get to plan a wedding?" my mother asks with a little too much hope in her eyes as she holds a sleeping Lily in her arms.

Jeff sits down next to me on the couch, and I subtly shake my head at him. *Please don't tell her. Not now.* She's in a good mood, and if we tell her that we sorta-kinda-not-technically got married without her there, I'm never going to hear the end of it.

"About that ..." He glances at me cautiously. "Henley and I have started talking about dates that would work with the school's schedule, and as soon as she's feeling up to it, we're going to take a look at some venues during her maternity leave."

Damn. He's good.

I reach out and squeeze his hand appreciatively.

My mom smiles brightly. "That's so wonderful. I'll call up to the country club and get you an appointment when you're ready. There's a new event coordinator who is just amazing, and the photos of recent weddings on the golf course have been breathtaking."

"That's really thoughtful of you, Mom, but I'm not sure the country club is what we have envisioned for our wedding," I say. We haven't done a lick of planning, but I already know that there's no way in hell we're getting married at my parents' country club. I'm sure it would be nice and all, but that would be celebrating *their* way. Not ours.

"But I think it could be *good* to explore all of our options," Jeff interjects, nodding at me and clearly trying to appease my folks. Which is probably smart because I have no patience or filter with her antics ever since the baby shower.

I smile politely. "Yeah, I guess it wouldn't hurt to look at the place," I say as my mom's face beams happily.

After a fair amount of doting and small talk, Jeff and my dad excuse themselves to haul the oversized teddy bear inside the house. I have no idea where we're going to put this monstrosity of a gift.

They're barely out of earshot when my mom turns to me. "You know, Henley, I was serious about my advice at the baby shower. You really should keep up with appearances. You don't want Jeff to lose interest before you even get married, do you?"

Um, what?

"I know you *just* gave birth, but look at yourself. You came home in your maternity clothes, and I can't remember the last time I saw you wearing any makeup."

Seriously. What?

"I'm just saying that you need to be mindful of yourself. That's all."

That's all? Oh, hell no!

"Mom," I scold, clenching my hands into fists to keep my arms from shaking. "I came home in my maternity clothes because even though I pushed out an eight pound, ten-ounce baby, I still look like I could be six months pregnant. *And that's okay.* Jeff loves me for being me in all of my ridiculous glory. He doesn't care if my makeup is fresh when he comes home every night, and he certainly doesn't care if I have a hot meal waiting for him on the dinner table. Lord knows that if I did, it would probably be burned to a crisp. This isn't the 1950s, Mom. He knows how to handle my neuroses and meltdowns. He knows exactly how to calm my fears. But best of all he's capable of loving me at my worst, which is probably more than I deserve at times."

A soft clearing of the throat comes from the doorway, and we both turn our heads. My dad is looking in at us.

"Lisa," my dad chides in a semi-loving tone from the doorway, "give the poor girl a break, will ya? It's been an emotional few days. Besides, I recall you staying in your pajamas for a week straight when we first got home from the hospital with Henley."

My dad gives me a sly, knowing smile. As an only child, I was often on the receiving end of her antics, and he understands how my mom can be a bit much sometimes. Overall, he does what he can to rein her in when she goes rogue. I appreciate the backup, for sure. But you'd think at this age she'd simply know better.

"Graham!" she gasps, but my father ignores her and redirects his attention to me.

"Um, we can't get it through the door," he confesses.

Of course you can't.

I sigh and run my fingers through my hair. It looks like we're the proud new owners of a giant teddy bear suit. "Let me guess, you need scissors and a trash bag?" I ask, standing up.

"Yeah, but you better make it a couple of trash bags. Have you seen the size of that thing?"

I nod. As I head down the hallway and into the kitchen, I hear my dad say, "I never would've guessed that when I came over today, I'd be murdering my granddaughter's first teddy bear."

Chapter Thirty-Three

THE NATURAL DISASTER

Motherhood.

It's the most glorious blur of snuggles and sleepless nights, and *holy swizzle sticks how can so much poop come from something so small.*

And speaking of poop, I'm convinced that diapers don't hold poop in. They simply redirect poop up the back and out the arm holes, defiling whatever adorable frilly outfit I've got Lily in on any given day.

Jeff is constantly telling me that I'm a natural. But really, we both know that I'm a natural disaster. In fact, this whole motherhood thing is one giant natural disaster.

Even still, I have no idea what the hell I'm doing. But she's still in one piece, and I haven't broken her yet. So I must be doing something right.

I guess.

I just feel like I'm missing out on something.

Chapter Thirty-Four

GIRL SCOUT TEARS AND THE PERFECT PENIS

A soft knock at the door breaks me from my trance. I've been sitting on the couch staring into the vast nothing of our family room for who knows how long. Lillian's asleep in her crib, and me ...

Well, there's about a billion and one things I could be doing. *Should* be doing, honestly. Laundry. Dishes. Vacuuming. Shaving my legs for the first time since Lily's arrival. But the only thing I've been able to will myself to do today is to sit here on the couch and pretend that I'm okay.

Thankfully, whoever it was, heeded the sign I taped over the doorbell that said "Baby sleeping. Ring this and die." It became a necessity after an overzealous troop of Girl Scouts rang the doorbell incessantly, waking Lillian after it took me almost three hours to get her to sleep. I may or may not have opened the door and unleashed the exhausted, stressed-out beast upon them. And then I felt so badly for screaming at them, I sat on the front steps and sobbed. And then I bought every last box of thin mints they had in their little red wagons because I felt so guilty. It was a two hundred dollar lesson in the simple art of telling people exactly what you do — and don't — want them to do.

Don't ring my doorbell.

Do give me all the cookies without judgment.

Lesson learned.

But whoever it is on the other side of the door knocks gingerly again.

Damn it! Go away.

I resolved around seven thirty this morning that I wouldn't be seeing anyone today when I elected to stay in the same clothes that I had been wearing the past three days. With Jeff out of town on business, it's a little luxury for me.

I bring the mug of hot chamomile tea to my lips and nearly choke the liquid down. It's cold. *How long I've been sitting here completely out of it?*

"Henley? Are you here?" Tara's voice calls out softly. She's taken the liberty of letting herself in with the key we've hidden underneath the flower pot on the front porch.

"Hen?" she calls out again, closing the door softly behind her. Her delicate footfalls traipse down the hallway toward me.

"Oh. Hey, T." I force a smile and try to add some enthusiasm to my voice, but fail miserably.

Tara sets her purse on the floor and takes a seat next to me on the couch. She eyes me cautiously. "I haven't heard from you in a while. I've been wanting to come see you and get some of those Lily snuggles and whiffs of her fresh baby smell that are sure to make my ovaries explode, but you haven't returned my phone calls."

Her voice isn't accusatory. It's just matter of fact. Sad, even. And even though she's not giving me a guilt trip, it's impossible not to feel like the shittiest friend in existence of shitty friends. I'm pretty shitty at everything these days it seems.

"I know ... Things have just been crazy busy." I swallow the anxiety and will confidence into my voice. My eyes scan the room, and I pretend not to see the disaster that lays before me. Dirty plates with half eaten sandwiches are stacked on the coffee table, and there are four baskets of clean laundry that need folding underneath the window.

My best friend is here for some long overdue girl time. The last thing she wants to hear is me melting down over the fact I still look five months pregnant when I'm six weeks postpartum.

I just don't understand how so many women bounce back so easily. Just last week a man at the bank asked when I was due. I simply bit my lip and said, "No hablo anglais," and diverted my attention across the room. But then he said, 'Y cuandu nace su bebe?' and I completely lost it. I bolted out of the bank faster than a toupee in a hurricane, without even bothering to get the cashier's check I needed. I had no business driving home considering I could barely see the road through my mass hysterics.

"Yeah, motherhood does make you pretty crazy busy," she deadpans before shifting her weight on the couch. "So how have you been? And I mean *really* been. Because I love the shit out of you, Henley, and you're not fooling anyone right now."

I sigh and fight the tears pricking the edges of my eyes. "It's going," I squeak. Mostly because life *is* going. It's just not taking me along for the ride.

Tara says nothing, but her look tells me just how worried she is. It's so quiet between us you can practically hear the foundation of my very being crack under the pressure I'm feeling. The guilt I can't understand. The sadness that consumes me.

"I've managed to keep us all alive the past few weeks, so at least I've got *that* going for me," I add, desperate to fill the silence.

Tara playfully slaps her hand against my knee. "Don't be so overdramatic. *Of course* you guys are all alive. That's because you're doing a great job, *Mom*. You've got this kick ass tiny human who loves you more than you can even comprehend. And from what I've gathered from Cam, Jeff's new gig seems to be going well. Things will start to level out soon. They always do."

She doesn't realize how many nights I've cried myself to sleep after Jeff had passed out, terrified that somehow I am going to fuck my daughter up beyond all comprehension. She's going to spend the majority of of her life in therapy, and it's all going to be my fault.

"I don't feel like I'm doing a good job. Most days, I'm barely hanging on by a thread."

"Spoiler alert — nearly *all* moms feel that way. Even the celebrity moms who have an army of nannies waiting in the wings."

"Really? Did you feel that useless, like your mom card should be revoked?"

Tara looks at me bewildered. "Are you kidding me? One day Cam came home to find me in the bathroom, boobs wrapped in cabbage to help ease the swelling, crying into a bottle of non-alcoholic beer because I didn't have three arms to help soothe the boys simultaneously when they were teething."

I suddenly feel absolutely ridiculous. And like a horrible friend. I never truly understood the trials and tribulations she went through with triplets. I can't even begin to imagine feeling *this* stressed out three times over. Tara deserves a fucking congressional medal of honor for getting out of bed each morning.

Just when I'm about to apologize for not being around more, she says, "What's really on your mind right now, babe? You look like hell, and based on the Pig-Pen-esque cloud of dirt circling around you, I'm questioning if you've showered at all this week." Tara wraps her arm around my shoulder, and I completely and totally lose it.

"I just have no idea what I'm doing!" I wail pathetically.

Every part of me feels like it is screaming *I am not okay!* even if the words never make it past my lips.

"Oh, Henley, no mother does. We're all just winging it hoping to do a better job than our own mothers did with us."

I press the heels of my palms into my eyes, trying to press away the tears. Every part of me feels like it is screaming "I am not good at this!" even if the words never make it past my lips. "I mean, what if I don't wake up when she's crying? What if I forget to feed her and she starves to death? What if I accidentally leave the window open and an eagle swoops in and carries Lillian off into the wilderness to be raised by a pack of wolves?"

Tara stifles a laugh, trying not to make light of my ridiculously irrational fears.

"Stop laughing! I'm being serious!" I smear the tears away from my eyes with the back of my hand.

"Sweetie, all of those things are virtually impossible."

"You don't know that! I just feel so ... so *blah* lately. Like no matter how hard I try, I just can't pull my shit together."

Tara sits up a little taller, trading her humor for a little more sympathy and advice. "Have you been getting out at all lately? Maybe a little retail therapy could help, or even going for a walk with Lily to get some fresh air?"

I shift in my seat and exhale long and hard. "I tried going to the gym earlier this week since my doctor cleared me. *Tried* being the operative word."

"Oh sweetie, that seems a bit aggressive. She's only six weeks old. What'd you do?"

"I did about twenty minutes of Zumba, followed by ten minutes on a defibrillator, and then twenty-four hours in the hospital."

"Wait ... what?! You were in the hospital?" she says in a panic.

"Well, no, but I may as well have been. By the time I bailed halfway through that Zumba class, I would have happily taken an extended nap in the morgue."

I don't tell her that the thought of having a night of uninterrupted sleep in the friendly confines of a hospital actually sounds inviting. This whole sleep when the baby sleeps thing is a crock of shit. I haven't been sleeping at all, and this zombie-state I've been living in isn't conducive to adulting in the slightest.

She laughs softly and shakes her head. "That sounds a bit like Cam's short-lived stint at CrossFit. Somewhere between putting his shoes on and reviewing the infamous workout of the day, he got CrossFit mixed up with croissant. He hasn't gone back since. But that little bakery he found with the chocolate filled pastries? They're on a first name basis now."

I smile weakly, appreciating the effort to get me to laugh. But the thought of laughter hurts my soul. "Just this weekend, I spilled breast milk right after I was done pumping and completely lost it. Jeff was all *'don't cry over spilt milk, Henley.'* and I wanted nothing more than to punch him in the face."

"He really said that?"

I nod in response, still upset over the incident.

"Breast milk is the *only* milk worth crying over. That shit is liquid gold."

We talk about nothing and everything like we always do, but I just can't get into the conversation. She tells me all about the latest antics of the boys, and how Cam surprised her with a weekend getaway for her birthday. Which only makes me feel shittier because I am, of course, the girl who forgot her best friend's birthday.

"I feel like I can't do anything right. I completely flaked on your birthday, and I so desperately want to disappear because all of this is so overwhelming. I've been a terrible friend, horrible and neurotic around Jeff, and I don't feel like I can really enjoy this newborn phase because I'm so focused on everything I'm doing wrong and simply not doing in my life."

Tara takes my hand in hers and squeezes gently. "All moms go through this, sweetie."

"Really, Tara? Do they really?"

"Well ... yeah. It's called motherhood."

"Did you ever think about running away and leaving it all behind when you were at home with the triplets?"

Tara snorts. "All the damn time. These boys, they're my Everest. Try as I may, I want to run away at some point each and every single damn day. It's like I will never be able to conquer the triple threat. You're not alone on the struggle bus, Henley. We're all along for the ride, but we all take our own turns behind the wheel."

Her words strike me like a hot iron, and I can't help but wonder how many women I know have been in these same shoes. I still don't understand why more women don't talk about how rough and exhausting it is to be at home with a newborn. Mommin' is some tough shit on every level imaginable. And sometimes, right smack in the middle of a beautiful, happy life, we find ourselves unhappy for reasons unknown. And I need to remember that that's okay.

Silently Tara pulls a dirty nursing bra out from underneath her leg and takes in her surroundings. "Hen, you *have* to take better care of yourself."

I divert my eyes, shamefully.

"Don't feel like you have to go out and run a marathon. Just start small. Take a shower right when you wake up and put on fresh clothes. Read a book. Leave for an hour or so to get your nails done. Lillian will be fine with Jeff or Auntie T or, God forbid, those nut cases that are your parents. But that little girl needs you to do whatever it is you have to do to be okay. Me and Jeff, too."

And instantly, I know she's right. First and foremost, I have to take care of myself — you can't pour from an empty cup.

"And everyone under the sun can tell you what an amazing job you're doing at being a mom—which, by the way, you are. But at the end of the day, *you* need to believe that in your heart of hearts."

I look at my hands, knotted together in my lap. "I know."

"Just do me one favor?"

"What's that?" I sigh. I'm not sure I'm humanly capable of one more favor, even if it is for my best friend.

"Promise me that you'll call your doctor and at least ask her to talk about postpartum depression? I don't know much about it, but I do feel like it's worth having the conversation with her. And, if anything, she can help you without any judgment. You spent nine months growing a human in your body and then in a matter of moments you birthed that baby and those hormones bottomed out, forcing your emotions and chemical balance to get out of whack."

And there's that word.

Depression.

The one I've been avoiding the past six weeks.

Why is it that we, as moms, are incapable of recognizing the symptoms when they slap us so obviously in the face? Why do we act like depression is such a bad word? It's not. It's something completely out of our control, but if we're honest with ourselves, we can control the outcome.

I look up at her, trying to hide the worry in my eyes. "Is that all PPD is? A chemical imbalance?"

"Eh, something like that. I'm not really one hundred percent sure," she admits and then gets lost in thought for a flashing moment. "I just wish PPD stood for something more awesome. Like post penis depression and not this postpartum bullshit."

We both snort, and a tiny smile plays on my lips. "God,

imagine that. Going into severe depression after having the world's most perfect penis for just one night only," I say.

Tara lifts her head to the ceiling, deep in thought. "No other man could compare. It'd be perfectly pink and glistening. Smooth, but not too veiny. Just the right length, and thick enough to make you wince at first, but not so much it hurts."

"Mmmm ..." I hum in a daydream. That *does* sound pretty perfect.

"Oh, and the manscaping would have to be impeccable."

"Good call. No woman has ever said '*I love a good hairball.*'" I try to joke.

We both manage to laugh softly, and the tone turns somber again. Tara looks at me softly, genuine concern etched across her face. I never once considered the possibility that these overwhelming emotions could be postpartum depression. But how would I know? I've got nothing to compare it to, and it's not like this is something I expected and was prepared to deal with. Depression is a bitch and can happen to anyone.

Clearly.

"Penises aside, there *is* help for postpartum depression," Tara affirms. "Talk to your doctor. Let her focus on you so you can focus on truly enjoying this time with your new family. Promise me, Hen." She wraps her pinky around mine and gives it a gentle tug.

"I promise," I whisper back, knowing just how important this promise is to keep.

The baby monitor lights up as Lillian starts to babble to herself. She didn't nap nearly long enough. I stand up to go and get her.

"Hey—" Tara reaches out and takes my hand. "Why don't I get some quality time with the little lady? I think you may feel a little bit better if you jump in the shower by yourself for a few minutes."

I look down at my shirt and take a whiff at my armpit. It *is* pretty foul, and I'm not sure if that questionable stain on my shirt is melted chocolate or something more toxic.

"Do I smell *that* bad?"

Tara shoots a narrowed look my way. "I've been around hobos who smell better than you, Henley."

And with that, I drag my exhausted, stank ass to the bathroom to de-funk my body.

Chapter Thirty-Five

MILK FACIALS AND SLIP N' SLIDES

One thing that doctors, classes, books and even Tara failed to tell me about was just how much having a baby changes everything about your life, but more importantly, your sex life. Before I got pregnant, sex with Jeff was constant. While I was expecting, the sex was off the charts orgasmically delicious, albeit embarrassing more often than not. Whenever I wanted it, I wanted it right then and there, and usually Jeff was more than happy to oblige. But now that Lillian is here, the sex — while mostly nonexistent — is more loving and intimate on a completely different level.

Jeff appreciates me and my imperfect skin, and takes the opportunity to worship every fiber of my being. I can't help but wonder if it's like this for everyone, or if it's a simple testament to Jeff's kind-hearted nature and pure soul.

The first time we had sex after Lillian was born was a total disaster. One night after dinner I had bravely proclaimed, "I want to do you tonight," to which Jeff happily complied. After the usual warm up, we quickly realized that sex at that moment was going to be an inevitable failure. Unless, of course, you consider the tip of his penis was inside me briefly as success. I was in so much pain that I cried, and Jeff panicked and pulled out. At first I thought it had been so long that we'd simply forgotten how to do it, but really, it was my body rejecting everything that Jeff was giving. My breasts leaked at mortifying and inopportune moments during foreplay giving Jeff a milk facial, my vag was dryer than the Sahara Desert, and the whole ordeal couldn't end fast enough.

We tried again the following week, and this time I didn't cry. I may have been so sleep deprived that I dozed off at the end, but Jeff knew better than to challenge it.

The third time Jeff was hellbent on bringing me to climax, and it was the first, and only time, I've actually faked it with him. He tried so damn hard, and I couldn't let him feel like a failure. I knew it was *my* issue. But when he gets it in his head that he's the one in control of my orgasmic destiny, there's no talking him down. And so I channeled my inner Meg Ryan a la *When Harry Met Sally* and gave a performance that made me want to thank The Academy.

I still feel bad about that.

But at least it made Jeff feel good about himself. As far as I can tell, he has no idea that I faked it.

Eventually, we found our rhythm again. It just took a lot of patience and the mentality that we had the distinct privilege of rediscovering each other. Things weren't exactly in all the same places that they were a year ago, and so Jeff turned it into a game learning how and where I wanted and needed to be touched in my new skin. He has a distinct way of making me feel radiant.

I'm truly the lucky one out of all three of us.

"She's snoring louder than a freight train," Jeff reports as he tiptoes back into our bedroom, shutting the door as quickly as possible.

"Thanks for getting her down for the night so I could jump in the shower."

"No thanks needed. I'm her dad. And that's what dads do. Besides, you were overdue. *Again*."

I don't argue because he's right, though a little recognition that I've been getting better would be nice. Talking to my doctor about all the stress and how overwhelmed I felt since returning from the hospital was a game changer. Hesitantly, I took her advice and accepted a low dose prescription for Zoloft and found a therapist who I didn't want to punch in the tit. I definitely feel better overall, and it's nice being able to talk to someone other than Jeff or Tara about leaky boobs and how I feel like a failure because I kept feeding Lily when, in fact, all she wanted was a fresh diaper.

I sorta feel like a brand new me.

Jeff saunters to the side of our bed. When he pulls off his T-shirt, I allow myself to quickly gawk at the glory of his pajama pants hanging low on his hips. The scruff on his face is sexy as hell.

Jeff crawls underneath the covers, turns off the light on his side table and pulls me close to him. "She's perfect. You know that?" he says, the glow from the television illuminating his proud smile.

"I do. Clearly, she takes after me," I jest. Between the two of us, any good qualities Lily has will come from Jeff. If she has the grace of a drunk panda with two left feet, then we'll know she takes after me.

"You took the words right out of my mouth, woman." Jeff kisses me softly. He tastes of peppermint mouthwash, and it makes me want to kiss him again and again until I'm dizzy.

His arms wrap tighter around me, and I relax into his protective hold. I love how he claims me as his without a single word and without going all caveman on me like the guys do in those romance books Tara left me to read. His touch is nothing but love.

A rerun of *The Late Night Buzz* plays softly in the background, and I can't believe how far we've come the past few months. He's a natural as this parenting thing, and can calm his baby girl down in less than two rap songs turned lullabies. And the days where I struggle to keep it together, Jeff manages to keep both Lily and me in one piece. The man is a miracle worker. And my personal lifeline. Witnessing him tackle fatherhood head-on has been nothing short of a turn on, and I want to spend the rest of my life repaying him for his infinite badassery.

Jeff starts to rub small circles on my back with his fingertips and I release a soft whimper. The delicate cadence has a soothing effect on me that I've come to crave.

I throw an arm over his hip and gently begin to mindlessly write naughty phrases on his ass with my index finger like I did when we first started dating. And just as I think he's dozed off into dreamland, he opens his eyes, narrowing them at me and says, "What are you talking about? You don't even have a cat!"

I giggle, surprised he was paying any attention. I had traced the phrase *feed my kitty*, but the euphemism was lost on him in a sleep-deprived stupor. I'll need to be more overt here.

"Let's try this again," I say and begin writing more words with my fingers now that I had his attention.

My fingers danced over his boxers, in what I imagined with a beautiful, flowy script as I inched dangerously close to his sensitive spots in the process.

"Umm ...?" Jeff narrowed his eyes at me, trying to concentrate.

"What'd I write?" I try to stifle my smile.

"Correct me if I'm wrong, *but I think* you wrote *stuff my muff ... part my pink c ...* and ..." his face grows increasingly red, "*yam my dam?*" He props his head up on his elbow and looks at me curiously.

"Actually, that last one was *jam my clam*," I correct him with an easy confidence like I was reading off a grocery list.

Jeff tries not to laugh. "You sound like Tara. But either way, if you're feeling it, I'm down to clown."

"Ew! Don't say that," I sit up abruptly.

"What? Those phrases are textbook Tara."

I shake my head because I couldn't care less about the mention of Tara right now. "No. There's nothing sexy about the phrase *down to clown.*" I shudder as the words roll off my tongue. There are some things you don't joke about, let alone joke about when you want to have sex. And the last thing I want is visions of Stephen King's Pennywise lounging in my loins as Jeff goes down on me.

"Oh. And jam my clam is?" He smiles smugly.

I want to yell that we're wasting time. That right now I'm *feeling* the good vibe, and he should just shut up and roll with it because who knows when I'm going to be craving him like this again. That any minute our dear, sweet daughter is going to lose her shit and one of us is going to run in there to take care of her no matter how close to orgasm one—or both—of us may be. That the longer we prolong this game of hide the pickle, the more engorged my breasts are going to get and the more likely I'll turn into one of those fountains where everyone stops and stares because fluid is freely flowing out of a body part.

You know exactly what I'm talking about, little marble boy who pees into the fountain.

Either way, he makes a good point. And so I tell him such as I lace my fingers through his with a shy smile. "Fair point. But this time it's different. *Trust me.*"

Neither of us says anything for a few moments, and he looks into my eyes like he's trying to gauge if I'm being serious or just fucking with him. *Which I totally want to be in the literal sense.*

"Are you sure?" He raises his brows.

I nod.

He looks at me unconvinced. "I know in the battle of sleep versus sex, sleep will win with you one hundred and ten percent of the time. I'm pretty sure you've fallen asleep during sex with me at least once in recent history." He fake coughs, trying not to show his bruised ego.

"Why are you questioning my libido, Jeff? Just shut up and kiss me."

His lips come crashing into mine with one fist in my hair and his other hand grabbing my thigh, hitching it over his hip. We make out like a couple of wild, horny teenagers who have been left alone for the first time.

And it's glorious.

We're a frenzy of tongues and moans and hands grabbing at flesh. And when he doesn't dare push things further, I realize he's waiting for me to make the next move.

I shift my weight and push myself up so I'm sitting, looking down at his handsome face. And then I pull my tank top up and over my head, freeing my breasts.

"God, you're so sexy." He watches me in awe.

I lean down and kiss him madly and fervently, letting one of my hands wander down his abs, and massage his dick to life. But to my surprise, the colonel is standing tall at attention and ready for battle. Jeff groans into my mouth, and before I can loosen the tie on his pajama pants, he's flipped me onto my back.

Slowly Jeff slides his hands down my body, gripping my waist with just enough force to make me purr. He trails kisses down between my breasts, taking care not to touch them (probably to avoid another milk facial) and across my stomach before deftly removing my panties, leaving me exposed for his taking.

He looks at my imperfect body reverently, but it doesn't make me uncomfortable.

It makes me feel alive.

And beautiful.

I reach out and grab his hands, placing them in between my thighs, encouraging him to touch me. As he delicately strokes my body, he kisses my swollen breasts ever so gently, and I say a silent prayer that the ladies don't overreact and go into fire hydrant mode.

My fingers stretch out, reaching to touch his length through his pajama pants, but he grabs my wrist and pins it against the mattress. He nails me with a look of sincerity and care. "You've spent so much time taking care of us. Tonight, let me take care of you, Henley."

Jeff wastes no time getting intimately reacquainted with what's below as he alternates using his hands and tongue to coax obscenities from my lips and shudders from my body. He's working in overdrive, and my body is responding in record time. We both know we're working against the clock. Lillian could wake up at any moment and who knows whatever freakish post-pregnancy thing my body could surprise us with next. Soon, I am a heaping mess of breathless lust and sweat and...

Holy shit, is that a building orgasm I'm sensing? *Stop the presses! Hallelujah!* I was afraid this day may never come. Or maybe that I may never come again.

Either way, I need him.

Inside of me.

This instant.

"Lube ... now," I pant as I writhe under his skilled touch.

While I know I *feel* like things are well oiled and ready to go, a little extra grease is just the ticket to keep the engine running smoothly.

Jeff complies and grabs a bottle of Liquid Astroglide from the top drawer of the nightstand. In one swift motion he flips open the lid, but when he squeezes some clear liquid onto his fingertips, the whole damn lid pops off and the entire contents of the bottle spill into his hand, dripping down onto his leg and our sheets.

We look at each other in stunned silence, and I can tell Jeff is thinking *what do I do now?!*

For a split second, I contemplate running to the bathroom to grab him a towel, but my body is throbbing, and common sense takes over. Opportunities these days feel rare, and even rarer is me feeling like I'm mere thrusts away from finally achieving orgasmic bliss after months of a post-childbirth draught.

It's been far too long, and a woman has needs, damn it!

"Oh, the hell with it!" I say, grabbing his wrist and slathering the lube across my nether regions, stomach and generally anywhere that my skin is exposed ... Which is basically everywhere.

I need *help*.

And I need *him*.

And I need both of those things right now.

"Get over here," I command, pulling Jeff on top of me and guiding his glorious length right in between my legs, giving it a few slick strokes in the process, and I can't help but smile at the obscenities he mutters under his breath when I do. I boldly grind my hips against Jeff, wordlessly begging him to enter me. But before he does, he holds his weight above my body and gives me that look of adoration. And I'm reminded that mere eye contact with Jeff is way more intimate than words will ever be.

"I love you, Henley. And I always will," he says with such promise as he leans down to seal those words with his kiss. He thrusts his body into mine and takes pause, allowing me to adjust. I wince, but try not to show any discomfort on my face because even though it's still a little painful post-baby, John Cougar Mellencamp was right ...

It *hurts so good*.

"Shit, woman." He shuts his eyes tightly and presses his forehead against mine.

Overwhelmed with sensation and desire, I throw my head back, exposing my neck and moan. Jeff seizes the opportunity and licks down my neck and begins to glide in and out of me with ridiculous ease.

The feeling is simply indescribable.

We easily fall into a quickening rhythm, our bodies turning into a goddamned Slip N' Slide and our bed a freaking amusement park. He holds his body weight up with one arm and gently starts to caress my breast with his other hand. It's still greased with the lube, and gliding all over my body. He knows this is a no-fly zone, but neither of us seem to care.

"Oh my God," I breathe and pray to no one in particular, digging my nails into Jeff's ass for dear life. I will be *seriously* pissed off if his dick slips out right now. All of my senses are heightened, and I'm in a liberating state of free fall where nothing matters except for this moment, this sensation, right here and now.

"Henley!" Jeff cries out, and for a split moment I fear I've clawed a chunk of skin from his left butt cheek. "I'm so close, I don't think I—"

And mid-sentence, he manages to hit just the right spot on my body that sends my muscles clenching as I sing an aria toward the rafters. And I swear there are fireworks behind my eyelids. It's all so very dizzying and breathtaking as I ride out the waves of euphoria.

The orgasm gods must be smiling down on me tonight because never have I ever climaxed *that* hard, *that* fast without the assistance of Walter, my secret vibrator. Jeff chases my orgasm with one of his own and collapses onto my chest in a dramatic *oomph!*

"Ow!" I wince, pushing him up and off of my boobs. "My boobs are so tender right now."

"Oh, shit! I'm sorry, babe." Jeff rolls onto his side and flashes me a lazy, yet apologetic love-drunk smile. He stares at me like he's seeing me for the first time. And maybe in a way, he is.

"What?"

Jeff inches toward me and rests his head on my pillow. "Remember when you told me that Tara said sex after a baby was like throwing a hot dog down a hallway?"

"Yeah," I pant, shooting a warning dagger his way. If he *dares* say anything about me being loose, then the life he saves will be his own. I pull the sheet up and over my breasts, trying not to appear as vulnerable as I suddenly feel.

"Well, she was wrong. Sex with you is better than ever. There's this unbridled, uninhibited quality about you. It's fucking hot." He leans over to give me a soft kiss on the cheek, and I feel the heat rising in my face.

And the moisture just barely below.

Fuck. There it is.

I pull the sheet up even further, tucking my head underneath, wishing the bed would swallow me whole.

"Aww, it's nothing to be embarrassed about, Henley. I just love that side of you."

I sigh. "I'm not embarrassed, Jeff. My boobs are leaking."

Chapter Thirty-Six

THE BEST DAY EVER

We kept our word to Father O'Donnell and eventually came back to see him with our extended families. But under a slightly different precedence, and one that Jeff had to sweet talk me into.

Okay. That's a lie. There wasn't much sweet talking required.

"All of our family will be in town, so why not?" he had asked late one night while I was nursing sweet Lily in the glider in her nursery.

I had absolutely no good response for him.

He's right. Why shouldn't we? Why wouldn't we? I'm not big on fanfare or even being the center of attention. And the little bundle in my arms gave me the perfect excuse.

When we shared the idea with Father O'Donnell, he was over the moon and swore he'd keep it a secret to ensure we had the best day ever.

He kept his word and then some.

When I opened the double doors at the back of the church, I fought back some tears. The altar was flanked by two lush bouquets of lilies so fragrant that I could smell them from the doorway.

"They're perfect for a baptism. And even more perfect for a wedding," Father O'Donnell said from behind me.

"How did you ...?"

"Don't ask. I'm a priest. I called in a favor. And one of the parishoners overhead *that* conversation and volunteered her services behind the lens, free of charge. It's not much, but I hope it'll make your day memorable — every bride deserves to remember the day she gets married. Needless to say, I'll be saying a few extra rosaries tonight."

I quickly closed the gap between us and gave him a hug.

"Thank you," I whisper in his ear. I am so touched by his gesture. The world needs more kind, nonjudgmental people like Father O'Donnell. He easily could have turned the other way in the hospital, but he's embraced our little family, imperfections and all.

"Did you bring the license?"

"Yes, Jeff has it. He's parking right now."

"Good. I'll give you guys some time. Let's meet back in my office in fifteen or twenty minutes?"

My cheeks hurt from smiling so much. Today really will be perfect. "Sounds good."

I retreat to the mother's room at the back of the church to nurse Lily one final time before everyone's arrival. I'm hopeful that she'll sleep through everything. My parents enjoy telling the story about how I screamed like a banshee throughout my entire baptism.

When she's done and fast asleep, I set Lily back in her carrier and walk out to find Jeff looking inside the sanctuary of the church from the double doors at the back.

"Is everyone here?" I ask.

"Yeah, I think so."

I do everything I can to reel in the nerves before he hears the quiver in my voice. I spin on my heel and give him a quick peck on the lips.

"Do you think they have any idea?" His voice is as calm as still waters.

"No ... none." I shake my head and try to fight my growing smile. Containing my excitement has become increasingly more challenging every day.

"You ready to go, Momma?" Tara asks.

"I am. And you?"

"Yep. I still can't believe you asked me to be her Godmother. I'm truly honored, Henley. I promise to keep all the corrupting to a minimum since the big guy upstairs will probably be keeping a close watch on me." Tara kisses my cheek. She's the closest thing I've ever had to a sister, and the only logical option for Lillian's Godmother.

"So about that ..."

Tara starts rummaging through her purse and pulls out her compact to touch up her makeup.

"Hmmm?"

"I have one more job for you today in addition to being Lillian's Godmother."

"What's that? Do you need me to run interference with Jeff's family? Because I can totally take them on."

I laugh softly. "No, I'm wondering if you'll be my Matron of Honor."

Tara jumps up and down like she's just won the lottery, and I'm pretty certain one of her boobs is about to pop out the top of her dress.

"Yes!! Absolutely, yes! When is the wedding?"

Jeff catches my gaze from across the room and smiles at me. He's talking with his brother Kyle right now, and from the looks of it, dropping the bomb on him with details of his new brotherly slash Godfather slash Best Man duties. My heart flutters and I look at the clock by the bathrooms.

"Um, it's actually in about three minutes."

"Exsqueeze me?" Her voice turns sharp.

"We're not here today for Lillian's Baptism. Well, we *are,* but that's not the only event."

"You can't get married today! You don't have a dress or flowers or any of that stuff you need to get married. And besides, I haven't had the chance to kidnap you and whisk you away to Vegas for your bachelorette party! I heard that all brides-to-be get pulled up on stage at the Thunder From Down Under male revue. If you're cute, they'll let you cop a feel. And with your rocking swollen boobs you would *totally* get a free feel." She winks.

Ew. No thank you.

"Tara, I don't need any of that. Like you said, that's all just *stuff.* The only things I need to get married are Jeff, my family and friends, and a license. Anything else is just gravy."

She opens her arms and pulls me into a massive hug. "Well, as your Matron of Honor, at least let me do one thing." She walks over to the table by the doors to the main part of the church and plucks a few flowers from the oversized vase. When she returns, she tucks a beautiful white lily in my hair. Then she somehow produces a safety pin from her purse and attaches a second white lily to Jeff's suit coat.

She tilts her head to look at me with a satisfied expression.

"There. It's not exactly bridal, but it will have to do."

"Thanks, T."

"Yes, thank you," Jeff chimes in, tugging at the lapels of his suit jacket. "You ladies about ready?"

I nod and turn to gather our daughter. Lillian is fast asleep in the baby carrier, and I lift her out with the greatest of caution, passing her into her daddy's arms. Jeff leans down and kisses her forehead delicately and my heart swoons at the sight. I loved him before. But seeing him like this with our daughter makes me fall in love with him all over again.

Tara reaches out and takes Lillian's hand between her two fingers. "You, little lady, you need to learn some etiquette. Don't you know it's in bad form to wear white to somebody else's wedding? I mean, if you're going to protest a wedding, you should really make it count. Like wear a black veil or set the church on fire or something. Really make a statement next time, okay? There is much you have to learn."

I love that she's already imparting ridiculous wisdom upon her goddaughter.

"Is everyone ready?" Father O'Donnell asks as he comes back to greet us.

Jeff and I both nod anxiously. Tara and Kyle smile and exchange a quick glance at each other, then awkwardly introduce themselves. Just as we start to walk toward the double doors at the back of the steeple, Tara stops me.

"Wait!" Panic and uncertainty flash in her eyes. "Before we do this, what am I walking into? Who all knows about your plan?"

"Well, besides Father O'Donnell, us, and you and Kyle? Nobody. But they're about to find out."

Her eyes go wide. "Seriously?"

"Seriously."

Tara fights a chuckle at the back of her throat. "Your mom is going to be so pissed!" Father O'Donnell nails her with a single look. "I mean miffed. Your mom is going to be so miffed."

The priest smiles in approval, and I simply shrug at her comment. "Eh. I just think she'll be annoyed that she didn't get to plan a wedding."

THE CEREMONY WAS small and surrounded by our closest friends and family, exactly as I envisioned it. I have no need for elegant dresses and string quartets. Those aren't what make a marriage work. But selfless love and humor and patience and empathy and passion do. And it's a good thing we've got a surplus of those.

Mom and Dad were utterly confused throughout the entire ceremony up until it was time for our vows. They thought the part after we baptized Lily was some weird new age shit. It makes me question when the last time they attended mass was. But when we began to recite the words we had written for each other, my mom gave an audible gasp causing everyone to turn toward her in stunned silence. She then proceeded to cry and run up to the altar to wrap both Jeff and me in one big mess of a hug. I love her, but damn she can be clueless sometimes. For all the grief about giving her a grandchild before a son-in-law, she barely noticed when I was giving her exactly what she wanted.

Well, exactly what *I* wanted. Her happiness about the situation was the least of my concerns. But at least she made peace with it from what I could tell.

And it was all kinds of perfect.

AFTER OUR "I DO'S" and signing the certificate with Tara and Kyle, we head to our favorite Italian restaurant to treat our loved ones along with Father O'Donnell to a nice dinner. A low key celebration for a low key ceremony felt right. Nothing else really matters beyond those who are here with us now, and the last thing either of us needed or wanted was a party that costs as much as a down payment on a new home. I did spring for one minor wedding-ish detail though ...

Mostly because I couldn't help myself.

On the round table in the middle of the room is a decadent,

four-tiered Spiderman wedding cake, inspired by the original sketch that Jeff's mom shared with me during our babymoon gone wrong. The bright red fondant frosting hid layers of red velvet and almond sponge cake. Elaborate black piping detailed Spidey's web, and I even found a small figurine of Peter Parker and Mary Jane to adorn the top. It's a surprise for Jeff, and far too much cake for such an intimate affair, but I don't care. He had dreamed of his wedding day longer than I had, so it was only fair to give him a piece of the dream. And did I mention I couldn't resist myself?

But he's beyond shocked that I was able to pull one over on him on such short notice. And I love how it reflects that there was nothing traditional about us or this wedding day. It took some time to realize just how important it is to love your own story. Even if it's not some perfectly scripted traditional fairy tale, it's still *yours*. It was a strange, unconventional path that led us here. But really, it wasn't strange at all.

It was quite perfect.

My heart skips a beat when I feel Jeff's palm on my thigh, squeezing gently. "You look absolutely beautiful today. Today and every day, in fact."

I feel the heat rise in my cheeks at the compliment, and I realize that this man is what brings out the beauty in me. Even on my worst days, he finds a way make me feel my best.

"Thanks, babe. You clean up nicely yourself."

Jeff leans over and softly presses his lips against my cheek, then buries his face in my neck inhaling slowly. It's a gesture entirely too intimate for this crowd, and I can't help but love it. He runs his nose across my jawline before stopping at my ear to nip my skin with his teeth. His hot breath sends a chill of anticipation down my spine. Jeff palms my thigh and squeezes oh so gently before sliding his hand up my leg, grazing dangerously close to the one place I want but can't have.

Well, I *could*, but that would just be awkwardly inappropriate for everyone. I mean, there's a priest here for crying out loud. I cross my legs and sigh, trying to stave off the desire that is building up inside.

Jeff pulls back and nails me with his lustful, panty-dropping, mischievous smile. The one that always seems to get me in trouble. And his hand slowly tugs at the hem of my dress. "There's something about weddings that makes me horny," he says so softly that no one else can hear.

"Oh, no you don't," I roar unable to control my laughter. That is exactly how we found ourselves in this perfect, beautiful mess in the first place. And I'd love for nothing more to enjoy this moment now, and *that* moment later tonight.

Thankfully, he begins laughing, too.

"You can't blame a guy for trying!"

I can't.

Nor do I want to.

I smile.

He smiles.

And our whole damn world is perfect.

A Note From The Author

Can we all just stop what we're doing and be honest for one goddamned minute here?

Motherhood is some tough shit. Fatherhood, too. All of this is true for parenthood in general.

But you know what?

If you have kids or little ones you love so much you consider them your own*, I want you to know that you're doing a fucking kick ass job at it. Don't let *anyone* ever try to convince you otherwise.

Even on your worst day when you forget it's your turn on carpool duty and Benny the hamster escaped his cage only to turn up dead in the washing machine and you completely lost your shit because you just stepped on a Lego that little Susie refused to pick up ... even THEN, you're still doing great.

Just remember that every parent under the stars has their highs and lows. I promise you June Cleaver lovingly uttered "Fuck off, you heathens!" under her breath to Wally and Beaver at some point.

Sure, there are days where we all feel guilty for feeding our little ones processed food off of BPA-laden plates. But recognize you love that little kid enough to make sure they have food in their belly.

And when you are so stressed out and angry that you have to step away from the situation and hide in the bathroom with a package of Oreos? You are smart enough to grasp the power of a "me moment" and how it's essential and healthy for *everyone* at some point each and every day. And sometimes *their* lives depend on that moment of reprieve. (Plus sometimes you simply don't want to share your Oreos.)

And when you're having a rough day and feel like the world's worst Mom, so you throw some cartoons on the TV and lock yourself in the shower to have a long, hard cry? You care so much that you don't want your children to see how sad you are, so you give them some time with their favorite colorful characters.

The point is, even when you feel like you're failing, you're doing a great job. Everyone takes their rightful turn behind the wheel of the proverbial struggle bus of parenthood at some point.

I've been the mom-to-be in that holistic, hippy-esque birthing class.

I've also been the mom who had an epidural within five seconds of walking into triage.

I've been the mom to make organic purees for her children.

And I've also been the mom who let her kid eat a Goldfish cracker off the dirty floor while shopping at Target.

Don't worry, it didn't kill him.

I've been the mom whose had her shit together and the one who runs to the grocery store in her pajamas because *I simply can't* exist as a functioning member of society on any given day.

And I've also been the mom who was so distraught after giving birth, that I didn't know my up from my down and I was truly terrified of fucking my daughter up beyond comprehension. I *now* know that I had been exhibiting some of the signs of postpartum depression and truly wish I'd had a friend in that moment to encourage me to talk to my doctor about what I was experiencing. If you feel like you, or someone you love, could use a little postpartum support — don't be afraid to reach out and ask for help from your doctor. You're not alone. You're a part of the league of extraordinary moms and simply reaching out to ask for help exemplifies your greatness and strength.

But the beautiful part is all of these "moms" are perfect. And right. And doing what is best for their baby in that given space and time with what they've got.

And that, right there, is motherhood at its finest.

There is more than enough competition out in the world, we need to stop comparing ourselves to the pristine images that litter magazines. And Facebook is this facade of what we *want* people to see rather than the reality that is our beautiful, disheveled life. And don't even get me started on Pinterest. Each time I log on I'm reminded just how gloriously I'm failing at life just because I can't repurpose a vintage towel rack into a wine bottle holder (look that one up — it's pretty amazing!).

I guess what I'm saying is that as women, we are all on the same team.

We need to spend less time judging each other and more time building one another up.

So regardless of if you had a water birth or c-section or totally abused the little epidural button in between contractions like me, let's celebrate the fact that we are raising some incredible, tiny human beings.

Keep on kicking ass, Mom.

* Barring any abductions or cult families. Because that's simply not cool, yo.

Acknowledgments

It would be amiss to not start my acknowledgments by thanking the two tiny terrors in my life for making me a mom and giving me the fuel for Birthquake fire. Then again, maybe I should lead off by thanking my better half for being a stallion and knocking me up so I was capable of having all the glorious and heinous pregnancy experiences depicted in this novel? But if we're going there, I may as well thank myself and my whorish tendencies. So thank you, Barb, for being the master of seduction and fertility. Your scandalous ways earned you some badass tiger stripes on your body and more pairs of mom jeans than you'll willingly admit. But in all seriousness, my family rocks. You three are the source of love and humor in my life which means you are my everything. I'd be nothing without you. Where you walk, I walk … always.

To those whose real life incidents inspired many a scene in this story … from breaking childhood bedframes to babymooning at their in-laws house to murdering a teddy bear to coping with postpartum depression … thank you for being so real and candid with me so I could create such a real and candid story.

If you ever need to incessantly nag someone for eighteen months to make sure what you're writing is actually funny and something worth reading, you're not allowed to bother Tracey Murphy. I've called dibs on her from now until the end of time. Tracey, thank you will never suffice. So instead, I hope you know how much I love you.

Alpha Angie. There's a special place in heaven for anyone who can wade through the drege of a first draft and actually give good advice to shape the story. Thank you for not giving up on me after all these years and for always being my first eyes. And tell that hubby of yours, thanks for letting me steal his name.

To my league of extraordinary beta readers — Angie, Tracey, Jenn, Kaitie and Heidi — thank you for giving your all to make Jeff and Henley so fantastic and gloriously awkward.

To the greatest humans I know—and you three know exactly who you are—thank you for being a constant support system and open exchange of ideas to make us all better in the long run. I adore our friendship.

Margaret Neal ... I don't know who you are or where you came from or how you came into my life, but I want to hop on a plane and fly to Australia just to hug you. You know what you did and I am forever in your debt.

Jenny ... I'm so glad you're far better at math than I am. Thank you for finding "the weird things."

Jenn, your ability to meticulously craft the perfect sentence as you make sense of my messy manuscript amazes me. We share a brain and you truly get me in ways I don't even get myself. Thank you for making my words look so damn good. I'm serious about taking my dual citizenship and coming to crash your couch and eat poutine while drinking pure maple syrup out of the bottle and watching hockey and doing all things cliche! I just can't quit you (nor do I want to).

Linda, Linda, Linda ... thank you for being my never-ending source of sanity in this crazy book world. You're the best publicist a girl could ask for and I'm so grateful to be on the Foreword Author team.

Virginia, you're a miracle worker who proofreads faster

than the speed of light. Thank you for giving BIrthquake your sweet, sweet lovin'!

NAJLA QAMBER!!! You, my dear, a freakin' design unicorn. You're one in a million. Somehow I can give you a small idea and you turn it into pure magic. Thank you for understanding my vision more clearly than I do.

Jade Eby of The Write Assistants ... I bow down to your formatting glory. Thank you for making the final stretch of publishing such a seamless process. I am so lucky to have you in my tribe.

To my author friends, each and every one of you manage to make me a better writer. May we all continue to write all the stories we harbor within and build one another up in this industry.

To all the bloggers in the our little bibliophile universe ... thank you for supporting us authors selflessly. We can't do this without you.

And finally, thank you to *you*, for reading this book and making it to the very last page. I hope you found these characters as charming and delightful and fun to read as they were for me to write. I love that you were open to take this journey with me.

I love you for it.

About the Author

BL Berry grew up telling lies. Eventually, those lies turned into elaborate stories and when she grew older she started writing them down. When she's not hiding behind her computer writing, you can find her spending time with her family or catching up on her favorite TV shows.

Rumor has it she'll sleep when she's dead.

Residing outside of Kansas City, she lives with her husband, two children and black pug. Each day her family thanks the makers of e-Readers, because without which they would be living amongst stacks and stacks of romance novels. Conversely, each day B.L. Berry thanks the makers of e-Readers for hiding her book-hoarding tendencies.

BL Berry loves to hear from her readers — you can connect with her at blberry@authorblberry.com, or on Facebook (www.facebook.com/blberryauthor), Twitter @blberrywrites and Instagram @blberrywrites. You can sign up for her newsletter here (http://bit.ly/1zCPOPr).

To learn more, visit www.authorblberry.com.

Also By B. L. Berry

An Unforgivable Love Story

The Art of Falling Duet
Love Nouveau
Love Abstract

Made in the USA
Columbia, SC
18 June 2019